THERE HAD TO BE
A BETTER WAY . . .

As Kinsman gazed at the richly blue Earth hanging above the horizon, the enormity of what he was about to do suddenly struck him.

He was ready to rebel against the United States of America, against the mightiest nation the world had ever known, against the three hundred million people he had sworn to defend and protect.

It was madness. They were outnumbered a hundred million to one. But it was their only hope of saving the world, and they were going to try . . .

"What happens in *Millennium* is not merely what is possible, it is to a large extent what is already on the drawing boards. It is quite an achievement."
—Gordon R. Dickson

"This is a highly successful fusion of SF and political thriller."
—*Publishers Weekly*

A SCIENCE FICTION BOOK
CLUB SELECTION

COMES THE MILLENNIUM . . .

"*Millennium* is the crowning achievement of Ben Bova's career to date . . . one of the most sheerly believable stories in science fiction."

—*Galaxy Magazine*

"Slick, snappy narrative, worthy convictions, all-too-plausible forecasts." —*Kirkus Reviews*

"Bova's novel hinges on the hope that somewhere, somehow, there will be enough people with enough vision to see beyond national boundaries and to act in the cause of humanity."

—*St. Louis Post-Dispatch*

". . . one of the most pleasant tales of terror I have ever read." —*Luna*

"One of the rare science-fiction books that deserves a wide audience." —*Chicago Sun-Times*

Millennium

A Novel About
People and Politics
in the Year 1999

Ben Bova

A Del Rey Book

BALLANTINE BOOKS • NEW YORK

To Barbara, with all my love

It is not death that a man
should fear, but he should fear
never beginning to live.

—Marcus Aurelius

Wednesday 1 December 1999: 0900 hrs UT

The digital clock on Kinsman's desk said nine. Not that the arbitrary time made any physical difference in the underground community. Up on the surface of the Moon it was sundown, the beginning of a night that would last three hundred thirty-six hours. But here, safely underground, a man-made day was just beginning in the city called Selene.

As the highest-ranking American on the Moon, Colonel Kinsman was entitled to a private office. It was small and functional. There was a desk tucked into one corner, but he rarely sat at it. He preferred slouching on the plastic foam couch that was set against one wall. It had been one of the first products of Selene's recycling facility. The plastic had originally come from packing crates hauled up from Earth. The foam was a fire retardation spray that had outlived its useful life and had been replaced by a fresh unit. A Belgian chemist—a visitor to Selene several years earlier—had hit on the method of converting the foam to a comfortable padding for furniture.

There were no files in the office. No paper in sight. Kinsman hated "paper shuffling," and preferred to talk out problems face to face. A computer keyboard sat on the desk; it was linked to Selene's main computer memory. Next to it was a picture phone with a small video screen, and another phone on a stand next to the couch. Two slingchairs completed the room's furnishings. The floor was covered with close-cropped grass, which was more practical than esthetic: green plants provided vital oxygen in this underground outpost on an airless world.

1

Three of the office's walls were covered with view screens. One showed Earth as it appeared from Selene's main dome, up on the surface. The other two were blank at the moment.

Kinsman was sprawled on the foam couch, one arm stretched lazily across its back cushions. He had once been lanky, but was starting to fill out now. His dark hair was touched with gray, and he wore it much longer than Air Force regulations permitted. There was no badge of rank on his blue coverall; it wasn't necessary: everyone in the underground community knew him on sight—even the Russians.

His face was long, slightly horsey, with narrow-set gray-blue eyes, a nose that he had never liked, and a smile that he had learned to use many years ago.

Facing him, sitting tensely on the front four centimeters of a slingchair, was one of Selene's permanent residents, Ernie Waterman, a civilian engineer. Tall, angular, gloomy. He looks like Ichabod Crane, thought Kinsman. But he smiled as he said, "Ernie, I don't like hounding you, but Selene can't really be self-sufficient until the water factory's brought up to full capacity."

Waterman's voice was edgy, ready for an argument. "So it's my fault? If we could haul up more equipment from Earth . . . "

"Wish we could." Kinsman glanced at the blue crescent glowing on the wall screen behind the engineer. "Dear old General Murdock and his friends in Washington say no. Too heavy and too expensive. We're on our own. But there's no reason why we can't build our own equipment right here in the shops, is there?"

Waterman gave a lopsided smile that was close to being a grimace. "An optimist, yet. Okay, look, so we've got some raw materials and some trained people. But where's the six million other things we need? We don't have tooling. We don't have supplies. It takes us four times longer to do anything, because we always have to start from scratch. I can't pick up the phone and order the stainless steel I need. Or the wiring. Or the copper or tungsten. We've got to mine it and process it ourselves."

"I know," said Kinsman.

"So it takes time."

"But you've been at it two years now."

Waterman's voice went up a notch. "Now, don't start blaming everything on me! I've only been up here a year, and I've been on this job just six months. I'm *supposed* to be retired—"

"Whoa, whoa, cool down," Kinsman soothed. "I didn't mean you personally. And you know you were going rock-happy in retirement, Ernie. You're not a man of leisure." Make him smile. No fights with the volunteer help.

The engineer's long face unfolded slightly with a small grin. "Yeah, well, maybe it was getting to me. But what bothered me most was your blue-suit skyboys trying to make like engineers. Those idiot solar ovens—"

"Okay, okay, you win." Kinsman threw up his hands in mock surrender. "You're on the right track, I know. I shouldn't push you. But the water factory's our key to survival. We need the extra capacity. If there's ever an accident and we lose what we have now . . . It's a long haul back to Earth. A long time to wait for a drink."

"You think I don't know? I'm pushing as hard as I can, Chet. It sure would be hopeful to get more equipment from Earthside, though."

"That's out."

With an elaborate shrug, Waterman said, "All right, so we'll keep doing it the hard way." He hesitated, then added, "But I don't see what the big hassle is. The factory's already turning out more water than we use. You could even refill that precious swimming pool of yours with fresh water every week, instead of recycling it."

Kinsman put on a grin. "The pool's Selene's one luxury. And the factory was originally overdesigned to make certain that we could accommodate extra people up here—such as retired engineers."

"With bad legs. Yeah, I know." Waterman was silent for a moment. Then, "But does Earthside know about the factory expansion?"

"What?" A jolt of electricity went through Kinsman. "Of course they know."

"I mean, about your trying to double its capacity?"

Kinsman remained silent for a moment, then answered evenly, "Self-sufficiency has always been our goal, Ernie. Water is the key to survival. Without water we couldn't even keep the grass under our feet alive."

"Yeah, but—"

"But what?"

Waterman spread his hands. "You've already got a big enough capacity to take care of more people than we have on the American side of Selene. Doubling it means we could provide water for the Russians, too."

"Is that so terrible?" Kinsman asked.

Waterman said nothing, but his face darkened.

"I didn't design this place," Kinsman said. "Selene got put together when the Russians were cooperating with us in the space program. We've got to live with them next door. All right, so far we've gotten along fine, much better than Earthside. But if the shoe starts to pinch, don't you think it'd be better if *we* have control of enough water to take care of both sides? Then, if something should happen to foul up their water supply, they'd have to ask us pretty please, wouldn't they?"

The cloud over the engineer's face vanished. He grinned. "I get it. Okay, you want double the capacity of the factory, you'll get double. Only stop breathing down my neck every day, will ya?"

With a relieved laugh, Kinsman said, "How about every other day? You know, Ernie, when I found out that you were an engineer, and interested in the water factory, I almost got religion. Waterman: just the omen we needed for the factory."

"Religion," the engineer said, his voice suddenly low and serious. "That's what you get when you find you can walk again, and do something useful again, instead of sitting in a wheelchair the rest of your life." He tapped the metal braces underneath his trouser legs.

"Low gravity is one of our tourist attractions," Kinsman said as he slowly ushered Waterman toward the door.

The engineer waved a hand. "It's not just the gravity. It's the whole attitude around here . . . the way people do things here. None of the red tape and bullshit like they have Earthside. No standing in lines or spending your days filling out forms. People have *faith* in each other up here."

And their faith has made them whole, Kinsman said to himself. He answered Waterman, "They're free, Ernie. We've got enough room up here to be free."

Waterman shrugged again. "Whatever it is, it's like a miracle."

"You don't miss Earth at all?" Kinsman asked, stopping at the door.

"Pittsburgh, Pa., I should miss? Hell, no! My two daughters yes. Them I miss. But the rest of it—it's just a crummy slum, from sea to polluted sea. It's going to hell so fast there's no way to stop it."

Kinsman thought of his last days on Earth, more than five years earlier. His sudden yen to see San Francisco one more time. The madhouse battling with the airlines to wrest a seat on a westbound plane. The shock of seeing a city he had loved turned into a vast slum: the once-gleaming towers rotting with decay, their elevators useless without electricity; the bridges rusting with neglect; the Bay dotted with houseboats and black with scum.

"And what about you?" Waterman asked. "Do you miss it? You've been here longer than almost anybody."

Kinsman avoided the question. "I can go back when I really want to. I'm not physically restricted."

"Oh, yeah . . . that's right. Makes a difference?" The phone buzzed.

"Duty calls," Kinsman said.

As the engineer closed the door behind him, Kinsman went back to the couch. Leaning over it, he touched the ON button next to the speaker grill.

One of the wall screens glowed, but no picture came up on it. Instead, the computer's honey-warm feminine voice tape said, "Colonel Kinsman, you asked to be reminded that the shuttle bringing new arrivals is scheduled to touch down at 0930 hours. Traffic control confirms that the shuttle is on schedule."

"Right," he said, and punched the phone off.

He left the office and started down the corridor toward the power ladder. Wonder what Ernie would do if I told him we'd share our water with the Russians in an emergency? Would he quit the job? Would he yell back to Washington?

Officially, the American settlement on the Moon was called Moonbase. The Russians called theirs Lunagrad. Officially, the two bases were separate and independent of each other. Military experts in both Washington and Moscow scowled whenever they thought of the brief rash of international amity that had resulted in the two bases being built side by side.

Technically, Moonbase and Lunagrad were each self-sufficient, each capable of surviving without help from the other. Actually, the Americans and Russians who lived with each other as neighbors all called themselves Luniks and their community Selene.

Now Kinsman strode through the big cavern that linked the two halves of Selene. It was a vast underground chamber with a high chalky white ceiling and rough gray stone walls. The Russians and Americans had turned it into an open plaza, with green lawns and treelined walkways. Tiny shops and refreshment centers, established by individual entrepreneurs from many nations, competed with the government-owned exchanges that provided a meager flow of personal goods from Earth. The plaza was always busy with off-duty people; it reminded Kinsman of an oriental bazaar—but restrained, quiet, in the soft, low-gravity, highly controlled lunar style.

Kinsman nodded and smiled hello to almost everyone as he went through the plaza. He knew all the permanent residents by name—there were only about a thousand of them.

But as he rode the power ladder up to the main surface dome, his thoughts returned to Waterman. How many of our people still think as if they're Earthbound? he wondered. By the time he stepped off the ladder and onto the rock floor of the big dome, he was scowling.

Follow the yellow brick road.

The dome was kept darkened; faintly luminescent arrows crisscrossed the fused rock floor, pointing the way to various destinations. Kinsman padded along the yellow arrows, heading for the main airlock.

The dome was as large as a modern cathedral, and just as empty. It was the biggest structure on the Moon's surface, a symbol of the eternal spirit of brotherhood and cooperation between the peoples of the United States and the Soviet Union. That spirit had died a little before the dome was finished, poisoned in a world choked by too much population and too few resources.

The sound of Kinsman's slippered feet scuffing along the fused rock floor was swallowed by the dark, sepulchral dome. He could feel the cold of the new lunar night seeping up through the rock. The dome's ceiling was also made from lunar stone, supported on a geodesic framework of aluminum scavenged from spent rocket stages. The main walls of the dome were transparent plastiglass, hauled up years ago from Earthside, kilogram by precious kilogram.

Rows of tractors and crawlers and other heavy equipment were lined up, mute and unmoving in their assigned places. Facing the main airlock, the right side of the dome was for American equipment, the left side for Russian.

That's political nicety, Kinsman told himself.

Crossing the dome floor, Kinsman didn't merely walk along, he prowled. His years on the Moon had led him to an unconscious compromise between his Earth-muscled legs and the low lunar gravity. The result was a gliding, almost floating slow-motion stride that resembled nothing so much as the silent, purposeful advance of a stalking cat. In the shadows thrown by the dim, faraway overhead lights, his bony long-jawed face and dark-browed scowl added to the impression of a hunting feline.

He came to the heavy metal structure of the main airlock and detoured around its once-gleaming walls, to the observation area. Despite the low lighting, he could see a faint reflection of himself in the plastiglass wall. His coverall seemed strained around the midsection. You're getting fat, he thought. Too much office work and not enough exercise. The curse of the middle-aged executive. Looking past his own image, he gazed out at the desolate lunar plain.

The Sea of Clouds.

It was a weary, pockmarked rolling plain of naked rock, pounded for eons by a constant rain of meteors and more recently scoured—close to the dome—by the landing jets of spacecraft. It was a frozen sea of stone, bare and utterly lifeless, with boulders strewn carelessly across it, like a half-finished construction job that the maker had abandoned, left to brood gray and ghostly in the light of the gleaming crescent Earth.

If it really were a sea, or even clouds, we wouldn't need the damned water factory. Kinsman's frown deepened as he thought of it. He hated to argue with people, despised the need to prod and pressure them. Maybe we won't need the extra water. But water is life and I don't want to have to refuse it to anyone, including the Russians. He glanced at the beckoning, lovely blue and white crescent of Earth. *Especially the Russians,* he added silently.

Turning slightly, he looked across the silent dome's wide expanse to the transparent wall on the other side. The tired, rounded humps of mountains huddled there, guardians of the lunar ringwall Alphonsus, a crater wide enough to hold any city on Earth, including its suburbs. The thought of a teeming, fetid, decaying city here on the Moon disgusted him.

He turned back toward the Sea of Clouds and looked upward for some glimpse of the arriving shuttle. No flare of jets. No glint of Earthlight on smooth metal. He saw the horizon, close enough almost to touch. And beyond it, the blackness of infinity. No matter how many times he confronted it the sight still moved him. A few bright stars could be seen through the dome's thick plastic wall. *The eyes of God,* he said to himself. Then added, *Superstitious idiot!*

The pressurized tractors of the ground crew were starting to move out of the big vehicle airlock and arrange themselves around the landing area. Lights were winking on out there, so the shuttle must be coming down. Sure enough, Kinsman saw a puff of bright color, dissipated in an eyeblink. Then another, and the heavy squat shape of the shuttle took form, falling like a stone in a nightmare, slowly but inexorably, falling, falling—

another puff of rocket thrust, then still another . . .

The bare rock of the landing area seethed into a miniature sandstorm, where it had looked a moment earlier as if nothing as Earthlike as dust could exist. The shuttle landed like a fat old man settling into a favorite chair: slowly, carefully, and then *plop!* The landing struts touched the ground and bowed under the spacecraft's weight. The engines shut off and the dust-and-pebbles storm subsided.

The ground crew's tractors clustered around the still-hot rocket, faithful mechanical puppies greeting the return of their master. A flexible access tube began snaking out from the personnel hatch of the airlock toward the main hatch of the ship.

Kinsman nodded to himself, satisfied with the landing. A new batch of ninety-dayers, almost all of them on their first tour of duty on the Moon. They would arrive calling this place Moonbase, the official designation given by Colonel Kinsman's superiors on Earth. Just as the new Russians called their base Lunagrad.

But those who stayed on the Moon, those who made their homes in the underground community—no matter how reluctantly at first—would come to call this place Selene. Kinsman had hit on the name several years earlier, and it had stuck, even among the Russians. The ninety-dayers who could see the difference between Moonbase and Selene would return for more tours of duty; Kinsman would see to that. The others would never come back; he would see to that, too.

Walking over to the airlock's inner personnel hatch, Kinsman watched the newcomers step in. They were girls, eight of them, all talking at once. And four silent men. Boys, really. All but the one in the lead bounced clumsily as they tried to walk in the low lunar gravity, a sure sign of the newcomer. The girls were wide-eyed, chattering, excited. Their first time.

Kinsman recognized the kid in the lead. He wore a captain's bars on his coverall lapels. *Perry . . . Christopher S.* The youngster saw Kinsman and flicked a salute. Kinsman nodded in return as Captain Perry led his file of newcomers toward the power ladder that went down to Selene's living and working areas.

The girls ignored him, still chattering and ogling the grave lunar landscape.

So damned young, he thought. Just kids.

But bringing up the end of the little group was a woman, not a girl. Tall, lithe, with short-cropped dark hair and a good figure beneath her gray-green coverall.

"A grownup!" Kinsman heard himself say.

Her dark eyes flashed wide. They were deep brown, large, startling. She smiled and answered, "I'm the den mother."

Kinsman stood there as she sauntered past him. He admired the way she filled the coverall as she tried to walk with dignity. It would be several days before she would become accustomed to the low gravity.

More than six hours later, at precisely 11 A.M. Eastern Standard Time, the President walked slowly, almost reluctantly, into the Cabinet Room. The members of the Security Council, already in their places around the polished oval table, all stood up.

"Sit, sit down." The President forced a smile and fluttered his hands at them. He took his seat at the head of the table as the others murmured two dozen versions of "Good morning."

The Secretary of Defense was not smiling as he sat down. "Mr. President, I must bring up a matter that just came to my attention this morning, and therefore is not on the agenda."

The President was black. Not very black. His complexion and his facial bone structure both showed decided Caucasian influences, a fact that had cost him votes. His close-cropped hair was peppered with gray, but his body had the slim-yet-soft look of a man who played tennis for exercise. He had a warm smile and a gift for making people feel he was on their side. Some said it was his only gift, but they were usually jailed as bigots—no matter what their color.

The Secretary of Defense was cold and spare, with a body as lean as a saber blade. His face was sharp-featured, with piercing gunmetal eyes. Behind his back he was called "the Hawk," which referred to his looks as well as his attitudes. The name secretly pleased him.

The President blinked at him. "Not on the agenda? Why not?"

"This information is barely a half-hour old. There wasn't time . . ."

Looking around the table at the others, the President tapped the single sheet of paper before him. "A half-hour ought to be enough time to revise the agenda. After all, that's what an agenda's for."

Nodding curtly, the Secretary of Defense said, "Yes, I realize that. But there wasn't time. The Russians have disabled three of our ABM satellites so far today—that's since midnight, Universal Time, which means seven P.M. last night, Eastern Stan—?"

"Don't get us all confused with time zones." The President raised his rich baritone voice. "What's the score over the past week?"

"Over the past seven days," the Defense Secretary said, shuffling through the papers in front of him, "the Reds have knocked out—yes, here it is—they've disabled seven of our ABM satellites, and we've hit only four of theirs."

The President shrugged. "That's not so bad. Was anybody hurt?"

"No, there have been no deaths or injuries since that captain rammed his spacecraft into one of their satellites. And that was purely accidental, apparently."

A four-star general in Air Force blue nodded. "We've investigated very thoroughly. There was no possibility of enemy action in that case. Unless the satellite was booby-trapped in some way."

"I don't want anyone hurt," the President said.

The Defense Secretary frowned. "Mr. President, we are playing for stakes of the highest sort here. It will be necessary to take some risks."

"I don't want anyone hurt."

With a glance at the general and the others sitting around the table, the Defense Secretary said, "We have been trying to complete our ABM network for the past two years. The Russians have been incapacitating our satellites to prevent us from finishing the network. If you'll look at these graphs"—he slid three sheets of paper toward the President—"you will see that they are now knocking out our satellites almost as fast as we launch them."

"And what about their satellites?" the President asked, without looking at the graphs.

The general answered sternly, "We're restricted in the number of anti-satellite missions we can fly. There are only so many trained astronauts available, and only a shoestring of funding to get the job done. Meanwhile, the enemy is increasing the frequency of his launches, putting up more and more ABM satellites. And his newest ones are decoyed and hardened—much tougher to find and eliminate."

The Secretary of State cleared his throat and said, "You keep calling them the enemy. We're not at war." He was balding, wore rimless glasses, spoke softly.

"Nonsense!" rasped a heavy-jawed, hulking man at the end of the table. His voice was a labored, tortured whisper; his face a perpetual red angry glare. "With all due respect, we *are* at war and have been for two years. Ever since we and the Reds started launching ABM satellites, we've been attacking each other. Each side knows that whoever finishes its ABM network first will have a tremendous edge—the satellites can destroy the entire strategic striking force of the other side. The nuclear stalemate will be broken."

He paused for a moment and took a deep, labored breath. No one spoke. Leaning heavily on his forearms, eyes blazing with pain or anger or both, he resumed the harsh whisper. "When one side completes its ABM network, it can dictate terms to the other side with impunity. We dare not let the Russians finish ahead of us. We dare not!"

The President fidgeted uncomfortably in his chair and looked away from the burly, angry-faced speaker.

The Defense Secretary said crisply, "Entirely correct. If the Reds complete their ABM network before we do, they'll be able to knock down our missiles as soon as we launch them. We will no longer have a retaliatory force. We'll be at their mercy."

"It *is* war," General Hofstader reaffirmed. "Just because there's no shooting on the ground and no casualties so far, don't be fooled into thinking that this is a game."

"And there will be casualties, sooner or later," said Defense.

"What? What do you mean?" For the first time, the President looked startled.

"If you will look at the graphs I gave you," Defense said, with weary patience, "you will see that we can't keep going the way we have been for very much longer. We need a minimum of a hundred-fifty satellites in low orbit to cover the entire world adequately against Russian and/or Chinese missile attack."

"The Chinese are so hopelessly broken up," the President mumbled, his face down as he spread the graphs out side by side on the table.

"They could still launch their handful of missiles at either us or the Russians," came the rasping whisper from the far end of the table. "They could start the pot boiling. And they're nearly desperate enough to do it."

Defense resumed, "We need a hundred-fifty satellites in orbit and functioning. We have been maintaining about eighty of them. Over the past few weeks, the Reds have been disabling them as fast as we could launch them."

"Why don't we repair the damaged ones?"

"Economics, sir," General Hofstader answered. "It's cheaper to launch a mass-produced unmanned satellite than to send a human repair crew out to fix one that's damaged."

The President blinked, puzzled. "But I thought that those lasers were so expensive . . ."

The general produced a tight-lipped smile. "Yessir, they are. But maintaining a man in orbit is even more so. It's costly enough just to keep our manned command-and-control centers in orbit, and they're aboard the space stations, which were already constructed when we began this program."

"I see." But the President shook his head as if he didn't really understand or necessarily believe all that he was being told.

"Meanwhile," Defense went on inexorably, "the rate of Russian launches is increasing. That's on the middle graph, there. Today they have thirty-nine ABM satellites functional and in orbit. Four weeks ago they had only thirty, even though we found and destroyed eleven of their satellites over that time span. Unless we do something about it, the Russians will complete their network in another year—eighteen months, at most. And we'll still be far short of having complete coverage."

"They'll have won," said the general.

"They'll be in here dictating terms to you," whispered the burly man at the end of the table.

The President rubbed at the bridge of his nose. "Well, what do you recommend?"

Defense nearly smiled. Tensing in his chair, leaning forward slightly, he ticked off points on his fingers. "First, we must increase our own satellite launches by at least fifty percent. Doubling the present launch rate would be preferable.

"Second, we must increase our kill rate of Russian satellites, otherwise they will pass us in a matter of months.

"Third, we must prepare for the possibility of striking their orbital command centers. One successful blow at a command center could incapacitate their entire network for months."

"Right!" snapped the general.

It took a moment for the President to realize what was being suggested. Then his mouth dropped open in sudden comprehension. "You mean attack their manned stations? That . . . that would kill people!"

"It would mean war!" said the Secretary of State, outraged.

"Not necessarily," Defense countered calmly. "Even if a few Russian technicians and cosmonauts are killed, they probably won't go to war over it. Our computer forecasts show less than a forty percent chance. Remember, neither side has publicly admitted that there are military operations going on in orbit. And they certainly won't attack when we have more functioning ABM satellites in orbit than they do."

"But that's precisely when they *would* attack," State insisted, his normally placid voice going high-pitched and nasal. "They'll attack when it becomes clear to them that we can complete our ABM network before they can. They'll attack before we finish it, before we have them hopelessly outgunned. That's what *we* would do. That's what you Pentagon people call a preemptive strike, isn't it?"

General Hofstader shook his head. The Defense Secretary frowned across the table at State.

The President said, "I don't want to run the risk of starting a nuclear war, and I don't want anyone hurt . . . unnecessarily."

"Sir, I am not making these recommendations lightly," Defense said. "The life of our nation is at stake, and—"

"I understand that," the President said. "But I still don't want any blood on my hands. You can increase your own satellite launches and shoot down more of theirs—your first two recommendations. But no attacks on people!"

"We may be forced to, eventually," muttered Defense.

The general added, "What do we do when they attack our manned stations?"

The Secretary of State leaned back and stared at the ceiling.

His voice slightly shaky, the President repeated, "No attacks on people. Not for now, at least."

The Defense Secretary nodded. "Very well, Mr. President. Now, for the first item on the agenda, these food riots in Detroit and Cleveland . . ."

It was late afternoon in Selene. The clock on Kinsman's desk read sixteen-fifty.

He had just come back into the office, after spending most of the day prowling around the underground community, popping in on people as they worked, listening to problems and gripes before they became major complaints, making certain that everyone knew there was a direct pipeline to the commander and no need to suffer through official channels to get things done.

His phone was buzzing as he slid the door back and stepped into the office. Flopping on the couch, he touched the ON button.

One of the wall screens lit up, showing the face of a young communications technician. One of the new girls.

Cute. "We're receiving a top priority message from Patrick AFB, sir," she said gravely, impressed with the seriousness of her job. "Captain Maddern thought you would want to see it as soon as the computer has finished decrypting it."

"Right," Kinsman said. "I'll be right there."

Top priority messages were always hand carried, by strict regulation. With the Russians living on the doorstep, it was virtually impossible to prevent interception of radio and phone links.

It took about five minutes for Kinsman to walk to the communications center. The corridor was narrow and low-ceilinged, and not very straight. Its walls were rough-hewn rock, sprayed with plastic to make them airtight. Catacombs, he thought. Got to get these walls finished or covered some day. The overhead lights were long tubes of fluorescents, dim in visible output but warm with infrared for the grass that lined the floor.

The communications center was a beehive of desks and electronics consoles and view screens that linked Selene with the three big manned space stations in synchronous orbit around the Earth. Through the space stations, the lunar base could communicate with any place on Earth. The Russians had their own manned space stations in orbit, as well, and a completely self-sufficient communications system of their own.

A broad balcony rimmed the busy working "pit" of the center. Kinsman went to the rail and glanced down at the humming, chattering jumble of people and machines below. He thought, Dante's Inferno . . . or maybe Marconi's.

The balcony was also jammed with desks and busy people, but not as many as in the "pit" below. Kinsman made his way around, one hand on the railing, nodding to those he recognized, until he reached the cryptograph area. It was separated from the rest of the balcony by thin plastic translucent partitions.

Inside there were four desks grouped around a minicomputer that was madly blinking its panel light. Only two of the desks were occupied at the moment. At one of them, Kinsman recognized the woman he had seen up at the dome when the shuttle landed. She was watching a message being spelled out, one word at a time, on the view screen atop her desk.

"They didn't waste any time putting you to work," he said, sliding into the desk chair next to hers.

She looked over at him. "Oh, hello." No smile this time. She turned back to the keyboard at her desk and touched a button that blanked the view screen.

"Is that the message for the base commander that's being decoded?"

She hesitated a moment. "It's classified," she said guardedly. "Only authorized personnel can see it."

Kinsman nodded. "You mean it might be a good idea to let the base commander read his own mail before showing it to strangers?" *Her eyes are incredibly beautiful!* he thought.

She smiled but stayed firm. "It's addressed to the base commander."

"You can let me see it."

She started to shake her head, then said, "You wouldn't be the base commander, would you?"

He grinned at her. "Caught me. I'm Chet Kinsman. Want to see my ID?"

"I'm afraid I'll have to. Why don't you wear your insignia?"

Kinsman reached into the breast pocket of his coverall and pulled out a worn, warped plastic card. "My holy picture."

"Holy picture?"

"People look at it and say, 'Jesus Christ, is that you?' "

She laughed, very prettily. "You've let your hair grow. I'm sorry I didn't recognize you. I'm new here."

"I know," he said, taking the card back from her. "What's your name?"

"Ellen. Ellen Berger."

"Welcome to Selene, Ellen."

"Do you know everybody in the base?" she asked.

"Just about. There's only about a thousand or so, including the Russians. Why do you ask?"

"I was wondering how you knew I'm a newcomer."

"Well, up topside, in the dome, you were walking like a first-timer. And besides, if you'd been here before

I would have known about it. You're much too pretty to go unnoticed."

Her eyes flashed. "So what the girls told me is true."

"Oh?"

"That you don't waste any time."

"Is that what they say?"

She nodded.

"Well, as long as I already have the reputation for quick decision—when are you off duty?"

"This shift ends at eighteen hundred."

"Fine. How'd you like to attend a surprise birthday party? Up in the rec dome, by the pool."

She didn't hesitate a moment. "Sounds wonderful."

"Good. Pick you up at twenty hundred."

"All right. Whose birthday is it?"

"Mine."

"You . . . yours? A surprise birthday party for you?"

Kinsman said, "I'd be a lousy base commander if I didn't know what was going on, wouldn't I? Are you good at looking surprised?"

"I don't know!" she said, laughing.

"Well, we'll give it a try. Now, how about a copy of my message?"

"A paper copy?" Her hand reached out toward the keyboard on her desk. "We're not supposed to make paper copies unless it's specially authorized. Paper's very scarce."

"I know. I planted four trees up here with my own hands. But there is the reusable plastic—in that bin next to the computer console."

She leaned across the desk and picked one of the reusable cards from the bin. Puzzling momentarily, she flexed it, then slid it into her typewriter. Instead of typing, however, she turned to the computer keyboard and very carefully, one finger at a time, touched a series of buttons on it.

"I've got to be careful," she said. "Working the keyboard is funny in this gravity, and I was never all that good at it anyway."

Abruptly the typewriter on her desk erupted into furious automatic action. It hammered out line after line with inhuman clattering speed, then stopped dead. Ellen pulled the plastic out of the typewriter and handed it to Kinsman.

"You've got to sign for it," she said.

Kinsman nodded, signed the desk book that she handed him, then gave it back to her. Getting up from the chair, he said, "See you at twenty hundred."

"You don't know my room location . . ."

"I'll find you," he said.

When he stepped out into the quiet and emptiness of the tomblike corridor, he examined the decoded message:

TO: COL. C. A. KINSMAN/CMDR, MNBS   1 DEC 99
PRIORITY: ONE-ONE-ZERO   REF: RMM 99-2074
SECURITY CLASSIFICATION: TOP SECRET

INCREASED ORBITAL OPERATIONS REQUIRE LOGISTICS AND MANPOWER SUPPORT FROM MOONBASE. URGENTLY REQUIRE YOUR LATEST ASSESSMENT ON MOONBASE CAPABILITY TO IMMEDIATELY SUPPLY LOGISTIC SUPPORT FOR TEN (10) MANNED ORBITAL SEARCH AND DESTROY SWEEPS PER DAY, PLUS MANPOWER SUPPORT FOR SWEEPS AND/OR BACKUP PERSONNEL FOR STATIONS ALPHA, BETA, GAMMA. PRIORITY RATING FOR THIS REQUIREMENT IS ONE-ONE-ZERO. CONSIDER POSSIBILITY OF YELLOW ALERT STATUS IMMINENT; RED ALERT POSSIBLE. REQUIRE DETAILED RESPONSE IN TWENTY-FOUR (24) HOURS.

B/G R. M. MURDOCK
COMMANDING OFFICER
USAF LUNAR OPERATIONS

Kinsman stood in the empty corridor, staring at the yellow plastic card in his hand. And suddenly he was trembling, his whole body crumbling while his mind saw it all again: the weightless, soundless, slow-motion nightmare fight; the cosmonaut's pressure suit revolving slowly, slowly against the backdrop of solemn staring stars; the face inside the helmet frozen in the sudden terrified realization of death.

They're going to do it, Kinsman's mind screamed at him. *They're going to make me kill again.*

Wednesday 1 December 1999: 2120 hrs UT

All space operations worked by Universal Time. Not only those in the lunar community, but all the manned activities in orbit, near the Earth.

In a small one-man spacecraft, Frank Colt flicked a glance at the fuel gauge readout on the instrument panel in front of him.

"Alpha to Mark One," said a voice in his helmet earphones, gritty with static. "Repeat: We read your fuel reserve as approaching redline."

Colt was in a standing position, weightless in the compact spacecraft. The outside of the vehicle looked something like a miniature shipyard, with booms and antennas and jointed grappling arms sticking out everywhere. Inside, there was room for one astronaut, standing like an old-time trolley car conductor.

Colt was an Aerospace Force major, one of the few black men among the astronauts. He had spent the past several hours maneuvering from orbit to orbit, chasing down "unidentified" satellites. A few hundred kilometers off to his left spread the achingly beautiful blue and white Earth. Dazzling clouds laced the south Atlantic, the coast of Africa was a thin gray haze on the horizon, approaching fast.

But Major Colt paid no attention to that. Inside his sealed pressure suit he itched and sweated, despite the suit's air blowers. His feet were constantly going to sleep, and he shuffled them from time to time to keep the circulation alive.

He was annoyed. His radar had acquired four "unidentified" satellites so far on this sortie, and they had all turned out to be decoys: nothing but metallized balloons. No markings, but everyone knew if they weren't made in the USA they came from Russia.

"C'mon Frank, give it up. You've got to start back now or else I'll have to ask Command for a stand-by rescue scramble."

"Stuff it," Colt snapped into his helmet mike. "Where they've got decoys they're decoying something. I'm closing in on another blip." His radar screen showed nothing but random sparkles.

The voice in his earphones sighed. "Man, you're more trouble than the rest of this outfit put together."

"You're pickin' on me 'cause I'm black." Colt grinned as he said it, in his old Motown accent. One of the pinpoints of light on the radar screen was getting brighter. It *was* a blip.

"Dammit, I'm just as black as you are! When're you gonna stop wearing your skin like a suit of armor?"

"When you stop wearing yours like a doormat." Colt touched the control studs on the panel before him. A surge of rocket thrust pressed at his back.

The radio voice from Space Station Alpha was silent. Shut him up, Colt thought, half guilty, half satisfied. They always made scrupulously sure to get a black controller on the board when he flew a mission. Colt's own skin was the color of richly creamed coffee. *Black enough.*

He watched the blip on the radar screen get bigger, brighter, then snapped the telescope eyepiece down from its overhead rack and locked it in position just in front of his helmet visor.

"Got it!" he yelped into the microphone. "Real one this time. Big mother, too."

Without even thinking about it, Colt eased his craft into a co-orbit with the Russian satellite. It was a precise maneuver, deftly done to use the least amount of fuel possible.

In his earphones, Colt heard a muffled voice in the

background say grudgingly, "The sonofabitch can fly, I'll give him that much."

He broke into a grin as he closed in on his quarry. It was a long thin needle of a satellite, built to present as small a radar cross-section as possible. Coated with radar-absorbing plastic, Colt guessed. The end that pointed toward Earth bore several glasslike lenses.

Colt glanced from the telescope eyepiece to his instrument panel. Fuel was too low to try an actual rendezvous with the satellite. Instead he flicked open the red safety cover over the grenade arming and launching switches. He tapped the first switch. The ARMED light glowed amber.

Carefully lining up his craft with micropuffs of rocket thrust, Colt let his hand hover over the FIRE switch. Without taking his eyes from the telescope, he pushed the switch and felt the quiver of the spring-loaded launcher hurling its half-pound of explosive. A tiny flash near the end of the Soviet satellite, and that was it.

Colt reached up and dialed greater magnification on the telescope. The satellite's near end was shredded by shrapnel. The lenses were all shattered, the metal ripped and gouged.

He nodded inside his helmet, satisfied. "Okay, Alpha, coming back now."

The radio voice said mechanically, "Set control channel frequency to 0415 for computer update on optimum transfer orbit."

Colt flicked out the numbers on the keyboard off to his right. "Freak 0415, check . . . Hey, what's today's score?"

"You got the only one so far—"

He grunted.

"—they got three of ours."

Selene's recreation dome was much smaller than the main dome, where the shuttles landed. It was set on slightly higher ground, so that you could stand at the edge of the swimming pool and see the main dome, the undulating dark plain of the Sea of Clouds, and the slumped shoulders of the ringwall Alphonsus. The main viewing attraction, of course, was Earth—hanging blue and white and gleaming against the dead-black sky. The planet was a fat crescent, more than half full, its light strong enough to bathe the lunar night with a far greater brightness than the full Moon lavished on Earth.

Kinsman and Ellen stepped off the moving power ladder together. She was wearing red slacks and a gray sweater that clung to her very satisfactorily. She carried her swimsuit in a tiny carryall bag.

"Nobody told me you could swim up here," she was saying. "I had to borrow a suit from one of the girls. I hope it's not too small for me."

Kinsman put on a leer. "There's no such thing as a too-small swimsuit. Not for a girl with your figure."

She made a sour face at him. "That's right. I forgot. They warned us back at Kennedy that you frontiersmen were the last refuge of male chauvinism."

"Now, remember to look surprised," he said, changing the subject, "when they tell you what's going on."

Ellen whispered back to him, "Okay, boss," as they walked through the humid atmosphere from the ladder hatch toward the row of metal lockers that lined one side of the dome. The lockers had started life as temporary life-support modules, fifteen years earlier when the first manned outposts were being set up on the lunar surface. They had fondly been called "telephone booths" by Kinsman and the other astronauts and scientists who had lived in them for two weeks at a time.

They entered side-by-side lockers. Kinsman simply unzipped his coverall. He was already wearing his trunks. He hadn't bothered to bring a towel. With electric heat lamps so plentiful in Selene, he had gotten out of the habit of toweling himself.

Stepping out of the locker, he scanned the pool area. A crowd was already there, filling the dome with noisy echoes of laughter and splashing. A few families had their children with them. A teen-aged boy and girl executed simultaneous dives off the thirty-meter platform, pinwheeling slowly in exact synchronization with each other. Impossible on Earth, but only marvelously difficult in one-sixth gravity.

The rec dome complex represented several years' worth of cajoling and arguing with General Murdock, who had absolutely refused to see the need for such luxury at Moonbase. It was only after Kinsman had procured a year's supply of Scotch for the base's three psychiatrists—and they began sending out reports on the vital need for recreational facilities—that the dome got built.

Murdock still didn't know, officially, that the Luniks had built a pool for themselves.

Pat Kelly spotted Kinsman, and padded up from poolside toward him, trying to look nonchalant about it.

"Uh, hi, Chet. About that order that came through this afternoon . . . " Kelly was a little guy, wiry, with a pleasant, open face marred by an oversized set of teeth and undersized squinting eyes. It made him look something like a rabbit. His quick, nervous way of moving and talking added to the impression. Sandy hair, darting pale blue eyes. He was very bright, young and coming on strong. He had already put in two tours of duty on the Moon, and was now working on his third. He had just made major, and Kinsman had picked him as his second-in-command.

"The order from Murdock?" Kinsman felt his innards go cold. "Any trouble?"

"No, no. Just wondering what it's all about. Why do we have to gin up a detailed report on our manpower and logistics by 1200 tomorrow?"

"Murdock wants to know how much help we can give the manned stations," Kinsman answered evenly.

"Yeah. That's obvious. But why? What's going on? What about this yellow alert?"

Shrugging, "Don't know, Pat. But you know Murdock; he's always been a wet-pantser."

Kelly still looked troubled. "Listen, Chet, is there really gonna be trouble? I've got a wife and kids down there. If there's gonna be real trouble, I want to be with them."

"I told you a long time ago to bring them up here. Even if the shit hits the fan Earthside, we can ride it out here."

"With half the place owned by the Russkies?" Pat's eyes widened in disbelief.

"If we have to fight here, at least it'll be with hand-guns, not nuclear warheads."

"You get just as dead."

Kinsman grabbed the younger man's shoulder. "Pat, if I could order you to bring your family here, I'd do it."

"You feel that strong about it?"

"They'd be much better off."

His face seemed to twitch, rabbitlike. "They're not in such bad shape. Good government housing. Got two whole rooms all for themselves. Pretty good location—no break-ins, not even any electricity rationing, except in the summer."

"Bring them here," Kinsman repeated.

"Really think I should?"

"I'll get the orders processed. Do it tomorrow."

He still looked undecided. "Maybe you're right . . ."

Great way to start a party, Kinsman thought. Trying to decide if your wife and kids are going to get blown up this month or next.

Ellen came up beside him. "The view here is incredible!"

Kinsman focused his attention on her. She was in a green and yellow bikini. "It certainly is," he said.

She flashed her eyes at him. "I knew you'd say that!"

"You gave me the straight line," he countered.

"Just testing," she said airily. "Like Pavlov and his dogs."

With a grin, Kinsman said, "Okay, so you've rung my chimes and I'm salivating."

"Hopeless case of chauvinism," Ellen murmured.

Kinsman was about to reply when Kelly nodded his head in the direction of the ladderway entrance. "Here comes Dr. Faraffa."

"Now you'll see what a real male chauvinist is like," Kinsman whispered to Ellen.

Dr. Faraffa was only slightly taller than Kelly, and had a broad, brown-skinned face with none of the aquiline features so often associated with Arabs. He walked straight to Kinsman, nodding briefly to Kelly as he passed the younger officer, ignoring Ellen altogether.

"Colonel Kinsman," he said in a voice as mellow and

brown as Turkish tobacco, "I have been informed by my associates at Alpha that there is some talk of a new crisis."

The word spreads fast. "I think any rumors to that effect," Kinsman said carefully, "are unfounded."

Faraffa stepped close enough for Kinsman to feel his breath on his face. It carried an odor of something sweet, almost cloying.

"Highly exaggerated? Perhaps. Such as the occupation of the oil sheikdoms by your Marines? That was once a highly exaggerated rumor."

Kinsman shrugged. "I'm not a diplomat. The Marines and the occupation are real. A new crisis is not."

"Not yet."

"Not yet," Kinsman repeated.

"If such a crisis does occur, I expect that all of the foreign nationals here will want to return to their homes," Faraffa said.

Only if they're fools, Kinsman thought. But he said, "We always make every effort to accommodate our foreign visitors."

"Of course."

"Within reason," Kinsman added.

Faraffa's eyebrows arched upward. Then, with a slight smile, he added, "I understand that this gathering tonight is to celebrate your birthday. Congratulations."

"Thank you." Kinsman could see from the expression on Ellen's face what she thought of the Egyptian's attempt to spoil the surprise of the party.

"It's very interesting," Faraffa went on. "You are the most visible man here in Selene. Everyone knows you and admires you, even the Russians."

With a shrug, Kinsman said, "My life is an open book."

"Not quite." Faraffa's voice became almost a whisper, but harder, sharper, a thin little dagger of sound. "I have attempted to learn more about your life. I am very interested in you, Colonel Kinsman. Yet, while the computer records are completely open, they extend back only a few years. Before that, your personnel file is a blank. A total blank. You are a man without a past, Colonel Kinsman."

Very evenly, Kinsman replied, "The personnel files go back to the point where I first assumed command of Moonbase."

"But no further."

"No further."

"Why is that? All the other files extend back to the person's birth."

Keeping his hands from shaking, keeping his voice low and steady, choosing his words very carefully, Kinsman said, "There's a résumé of my career up to the point when I became Moonbase commander. My birth date is given."

"Indeed."

"There's no need for more detail."

"A man without a past," Faraffa repeated. "It makes one wonder what you are hiding from us."

"Modesty," Kinsman said, feeling his voice becoming edgy. "I have a highly developed sense of modesty."

"Or secrecy?"

"Call it privacy. If you need to know anything about me, ask me."

"No," Faraffa said. "I shall ask my government. Perhaps they can learn more than I can."

Never. The information was erased from all the tapes. There are only two people left alive in the States who know. "Why all this interest in my early life?" Kinsman tried to make his voice sound light again.

Faraffa shrugged elaborately. "Ahh . . . call it curiosity, Colonel Kinsman. I am a scientist, after all. Scientists are intensely curious. Especially when they find a mystery."

"There's no mystery," Kinsman lied. "Ask me what you want to know and I'll tell you. Including the three months I flew patrol out of Cyprus."

Faraffa's head rocked back. "So you *were* part of the so-called Middle East Patrol Force."

"Yes, I was."

"I thought as much." The Egyptian nodded and smiled, more to himself than at those around him.

"All you had to do was ask," Kinsman said, feeling cold sweat trickling down his ribs.

"Yes, of course." Faraffa made a stiff little bow,

more with his head than his torso, and walked away without a further word.

"Do you have many foreign visitors here?" Ellen asked.

"About forty or so—mostly English and West European. A few Japanese, a couple of Africans and Indians. And Faraffa."

"No Israelis?"

"Not while Faraffa's here!"

There were more than fifty people already by the pool, in their swimsuits, and more pouring into the dome every minute. The prevailing skin tone was white, with a few browns and only two blacks.

Several people were swimming, and the usual handful of muscular exhibitionists had pushed the teen-agers off the high platforms to make spectacular—if poorly co-ordinated—low-gravity dives. They sliced downward in dreamlike slow motion. The water splashed around them with equal languor. Most of the people were sitting around the pool or standing, talking, with drinks in their hands.

There were only a few Russians in the crowd, Kinsman noted. Leonov's not here, he thought. What orders did he get today?

"Ah, there you are!"

Kinsman turned to see Hugh Harriman knifing through the crowd, drinks in both hands, bearing down on him like a heat-seeking missile. Harriman was short, round, bald, bearded, pop-eyed, loud, irreverent, dirty-mouthed, a professed coward and probably the brightest human being within roughly 384,405 kilometers.

"Our esteemed leader!" Harriman bellowed. "Have a drink!"

Kinsman took the proffered plastic cup, as people in the crowd turned to watch, and handed it to Ellen.

"Oh, shit!" Harriman snapped. "Might've known you'd have a gorgeous woman with you. Should've brought an extra drink. Give you this one except I've already pissed in it."

"That doesn't matter." Kinsman took the cup from him. "Alcohol purifies everything."

"You sonofabitch!" Harriman yelped.

"Ellen," Kinsman said, "this is Hugh Harriman. He's half Irish, half Jewish-American, half Spanish . . ."

"Portuguese, dammit! Watch your mouth, Kinsman!"

"This is Ellen Berger," Kinsman finished.

Harriman's bellicose expression suddenly melted into baby-blue innocence: all rolling eyes and a cupid's-bow smile. "Charmed, I'm sure." He reached for Ellen's free hand and kissed it.

"I'm pleased to meet you," Ellen said. "What do you do here at Moonbase?"

"Selene, my dear. Selene. That's the name we have given to this haven of refuge." Harriman paused for a breath, instantly glared at Kinsman, who was sipping the drink, then smiled back at Ellen. "I'm a political exile, my dear. An unfortunate victim of diabolical forces. Would you care to hear the story of my life?"

"He's a secret agent," Kinsman said, "but we haven't figured out which side he's working for—or against."

Ellen shook her head. "I don't think I believe either one of you!"

"Doesn't matter," Harriman said.

Kinsman asked, "Who set up the bar? What's going on around here tonight?"

Harriman went back to glaring. "Fuck off it, Kinsman! You know damned well this is a surprise party for you. But you don't know what the *real* surprise is."

Kinsman was about to answer when a clamor erupted from the general direction of the ladderway, and a deep voice proclaimed: "Greetings and felicities from the peace-loving peoples of the Soviet Union of Socialist Republics to the money-grubbing imperialist lackeys of Wall Street!"

Suddenly Kinsman felt better. "Leonov." He grabbed Ellen by the wrist and towed her through the crowd toward the ladderway. "It's Piotr Leonov, the commander of the Russian half of Selene."

Leonov was flanked by two smiling Russian women in zipsuits. Damned good figures, Kinsman noted automatically. The Russian was in full uniform, with colonel's insignia on his shoulders. He was slightly shorter than Kinsman, a bit heavier. His face was dominated by ice-blue eyes, very expressive, and a full-lipped Slavic mouth. His hair was already iron gray, but it flopped boyishly over his forehead; he was constantly brushing it back with his hand.

"Chet! Bloated reactionary plutocrat! Happy birthday!"

He grabbed Kinsman around the ribs and lifted him off the ground.

"Hey, Pete, whoa!" Kinsman laughed.

With his feet on the ground again, Kinsman said, "Good to see you. I was afraid you wouldn't be coming."

"What? Miss the birthday celebration of my fellow Lunik? My friend?"

Nodding toward the two girls, Kinsman said, "You seem to have a few friends of your own."

"Hah! Secret police. They have come to spy on you and keep an eye on me."

The girls smiled and tried not to look uncomfortable.

I wonder how much truth there is to that? Kinsman asked himself.

Time was almost meaningless in Antarctica. It was daylight. It had been so since September and would continue to be so until March.

The coldest air on Earth settles atop the mile-high plateau that rims the South Pole. Dense, frigid, this high-pressure air spills down the plateau walls like an invisible waterfall. Invisible, but palpable, audible. It howls across the glaciers and snowfields with gale force, driving blizzards when there is moisture aloft.

Today the sky was clear, the air utterly dry. But Captain Ernest Richards still shivered inside his electrically heated parkasuit. The wind cut through the plastic and foam insulation and electrical warmth with remorseless indifference.

Richards stood outside the big crawler, mentally counting the days until he'd be relieved of duty and on his way back to civilization. Like most of the men who served under him—scientists and Navy alike—he had grown a beard during his six-month tour in Antarctica.

Now it was flecked with ice, condensed and frozen moisture from his own labored breath.

One of the enlisted men slowly approached him. He was so heavily muffled in parka and hood that Richards couldn't identify him until he was only a couple of meters away. Even then, his goggles and beard hid most of his face.

"Sir, the scientists say we're right on top of a big deposit. Scintillation signals are very strong, and are getting stronger as we head northwest."

Richards nodded. "Very good. Can we track the signals from the crawler, or do we have to stay on foot?"

"Looks like they wanna stay on foot, sir. They're picking up rocks and jabbering among themselves."

Inside his hood Richards scowled. "Damnation. I'm going inside to make a radio check."

Richards watched the sailor trudge back to the group of scientists who were clustered around a big rock outcrop, bending or kneeling like fur-wrapped pilgrims who had finally arrived at their shrine.

The valley was dead dry, one of those strange Antarctic deserts. No snow, no vegetation, no soil. Rocks and gravel and more rocks. White-topped mountains glistened all around them in the howling wind, poking their sparkling peaks into the painfully bright sky. But here in this bone-bare valley there was no water, not even frozen. No life of any kind. Except the duty-driven Americans, searching for coal deposits to feed the voracious cities back home.

Slowly, stiff with cold, Richards walked back to the crawler. His boots crunched on pebbles. The metal rung of the ladder felt burning cold, even through his heavy gloves. He clambered up and pushed through the hatch, into the rear compartment of the big vehicle.

Warmth. Glorious soaking thawing warmth. It took half an hour and a pot of coffee before he felt human again. He sat alone in the drive compartment, parka off, feet planted directly in front of the heater outlet. He finished a radio check with McMurdo and settled back in the big padded driver's seat. He could watch the geologists from here.

Suddenly they all gathered together in a tight knot.

Richards sat up straight and watched through the bulging bug-eyed windshield of the crawler. They were pointing at something and talking about it. Heatedly. Arms waving and gesticulating. One of them pointed to the crawler and then off to the sawtoothed horizon. He detached himself from the group and sprinted for the crawler.

Puzzled, Richards pulled himself out of the seat and ducked through the hatch into the rear compartment, where the bunks and work tables were.

The outside hatch opened, letting in a slug of frigid air. The man was the same sailor who had spoken to Richards before. Pushing his hood down off his head, he said excitedly, "Captain, sir, they've found a marker out there! Made of metal. Russian writing on it."

"Russian?"

"Yessir. Dr. Carlati says it looks like the Russians have been here before and staked a claim to this valley."

Richards frowned. "Stop talking like a Western movie, dammit. This is international territory. Nobody's got a right to claim any damned thing."

The sailor shrugged. Richards reached for his parka and hauled it on. Zippering it up, he muttered, "Come on, let's see this. Do any of the scientists read Russian?"

"Dr. Carlati does, sir."

As he climbed down from the hatch and set foot on the rocky ground again, Richards heard the sailor call out from above him, "Hey, look there, sir! Another crawler coming up the valley."

Richards saw it. A dark speck edging along the gray rocks. He looked up the ladder at the sailor, who was still standing in the hatch. "Get a carbine out of storage and load it. Bring it with you."

"Should I radio McMurdo, sir?"

Caught for a moment between two priorities, Richards shook his head. "No. Bring the carbine. We'll fill in McMurdo after we've talked with the Reds."

By the time Richards and the sailor got to the group of scientists, the Russian crawler was close enough to make out its red star insignia.

"The richest deposit of coal I've ever seen," one of

the geologists was saying. "This must be what the Montana beds were like before the sixties."

"Yes," said another parka-muffled man. "But apparently *they* were here first."

"There's plenty here for everybody."

Naïve fool, Richards thought.

The crawler was advancing on them, looming bigger and more menacing with every clank of its treads. Richards stood there watching it, no longer aware of the cold or wind. The scientists seemed tense, too.

One of them said, "Do you think Podgorny might be with them?"

"Is he here this year?"

"That's what I'd heard."

"I haven't seen him since the Vienna conference."

Richards broke into their conversation. "I think you civilians had better get back to the crawler. And Jefferson, go get two more carbines."

Dr. Carlati stepped in front of him. "Captain, you're being too dramatic. What could cause trouble?"

"Do it!" Richards bit off the words, then looked past Carlati at the advancing Russian crawler.

Jefferson raced for the American vehicle, disappeared inside, then reappeared a moment later with a pair of carbines cradled in his arms. He ran back toward Captain Richards as the scientists fidgeted irresolutely around him.

The sailor stumbled over a rock and fell face forward. One of the guns went off with a single sharp bang.

Immediately, an answering *crack-crack-crack* came from the Russian crawler. Chips of stone sprang up around the sprawled sailor. Richards saw a man sitting atop the Red vehicle, pointing an automatic rifle at them.

"Get down!" he screamed at the scientists. Pulling the carbine from the stunned sailor standing next to him, he turned it toward the advancing crawler. It loomed huge and gray now, like an army tank. Richards cocked the carbine, hearing one more *crack* as he did so.

An incredible force slammed his chest, knocked him

over. He never felt hitting the ground, but suddenly he was staring at the sky. Hooded faces slid into his view. They were blurry. The pain! His body was in flames.

"My God, they shot him!" It was a distant voice, fading, fading.

"I think he's dead."

Kinsman had drifted away from the crowd around the pool. Nursing his third drink (Or is it my fourth?) he stood apart from the laughing, chattering people, near the base of the transparent dome. He turned to look out at Alphonsus's weary ringwall, billion-year-old guardian of nothingness.

In the distance he could hear snatches of conversation.

". . . Takamara says there hasn't been a dolphin seen in the North Pacific all year. They've gone the way of the whales, looks like."

". . . get back in time to do some Christmas shopping. The kids will be so excited . . ."

". . . just rounded up the whole department and marched them off to an internment camp. Claimed they were deliberately holding back on developing the new pacification gas."

"The whole damned department?"

"Eighteen men and women. Took their families too. They're all in Nebraska somewhere, getting reeducated with electroshock and mindbenders."

"Without a trial? Or due process?"

"Hah!"

"They can't do that! It's against the Constitution."

"Don't say it too loudly. You could get a paid vacation in Nebraska too, you know."

Hugh Harriman came up beside Kinsman. But now the little round man was quiet and serious. With a lift of his eyebrows, Harriman asked, "What's this I hear about a yellow alert?"

"Christ," Kinsman muttered. "Aren't there any secrets in this town?" *There's one. But maybe they'll find out about that, too.*

"I know we mere civilians aren't supposed to know," Harriman said, "but how serious is it? Are you and

Leonov going to arm-wrestle, or is this the real thing?"

"I wish I knew."

Harriman gulped at his drink. "That bad?"

"It won't be arm-wrestling."

"Damned fools."

A thought struck Kinsman, and he almost smiled. "Hey, if we're ordered to seal our half of the base from all foreign nationals, what the hell are we going to do with you? Brazil still hasn't come through with your papers, have they?"

"Of course not, the bastards. It's been almost two years now. I'm officially a stateless person. Another few months and I won't be able to stand up straight on Earth. They've got me by the balls—invite me up here with their sociology team and then revoke my citizenship."

"Cheer up. Socrates got hemlock."

"The world's still not ready for us philosophers," Harriman said with a sigh.

"You mean gadflies."

"Whatever. You know who've they put in my chair at São Paulo? A dimwitted colonel. A colonel in the fucking army is the chairman of the philosophy department in the largest university of Brazil! A colonel!"

Kinsman knew it was bait. He said only "Hmm."

"*You* could qualify as a philosophy department chairman in São Paulo, Chet."

"Something to think about when I retire."

"You should live so long."

"That's not funny. Not tonight."

Harriman stared at him for an instant, mouth open and ready for his next reply. But when he realized what Kinsman had meant he said, "Yeah. They're closing down all the schools. Luxuries, you know."

He walked away. Kinsman turned and looked outward again, feeling the numbing cold of infinity seeping in despite the heated curtainwall, watching the tantalizing beauty of Earth hanging there. Eight billion people getting ready to destroy themselves.

A hand on his shoulder. Ellen.

"You're supposed to be having fun, whether you like it or not."

"Oh, yes, sure."

"I think there's some sort of grand unveiling coming up." She gestured back toward the pool.

There was a huge package at poolside now, covered by a blue plastic tarpaulin. It had an odd shape; Kinsman could not make it out.

"They sent me here to bring you back," Ellen said.

She had changed back into her slacks and sweater. But her close-cropped hair was still glistening from swimming. Her skin—"I can think of better places for us to go," he said.

She smiled but said nothing. They walked together through the crowd that was clustering around the mysterious package. Their chatter and murmurs faded to an expectant hush as Kinsman and Ellen approached.

Piotr Leonov was standing beside the veiled shape, grinning broadly. Everyone else was silent now.

"Ah . . . the guest of honor approaches. The magic hour has come."

Kinsman tried to look relaxed, but he was really burning to know what was under the wrap.

"Before I unveil your birthday present, I have a speech to give . . ."

Everyone groaned.

"Wait, wait." Leonov held up a calming hand. "It is not a political speech. It is short. Only two sentences."

"We're counting!" came a voice from the crowd.

"Very well. One: We did a great deal of research into your background to select this present, Chet."

The face of the dead cosmonaut drifting helplessly. Kinsman drove the picture from his mind.

"And two: Every permanent resident of Selene gave up two months' worth of personal freight space to get this—thing—up here. Dr. Nakamura lent his personal assistance and used family connections to acquire the—ah—object. And the dedicated workers of Lunagrad provided the necessary technical assistance to make the thing work correctly."

"That's four sentences, Leonov!"

The Russian shrugged. "I am within a factor of two of my original estimate. That's quite good, compared to what some of you scientists have been doing."

General laughter.

Turning back to Kinsman, Leonov finished, "Very well, then! From all of us Luniks, Chet—Lunagrad, Moonbase, Selene—Happy birthday!"

He tugged at the plastic tarpaulin and nothing happened. Everyone roared. Suddenly red-faced, Leonov pulled again, harder, and it slipped to the floor. Revealing a gleaming ebony baby grand piano.

Kinsman felt his jaw drop. "Holy God in heaven."

For a long moment he simply stood there, too dumfounded to do anything but gape. Then everyone was clapping his hands. Somebody started singing "Happy Birthday." Ellen stepped up to him and threw her arms around his neck and kissed him. More applause.

"You do know how to play it, I trust?" Leonov asked.

Keeping one steadying arm around Ellen's waist, Kinsman said, "Haven't touched a key in years and years. I used to be pretty good."

Pat Kelly came up beside them. "We found out that you were a child prodigy."

"Dullshit," Kinsman snapped. "I had a recital when I was fifteen or so—my parents pushed me into it." *It killed them when I joined the Air Force.*

"Play!" Leonov insisted. "I had to keep this thing in hiding in Lunagrad for weeks. I had to find someone to tune it, since there is no such talent in your den of capitalist Babbitts. Now, play something—Tchaikovsky, at least."

Shaking his head, Kinsman said, "You'll be lucky if I can remember 'Chopsticks.' "

He sat at the bench and stared at the keys. Black and white. Like morality. His hands were shaking. Why? Scared or excited or both?

He touched the keys, played a few experimental notes, ran through a few scales. *The hands remember.* Then he knew what the first music played on the Moon should be.

He actually closed his eyes. Involuntarily. He was surprised when he realized he had done it, and snapped them open again. By then his hands were well into the opening bars of the "Moonlight Sonata."

The crowd was absolutely silent. The soft, measured notes floated through the dome, nearly three hundred years and almost half a million kilometers from their place of birth.

He got about halfway through the first movement and then flubbed. He tapped out a few notes from a childhood exercise and then stood up. Everyone applauded.

Leonov came up to him. "Congratulations! But you must move the instrument from this dome. Too humid. It will never stay in tune here."

Kelly said, "We can put it in your quarters, Chet. We checked. There's enough room.".

"No," Kinsman said. "Everybody ought to be able to use it. Put it in the assembly hall downstairs."

"They'll ruin it in a month. The kids—"

"No they won't. And we'll borrow Pete's tuner when we need him."

"Agreed," said Leonov. "On two conditions."

Kinsman cocked a brow at him.

"First, that you allow my frustrated musicians to use the instrument now and then."

"Of course."

"And second," Leonov raised two fingers, "that you *keep* it here, on your side of Selene so that I don't have to listen to them!"

"Sure," Kinsman said. "And your secret police can plant their bugs in it, too."

"Wonderful. That will make them very happy."

Harriman was standing beside Ellen. "Regular Renaissance man, aren't you, Kinsman? Musician, soldier, astronaut . . ."

"I used to be a swordsman, too, on the Academy's saber team."

"Humph. Goddamned Cyrano de Bergerac in our midst!"

"My nose isn't that bad," Kinsman said.

"I like your nose," Ellen said.

Harriman tried to make his round face frown, and almost succeeded. "I'm consumed with jealousy," he groused. "You get to do everything, Kinsman. I can't play a note. I can't even get my stereo to work right."

With a laugh, Kinsman answered, "Playing piano is

like politics, Hugh. The secret is not letting your left hand know what your right hand is doing."

Several other people tried their hand at the piano. The dome rang with concussion rock, Chopin, soul, Strauss. One of the new ninety-day girls ran through some of the neo-oriental style that was getting popular Earthside.

"Bah! Peasants and degenerates," Leonov grumbled at last, and plopped himself down on the piano bench. He pounded out some heavy-handed Mussorgsky, then broke into melancholy Russian folk tunes.

When Leonov finally got up from the piano, he began saying goodbye to everyone. "I must return to the workers' paradise," he told Kinsman.

"Thanks for the surprise. Feel free to come over and use it any time. It belongs to all the people of Selene— Moonbase and Lunagrad alike."

Leonov closed his eyes briefly. It was a gesture he used in place of a nod. "I understand." He hesitated and carefully refrained from glancing over his shoulder. "My friend, we must get together for an inspection tour of the route for the buggy race. Just the two of us. Do you agree?"

"Away from the lipreaders?" Kinsman smiled grimly.

"Exactly."

"All right. Tomorrow?"

Leonov blinked slowly again. "I will call you."

"Good."

"Happy birthday, comrade. May you have many more of them."

"May we all."

"Indeed."

The party was breaking up. Leonov and his two girls left, followed by a trail of admiring glances.

"They *are* intelligence agents," Harriman assured a young blonde with whom he was sharing a joint.

Finally Kinsman found himself walking slowly down a smooth-finished corridor with Ellen, his arm around her waist, her head leaning sleepily on his shoulder.

"It was a great party," she said softly. "Nice of you to arrange it for my first day."

He laughed. He had enough alcohol in him to feel relaxed, but not enough to be uninhibited.

"They're a great bunch of people. Salt of the Earth."

"You mean the Moon."

"Right. They're good people. This is really just a small town, you know—a frontier town. Everybody knows everybody else. We all help each other. Got to . . . It's too damned dangerous up here otherwise."

"I never saw anyone look so surprised," Ellen said, her voice light with laughter.

"They really got to me with that piano," Kinsman admitted. "I never expected that."

They stopped in front of the door to her quarters. "Would you like some coffee?" she asked.

He pulled her to him and kissed her. Her breath caught and then speeded up and she clung to him. But his mind was racing, filling his head with old dead pictures, battling against his body.

Finally he said, "I . . , guess we'd better call it a night. Thanks. It was fun."

She looked surprised, puzzled, almost hurt. Then she tried to mask it. "No coffee?"

"Thanks, no. Ellen . . ." He couldn't say it. "I'll see you tomorrow. Good night."

"Good night and thank you."

He turned and hurried down the corridor. *Goddamned fool!*

He strode right past his own quarters, prowling the corridors, sleepless, angry with himself, knowing that he had behaved idiotically.

Without consciously directing himself, he wound up back at the rec dome. It was empty now. The litter of the party cluttered the floor. The overhead lights were out, but the pool lights glowed and shimmered softly. Earth hung bright and motionless overhead.

Kinsman sat down at the piano and tinkered with it. He got all the way through the first two movements of the "Moonlight Sonata," decided against risking the third and botching it. He tried Bach. It was miserable and so was he.

Then he felt her hand on his shoulder. He knew it

was Ellen without looking up. She sat on the bench beside him. "Whatever it is, it's all right," she said.

It was like the first time he had flown in orbit. The freedom of weightlessness. Free fall. All the bounds of Earth slipped away. Nothing else in the universe except himself and this lovely warm woman. Kinsman even forgot the crowded, beckoning, troubled Earth and the star-eyes of God that watched him.

Thursday 2 December: 1550 hrs UT

Orbiting nearly 40,000 kilometers from Earth, Space Station Alpha was a set of concentric rings connected by spokelike tunnels. At the central hub spacecraft docked. From a distance, it looked something like a dozen bicycle wheels of different sizes nested within each other. Closer up, you could see that things were nowhere near that neat: antennas and equipment pods and odd-shaped structures poked out from the wheels every few meters. Like all human cities, it was suffering from urban sprawl.

The military section of Alpha was comparatively small. Of the station's constantly changing population, only a hundred or so were actually Air Force personnel. Officially, they belonged to the U. S. Aerospace Force, but the old name still clung, and they called themselves "Air Force." They handled the docking facility, the major radar and communications centers, and the electrical power generation and distribution systems. So although there were nearly a thousand scientists, technicians, administrators and even tourists aboard Alpha—and they came from every non-Communist nation in the world—the Air Force still controlled the satellite station.

Frank Colt was supervising the overhaul of his space-craft. The one-man tug was standing in the middle of a large hangar that was jammed with other tugs, and the men and women who labored over them. The hangar was next to the hub of the station, and therefore effectively weightless.

Technicians and equipment drifted easily in the nearly zero gravity, hovering over the bristling, gadget-loaded tugs. The spacecraft had once been gleaming and polished. Now they looked used, their metal finish glazed by long hours of solar particle bombardment, their anodized colors blackened around the rocket thrusters. Each tug was moored in midair with rigid braces so that the tech crews could get at every part of them. Some were oriented in one direction, some in another. "Up" and "down" made little difference to the humans or the equipment. The entire volume of the big hangar was being used, and people entered or left the area by hatches set into the "deck," the "overhead" and all four bulkheads.

Colt pointed with one hand and gripped his technician's shoulder with the other. "That's the one," he yelled over the clamor of machinery that echoed through the hangar. "That's the humper that froze on me."

The technician was white, with red hair and freckles. And new to Alpha. He hung onto a handgrip set into the tug's skin and peered at the tiny jet nozzle of the maneuvering thruster. "Looks okay to me," he said, then added, "sir."

Colt pushed his face next to the tech's. "Listen, sergeant. I don't give a shit how it looks to you. It froze on me. Get it out of there and find out what's wrong with it."

"Take out the whole thruster assembly?"

"Perform a hysterectomy if you got to. Just find out what's wrong with it and fix it."

"But my shift is over in ten min—"

"Sergeant, your shift is over when I'm satisfied that this thruster works right. Understand that? And the way I'm gonna test it is to bring you along with me on a checkout flight. Now, you can either bust ass in here or get killed out there. Take your pick."

The sergeant's face went a deep red. But before he could say anything, the loudspeaker blared: "Major Colt, top-priority communication from Earthside. Acknowledge immediately."

Colt glared over his shoulder at the loudspeaker, set into a distant bulkhead. Then he looked back at the technician. "I'll be right back, sergeant. Neither one of us sleeps until that thruster works perfectly."

After Colt pushed away and went glide-striding toward the nearest hatch, the technician muttered, "Black sonofabitch."

Officers' quarters aboard Alpha were styled after the wardrooms of submarines. Compact. Functional. Barked shins and numbed elbows until you learned how to live gracefully inside a fully furnished telephone booth.

Colt plopped down on his bunk, automatically ducking to avoid the cabinets set above it. He touched the ON stud of the communicator panel on the bulkhead beside his bed. The view screen next to the panel glowed to life.

The screen showed one of the communications techs, a cute young blonde that Colt had occasionally dated when they had been in Florida. It frosted enough people that Colt made certain to keep on dating her. "The message is from General Murdock, sir," she said with conspicuous formality. "Personal and scrambled."

Colt scratched his chin. "Okay, pipe it through . . . and you can at least smile for me, sugar."

She smiled.

"That's better."

The screen went into a crazy flutter of colors as Colt leaned across the arm's-length span of his compartment and pulled his codebook from the writing desk. "Goddam crap," he muttered as he found the right page, then with a lean extended finger picked out a sequence of numbered buttons under the view screen.

The picture stayed scrambled, but he heard a man's

voice say, "Please identify yourself for voice-print verification."

Scrambled Earthside too? Colt was impressed. Even for Murdock, this was elaborate. "Franklin D. R. Colt, 051779, Major. USAF."

There was the slightest instant's delay, then: "Thank you, Major Colt. Go ahead, please."

The picture cleared up and showed General Murdock sitting at his desk.

"There you are," the general said.

"Yessir."

Murdock was round, bald and nervous. Colt had never seen him look happy or pleased. The general had a little gray mustache, hyperthyroid eyes, and an apparently endless supply of the jitters. His hands were never still. "I'm having you reassigned to Moonbase, Colt. The paperwork is already on its way to you. I want you to leave on the next available shuttle."

Colt immediately thought of the technician he had left slaving over the tug's faulty thruster. "May I ask why, sir?"

"It's . . ." Murdock seemed to glance around furtively, even though he was alone in his own very secure office. "It's part of the build-up we're putting into effect . . . to protect our ABM network and prevent the Reds from completing theirs."

"Then why'm I being sent to Moonbase? I oughtta be out flying double shifts, knocking off as many of their satellites as I can. You'll need every qualified astro—"

"We've got a batch of replacements coming up. Leaves are being canceled, new men sent up ahead of schedule. There'll be plenty of manpower for orbital missions."

With a shake of his head, Colt objected, "But, look, sir, it sounds blowhard to say it, but, hell, I've got the highest score of any of the rocket jocks here. If you want—"

"I don't want any arguments, dammit!" The general's normal tenor voice rose higher, and his face started to show splotches of purple. "You flyboys turn every order into a debate. I want you on Moonbase."

"But I don't understand why, sir."

"You know why. I don't have to draw you any maps."

Colt rolled his eyes heavenward. "Sir, this may surprise you, but I can't read your mind."

"Dammit, Colt!" Murdock actually drummed his chubby fists on the desk, like a little boy about to have a tantrum. "Do I have to spell it out? You know Kinsman's commanding Moonbase. He refused rotation last year, and those fools on staff decided to let him have his way."

Now it was becoming clear. Colt almost smiled. "You want me up there to look over Chet's shoulder during the build-up."

"That's right."

"Because you don't trust him."

Murdock glared. "I've had to deal with Kinsman for more than fifteen years. He's too flighty. Too easygoing. Too unreliable."

It was unkind to tease the general, but Colt couldn't resist. "Then why don't you relieve him? Rotate him out of Moonbase. Nobody's supposed to serve on the Moon for more'n a year, anyway. He's been there—how long now? Three years?"

"More like five," Murdock answered, his bald head glistening with sweat. "But it's not that simple. Where would I find another qualified man of high enough rank who's willing to stay on that rockpile for a year straight? Would you do it?"

"Hell, no!"

"You see? And besides, Kinsman's got some medical disability in his record—a heart flutter or something like that. It's probably faked, but if he's relieved of duty he could stay on the Moon as a medical case. Who'd want to take over as commander with *him* standing at his shoulder?"

Colt wanted to laugh, but instead he probed deeper. "Yeah, but Chet gets the job done, doesn't he? Moonbase is coming along fine, everything on schedule or ahead?"

Murdock didn't take the bait. Instead, he leaned forward confidentially and lowered his voice: "Listen, Frank. I know Kinsman. And I know a good deal more about him than you do; things nobody else knows. I don't want him up there with a totally free hand if a crisis comes up. He'll crack. Or he'll jump the wrong way. He's gotten very friendly with the Russian commander, Leonov. He's just too soft all around. I want you there so that you can take command, if and when the crunch comes."

Colt heard himself say, "Chet and I were buddies. We've been through a lot together."

"I know that," Murdock answered. "He trusts you. But I also know that when the chips are down, you'll react like an American and an officer—not like a weak-kneed neurotic."

Neurotic? The word made Colt's stomach tighten.

"In an emergency situation," Murdock continued, grim-faced, "I know that you'll put your orders and the nation's welfare above your personal feelings."

Colt's eyes widened as he realized what Murdock was saying. "You mean you think Chet would commit *trea-son?*"

"I'm not accusing anyone of anything," Murdock said, obviously forcing himself to speak calmly. "I'm just being careful."

"Thanks," Colt said.

As he packed his meager travelkit, Colt began to understand what Murdock was doing. *The sonofabitch is using me! Because I'm a friend of Chet's. Gonna look great. Like Brutus sticking in his blade.* He zipped the bag viciously and hefted it in one hand. And he knows I'll do it, too. I've come too far and fought too many of those lily-white bastards to back down now. Never duck a tough job. Never turn down a chance for a promotion. Don't give 'em a chance to pass you over. And if I have to step across Chet's body to get the next step up . . . Shit, if I don't do it, somebody else will.

As he reached for the door to his compartment, Colt remembered the technician working on his tug. *Fuck him. Let him work his white ass off.* And he stepped into the corridor and strode off for the Moonbound shuttle.

"When you said we were going for a walk, I didn't realize you meant up here," Ellen said.

She and Kinsman were in pressure suits, walking slowly and carefully across the inlet of Mare Nubium that covered Selene and lapped up to the base of Alphonsus' ringwall.

Kinsman hated the pressure suits. It was like being inside someone else's skin. Sluggish, difficult to move, even in the gentle lunar gravity. They always smelled of plastic and someone else's sweat. He was annoyed with himself for not having ordered a special suit custom-made for him.

"Everybody ought to see the surface," he said to Ellen. "Too many ninety-dayers come here and stay down below all through their tour. Might as well be in the Pentagon or the New York subway."

"What's that?" Ellen pointed toward the rounded plastic of a surface dome, more than a kilometer away. He couldn't see her face behind the glare-proof visor. The pressure suit transformed her into an anonymous hulking figure. Her voice was an electronic approximation in his helmet earphones.

"That's the original Lunagrad dome," Kinsman explained. "Leonov's people still land their shuttles over there." *And why did Pete beg off meeting me today? What's going on with him?*

She stepped closer to him, waddling ponderously. "How come the two bases were built right next to each other?"

"That was back in the eighties, when the watchword was cooperation. We were going to share most of the facilities: electric power, water factory, the farms . . . Cheaper for both sides."

"It didn't last long, did it?"

"Earthside politics," Kinsman said. "The food shortages, the energy crunch—we started getting orders to make Moonbase self-sufficient. Not to depend on the Russians for anything. They got the same orders. But we'd already been living together for ten years."

"You've been up here ten years?"

"More like fifteen, off and on. Past five years

straight." He spread his arms and turned slowly. "Well . . . What do you think of it?"

She may have tried to shrug inside the suit; it was impossible to tell. "It looks so barren . . . desolate. And it's so *empty!*"

"We've got lots of space," Kinsman agreed. "And energy—free, almost, from the Sun. What we don't have is water. Have to process it out of the rocks. Funny: energy's cheap here and water's expensive. On Earth it's just the other way around."

"Water isn't cheap on Earth," Ellen said. "Not drinkable water."

Kinsman shook his head, even though Ellen couldn't see his gesture. "You'd think that would be the last thing they'd mess up on a planet brimful of the stuff."

He took her gloved hand and guided her up the gentle slope of a small crater rim. The ground was pockmarked with craterlets a few centimeters across. The blower in Kinsman's suit hissed at its highest speed; still it felt hot inside.

"The horizon's so close," she said.

"The edge of the world. Makes you half think you could fall off."

"I thought we'd be able to see the stars better."

"Your visor's pretty heavily filtered. And the glare from Earth doesn't help much."

"It's just so *dreary!* I've never seen such desolation."

What did you expect? he said to himself. Aloud, he asked, "What brought you up here?"

She turned ponderously to face him. "I was working in the Pentagon and heard of an opening for a chief of the cryptography section. I grabbed at it. Then they told me where it was."

"But you came anyway."

"For a chance to be a section chief? I'd go a lot farther than the Moon for that kind of advance."

Kinsman felt his brows knit. "Are jobs that hard to come by in Washington?"

"Everywhere. Especially when you start working as late as I did. A man can get married and have a child, and nobody penalizes him. But a woman loses at least a year from her career profile—and don't think the personnel people don't mark that down in red."

"You have a baby?"

"She's nine, now. With my ex-husband. In Arizona, last I heard."

"So you came up here," Kinsman said, "to the land of opportunity."

"That's right. I want to be head of the whole communications department."

With a wry grin, he said, "I'll see what I can do about that." Then, more seriously: "You know, Pierce *is* due for rotation Earthside. He's been running Communications for more than a year now . . ." He let his voice trail off.

But Ellen's voice was eager. "Do you think I could move into his job? I mean, I know I can handle it. Back in the Pentagon I was really running the whole office, except that my boss—"

"Whoa," Kinsman said, raising his gloved hands. "Slow down. It's up to Larry to name his replacement. And I'm not sure that putting a new arrival into the slot right away would sit too well with the rest of the crew. Especially the guys who've been there for a while."

"Larry? You mean Mr. Pierce?"

"Yeah. Talk to him about it. It's his decision."

"I will," Ellen said.

They stood next to each other in the lonely vacuum of the roiled bare rocked lunar plain, and Kinsman realized that they had nothing more to say to each other. "Come on, we ought to be getting back," he told her.

She paced along beside him as they headed over the uneven ground, back toward Selene's main dome. "You're held in very high esteem around here," Ellen said, after a long silence.

"Rank hath its privileges."

"It's more than that. You were one of the first astronauts to stay on the Moon for any length of time . . ."

"A regular pioneer. Way back in the eighties."

"And you saved a few lives when the first temporary bases were set up."

"Everybody saved a few lives back then. There was

no way you could survive without your buddies' help."
How much more does she know?

"You're a very dashing and romantic figure."

"Sure. And rain makes applesauce."

"You are," Ellen insisted. "Women talk. From what
I hear, you can have your pick of the women here, and
you often do."

"Well . . . "

"But no lasting relationships. Nothing permanent.
Nothing even long-term."

I'm being cross-examined! he realized.

"That's smart," Ellen went on. "No ties, no commitments. Very smart."

"Dammit all, Ellen, this is getting ridiculous."

"Is it?" Her voice sounded amused. "I think it's fascinating. I'm trying to understand you . . . and myself.
I don't go to a party with a guy the first day I meet him
and wind up in his bed. And I had to *chase* you!"

"I'm old and tired . . ."

"I know better. You're in excellent condition."

"I had no intention of getting you in bed."

"Getting me in bed? Just like that. I had nothing to
do with it. It was all your idea. Tarzan finds a mate and
swings her up to his tree."

"Come on, you know what I mean."

She laughed. "Chet, you're priceless. The last of the
heroes. You really ought to be carrying a sword and
wearing shining armor."

"And a hat with a feather in it?" All he could see in
her visor was the reflection of his own blank-faced helmet.

"It would look good on you."

"Maybe it would, at that."

They walked in silence for a few slow, dreamlike lunar strides.

"How about dinner tonight?" Kinsman asked.

She hesitated long enough to let him know that she
considered it very carefully. "I'm afraid I've already
made a date with Mr. Pierce. He asked me this morning."

Kinsman didn't say anything for a moment. Then,
"Well, I've got to get back to my office and play at

being base commander for a while." And see why Leonov backed down.

"Chet," Ellen said. "I don't want to make any commitments, either."

"Sure," he said. "That's very smart."

Jill Myers was just finishing her rounds at Selene's hospital. Like most of the underground community, the hospital was built in two interconnecting sections, one American and one Russian. Nearly all the facilities were duplicated.

At first glance, Jill didn't look much like a doctor. She was short, barely a meter and a half, and had a child's round, snub-nosed face. But she also had strength and skill and a quality that was rare in a physician: empathy.

The hospital was large and well-staffed out of all proportion to Selene's total size. This was because most of the permanent lunar residents—Russian and American—were on the Moon for health reasons: bad hearts, bad lungs, muscular diseases. Jill herself had developed an intolerable series of allergies that had incapacitated her Earthside. Here in the controlled environment of the lunar community she was virtually perfect.

Jill looked tired now as she left the last of her patients and headed for the hospital's core of administrative offices and monitoring stations. She got as far as the first monitoring station, a horseshoe-shaped set of desks covered with view screens and computer-linked sensors that watched over a dozen patients' heart rates, respirations, alpha rhythms and so on. The girl sitting in the curve of the horseshoe called to her, "Dr. Myers, phone for you."

Jill stopped and accepted the handset the girl was holding out. Leaning tiredly against the edge of the desk, she watched the nearest view screen crackle with momentary interference; then it cleared to show a bearded, dark-eyed man that Jill immediately recognized as one of the Russian doctors.

He looked very grave.

"Alexei, what's wrong?" Jill blurted, as her free hand unconsciously went up to smooth her brown hair.

"We have a difficult situation on our hands," he said, in smooth English. "Cardiac infarction. Our emergency equipment is all in use. If you can't loan us an aortic pump system, I'll have to decide which man to let die. It's a choice I'd rather not make."

"Of course. Can you move the patient here?"

"Not without a pump in him. He's too feeble."

"I'll be there in fifteen minutes," Jill said. "No, ten."

"Good."

Turning to the monitoring nurse, she said, "Put me through to the base commander, and while I'm talking to him, get the emergency crew across to Dr. Landau with a heart pump wagon."

Pat Kelly's face showed up on the view screen. "Kinsman's off someplace," he said, with a faint grin to show what he thought of his commander's absence. "Not to be disturbed except for cataclysms."

Jill outlined the problem in two sentences. Then, "I'm taking an emergency unit to the Lunagrad section."

Kelly hiked his eyebrows. "Regs don't allow that, you know."

"Then either find Chet in the next three minutes or break the regulations yourself! There's a life at stake."

"Not one of ours."

"Oh, you're not a member of the human race? I'll remember that the next time you come in here. I'm going. What you do with your regulations is your problem, but I can make a medical suggestion—"

"Okay, okay." Kelly threw his hands up. "I'll write out the order and ask Chet to sign it when he gets back to his desk."

"All right," Jill said. "Thanks."

"Don't thank me. I'm just doing what Kinsman would do if he was here. If it was up to me . . ."

But Jill had already dropped the handset and was racing down the corridor toward the Russian half of the hospital.

Four hours later, she was slouched on a softly padded sofa, sipping a glass of scalding tea. Alexei Landau sat next to her. He was tall, with the broad shoulders and strong, sure hands of a surgeon. Behind his beard he was smiling.

"There is an old Russian proverb that I just made up: If you have five cardiac emergency units available, you will get six cardiac emergencies."

Jill smiled back at him. "At least we got him in time."

"Hmm, yes. But he's going to need support for many days. Weeks, perhaps."

"We can bring him back to our side. There's plenty of room."

Landau shook his head. "No. The rules forbid us to send our people into your part of the hospital."

"Rules!" Jill snapped. "If we played by their rules, your patient would be dead now."

The Russian shrugged elaborately.

"I'll have Kinsman talk to Leonov. They'll work it out."

"I doubt it. Leonov is due to leave shortly anyway. We don't know who will be taking his place."

"Chet Kinsman will figure out a way to do it," Jill said, dismissing the problem. "Who is the patient? He looked vaguely familiar to me."

"He should. He is Nicholai Baliagorev."

"The ballet master?"

"Yes."

"I didn't know he was here!"

"He just arrived. They sent him here to rest his heart, but the rocket flight was too much for him."

"Oh, Alex, we've got to save him! We can't let a man like that die because of red tape."

Landau shook his head wearily. "Red tape has killed more people than bullets, dear girl. Far more."

It was still night on the Sea of Clouds, and would continue to be for another week. But the waxing crescent of the Earth, more than half full now, cast a soft light on the lunar landscape.

Kinsman stood on a slight rise that overlooked the broad undulating plain, listening to the sound of his own breathing and the suit's air blower. A pair of dune buggies were inching their way across the plain, and not far from where he stood, a group of pressure-suited Americans and Russians were deep in conversation.

Next to him stood Colonel Leonov, in a bright red pressure suit almost identical to Kinsman's own, except for slight styling differences in the helmet and backpack.

"It should be a good race," Leonov said. Kinsman heard the radio voice in his helmet earphones.

"Yeah," he answered. "And this year we ought to win, for a change."

"Hah! Wait until you see the special buggy we've put together."

"Not another rocket job?"

"You'll see."

While they talked, Kinsman took a pad from his belt. Clumsily, with his gloved hands, he wrote, "Is your suit bugged?" He held the note up before Leonov's visor.

"I checked the suit out personally before putting it on," Leonov answered. "It is perfectly safe."

"We ought to take a look at this crater," Kinsman said, clumping up to the rim of a thirty-meter-wide depression. "It's close enough to the route of the race to be marked off, don't you think?"

"That depends on how steep the interior is." Leonov followed him.

They walked slowly down the interior slope, picking their way through rocks and loose rubble by the lights on their helmets, until they were out of sight of the race committee and the standing crawlers and buggies. Out of sight meant out of radio contact. They could talk to each other now without fear of being overheard.

"What happened yesterday?" Kinsman asked. "Your message wasn't very clear."

"Too much to do. I couldn't get away. It would not have looked right to drop important business because of the race committee."

Nodding, Kinsman changed the subject. "I got a call from one of our doctors. She wants us to transfer a heart patient of yours to our end of the hospital."

"Yes, I know. Baliagorev, the former dancer."

"She says your regulations won't let us take him in."

Leonov answered, "Of course. And *your* regulations do not allow you to take him without permission from your superiors Earthside."

"Hell, Pete, I'll just do it and get them to okay it after the fact. There's a human life at stake."

"Yes. But your superiors are much easier to handle than mine. Mine would absolutely forbid transferring one of our citizens to your end of the hospital. Absolutely."

"Then he's going to die?"

"No, he's on his way to your side of the hospital. I gave the order this morning before I came out here to join you."

Kinsman stopped dead on the gravelly slope, sending a few loose pebbles rattling noiselessly down toward the shadowed bottom of the crater. "You . . . Pete, sometimes you astound me."

"You think it's impossible for a good Communist to be flexible? To fly in the face of authority? You think only you Americans have feelings?"

"Oh, hell."

Leonov put a hand on Kinsman's shoulder. "Old

friend, I am being relieved of duty. I am being sent back to Mother Russia, to my wife and little ones. We will never see each other again."

"Shipped out? When?"

"In two weeks. Perhaps less. I'm not certain yet who my replacement will be, but the indications are that he will be a hard-liner. A good Marxist and a good soldier. Not a soft-head like me. Not a collaborationist who attends capitalist parties and wastes the peoples' time and money on frivolities."

"You're in trouble?"

"I'm always in trouble," Leonov said, trying to sound jovial. "That's why I was given the Lunagrad post in the first place. This is, even better than Siberia—a banishment that appears to be a promotion. Most of the people in Lunagrad are exiles."

"If they're anything like the people in our half of Selene," Kinsman said, "they wouldn't want to go back to Earth. It's too crowded down there, Pete. Like rats, that's the way they're living."

"I know. But our superiors don't realize that. They are still living in the past. They still think of Lunagrad as a sort of exile for troublesome officers."

"They're calling you back, though."

"Yes. The game is becoming serious. They have finally realized that we supply most of the oxygen and foodstuffs and fuels for the space stations. Lunagrad—forgive me, Selene—is a vital logistics center for the orbiting platforms. And the men in those stations direct the work on the ABM satellite networks. So we here on the Moon hold the key to all the military operations going on in orbit around the Earth. That is why I am being replaced. They want a reliable soldier up here."

Kinsman turned his head inside the helmet of his pressure suit. His nose wrinked at the scent of plastic and sealant grease. The rim of the crater blocked everything from view with a continuous wall of solid rock. He and Leonov could not see the other men, the buggies and crawlers, the lunar plain, even the ever-watchful Earth. There was nothing to be seen except the rockstrewn crater slope, the solemn unblinking stars overhead, and this other human being standing before him. Kinsman's eyes saw only the outside of a bulky, impersonal pressure suit; even the visor was blank. But he could sense the man inside, the soul that animated the plastic and metal.

"Pete, I'm not supposed to tell you this," Kinsman said, "but something big is brewing. I don't mean just tinkering with the ABM satellites; that's been going on for a long time. I think they're going to take the next step."

He could sense Leonov nodding slowly. "Yes. That is why they want to remove an unreliable officer from command of Lunagrad."

"They're sending up a 'good soldier' to be my second-in-command, too," Kinsman said. "Pat Kelly's being sent back Earthside, and Frank Colt's coming up to keep an eye on me."

"Colt? The black one. Yes . . . I remember him."

"Dammit all!" Kinsman balled his fists. "They're going to have their war. They're going to start killing people in orbit, and they'll end up destroying everything."

"History is inexorable."

"Stop talking like a goddamned robot!" Kinsman snapped. "This isn't abstract. It's you and me, Pete! They're going to try to make us kill each other. Those shitheads won't be satisfied with tearing the Earth apart; they're going to send us orders to go to war up here."

"I won't be here," Leonov said quietly. "I'll be home in Kiev with my wife and children, waiting for your missiles to fall on us."

"And you're just going to let them do it to you? You're not going to try to do anything about it?"

"What *can* we do?" Leonov's voice deepened to a growl. "We've talked about this many times, Chet. But what good is talk? When the actual moment comes—what can I do? What can you do?"

"I can refuse to fight," Kinsman heard himself say. "And so can you, as long as you're in command here. We can stop them from making war here on the Moon."

"Bravo. And what about the eight billions of human beings on Earth?"

Kinsman stared at his friend. He had no answer.

It was almost fully dark in Washington. Streetlights and store windows were lit, because the danger of darkened streets was far worse than the drain on fuel from turning the lights on. Commuters were scurrying for the armed buses that would speed them to the relative safety of the protected suburbs, leaving the city to the poor, the black, the angry.

The President stood at his office window, gazing across Lafayette Park to the National Christmas Tree. It soared more than twelve meters high, a triumph of plastic and chemical fluorescence. A Marine honor guard paced around it with bayoneted carbines.

"Nobody comes to see it any more," the President murmured. "When I was a kid we used to watch the tree being lit up on television every year. The first time I came to Washington we saw the Christmas tree. Now nobody comes at all. Nobody pays any attention to it . . ."

The Secretary of Defense coughed politely. "These papers, Mr. President—they require your signature."

Reluctantly, almost petulantly, the President turned away from the window. "We ought to do something. There must be millions of kids who'd like to see the tree."

"They see it on television," said the Defense Secretary. "It's difficult for them to get to the city." He was standing in front of the President's broad real wood desk, unconsciously tapping a thick sheaf of papers resting on the desktop.

"Um, well, I suppose so." The President shook his head and then dropped his chunky body into the high-backed plush swivel chair behind the desk. He looked much too small for the chair, for the broad desk itself.

"Now, what am I supposed to be signing here?" he asked.

"These are the contingency plans, part of our follow-up on the ABM satellite problems."

"Oh. And what's different about these that they need my signature?"

The Defense Secretary's narrow, sharp-featured face clouded momentarily. "The contingency plans cover the possibility of a Red attack on our manned space stations. They provide for manpower and logistics back-up to prevent such an attack from succeeding."

"Beefing up the stations' defenses?"

"Exactly."

"What's this going to cost? Are you sure we need it?"

"Sir, it's obvious that the Russians are up to something big. There's been a shooting incident in Antarctica. One of our Naval officers was killed."

"What?"

Defense raised a calming hand. "We've only gotten a scrambled report out of McMurdo Station. They're investigating the incident. Our monitors have also intercepted similar reports from the Russian base at Mirnyy. All we know for certain at the moment is that a team of Russians and a team of Americans fired on each other. One American officer is dead."

The President's hands were trembling. "They killed one of our men?"

"Apparently. We'll know more shortly."

"I want a full report as soon as the information becomes available."

"Of course."

"No matter what hour of the day or night. Do you hear me? A full report."

"Yes, sir. Certainly."

His voice still hollow with shock, the President went on, "Now, what's this got to do with the space stations?"

Defense said, "It's all part of a pattern. They're getting tough in Antarctica. They're building up their troop concentrations in Syria. Intelligence reports show that they intend to replace their present commander of Lunagrad, a coexistence type, with a hard-line full general straight out of the Kremlin. They're up to something big."

Wordlessly, the President reached for a pen from the holder on the desk and scribbled his signature at the bottom of the last page.

"Thank you, Mr. President."

Defense snatched the papers off his desk and strode quickly out of the office.

In the anteroom outside, the burly, angry-faced man paced across the plush carpeting. He walked with a slight limp, as if his feet weren't meant to be in the shoes he was forced to wear.

He glared up at the Defense Secretary. "He signed?"

The harsh tortured whisper made Defense want to shudder. "Yes, of course."

"He realizes that the plan includes preparations for an attack on the Russian space stations?"

"No." Defense shook his head. "That didn't come up in our conversation."

The angry one almost smiled. "So be it. We can explain the value of a preemptive strike to him later. Gradually. If time permits."

The meeting of the Internal Security Committee had been long and bitter and sometimes loud. The Kremlin had often enough rung to the shouts of angry men, and many times such rancor had led to violence.

Prime Minister Bereznik was determined to restore harmony.

"Comrades!" he said sharply, slapping a heavy palm on the table before him. They all jerked their attention to him, dropping their hot arguments for a moment.

"Comrades, we should direct our energies to the solution to this problem. Wrangling will produce no positive results."

"But firing on our scientific expedition is an inexcusable provocation!" General Kemenevsky shouted.

"But we killed one of their men," said the Foreign Minister, his puffy face florid with passion. "There was shooting on both sides."

"They are increasing their orbital missions," repeated the Intelligence Minister. "More satellites, and more attacks on our satellites."

The Prime Minister glared in helpless frustration. Sometimes he wished he had Khrushchev's boldness; it was canny old Nikita who had often carried a pistol to these meetings.

"My father gave his life for the Soviet Union at Stalingrad," the general was saying heatedly, "and I will not allow *any* foreign transgressor to destroy what he fought and died to preserve."

"But what of the Chinese?" someone asked, his voice quavering up from the general din around the table. "What are they going to do?"

At the far end of the table, the Nameless One got to his feet. All the arguing stopped dead. He was not truly nameless, of course, but he insisted on using his unpronounceable Tadzhik tribal name; so the Russians jokingly called him the Nameless One. What he thought of the joke no one knew; he neither smiled nor complained.

Ah, thought the Prime Minister, a little clear thinking will enter the discussion. I was wondering how long he would remain silent. But he suppressed a shudder as he nodded at the Nameless One. The man was uncanny, frightening in the way a snake is: inspiring a terror that goes far deeper than rational understanding.

"It is clear," he said in his icy, quiet, slightly sibilant tone, "that we face a crisis of will." The Nameless One was neither tall nor imposing from the standpoint of physical size. His face was thin, with a slightly oriental cast to the glittering, hypnotic eyes. His ears were slightly pointed; his hands, long and thin and graceful.

"Our people urgently need the coal that our scientists have discovered in Antarctica. The Americans desire the coal also. Our strategic deterrent is matched by their missiles. Our ABM satellite network is incomplete, and so is theirs. We are in a stalemate, unless . . ."

He let the word hang while the various ministers and military officers leaned forward in their chairs.

"Unless," he went on, "we are prepared to steel ourselves for the next step."

The general nodded firmly. "Orbit the bombs."

"Exactly," agreed the Nameless One.

"But that would be in violation of a treaty that we solemnly—"

The Prime Minister rapped his knuckles on the arm of his chair. "That treaty was signed more than two decades ago. The world is very different today."

"Yes, but . . ."

"We have no choice," said the Nameless One, with infinite calm. "If we are not prepared to keep the Americans from attacking us, we will lose everything. The orbiting bombs will be a threat that the Americans—and the Chinese, as well—cannot ignore."

The discussion went on well into the night. But at least, thought the Prime Minister gratefully, it is a discussion and not a brawl.

The Nameless One did most of the talking.

It was nearly midnight in Selene before Kinsman got to the hospital. He looked in on Baliagorev, in the intensive-care unit. Jill Myers was there, and they wound up having coffee together in the hospital's tiny automated cafeteria.

The place was deserted. They got their steaming drink from the dispensers and sat at the nearest table. It wobbled on uncertain legs.

"Damned place always smells of antiseptic," Kinsman grumbled. "And the light panels are too bright—glaring."

Jill laughed tiredly. "Yeah, boss, how about that? I'd look a lot better in candlelight."

"You look fine, kid. Tired but happy." It was true. There were fatigue circles under her eyes, but Jill was smiling.

She slumped back in her plastic chair. "Well, it's been a long day, but a good one. I think Baliagorev will make it."

"And you've got Landau orbiting around you."

"Alex? Oh, he's an old friend. We met years ago . . ."

Sipping gingerly at the searing coffee, Kinsman said, "I was watching you two back at the ICU. Do you realize that you actually fluttered your eyelashes at him?"

Jill's face went deep red. "That's not true!"

"Oh, no? He's asked to stay here overnight."

"He wants to be with his patient."

"And rain makes applesauce. He wants to be with you, sweetie."

She grinned, but her hands seemed to go out of control. They fidgeted around the coffee cup and then up to her face. "You're kidding. You really think so?"

"Looks pretty obvious to me. I wouldn't be surprised if he ran the old man halfway around the Ocean of Storms just to get him to keel over."

"You're terrible!"

Kinsman smiled back at her. "Yeah, I guess I am. But I'm not the only one who's noticed the way you two have been looking at each other. Half the hospital staff is sighing with romantic rapture about you. The female half."

Jill tried to frown, but her pixie face wasn't made for it. "What about you and this new girl in the communications department?"

Kinsman scratched at his stubbly chin. "She wants to be the department chief. At least she's honest about it. She reminds me of a girl . . . You knew her, too. That photographer in the orbiting lab."

"Lord, that was *ages* ago."

"Never forget a face," Kinsman said. "Can't remember her name, though. But she was the same as Ellen. Lots of ambition."

"So there's nothing serious going on with you?"

"Has there ever been?"

Jill ran a finger along the lip of her coffee cup. "Don't you think it's about time that there was? You're getting a little elderly for the playboy life-style."

"Yeah. Maybe. And I'm too young to be a *roué*."

She smiled. "So what are you going to do about it?"

What can I do? he wanted to shout. But instead he merely mumbled, "It's a lousy time to get my personal life tangled."

"Why?" Jill asked. "What's so lousy about this particular time?"

He hesitated. "Things . . . things are brewing. Trouble's coming. Big trouble." He reached across the table and grabbed her wrist. "Listen, kid: you and your Russian friend better grab whatever fun you can get, here and now. Because in the next week or two the lid could blow off. All hell's going to break loose. And soon."

Saturday 4 December 1999: 1830 hrs UT

Kinsman stood at the airlock hatch in the main dome, waiting for it to open. Outside, the shuttle rocket sat squat and ungainly, connected to the tube by flexible access tunnels.

The hatch popped ajar with a sigh, then swung smoothly back. Kinsman felt a slight stir of air as the pressure in the dome equilibrated.

Frank Colt stepped through the hatch and into the dome. He carried a single small travelkit, and was wearing a regulation Air Force blue uniform, the way officers did Earthside, with a chest full of decorations. Not the usual lunar coverall.

Kinsman was always surprised at Colt's lack of physical size. The black astronaut had a giant's strong personality, but physically he was slight. A black Alexander Hamilton, Kinsman thought. Tough, waspish. Then he remembered that Hamilton had been killed in a duel by a man later found to be a traitor to the United States.

At the sight of Kinsman, Colt snapped to bayonet-stiff attention and saluted crisply. Suppressing a grin, Kinsman returned the salute, then reached for Colt's hand. "Frank, you old ass-kicker—good to see you. Welcome aboard."

Colt grinned widely. "How're you, pal? Still letting your hair grow, huh?"

With a glance at Colt's close-cropped fuzz, Kinsman countered, "Jealous?"

"Shit, baby, if I let mine go natural I'd never get a helmet over it."

Laughing, they made their way toward the power ladder.

"You can drop your bag off at your quarters and have dinner with us," Kinsman said as they stepped aboard the moving rungs.

"Sure, sure. But shouldn't I be presenting my orders and officially checking in?"

"We can do that tomorrow. You must be hungry. That food on the shuttle hasn't improved any, I'll bet."

Colt laughed as he clung to the handgrip in front of him. "Hell, no."

They rode down four levels in silence, the only sound being the distant whine of the ladder's electric motors. Then Colt said, "Maybe I can wait a couple more days and officially take my new post on Pearl Harbor Day. That'd have a nice touch to it."

"Pearl what?" Kinsman asked.

"Pearl Harbor, December Seventh. World War II. It was in all the papers."

As they stepped off the ladder, Kinsman said, "You've got an odd sense of humor, Frank."

"History, man, history. It's my big subject."

Half an hour later they were in the cafeteria. It was a small place, with only a couple of dozen tables. Most of them were filled, but the acoustic insulation kept the background noise down to a muted murmur.

Colt's face was grim as he sat down. "Aren't those Russians over there?" He cocked his head in the direction of the table where Jill Myers was sitting with Landau and one of the Russian medi-techs.

Kinsman nodded. "We've got one of their people in our intensive-care unit. Heart condition."

"Chet, this is *supposed* to be a military installation. It's bad enough to be sitting right next door to the enemy—"

"Hey, relax," Kinsman said. "These people aren't enemies of ours."

Colt shook his head warily.

Kinsman went on, "There's not enough military activity here to make it worth worrying over. You know that, Frank."

"Suppose you stopped supplying food and oxygen to the space stations? What then?"

"Come on."

"No, I'm serious, man." Colt jabbed a fork into his steak, the first he'd had in months. "Suppose they knocked out Moonbase, or took over. How'd our guys in the space stations get supplied?"

"From Earthside, of course."

"Yeah? You know how long it'd take to set that up? And the cost? If they knock off Moonbase, they cripple our space stations. They win the battle, man. They own everything from a hundred klicks off the Earth's surface. And that means they own the Earth!"

"It won't happen, Frank."

"It could." Colt attacked the steak with vigor. "That's why I've been assigned here. Murdock's worried about just that."

Kinsman suddenly wasn't hungry any more. "I guess I should've taken a look at your orders, after all."

"Wouldn't do you any good. But Murdock gave me a personal call—he thinks you're a mushmelon and he wants me to make sure this place doesn't get bagged. That's why I'm here."

"Terrific," Kinsman said. He pushed his tray away from him. "And the next step will be to get prepared for taking over Lunagrad."

"Could be."

"That's stupid," Kinsman snapped.

"Is it?"

Hold it, Kinsman told himself. Don't let them start a fight between the two of us! With an effort, he forced his temper down.

"Frank, do you remember Cy Calder?"

"Who?"

"Way back in the early days, when we were training. Cy Calder. He was a newsman for . . . "

Recognition dawned on Colt's face. "Oh, yeah, the old dude. Man, he must've been ninety years old."

"Not quite," Kinsman said. "He told me a story once . . . about when he flew a bomber in World War I."

"I didn't know he was a pilot."

"One of the first. He used to fly bombing runs in the early months of the war. Open cockpit, scarf-in-wind kind of stuff."

"No shit."

Kinsman grinned at the memory of Calder's story. "He flew a two-man bomber. Cranked her up to maximum altitude over the trenches—about five thousand feet. All the soldiers in the trenches shot at any airplane. They hated the fliers."

Colt laughed.

"Cy flew mostly at night. Never saw another plane in the sky. Then one night, as they were coming back from a bombing raid on some farmhouse, they passed a big German Gotha bomber coming back from a raid on the Allied side of the lines."

"Yeah?"

"Cy waved at the German pilot and the guy waved back. They were both excited just to see somebody else up there."

"Those were the days," Colt muttered.

"Well, a couple minutes after they passed each other, Cy's gunner turned around to him and started yelling, so he could be heard over the engines, 'That was a *German!* What the hell were we waving at him for? Turn around, let's shoot the bastard down!' "

Colt nodded.

"Cy pushed the gunner back away from him and told him, 'You silly sonofabitch, it's dangerous enough up here without shooting at people!' "

Colt started to laugh, but it never got to be more than a chuckle. "Okay, I dig it. It's dangerous enough up here without shooting at people. But I've got my orders. And maybe your Russian pals never heard that story."

"Anybody who's spent any time on the Moon knows that story," Kinsman said slowly. "They've saved our guys a thousand times and we've saved theirs. Most of their people speak English and a lot of our people know Russian. We live together, Frank. In peace."

"Sheee-it," Colt deliberately exaggerated the accent. "Next thing you know you're gonna start singing Gospel songs. You live in peace, huh? For how long, pal? How long? What happens when they get orders from Earth-

side to do it . . . " Colt slowly squeezed his thumb
down on the tabletop, as if he were squashing a bug. Or
pressing a FIRE button.

Kinsman said nothing. Colt went on, "It's getting
down to the big crunch, man. All this messing around
with the satellites. And some Navy dude got himself
shot down near the South Pole—"

"What?" Kinsman felt a lightning flash of fear-
surprise in his guts.

Colt nodded. "Yeah. Couple days ago. Things are
warming up."

"In Antarctica? They're shooting at each other in an
international zone?"

"Why not? World's biggest coal beds down there.
They're gonna fight over it—or something else. Maybe
the Middle East again; there's still some oil left there.
It's coming, baby. Lotta hungry people and not enough
resources to keep 'em all going. They're going to fight
over it, sooner or later. Nothing we can do to stop it."

Kinsman started to reply, but there was nothing he
could say. He sat there, defeated. Then he saw Pat
Kelly coming up holding a dinner tray.

"Mind if I join you?" Kelly asked. He didn't wait for
an answer, but put his tray down next to Colt's and
pulled out the chair.

"Frank, you know Pat, don't you?" Kinsman asked.

Colt nodded as Kelly sat down. "Just made major,
didn't you?"

"Yep," Kelly answered. "Pretty soon I'll outrank
you, Flash." His usual rabbit's face looked different:
tense, almost angry, flushed with eagerness.

Colt flicked him a lazy glance. "I'm not planning on
retirement that soon. And what's this 'Flash' crap?"

With a shrug, Kelly said, "You've got a reputation
for being a hotshot jock, you know."

"No, I don't know. Tell me."

Kinsman sat there and watched it happen. He felt
helpless and fascinated at the same time. Kelly was a
good man, bright and dedicated. Frank Colt was just as
bright, maybe more so. And whatever was burning inside Colt was far hotter than Kelly's flame, Kinsman
knew from long experience. There was something about

Colt that called lightning down from the sky. Men either loved him like a brother or hated him.

Kelly was tight-lipped. "Look at you, wearing that uniform. Like you're at an Academy parade. You know damned well that we don't do that up here. But you've got to be the superhero. All-time champion hotshot."

"And you keep your uniform stowed in a closet so everybody'll think you're Mr. Nice Guy, huh? Ever been shot at?"

"That's got nothing to do with—"

"Hell, it don't! Know why you're here, Mr. Nice Guy? D'you know why you can prance around on the Moon and collect rocks and advances in rank every three years?"

"Now, wait—"

Colt shut him up with a long forefinger jabbed toward his face. "You're here on the Moon, *Major* Kelly, because it's cheaper to supply our orbiting stations from lunar resources than from Earth. That's it. I don't give a shit how many scientists you've got here or how many cripples you've saved. The only reason the taxpayers of the United States support this fairy palace is because it's cheaper than boosting supplies into orbit from Earthside. Got that?"

Kelly was white-faced now. "That's about what I'd expect from you. Did you bring any bombs with you?"

Colt leaned back in his chair and laughed. "Shit, baby, you know bombs are outlawed in space. We signed a treaty with the Russians about thirty years ago. No weapons of mass dee-struction. I bet if you were to swing a search-and-destroy patrol through Lunagrad right now you wouldn't find more'n three or four nukes."

Kinsman butted in. "Both you guys are supposed to be officers and gentlemen. How about acting that way? You're giving everybody a helluva floor show."

Kelly glanced over his shoulder. The people at most of the other tables were staring at them. Including the Russians. Colt just sat back and toyed with his fork.

Very quietly, Kelly said to Kinsman, "Chet, you had me just about convinced to bring my family up here. But I can see that it's useless. It only takes a few Neanderthals to ruin everything, whether it's Earthside or on the Moon."

He got up and walked stiffly out of the cafeteria, leaving his untouched tray at the table.

Colt pursed his lips and looked at Kinsman. "He's too soft to be an officer."

"He's a good man, Frank."

"Yeah, but nice guys finish last. And in a two-man race, only the winner survives."

They finished their meal in silence, with Kelly's food getting cold beside them like a mute reminder of their differences.

Kinsman took Colt back to his own quarters after dinner. "I've got a bottle of homebrew," he said as Colt plopped on the living-room couch. "See what you think of it."

Kinsman slid back the partition to the kitchenette and reached into a closet built in above the microwave cooker. He pulled out a bottle of colorless liquid. "It's sort of a cross between vodka and tequila. The guys in the chem lab made it."

Colt was sprawled happily on the couch. "Y'know," he said, accepting the plastic cup Kinsman handed him, "I had forgotten what luxury you cats live in. A living room, a bedroom, a kitchen, all the electric power you want, all sorts of view screens and gadgets—*fan*tastic!"

Kinsman pulled up the only other chair in the room, a webbed affair that had been salvaged from a wrecked dune buggy.

"Well . . . I guess it *is* pretty soft, compared to the orbital stations."

"Compared to Earthside, man!" Colt said fervently. "Compared to Earth."

He hoisted his cup and Kinsman returned the salute. Kinsman sipped at his drink, carefully letting the burning liquid slide over his tongue. Colt gulped.

"Aargghhh!" Colt squeezed his eyes shut and shook his head. "Wow! That's some helluva chem lab you got, man."

"They do good work," Kinsman admitted, grinning.

"On their own time, of course. No taxpayers' money wasted on frivolities."

"On their own time," Kinsman said. "And under careful supervision of the management. I won't let any bootlegging operations get started around here."

Colt took another swallow. He held the cup up and admired it. "Real rocket fuel, all right." Then he downed the rest of it.

Kinsman put his cup down on top of the phone console next to the couch. Colt did the same.

"Frank, you really shouldn't clobber kids like Kelly the way you did."

"Hey, he jumped *me!*"

"I know. He's scared. He's got a wife and kids sitting next to a SAC base."

"So whattaya want me to do? Turn the other cheek?" Grinning, "That'll be the day."

Colt spread his hands. "Look, Chet, I'll try to go easy on these peaceniks you've got up here. But I've got a job to do, and I'm gonna get it done. If it takes splitting heads, or bruising delicate egos, I can't help it. This base has got to be prepared for an attack."

"I know," Kinsman admitted. "But just don't go out of your way to batter people. Most of them aren't in your league. It's unfair to sock 'em so hard."

"Yassuh," Colt joked, or maybe he was only half joking. He got up from the couch and started shuffling, with stooped back, toward the door. "Us colored folk know our place, massah. Don't want to make no trouble, no how."

"Go to hell," Kinsman said, laughing.

"See ya," Colt said at the door.

"Can you find your way to your quarters okay?"

"Blindfolded."

"Good night, Frank."

As soon as Colt shut the door behind him, Kinsman leaned over and touched the ON button of the phone console. The screen lit up but showed no picture.

"Pat Kelly, please," he said.

For a moment the phone hummed to itself, then the computer's tape voice replied, "Not in quarters."

"Find him."

It took several minutes before Kelly's face appeared on the screen. He still looked tight-lipped, tense.

"Where are you?" Kinsman asked.

"Corridor C, area twenty. I was taking a walk . . . cooling off. Thinking."

"Okay. Now, listen. I want you to get something into your skull. Colt's going to be deputy commander. But I'm creating a slot for an aide to the commander. I want you to take the job. You won't have to go Earthside. You can bring your family here."

Kelly's voice was dead flat. "Not while he's here. It won't work."

"It will work if you make it work," Kinsman answered. "I've known Frank Colt since flight school. There isn't a helluva lot we agree on, except that we're friends. Brothers, almost. He saved my life once. I've helped him through some rough times, like when he lost his wife."

"I didn't know . . . "

"But as close as we are," Kinsman went on, "I'll never know what it's like to be black. And neither will you. He's fought goddamned hard to get where he is now. He's had to jump over hurdles that we can't even imagine."

"Come on now, Chet," Kelly said. "That poor little underprivileged kid from the ghetto . . . I've been hearing that routine all my life. It's phony as hell."

"People still burn synagogues, Pat. And they still kick niggers. It's getting worse, not better. Frank's got the scars to prove it."

"And I'm supposed to—"

"You're supposed to act like an adult," Kinsman snapped. "You do the job that needs to be done and you bring your family up here. They'll be safe."

"Even with *him* around?"

"Even with him around," Kinsman said.

Kelly looked doubtful. But some of the anger had left his face.

"Start the paperwork tomorrow first thing," Kinsman said. "That's an order. You're now my aide. And your family comes up on the next available shuttle space."

"Well . . ."

"And while we're at it, get into the personnel files

and find out how many people in Selene have immediate family Earthside."

"My God, are you going to start a rescue service?"

"Call it an immigration service," Kinsman replied. He snapped off the phone and Kelly's face faded from the screen.

But Kinsman sat staring at the view screen on the opposite wall of the room. It showed Earth. "You know damned well you can't accommodate all of them," he whispered to himself. "I can't save them all. God, there's eight billion of them!"

He didn't sleep that night. He got into his bed and turned off all the lights and view screens and stayed wide awake.

Eight billion of them.

And ye shall hear of wars and rumors of wars . . . For nation shall rise against nation, and kingdom against kingdom: and there shall be famines, and pestilences, and earthquakes . . . And woe unto them that are with child, and to them that give suck in those days!

But pray ye that your flight be not in the winter, neither on the sabbath day:

For then shall be great tribulation, such as was not since the beginning of the world to this time, no, nor shall ever be.

"Holocaust," he whispered to himself.

Sitting up in the sweaty, wrinkled bed he stared at the view-screen picture of Earth floating in the black void. ". . . famines, and pestilences, and earthquakes . . . nation shall rise against nation . . ."

He closed his eyes and saw the dead cosmonaut again. Hanging in space. Oxygen lines ripped out. "By my hand."

Kinsman held his hands out before him in the shadows of the darkened room. *So you're going to survive while everybody else dies. You're guiltier than they are. You've killed. You didn't push any buttons; you did it the old-fashioned way. With your own hands.*

"And if thy right hand offends thee, cut it off." The sound of his own voice in the darkness startled him. He knew it wasn't the correct quotation, but it fit. It fit.

Sunday meetings. The Sunday they found that a squirrel had gotten into the Meeting House and chewed up half the leather upholstery of the benches.

"Serves us right," his father had said. "Upholstered benches are an affectation."

This from the richest Quaker in Pennsylvania. A strange collection of contrasts, he was. *Wish I had known him better.*

The school kids teasing him because he was a Quaker. Calling him William Penn. The tough ones, the big ones, ganging around him. "Let's see you quake, Quaker." How to get your nose broken. How to learn to talk your way out of a fight.

But there's no way to talk us out of this one.

Never to fly a plane again! If they wipe themselves out, there will be no airplanes. No airfields.

"Who're you trying to kid?" he asked himself. "You couldn't handle one now. Not after years of living in low-gee. You're soft as a sponge. And you're no kid any more; pushing fifty. You couldn't handle anything hotter than a glider."

Why do they have to have their war? In a half-century of Cold War, haven't they learned anything? Why must they blow up everything?

But he knew why. For the same reason that he had killed the cosmonaut. Exactly the same reason. It wasn't necessary. It wasn't. But you get the fury into you and you can't stop. Not until it's too late.

The alarm buzzer sounded. The bedroom lights slowly turned on and rose to full intensity. Time to get up.

Kinsman pulled himself up to a sitting position. *To hell with everything and everybody,* he told himself. *This is the way it is, and this is the way I've got to play it.*

Things always look different in the light of day. *Even when the light's artificial.* Not easier. Not better. But more rational. You can deal with things logically in day's light. In the dark, strange shapes haunt the shadows.

Kinsman put in a phone call for Leonov, then dry-

showered and dressed while he waited. Finally the
phone buzzed and the communications tech told him
that the Russian commander was on the line.

The screen went gray, there was no picture. But Leonov's voice was strong and clear. "I didn't realize capi-
talists got up so early in the morning."

Kinsman shot back, "That's how we stay ahead of
you centralized bureaucrats."

"Hah! A provocation."

Getting serious, Kinsman asked, "You've heard
about this Antarctica thing?"

"Yes."

He waited for Leonov to say something more. There
was nothing to say. "Any further word on your replacement?"

"No, not yet."

Leonov's voice sounded strained. *They're bugging his
line*. Then he realized, *And probably mine, too*.

"We've got to get together, Pete, and discuss things.
The buggy race and all . . ."

"I can't," Leonov immediately replied. "Not today.
Too many other problems to attend to. Possibly in a
day or two."

Nodding to himself, Kinsman said, "Yeah. Okay.
Call me."

He shut off the phone, stood there naked beside the
bed for a few more uncertain minutes, then punched the
phone keyboard again.

"Get me a flitter," he said to the flickering gray
screen. "Long-range flight. I'll fill out the flight plan in
the operations office. Be there in half an hour."

Sunday 5 December 1999: 0945 hrs UT

Kinsman rode alone across the ghostly landscape. The flitter boosted into a high arc, gliding silently through the long lunar night. The ground below was softly lit by Earthlight, a jumbled primeval panorama of gray rocks and craters.

He was strapped into the pilot's seat of the tiny rocket-driven craft, racing over the highlands east of Aristarchus. The Sea of Tranquillity was a dark smear on the horizon ahead of him.

He flew alone. The craft was pressurized, so he could keep the visor of his helmet up. The pressure suit was bulky and uncomfortable, but he willingly kept it on. If anything happened to the flitter, the suit could save his life. It had happened before.

The highlands slid by, far below, pocked and roiled mountains sandblasted and worn smooth by eons of meteoric infall. The only sounds inside the flitter's cockpit were the faint hum of electric motors and the even fainter hiss of the air circulators.

This is silly, he told himself. A damned stupid waste of time. But the craft was locked into its course by the unyielding laws of ballistics. The pilgrimage, once begun, had to be carried through to its destination.

By twisting around in the pilot's seat and leaning as far forward as the seat harness would allow, he could see Earth beckoning to him. He leaned back again and checked out the instruments on the panel before him. But this occupied only a fraction of his attention. He kept seeing Jill's face, and Kelly's and Pete Leonov's and those of the people he knew in Washington, New

York, Los Angeles. Worst of all he kept seeing children: playing, running, in school, at sleep, all wiped away in the searing glare of a fireball.

Keep thinking with your tear glands, he raged at himself. That's a terrific way to solve a problem!

His helmet earphones buzzed. Flicking a switch on the control panel, he said crisply, "Kinsman here."

"Comm center. We're picking up a news broadcast from Earthside. Officer of the Day thought you would want to hear it."

"Okay, pipe it through."

There was a barely discernible click and a momentary hum. Then: " . . . of Captain Ernest Richards. White House spokesmen have emphasized that the shooting took place in international territory, although last year the Soviet Union and several East European and Asian nations served notice that they intended to exploit the mineral resources of Antarctica.

"The United Nations has debated the issue since the opening of its session this fall, with the United States taking a sharply differing position from that of the Russians.

"Senator Russell Montguard of North Carolina has called the shooting of Navy Captain Richards, quote, An act of international murder; yes, an act of war. Unquote. Other reactions from around the nation and around the world include . . ."

Kinsman snapped the radio off. *Now it's an international incident. An act of war. Just the excuse they've been looking for.*

The control panel's lights and instruments winked at him, red, amber, green. The computer readout screen flashed numbers. The radar and lidar altimeters told him it was time to prepare for landing.

The rocket engine fired without Kinsman's aid, programmed by the automatic sequencer. He felt inordinately heavy for a few moments. Then the thrust shut off and almost simultaneously he felt the springy bump of the craft's landing struts touching down on the Sea of Tranquillity.

The guidance system checked the local landmarks and peered at the arrangement of stars overhead

through the craft's stereo telescope. Then it agreed, with
a bright green circle drawn on its view-screen map, that
they had indeed touched down precisely at the programmed destination point. All the lights on the control
panel turned a steady green.

"Proud of yourself, aren't you?" Kinsman asked the
humming machinery.

He slid his helmet visor shut and sealed it, then unstrapped from the seat while the pumps sucked the air
out of the cockpit with a diminishing clatter and stored
it in the tanks built into the craft below the cockpit.

Within a few minutes he had clambered down from
the cockpit and was walking across the sandy lunar soil,
leaving footprints that would last for eons.

He topped a small rise and there it was: the seismo-
meters, the laser reflector, the stiffly proud flag, the
gold-wrapped lower half of the lunar module. Just as
they had been left thirty years earlier. The only change
was the clear plastic cover that had been carefully
sprayed over the ground to protect the original footprints of Armstrong and Aldrin.

"Tranquillity Base," Kinsman murmured.

Picking his way around the assorted hardware left by
the astronauts, Kinsman stepped around the lunar module until he found the plaque. It was still polished and
gleaming, even in the feeble light from Earth:

HERE MEN FROM THE PLANET EARTH
FIRST SET FOOT UPON THE MOON
JULY 1969, A.D.
WE CAME IN PEACE FOR ALL MANKIND

Kinsman stared at it for a long time, especially the
last line. Then he lifted his eyes toward the beautiful
Earth and muttered, " 'Nation shall not lift up sword
against nation; neither shall they make war any more'
. . . At least, not *here*."

A flicker of movement caught his eye. Stepping
away from the lunar module, he looked upward as far
as his helmet would allow his vision to rise. A puff of
light—rocket thrusters—the tiny gleam of another lunar
flier solidified into a full-sized craft, engines firing si-

lently, landing struts poking rigidly outward. A Russian flitter.

It touched down close enough for Kinsman to watch its noiseless landing. The bubble canopy opened and a red-suited figure lurched out of the cockpit and climbed slowly down the ladder.

Kinsman walked toward the newcomer. "Pete?" he called into his helmet microphone.

"Yes," Leonov's heavy voice answered.

Kinsman's spirits soared. "How the hell did you know I'd be here?"

Leonov trudged over to him and laid a heavily gloved hand on Kinsman's shoulder. "My spies watch you very closely," he said flatly. "And so does my radar. It was rather simple to fix your trajectory and puzzle out your destination. No?"

"And you came out after me."

"Officially, I am discussing the need for tighter security with our radio astronomers at the Farside Station. As far as my crew and intelligence officers back at Lunagrad are concerned, we have made this stop here to see what you are up to."

"I'm making a pilgrimage in the desert," Kinsman said. "When I saw your ship, I was hoping you were doing the same thing."

"To a shrine dedicated to American success? Hardly."

"There are medals for Gagarin and Komarov in there." Kinsman hiked a thumb in the direction of the lunar module.

"Yes, I know." Leonov hesitated a moment, then, "What really brings you out here?"

Kinsman said, "I couldn't sleep."

"Neither could I."

"What are we going to do about it?"

"Chet, my comrade, let's not begin to torture ourselves again."

"There must be something we can do!"

"Hah! I'm going to be replaced in ten days, and you have your black superpatriot snarling at your heels."

"So whatever we do, it's got to be done in the next ten days."

Leonov said nothing. Kinsman could sense his disapproval.

"Come on, Pete," he snapped.

"Do you have a plan of action?" the Russian asked softly.

"I wish I did." Kinsman stamped his booted foot, stirring up a cloud of dust. His legs felt itchy, and it was impossible to scratch them with the cumbersome suit on.

"So. You talk and worry and stay awake nights—but you have no idea of what can be done."

"Do you?"

Leonov raised both hands above his helmet. "Spare me this endless self-flagellation!"

"Now, don't get excited," said Kinsman. "Before we can lay any plans, we've got to agree on how far we're willing to go—"

"In what direction?"

"Well . . . " Kinsman suddenly realized that he had known the first step all along. "To begin with, suppose you refused to return Earthside. Suppose you requested that you remain in Lunagrad? What would happen?"

The shoulders of Leonov's suit moved vaguely, as if he were shrugging inside it. "I have several weeks' leave due to me. I could ask to spend it in Lunagrad rather than at home. But it would be a very suspicious move."

"Suppose you refused to relinquish command of Lunagrad?"

"Mmm . . ." The Russian's voice grew somber. "That would be a direct disobedience of orders. Treason against the State. Very serious."

"What about your wife and children?"

"The children are away at school . . . I doubt that the security police would bother them. Nothing like that has been done in more than twenty years, despite the horror stories concocted by the Western press. Although, frankly, I would be worried for them."

"And your wife?"

He almost laughed. "My darling wife would be quite happy to see me shot. It would free her completely."

"Oh, I didn't know . . . ."

"It isn't something one boasts about."

An embarrassed silence settled over them. Finally Leonov asked, "Well, you obviously have something in mind. What is it?"

Without letting himself stop to think, Kinsman answered, "Declare independence."

Leonov said nothing.

"Make Selene a nation, declare our independence from both the United States and the Soviet Union and apply for membership in the United Nations."

It took a long time for Leonov to reply. "I thought so. I was afraid that would be your brilliant idea."

"Look at it point by point," Kinsman urged, starting to feel some excitement. "First, we don't want to fight here on the Moon. If we unite, we won't fight. The only way we can unite is for both of us to stop taking orders from Earthside. The only way we can stop taking orders is to declare ourselves independent—"

"We would starve to death in a matter of weeks."

"Not so!" Kinsman snapped. "Moonbase's water capacity can more than take care of all our needs. If we combine it with yours, we can irrigate more farmlands and grow enough crops and livestock to be completely self-sufficient."

"If we have enough water."

"We do. And we'll have even more in a few months—plenty. Enough for everything we want to do and an emergency back-up supply as well."

Before Leonov could say more, Kinsman went on, "The only way to make our independence stick is to have the UN recognize us. I think there are enough small nations in the UN that are fed up with both the West and the East."

"That debating society!" Leonov threw up his hands. "Chet, my lunar brother, I expected better of you. This idea of independence is nonsense, idiocy. It cannot work. I myself have thought about it a thousand times. But it cannot work!"

"But if the UN would recognize an independent Luna—"

"Hah! So what? What good would it do? Long before the question of our glorious independence is even placed on the debating society's agenda, both Lunagrad and Moonbase will be buried alive under troops from Earthside. Our courts-martial would be finished and our bodies fertilizing pig farms before the UN bureaucrats could lift a finger."

"But—"

"Admit it!" Leonov nearly shouted. "We have no military strength. You could not even be sure that enough of your Moonbase people would go along with your insane idea. All you would do would be to foment civil war inside your own community."

Kinsman shook his head. "No. That much I'm sure of. You forget, I've been selecting the permanent residents of Moonbase for the past three years. I know who they are and what they'll do. The ninety-dayers—yes, we'd have trouble with some of them. But nothing we couldn't handle."

Leonov snorted. "Well, I know what would happen in Lunagrad. Half the populace would shoot the other half, and I have no idea of who would be left alive when the smoke cleared. Possibly no one."

Despite himself, Kinsman grinned. "I thought you said Lunagrad was filled with exiles."

"Yes—but they are *Russian* exiles. Not citizens of Selene."

"And they're not sufficiently intellectual to see that a free Selene is to the advantage of everyone, including Mother Russia?"

Leonov's voice went from scornful to curious. "What do you mean?"

"If we declared our independence, it would startle both America and Russia. If we stopped supplying air and water and propellants to the space stations, it would upset their orbital operations quite a bit . . ."

"For a month or two, possibly. No longer."

"All right." Kinsman glanced at the ungainly lunar module squatting off in the distance. He couldn't see the plaque from where he was standing. "But we'd cause enough of a fuss, enough of an upset to their plans, that they'd be forced to delay this war build-up. This Antarctica incident would be pushed out of everybody's mind. By turning their attention to us, we could stop them from going to war against each other."

Leonov sighed. "I wish it were that simple, my friend. But it is not. Nothing will stop them from fighting their war. They will bow only to superior force, and there is no force superior anywhere on the Earth or the Moon. When China was a possible threat to both the USSR and U.S., they both made moves toward peace. But once China fell apart, they both drove directly toward war. History is inexorable, just as Marx said."

"No, it doesn't have to—"

"Chet, you are being naïve! Assume the best possible results. Assume that your most optimistic hopes come true: We become independent and the UN recognizes us. Your nation and mine do not interfere. Their war is averted. For how long? Six months? A year? Have we provided more food for anyone? More energy? Sooner or later we will be exactly where we are now: standing here helplessly and watching them build up for war. *There is no way to avoid it!*

"The Earth is too crowded, resources are too scarce. Why do you think they are shooting at each other in Antarctica? Both of them *need* that coal!"

Kinsman reluctantly agreed. "Even with the breeder reactors there's not enough energy for everybody."

"Even with the breeder reactors," Leonov echoed. "And the fusion machines won't be able to produce enough energy to solve the problem for another five or ten years."

"If we could hold off the war that long—"

"We could not even hold it off for five months," Leonov said.

"You're right," Kinsman admitted.

"So, my idealistic friend, declaring independence for Selene will achieve nothing. It will change nothing."

Coldly, Kinsman answered, "It will guarantee that nearly a thousand human beings will survive the war, without being killed off later by fallout or disease or starvation."

Leonov was silent for long moments. He paced toward the lunar module, then stopped as the American flag came into view from behind its spidery bulk.

"Do you seriously believe," he asked slowly, without turning back to face Kinsman, "that any of us could watch our homelands being destroyed without going mad? Do you honestly believe that their war will not destroy us, too?"

Forcing his voice to stay calm as he walked to stand beside his friend, Kinsman answered, "We could get through it without fighting. If we tried."

The Russian's voice was infinitely sad. "No, old friend. I might trust you and you might trust me, but to expect nearly a thousand Russians and Americans to trust each other while they watch their families being killed—never."

Kinsman wanted to scream. Instead, he heard himself whisper, "But Pete, what can we *do?*"

"Nothing. The world will end. The millennium is rushing upon us. A thousand years ago, most Christians believed that the world would end at the millennium. They were off by a factor of a thousand years. It will end now. And there is nothing we can do."

The flight back to Selene seemed longer and lonelier than the flight out to Tranquillity Base. Kinsman tried to blank everything out of his mind, think of nothing whatever. Impossible.

The world will end. There is nothing we can do.
Wrong! It had to be wrong. There must be something that can be done. Something!

As he gazed at the richly blue Earth hanging above the horizon, the enormity of it struck him. He was ready to rebel against the United States of America, against the mightiest nation the world had ever known, against the three hundred million people he had sworn to defend and protect. *Leonov's right. It's madness.*

Kinsman's mind flooded with images: Thanksgiving dinners, sitting in school watching filmstrips about the Declaration of Independence, the maddening drive each morning from Virginia through Crystal City to the crumbling old Pentagon, the first time he had ever seen the Grand Canyon, pledging allegiance to the flag as a solemn little kid and then the special flip of saluting the same flag at retreat that first day he wore his shiny new gold lieutenant's bars, barrel-rolling a T-39 under the Golden Gate bridge, "Don't Give Up the Ship,"

"Send Us More Japs," "Give Me Liberty or Give Me Death," "Government of the People, by the People . . ."

We're the people! he told himself. *They've got no right to make us fight their goddamn war.*

All that history, all that training, three hundred million programmed people . . . How could Selene hold out against it? Outnumbered a hundred million to one. Each man, woman and child in Moonbase trained and indoctrinated since birth. "My Country, 'Tis of Thee . . ."

And then he remembered a line from a physics class (or was it history?)—a chalk-dusty little man of a teacher with a pinched face and the same gray suit every day of the semester saying: "Give me a lever long enough and a place to stand, and I will move the Earth."

Is 400,000 kilometers long enough? Kinsman wondered.

To anyone who took notice of such things, Jill Myers and Alexei Landau made an incongruous couple: the tall, bearded, grave Russian and the tiny moonfaced American girl with short-clipped brown hair.

At the moment no one was noticing. Jill and Landau stood in the midst of a knot of people who were watching a TV newscast from Earthside. They were in Selene's central plaza, the wide high-domed arcade that had started as a large natural cavern, been converted to the quartermaster's depot, and grown into a multitiered complex of privately owned shops that seemed to grow organically around the government-issue outlets.

But there was little buying and selling right now. The crowd stood in tense silence in the middle of the arcade, watching the big view-screen set up in the archway at the far end. An Earthside newscaster was grimly narrating the day's events, while the screen showed videotapes of the American base at Antarctica's McMurdo Sound and aerial views of the dry valley where the Navy captain had been killed.

The scene switched to Washington, the old Pentagon, gray and forbidding.

"While no word has yet been received from the White House," the newscaster was intoning, "highly placed Pentagon officials have hinted that American military units around the world have been alerted for possible action. Satellite monitors have identified a Russian task force steaming at top speed for Antarctica from Vladivostok, and East European troop maneuvers continue in Poland and Czechoslovakia, under the guise of winter exercises . . . "

Jill turned to Landau. She had to crane her neck to talk to him, but the inconvenience never entered her mind. "Alex, do you think they're going to do it this time?"

He shook his head. "Madmen, all of them. Insanity. It comes from heavy metal pollutants in the air—they cause brain damage."

"Be serious," Jill insisted. The people around them began to glare and shush them.

Landau took her by the arm and started pushing through the crowd. "I am being serious. It begins to look as if the end of the world is really at hand."

Jill felt a shudder go through her. She let Landau lead her out of the crowd, then toward the power ladder that led downward toward the living quarters area. He slid his arms around her shoulders and pulled her close.

"If we only have a few weeks, little one, let us use them wisely."

By the time he got back to his office, Kinsman realized that he couldn't face the evening alone. He called Ellen and asked her to dinner.

In the small view-screen of the picturephone, she seemed genuinely happy to hear from him. "Dinner would be fine. Why don't you come to my place?"

He hesitated. "You're busy enough . . . "

With a smile, she said, "Don't be silly. I like to cook."

And she cooked well, Kinsman decided. Lunar food consisted almost entirely of home-grown vegetables, a precious smattering of chicken, pork and lamb, and an occasional luxury item such as beef or spices from Earth. Ellen's dinner was mostly soybeans in various disguises, plus a dessert of barbaric splendor: Cherries Jubilee.

Kinsman had brought one of his own rare bottles of Burgundy, and they were savoring the last of it when Ellen told him her news.

"Larry Pierce is going back home on the shuttle next week."

Kinsman felt his eyebrows rise. "He told you that?"

She nodded.

"He hasn't sent through a request yet."

"He will. He wants to get back to his family, with all this talk of emergencies and war."

"He'd be smarter bringing his family up here."

"That's not the way he sees it," Ellen said. "He wants to go home. And he's going to recommend me to take his place."

For a moment Kinsman didn't answer. He glanced down at his wine glass—a product of a Czech artisan from Lunagrad—and saw that it was empty. "So you're going to be head of the communications department. Congratulations."

She looked at him steadily. "I still need the base commander's approval, don't I?"

"Is that why you asked me over here? To cement the deal?"

Instead of getting angry, Ellen grinned at him. "You're still the total chauvinist, aren't you? You think I got Pierce's recommendation in bed."

"Didn't you?"

"It's none of your damned business," she said, still looking gleeful. "You can stew in your own male juices over that."

"That's a very female attitude," he said, grinning back at her.

"It may interest you to know, in your capacity as base commander," Ellen said haughtily, "that my aptitude scores and career record rate me higher than anyone else in the communications department. Mr. Pierce told me that I've got the best background he's seen in years."

"You've got a lovely foreground, too."

She grimaced. "You're beginning to get me irritated."

With a shrug, Kinsman said, "You're telling me that the personnel computer would select you as Pierce's replacement if I just asked it to evaluate the background information it's got in its memory files?"

"That's exactly what it would do."

"You think so."

She got up from her chair and headed for the phone, next to the living-room sofa. "Want to call and try it?"

Kinsman pushed his chair away from the dinette table. "No," he said laughing, "I'll take your word for it."

"That's big of you."

He got to his feet and walked over to her. She was no longer smiling; she seemed balanced between joy and real anger.

"I was only kidding," he said.

"Like hell you were."

"Well, maybe I exaggerated——"

"Dammit, Chet, I've earned that promotion. I'm better qualified than anyone else for the job, and Larry knows it!"

"Okay. I'll take his word for it."

They stood face to face, and suddenly Kinsman felt awkward. "Then dinner tonight . . . was to celebrate?"

"Is that so strange?" she asked. "Wouldn't you do the same thing?"

"I did," he heard himself reply.

"You called me to celebrate? What?"

"I called you because I didn't want to be alone," he said.

"Neither do I."

Thursday 6 December 1999: 0345 hrs UT

Kinsman pulled himself up to a sitting position on the bed. It had been years since he'd smoked, but he badly wanted a cigarette. Instead he sat staring into the darkness of Ellen's bedroom, running his tongue across his lower teeth. They felt gritty.

She turned beside him. "You're not sleeping?"

"No."

"What's the matter?" Her voice sounded hollow, as if she were stifling a yawn.

"Can't sleep," he said simply.

"You're really worried about this war emergency?"

He nodded, then realized that she probably couldn't see him in the dark. "Yeah."

"They've had these crises before. It'll blow away," Ellen said.

"Not this time."

She put her hand on his back. "Do you really think so?"

"This time it's for real." He turned toward her, and could barely make out her face in the shadows. The only light in the room came from the digital clock on the nightstand next to her side of the bed. "I'm going to try to talk Pierce out of leaving. I have to. I'll tell him to bring his family up here where they'll be safe."

He could see her eyes widen. "It's that serious?"

"We're going to declare our independence from Earth. Leonov and I. I want as much of everybody's family as possible to be here when the shit hits the fan."

Ellen said nothing.

"I'm hoping our declaration of independence—and

our stopping the supplies to the orbital stations—will throw a monkey wrench into their war preparations."

"Will the Russians really—?"

"Pete's saying no, but he means yes. We'll work it out."

Her voice was utterly calm. "And if you don't?"

He shrugged. "At least we'll have brought as many families up here as we can. We'll survive here."

"Is that why you haven't gone back to Earth for so many years? You've been worrying about this moment?"

He looked off into the darkness. "I never thought of it. Not consciously, anyway. Maybe you're right. Maybe I have been—"

"Then your medical record is faked?"

He turned back toward her. "How did you know . . .?"

Her voice sounded faintly amused. "I told you that I tried to find out everything I could about you. I have access to the personnel computer, so I took a peek at your record."

"Hmm."

"There's nothing secret about your file, is there?"

"No . . . " But he felt all the old fear welling up in him.

"The file does go blank, just as Dr. Faraffa said. It makes you very mysterious."

He didn't answer.

"And there's a medical notation about a heart condition."

"Officially," Kinsman said slowly, "I'm supposed to have a heart condition that makes a full Earth gravity dangerous for me. It's only a little hypertension, but Jill Myers wrote it into the file so that I can stay here in Selene indefinitely."

"Officially," Ellen murmured.

"Unofficially," he explained, "it's because I don't want to give Murdock or any of the Earthside brass a chance to call me back there and keep me down there. I decided a long time ago that this is where I want to be. This is my home."

He could sense Ellen shaking her head. "Those are

the official and unofficial reasons. But what are the real reasons?"

The fear was still inside him, but it felt strangely muted, distant, fading.

"Chet," Ellen said, tracing a finger along the length of his thigh, "you haven't told me anything that you wouldn't tell Pat Kelly or one of your other buddies. I don't care about the politics; I want to know what's going on inside your head."

"Why?"

"I told you," she answered. "I want to know about you. All about you. Everything."

A picture of Samson and Delilah flashed through his head. "You want to know why I haven't gone back Earthside for more than five years."

Her answer was so immediate it startled him. "I want to know what you're afraid of."

"It's too beautiful," he said. "And too ugly. It's too big and exciting, and too small and crowded. It's . . ."

"It's home," she said for him.

Nodding. "Right. Everybody up here knows that. All the permanent Luniks. We feel like exiles, no matter how much we tell each other that Selene is better than New York or Moscow or London or Tokyo. It *is* better up here! That's the hell of it. We have more freedom, more living space, more food and energy, a better, more intelligent society . . . "

"But Earth is home."

"The elephants' graveyard," he said. "If I spent a few days on Earth—especially if I got into whatever's left of the countryside, saw a blue sky with clouds, or a hill covered with grass, trees . . . "

"They're mostly covered with housing developments."

"Not all of them. I can see them from here, through the 'scopes. Colorado, the Canadian Rockies, the Mongolian grasslands . . . There are still herds of horses running wild out there! And the oceans! If I stood on a beach and watched the breakers coming in . . . "

He stopped. His voice had risen; he was losing control.

Calmer, he said, "You don't have to worry about

Pierce staying. I know him. He'll take the shuttle and go back to his family, no matter what I tell him. He'll head for the elephants' graveyard, all right."

"And we'll stay here."

"Right."

"And we'll survive."

"Yes."

Ellen sighed. "We're the strong ones, aren't we?"

"I wish I knew," he said.

"Are we going to have a life together, Chet?"

He looked away from her and mumbled again, "I wish I knew."

"What's the secret, Chet?"

You knew she was going to dig deep; don't act surprised, he told himself. For a long moment he was silent, trying to identify the feelings boiling inside him: anger? fear? pain?

"Whatever it is," Ellen said softly, "it won't hurt half so much after you've shared it."

No! he warned himself. How do you know you can trust her? How do you know . . . ?

But he heard himself saying, "It was on an orbital mission, years ago. Before we started cooperating with the Russians in space. I was inspecting one of their satellites . . ."

His mind detached from his body. He watched himself numbly reciting the ancient story, sitting there in bed beside this beautiful woman and opening himself to her as he had never opened himself to anyone in his life.

"It was a big mother, just launched. Our intelligence spooks were afraid it might be an orbital bomb. The cosmonaut came up in a separate capsule, while I was in the midst of examining their satellite. We fought—like a couple of sea elephants barging into one another. We didn't have any weapons. We just pawed at each other."

He was floating again. Weightless.

"I could have backed off and gotten back to my own spacecraft, but I stayed and fought. Very patriotic. Very full of righteous wrath. I fought. I pulled out her air hose. I killed her."

"Her?"

Nodding, seeing her face in the bulbous helmet behind the heavily tinted visor, screaming silently, going rigid.

"I didn't know it was a girl." His voice was as dead as she was. "Not until I had already ripped out her air line. That's when I got close enough to see into her helmet."

He stopped.

"And you've been carrying around this load of guilt about it ever since." Ellen took one of his hands in both of hers.

"I swore to myself that I'd never kill anyone again . . . I wouldn't let them make me kill anyone . . ."

"Chet, it wasn't your fault."

"Bullshit! *I* fought the cosmonaut. I *wanted* to kill! I wanted to rip the sonofabitch's air hose right out of his helmet! I didn't have to. But I wanted to."

"And you didn't know it was a girl."

"No."

Ellen started to say something, but he went on, "Now I've got to convince Leonov that he can trust us, trust *me*. With this thing sticking in my guts. And he probably knows about it; they have intelligence files on it. How can he trust me? How can he trust any one of us?"

"But you trust him, don't you?"

"He never killed any of us."

Ellen asked, "Had you killed other people, before, when you were flying combat missions in airplanes?"

"I guess so. But that was different . . . remote . . . It wasn't hand to hand. I never knew."

"And if it had been a male cosmonaut," Ellen went on, "would you feel so guilty about it?"

He stared at her. "No, I guess not."

"Why not?"

"I don't know," he said vaguely. "Men expect to fight, I guess. It's different . . . more even."

"Bullshit, to use a male word." Ellen pulled herself up to a sitting position. "Chet, you've let this thing hang around your neck for how long now?"

He shrugged. "Fifteen years . . . seventeen, actually."

"That's long enough," Ellen said firmly. "It's over. It's done with. You can't bring her back. And it wasn't your fault, to begin wi—"

"I had all the psychology lectures," he snapped. "It *was* my fault. Nobody else's."

"So you've got a built-in excuse for keeping a wall around yourself and not taking any chances on getting hurt again."

"*Me* get hurt?"

"Yes, you! You're not worried about some Russian woman you never knew! You're worried about Chester Arthur Kinsman, worried that people won't like you if they know you killed somebody. Worried that Leonov won't be your buddy any more. That's what's eating at you. Not her. She's been dead for seventeen years."

"Don't tell me what's churning in my guts!"

"Why not?" Ellen blazed back. "You're so sunk in self-pity that you think you've got to save the whole world to make up for one mistake."

"It's not self-pity!"

"Whatever it is," and suddenly Ellen's voice went low and calm and measured, "whatever it is, Chet, you've got to tell Leonov about it."

He felt hollow inside. No longer angry. Not even fearful. Empty. Nothing there but a dull, distant ache.

"I don't know if I can," he said.

"You can."

"It's not that easy. Admitting it to you—even admitting it to Pete—won't exorcise the demon completely."

Ellen put her hand on his cheek. It felt cool and soft to him. "It will always be with you, Chet," she said. "You'll never get rid of it completely. But you can't let it stand in your way."

He knew she was right. Still, it scared him.

Pierce's request for a transfer and return to Earth was on Kinsman's desk when he got to his office the next morning. He called the communications chief and tried, briefly, perfunctorily, to argue him out of it. Pierce was politely adamant. And he recommended Ellen Berger to take over his position.

Tight-lipped, Kinsman agreed. Pierce smiled and thanked him.

Leaning back in his desk chair, Kinsman punched a button on the desktop controls and an Earthside news broadcast filled the main wall screen. The view was of the speaker's podium in the General Assembly chamber of the UN building in New York. The Russian delegate was fulminating, glaring at the Americans sitting in the front row, his brows knit angrily, arms gesticulating. The English interpretation was being spoken in a voice as calm and flatly unemotional as Selene's computer:

". . . the capitalist imperialists were obviously guilty of invading territory that was clearly marked by officials of the USSR, provoking the incident deliberately. This aggression was rightfully repelled, as American aggression has been repelled by freedom-loving peoples all over the globe."

There was a commotion, and the TV camera swung to the American desk, where the chief delegate was on his feet, bellowing: "Mr. Chairman, how long must we listen to this pack of lies and distortions? There can be no meaningful resolution—"

The Russian speaker pounded the podium with his fists and shouted something unintelligible. The whole American delegation came to its feet, yelling.

Kinsman watched, stunned, while the cameras panned across the huge chamber. It looked as if a riot were about to break out. Shouting, screaming, arm-waving. The only person who remained in his seat was the Chairman, up at his desk above and behind the podium. A slim, dark Latin American with big sad eyes, he merely sat there shaking his head.

The last, best hope of mankind. Kinsman snapped off the newscast. He sat staring at the blank screen for a moment, then got up from the desk.

Better make the rounds, he told himself. He knew he would start with the water factory.

He spent half the morning there, listening to Ernie Waterman, over the noise of the construction crews, complain about how difficult everything was. Yet they were making considerable progress, Kinsman saw. The dour-faced engineer was cautious to the point of being morose, but Kinsman knew that Selene would have plenty of water for all of its needs, even if they suddenly doubled.

The water factory was actually half an ore-processing plant and half a water-purification facility. The rock crushers dwarfed human scale, taking in fresh loads of ore from the mining vans that came from as far south as the Straight Wall and as far north as Fra Mauro.

Kinsman clambered over the big crushers, feeling the rumble of their heavy machinery in his bones. This was the most expensive equipment in Selene, hauled up from Earthside over a ten-year period. Selene's technicians could repair and maintain them, but it would be another decade before they could even attempt to build such machines on their own.

Following the conveyor belts that carried the crushed rock, Kinsman came to the electric arcs humming steadily inside their stainless steel jackets. From here onward the factory was a maze of plumbing: pipes overhead, underfoot, lining kilometers of tunnels, sweating beads of precious ice-cold water no matter how much insulation the engineers put on them. Kinsman stepped over, ducked under, squeezed between the pipelines that carried Selene's lifeblood.

Waterman dogged behind him, unhappily cataloguing his real and extrapolated problems all the way through the factory.

Finally, as they walked through the relatively quiet corridors of the factory's office and control area, Waterman said, "I still don't see what the rush is all about. I wish you'd let me ease off; some of these guys have been working their tails off."

Kinsman stopped in front of the window that looked in on the computer control section. Watching the nearly unattended machine's lights flickering in some internally meaningful pattern, he answered, "Ernie, we've got a yellow alert slapped on us. We've got to be prepared for any emergency. Earthside might suddenly need double, triple the rocket juice they want now."

"Then we ought to be beefing up the electrolysis facility, not the water production."

"First things first," Kinsman said. "Hydrogen and oxygen propellants come from the water. If we want more rocket propellants, we have to increase the basic water supply."

"Yeah, eventually, but in an emergency—"

"First things first," Kinsman repeated. The tautologist's handbook: when in doubt, fall back on slogans.

"But what about the interconnects with Lunagrad?" Waterman asked. "Why in hell do we have a full crew working to connect them with our increased supply lines, when we're just going to have to cut them off when the fighting starts?"

"There isn't going to be any fighting," Kinsman said firmly. "Not here."

Waterman's jaw went slack. "Wh-what do you mean?"

"Just what I said, Ernie."

"I don't get it."

"You will," Kinsman said. "You will."

And he left Waterman standing there in the corridor, scratching his head unhappily.

Kinsman worked his way through the underground farm areas, the shops and laboratories, the computer section, the communications center. He did this almost every day, but in no set pattern. Say hello, look for problems, listen to gripes or suggestions. Maintain a high profile, good visibility. Everyone knew him. More important, he got to know everyone in Selene; even the ninety-dayers.

The hospital section was always the quietest, most relaxed and sanest part of his rounds. As soon as he stepped through the big double doors of the hospital lobby area, Kinsman could feel himself calm down. Soft pastel walls, soft voices—even the intercoms and the PA systems were muted. Pleasant place to be, he thought, as long as you don't let them get their hands on you.

But today was different.

Two nurses scurried past him, pushing small wheeled consoles. They looked worried, and they went by so fast that Kinsman didn't notice just what kind of equipment they were rolling. They disappeared down a corridor that led off from the lobby. A harried-looking young doctor hustled after them.

The PA system came to life. A man's voice, sharp and unusually loud, called, "Dr. Myers, Dr. Myers. In the ICU immediately!"

The Intensive Care Unit. My God, Baliagorev! Kinsman sprinted down the same corridor that the nurses had taken. *That's all we need, for him to conk out on us. Talk about international incidents.*

He flashed past the ICU monitoring station, where a male nurse spun around from his desk of view screens and called, "Hey, you can't . . ." Then, recognizing Kinsman, he said weakly, "Sir?"

Kinsman saw a huddle of white uniforms ahead of him. He skidded to a stop, then shouldered past the outermost ring of nurses.

"I do not want to talk to any of you enema-wielding vampires! I want Dr. Myers!"

It was Baliagorev. A wisp of a man, feather-frail. But his voice was like iron. He was pale, face seamed with age. A dozen tubes and wires connected to various parts of his body. Someone had cranked his floater bed up to a sitting position.

One of the consoles that the nurses had wheeled in was a videotape reader, Kinsman saw. The Russian reached toward it.

"Don't! You'll pull the IV loose!"

"Then take it away!" Baliagorev roared. "When I want to be entertained by brainless tapes, I will tell you. Now, where is Dr. Myers? Where is she?"

Pushing his way through the remaining knot of nurses and the young doctor, Kinsman said, "She'll be here shortly, sir. I'm Chet Kinsman, the commander here. I'm glad to see that you're feeling so strong."

"I feel miserable," Baliagorev snapped, in impeccable English. "How would you feel, wired up like a marionette?"

"Well, I . . ."

The Russian shook his head. "I am a simple man. I can accept the fact that my countrymen regard me as a revisionist fool. I can accept the fact that my own heart has turned traitor on me. I can even accept the fact that

I am surrounded by Yankees who have all the cultural
sensitivities of a Latvian smuggler. All I want is to see
Dr. Myers. Why can't this one simple request . . ."

"Here I am, maestro."

Kinsman turned and saw the others clear a path for
Jill. Behind her strode the Russian doctor, Landau.
Both of them had funny expressions on their faces:
happy but—embarrassed?

"Ahhh, Jillyushka, my ministering angel—where
have you been?" Baliagorev's tone completely changed.
He went from truculence to grandfatherly sweetness in
an eyeblink.

Jill grinned at him. "Well, there *are* other patients in
this hospital, and—"

"Nonsense! You were off in some corner kissing this
bearded oaf."

Landau's face went beet red. Jill giggled. Kinsman
turned to the other nurses and said quietly, "I think the
emergency is over."

They started filing out of the tiny room, whispering
among themselves.

"Don't you go," Baliagorev called to Kinsman. "I
have a request to make of you."

Kinsman stopped at the open door, looked back at
the Russian.

"I should like to stay here in the American sector,
rather than return to Lunagrad, at least for a while."

Kinsman didn't know whether to laugh or frown. "I
thought we Yankees had the cultural sensitivities of
Latvian smugglers."

Completely unflustered, Baliagorev answered, "When
you have spent as much time as I have in the tyrannical
grips of hospital orderlies and nurses, you learn that
there is only one way to treat them—with contempt.
However," his tone softened, "I sincerely wish to remain here."

"Well . . ." There's something crafty about this old
man. "May I ask why?"

Baliagorev shifted his gaze to Landau momentarily,
then looked back at Kinsman. His eyes were ice-blue.
"Put it down as the whim of an old man. The women

here are much prettier. The nurses in Lunagrad are *awful*—huge beasts, ungainly, hopeless."

"That's not true," Landau murmured.

"Bah! Why should I hide it? I want political asylum. I was seeking asylum in France when my countrymen arrested me and carted me to a hospital in Siberia. A *psychiatric* hospital! That's where my heart broke."

Kee-rist! Just what we need. Kinsman kept his eyes off Landau as he answered, "This is a very touchy time to ask for political asylum, you know."

Baliagorev pursed his thin, bluish lips.

Jill cut in, "There will be no discussion of politics of any sort whatsoever as long as my patient is in Intensive Care." Turning sternly to Baliagorev, she shook a stubby finger at him. "We haven't brought you back from clinical death just so you can kill yourself with excitement over politics!"

Landau broke into a laugh. "She's right, Nicholai Ivanovich. This is no time to discuss politics."

The old man raised his wispy eyebrows. "Very well. You have performed your miracle, and you don't want your Lazarus to suffer a relapse, eh? But will *you* be discussing politics with any of our countrymen?"

The Russian doctor shook his head gravely. "No. I promise you."

"You can trust Alexei," Jill said.

"I'm sure *you* can trust him," Baliagorev muttered. Then, with a crooked grin that threatened to turn into a leer, "Admit it, Jillyushka, you were necking with this bearded rascal, eh?"

"As a matter of fact, yes, I was," she admitted cheerfully. "And you'd better stop teasing, or I'll put nothing but male nurses in here with you."

The Russian hesitated only a moment. "Hmm . . . if they are young and tender—"

"You're impossible!"

Kinsman managed to say, "All right. Listen, Jill, Alexei, your patient will have to stay here several more days?"

"At least a week," Landau answered.

"I could arrange to have a relapse," Baliagorev said.

Kinsman raised a hand. "Let's let things work themselves out for a week." Before they could say anything else, he ducked back out through the doorway and headed down the corridor.

But he heard the ballet master's voice saying gently, "Now then, Jillyushka, there is no reason why you could not become a first-rate dancer here on the Moon. With this low gravity, and me to instruct you, we could work miracles."

Kinsman shook his head and wished he felt good enough to smile.

The corridor lights had just turned down to their evening level as Kinsman padded from his office toward his quarters.

Got to talk to Leonov again, he was telling himself. Maybe he can get his kids to visit him here before—

"Chet, Chet, wait up, will you?" It was Jill Myers scampering after him. She had a child's wide grin on her face.

He smiled back at her as she ran up and said breathlessly, "He's proposed to me!"

"That dirty old man?"

"No, not Baliagorev," Jill replied, beaming. "Alexei! We're going to get married!"

Something inside Kinsman went cold.

"You're invited to the party," Jill was saying. "It's already started, over at my quarters!"

"Married," he repeated.

"Yes! 'Here comes the bride' and all that stuff. Isn't it wild?"

"Why?"

Her grin froze. "Why what?"

"Why does he want to marry you?"

She planted her hands on her hips. "I *presume* it's because he can't live without me, and wants to spend the rest of his life with me. A lifetime commitment— but you wouldn't understand that, would you?" Her eyes were snapping at him.

"Dammit all, Jill, you know that's not what I meant. You two can live together without having a legal contract drawn up. Why talk about marriage? What's behind it?"

"Argh! Chet Kinsman, you *stupid,* insensitive—"

He reached out and put two fingertips over her mouth. "Jill, we've known each other too long to pull punches. He loves you, okay. I can believe that. You love him. Fine. But where does marriage come into it? Does he plan to try to become an American citizen?"

She pushed his hand away, but her tone was quieter, less angry. "I . . . we haven't even discussed it. I thought I'd move into Lunagrad with him."

"Uh-huh. And suppose he figures that he wants asylum, like Baliagorev . . . or that he's scared the Russian security people will nail him for the old man's defection?"

"Chet, that's a shitty thing to say."

"I know. I'm a bastard. But I'd rather have me hurt your feelings than have him break you in half—him, or anybody else."

"I love him, Chet. I want to be with him wherever he goes."

A lifetime commitment, even if our lives only last another week. "Jill, you can *be* with him. Hell, you've been living together for the past few days, haven't you?"

"Few days?" she echoed, wide-eyed. "We're talking about a pair of lifetimes!"

"You two can live together as long as you want to," Kinsman went on, "but when he brings up the idea of marriage—that gets into legal and political problems."

"Chet, you're talking like a big brother. I'm old enough to take my own risks."

He shook his head. "Don't rush things, Jill, there could be—"

"You can't stop us," she snapped.

"Yes, I can. Or Leonov could. You know that."

Clenching her fists, Jill said in a barely controlled whisper, "Chet, just because you can't work out your own head well enough to make a lasting commitment to anything or anybody doesn't mean that I'm as scared and mixed-up as you are. I love Alexei and I'm going to marry him."

"On the strength of a few days' living with him."

"We've known each other for three years, off and on. Why do you think he came up to Lunagrad?"

Kinsman actually took a step backward at this news. She came after him, a furious little sparrow pursuing a confused cat. "You must think I'm some brainless child that you've got to protect and watch out for. Well, if either one of us needs a keeper, *Colonel* Kinsman, it's you! You haven't got the brains to realize when somebody loves you. But I do! And I'm going to enjoy his love as fully as I can. Understand *that,* big brother!"

And suddenly Kinsman was laughing. "Okay, okay," he said, putting up his hands as if to fend her off. "So I'm a suspicious old bastard."

"You're an idiot."

"That too."

"And, and . . ."

"I'm trying to protect you," he offered.

"I'll protect myself, thank you. And even if what you think is true, I'd rather face that than spend one minute less with Alexei than I have to."

"Okay," Kinsman said. "Message received and understood."

"All right."

"Umm . . . Am I still invited to the party?"

"You'll behave yourself?" She was starting to grin again.

"I'll be the model of decorum."

"No politics?"

"I'll just sit in a corner and won't even open my mouth—except to sip a little medicinal brandy."

"Then you can come."

"Thank you, ma'am. I'll just run right along and change into my good coverall."

She sniffed at him, then suddenly threw her arms around his neck and squeezed mightily. She had to stand on tiptoe to manage it.

"Oh, Chet, I'm so damned happy! Don't spoil it for me."

"I won't," he said. But he was already wondering, Will Pete Leonov be at the party?

He wasn't. A few Russian medics were there, crammed in with the crowd that bulged Jill's two-room quarters. But Leonov and all the other Russian military and administrative personnel were conspicuously absent.

The place was impossibly jammed. The party was already overflowing out into the corridor by the time Kinsman got there. He had brought a bottle of Earthside Scotch with him—everyone brought their own bottles to these parties. When Kinsman had pulled the Scotch from his kitchenette cabinet he saw that it was the last one and told himself, Got to get the guys to bring me reinforcements on the next grocery run. Then he realized that there might not be another replenishment mission; the shuttle flights from Earthside could stop at any moment. *No!* he raged to himself. They'll take a few weeks to bring things to a real boil. Ten days, at least.

Kinsman wormed his way through the crowd, holding his bottle over his head. He realized he could never spot tiny Jill in this mob, so he looked for Landau. He found him in the bedroom, standing to one side of a slightly smaller knot of people who were standing, sitting on the bed, slouching on other pieces of furniture, squatting cross-legged on the floor.

Jill was beside Landau, Kinsman saw as he made his way through the noisy conversations and laughter. Her back was to the doorway, so she couldn't see him approaching. He wrapped his free arm around her, pulled her to him, and kissed her mightily.

"Congratulations," he said at last. "I didn't get to say that before." Releasing her, he put his hand out to Landau. "And congratulations to you. You're getting the best girl there is."

"I know," he said. "Thank you." Somehow he looked very happy and very serious at the same time.

Within minutes Kinsman was sitting on the floor, a plastic cup of Scotch in one hand, his back propped against somebody's knees, listening to a discussion that was getting steadily drunker and less coherent. Ellen was nowhere in sight. He wondered if she had been invited to the party. Maybe she's on duty at the comm center?

Then Frank Colt pushed his way into the bedroom. For a moment he stood in the doorway, looking uncertain. At least he's wearing fatigues, Kinsman thought. Landau started to extend his hand. Jill reached up and put a hand on his shoulder. "Kiss me, I'm the bride-to-be."

Colt pecked at her, then shook hands with Landau. Before he could sit down, though, a swarthy lean-faced man sitting on the other side of the bed said, "Here comes supermouth."

Kinsman started to say something, but Colt got there first. "Hey, it's a party—save the brain-damage stuff for later."

The guy was potted. Kinsman knew him slightly: a civilian engineer, one of Ernie Waterman's people. His name was . . . Kinsman searched his memory, then it clicked: Jerry Perotti.

"You been pretty mouthy all day long, Colt—why get shy with us here? Give us all the benefit of your keen military mouth."

"Stuff it," Colt said.

Everyone else in the room went silent. Kinsman's brain seemed to be working in slow-motion. He panned across the room, looking at the faces of the people: surprised, amused, upset. Perotti looked sore. God knows what Frank did to him today. Colt himself looked tense but fully in control, almost smiling. The fastest gun in the West, facing yet another foolhardy challenger. I ought to stop this right here and now . . .

"No, I won't stuff it," Perotti was saying. "You and your goddamned gold braid. Who the hell do you think you are?"

Colt abruptly turned and took three strides into the bathroom. Before anyone had a chance to say or do anything he came out again and tossed a roll of toilet paper at Perotti, who involuntarily snatched it one-handed, against his chest.

"Here, that's what we use on assholes," Colt snapped.

There was a split-second of shocked silence, then everyone broke up. They roared. Everyone but Perotti. He pushed himself to his feet in the midst of the laughing people, face darkening. He slammed the toilet-paper roll down on the bed and stomped out of the room. Colt stood back from the doorway and let him lurch past.

"Another notch on the old six-gun," Kinsman mumbled, suddenly realizing that the combination of lack of sleep, tension and Scotch had made him drunk already.

Colt spotted him and came over to squat on the floor beside him.

"What is there about you that makes some people instantly want to give you a hard time?" Kinsman wondered aloud.

"Skin, man," Colt said.

"Oh, hell, Frank. There are dozens of black people in Selene. We had a whole delegation from Chad here last year. Nobody threw knives at them."

"Yassuh, but they's nice folks," Colt put on his Mississippi yokel accent. "Me, I'm a sonofabitch. If you're white and a sonofabitch, nobody hardly notices. But if you're black, it all hangs out."

The party glided on. Kinsman drank slowly, steadily, maintaining a soft glow that blurred the edges of reality just enough to make everything pleasant.

In the apartment's main room, the drifting currents of humanity had washed Pat Kelly and Ernie Waterman into the same corner. They made an incongruous pair: the tall, hound-sad engineer and the stubby, rabbit-faced officer.

"Just how serious is this yellow alert?" Waterman was asking.

Kelly rubbed his nose with a hand chilled from holding an iced drink. "About as serious as they come. I've been working all day on the logistics programming."

"I mean, shouldn't we be pretty damned careful about these Russians? They're right in our laps, for Chrissakes."

"I know," Kelly said. "I told Chet about that. And now he's got 'em in the hospital and marrying into our people."

Waterman shook his head dismally. "You know what he said to me? He said that we're not going to fight up here."

"Yeah? He said that?"

"That's exactly what he said. Now, how can he keep from fighting here? If the orders come through, he has to obey them, don't he?"

"He does," Kelly said, "or somebody else will. That's why they brought Colt up here—superpatriot. It'd take only a one-line message to relieve Chet of command and put Frank in."

"That might not be such a bad thing," Waterman mused.

"I wouldn't worry about it," said Kelly, looking worried. "Chet's a nice, easygoing guy. Great to work for. Likes to have everything friendly and relaxed. But when the orders come, he'll follow them. Got no choice. When we get right down to the nut, Americans will act like Americans, and Russians will act like Russians. Friendships end when the missiles are launched."

"You think so?"

"You don't?"

Waterman shrugged. "He seemed so damned determined to get the water factory's output up to the point where the Russians can use it. You think maybe he's planning to let them walk in and take over?"

"What?" Kelly looked startled.

"Well, he says there won't be any fighting up here. The only way he can guarantee that is to let the Reds take over without firing a shot. Right?"

"That's lunacy!"

"Maybe so, but do you see him making any plans to take over Lunagrad?"

"We've got contingency plans . . ."

"When's the last time *he* took a look at 'em?" Waterman asked.

Kelly hesitated, then, "No! Chet wouldn't do that. He's easygoing, but he's not a traitor."

"Maybe he don't see it as treason." The engineer waved a hand at the chattering crowd all around them. "Maybe he thinks that any kind of fighting up here would kill everybody, so he won't fight, no matter what."

"Like the peace nuts back when we were kids?"

"Uh-huh."

"Jesus Christ," Kelly muttered. "I sure as hell hope that's not what's on his mind."

Waterman looked as if he were about to cry. "It could be. He could be ready to sell us all down the river, just to avoid fighting."

"Hell! You know what that means, don't you?" Kelly looked genuinely distressed now.

"What?"

"I'm gonna have to go to Frank Colt and get *him* to review all our emergency contingency plans—behind Chet's back."

"If that's what's gotta be done . . ."

Kelly grimaced. "I hate to go around Chet. He's a nice guy and all that." His frown deepened. "And I hate like hell having to work with Colt."

"If you've got to, you've got to," Waterman said.

Kelly nodded unhappily. "Yeah, I've got to."

More people jammed into the party. Others left. For a long time Kinsman could see neither Jill nor Landau in the roaring, body-crammed apartment. He spotted Kelly and Waterman talking solemnly together off in a corner, looking grimmer with each word. Then Jill and the Russian reappeared. The apartment started to get a little less crowded. People were drifting homeward.

Kinsman threaded his way carefully through the living room and back into the bedroom, marveling at how well and steadily he was walking. Colt lay sprawled on the bed now with a bosomy redhead sitting alongside him, propped up on a pair of pillows. She was wearing a wine-red party dress, low in front and short skirted. One of the newcomers, Kinsman realized.

Jill and Landau came into the bedroom; the Russian standing protectively beside her.

Colt gave them a long look. "Ain't gonna be easy for you two, y'know," he said. His drink was perched precariously on his stomach, his hands clasped behind his head. Only someone who knew him as well as Kinsman did would realize how drunk he was.

"I was married to a girl that looked kinda light. She wasn't white, but try telling that to some drunk Florida rednecks." Colt's voice was absolutely flat, no emotion detectable. Like a pathologist reciting the details of an autopsy.

"We are intelligent people here," Landau said. "Jill and I can live in Lunagrad without difficulties."

"You mean your security people will let her in? Without worrying that she might be a spy? I just don't believe it."

Jill said, "We can live here."

"Then I have to try to find out if he's spying on us," Colt shot back.

"Come on, Frank," Kinsman said, knowing that his speech was slightly slurred. "Don't piss on the wedding cake."

Colt looked over at Kinsman. "Hey man, you still up and around?"

"Well, it *is* a lot easier if I hold onto a wall or something."

Landau said, "Wait, this is serious. Suppose my government makes it impossible for Jill to live in Lunagrad? Could I take up residence here in Moonbase?"

" 'S'okay with me," Kinsman said. "But I don't think your own people would let you do it. Leonov had to break six hundred rules to let Baliagorev come here to have his goddamned life saved."

"But—"

"No buts," Colt said. "This is *very* serious. You guys might have gotten along as friends up here so far, but things are changing very fast."

"Frank, old buddy," Kinsman said, holding himself stiffly erect, "I don't pull rank often, but I don't want this stupid crap to go any further." He turned to Landau. "Alex, husband-to-be of the woman who is virtually a sister to me, if you want to live here, you are welcome to. I am not going to permit this chickenshit from Earth to make a mess of things here. No way. Not now. Not ever. Not as long as I'm in command here."

Colt chuckled lazily. "That's a great way to make me commander of Moonbase, pal," he said.

Kinsman found himself tottering down the corridor toward his own quarters, with no idea of what time it was, or how the well-built redhead got attached to his arm.

By concentrating so hard that it made his head hurt, he could remember the talk with Colt and Jill and Landau. The tense silence that ended it. Going back to the bar in the living room for more Scotch. The girl popping up beside him . . .

With an effort, he focused his bleary eyes on her. Even in the unflattering overhead lights of the chilly corridor she looked good. Young, soft, large-eyed and full-lipped. Big boobs. The dress had slipped off one shoulder and her hair was disarrayed. She smelled of lost and forbidden memories: flower gardens and soft summer evenings.

She smiled up at him. "You got awfully quiet."

"I am old enough to be your father," he said, feeling stupid.

"Oh, don't be silly," she said. "You're cute."

Cute? Holy shit. Cute! He scowled at her, but she only smiled all the more. Ellen doesn't show up at the party, and I'm dragging teen-agers into bed.

"Cute," he muttered at her.

He knew why. He didn't like it, but he knew. Don't ever put yourself in a spot where your survival depends on one individual. Don't let yourself become vulnerable to Ellen or anyone else. Armor plate, flyboy. Surround yourself with it. Otherwise it's too fucking easy to get shot down.

"Cute," he grumbled at her again.

She laughed and slid her arm around his waist and snuggled closer as they walked.

What the hell, he thought. Maybe she's a good lay.

Tuesday 7 December 1999: 1025 hrs GMT

"Good morning, cheerful campers! And how's our peerless leader today?"

Through the haze of a throbbing headache, Kinsman squinted up at Hugh Harriman. The little round man was smiling broadly and clasping something behind his back.

"Go away," Kinsman muttered.

"Now, now, don't be testy." Harriman was standing in the doorway of Kinsman's office. He walked all the way in and leaned over the sofa slightly to peer into Kinsman's eyes.

"Nicely bloodshot," he announced. "Must have been a good party."

Kinsman leaned back on the sofa and rested his aching skull against the cool stone wall. "It was quite a party, I'll grant you that." Then, remembering, "Hey, where the hell were you last night?"

"I thought you'd never ask." Harriman plopped himself down on the sofa beside Kinsman and revealed what he was holding: a thermos bottle. "But first," he said, unscrewing the cap, "try some of Old Doc Harriman's sure-fire hangover cure. Never fails."

Kinsman watched warily as Harriman poured a reddish liquid into the cup that had been the top of the thermos. He took the cup, but asked, "Aren't you having any?"

Harriman's eyes went round with injured innocence. "Suspicious this morning, aren't you? Well, if you insist." He hoisted the thermos in salute and put it to his lips.

Kinsman sipped from the cup. It had been a Bloody Mary originally, that much he was sure of. But Harriman had added things to it. It tasted almost sweet, very smooth, instantly soothing.

"Not . . ." his voice was a choked whisper, "not bad."

"Good! A little LSD never hurt anyone." Harriman seemed genuinely pleased. Wiping a bit of red foam from his mustache with the back of his hand, he went on, "Now, to answer your original question . . ."

"My question?"

"You *are* accelerating slowly this morning! You asked why I wasn't at the party last night."

"Oh, yeah." Kinsman could feel his whole nervous system vibrating like the strings of a harp that had been wedged into a supersonic wind tunnel.

"I was doing a bit of homework yesterday, and I got so engrossed in it that I stayed up all night. Haven't been to sleep yet."

Impressed, Kinsman said, "You look damned chipper for a guy who hasn't slept at all."

"That's because I've been stimulating my brain with creative thought, not soaking it in alcohol."

"Touché."

"Ah! A linguist. I didn't know. Well . . ." Harriman's face suddenly went completely serious. The smile vanished, the eyes became intense. "You realize, of course, that everybody in Selene knows you've been muttering about refusing to follow orders and declaring us independent of Earthside control."

"There are no secrets here," Kinsman admitted.

"Not the way you handle 'em, at least! At any rate, I've been spending the past few days casually talking things over with lots of people—Americans, Russians, foreign visitors, permanent Luniks, ninety-dayers. I've also gone over the personnel records of most of the people here, their psychological profiles mainly . . ."

"How the hell did you get access—?"

Harriman held up a pudgy hand. "You think you're the only one who has a way with women around here? After all, I'm considered a dashing and romantic figure by some of the weaker broads. Besides, I told the kids in charge of the computer files that I wanted to search for people who might be interested in starting a university here. They fell for it."

Kinsman said only "Hmm."

"It's your own fault, Chet! You run a very lax operation here. No wonder they sent Colt up to tighten security."

"Don't tell me my troubles."

"All right. Near as I can compute it, about eighty percent of the permanent Luniks would support a move for independence. And the surprising thing is that the ninety-dayers are split about fifty-fifty. You can carry it off, frlend, lf you want to."

Kinsman shook his head, and immediately regretted it. The throbbing grew worse. "I've thought it all over. Declaring independence won't change things Earthside. They'll still start their war; all we'll be able to do is delay them."

Harriman blinked at him, owlishly. "You mean you haven't figured it out? You're kidding! A brilliant military mind like yours? Not even Leonov has seen it?"

"Seen what?"

"How to make Selene independent and stop the friggin' war before it starts!"

Suddenly Kinsman forgot his headache. He straightened up in the sofa. "What the hell are you talking about?"

Harriman laughed. "My God! Are philosophers really the only people who can truly think?"

"Hugh . . ."

Running a hand over his bald pate, Harriman said, "I thought you had already worked this out for yourself."

"Worked *what* out?"

"Taking over the satellites."

"What?"

With a heavenward roll of his eyes, Harriman explained, "Look, neither the U.S. nor Russia has enough ABM satellites in orbit to provide a really effective shield against a missile attack. Right?"

"Not yet."

"How many satellites have to be on station for an orbital ABM network to be considered workable?"

"That's classified information, Hugh."

"So's my hairy ass! Anybody with a pencil and paper can figure it out, for Chrissakes! You want to be sure you've got several satellites over every enemy launching area, every minute of the day. If the satellites are in low orbit—which they are, to save on laser power—then you need between a hundred and a hundred fifty to do the job right. Right?"

With a grin, Kinsman said, "You're giving the numbers, not me."

"All right. How many workable satellites does the U.S. have in orbit right now?"

"Classified."

Harriman glared at him. "How many do the Russians have up?"

"Ask Leonov."

"How many are there between the two?"

Kinsman started to open his mouth, then it struck him.

"Ah-hah!" Harriman crowed. "Dawn is breaking inside that murky skull. There are *already* more than a hundred satellites in orbit and in perfect working condition. Right? And if you and Leonov could grab *all* of them, Selene would have an ABM network that could prevent *anybody* from launching *anything!* Right?"

Kinsman heard himself say, "Including troop shuttles to take Selene away from us."

"Exactly right," Harriman said. "You get an *A*. Go to the head of the class."

Suddenly Kinsman was out of breath, winded as if he had sprinted through an obstacle course. "Hugh, if we could do that—"

"It would guarantee Selene's independence, our freedom from attack, and it would prevent them from starting their war—at least, they wouldn't be able to launch missiles at each other."

"But—" Kinsman was still trying to catch his breath. "But to seize control of the ABM networks, we'd have to take over the manned space stations."

"Right. Which is probably why you hadn't thought of the idea yourself."

"Why?"

"Simple psychology, friend," Harriman explained. "Despite your lofty military rank, you're not a violent man. You don't want to hurt anybody. You could see your way to making Selene independent, because you didn't think there would be any fighting involved. But taking the space stations is another matter. Those guys in the stations aren't Luniks. They'll fight you."

Kinsman nodded.

"It'll take bloodshed," Harriman said, very gravely. "There hasn't been a political movement in all of history that hasn't spilled blood. Dammit."

Pat Kelly had spent much of the morning searching for Frank Colt. After a fruitless couple of hours trying to get the computer-directed phone system to track him down or page him, Kelly finally left his cubbyhole office and the work he was supposed to be doing, and set out himself to look for the black major.

It was nearly noon when he found him, out at the catapult launching facility, at the extreme end of the longest tunnel in Selene. The facility was mainly underground, but the ten-kilometer-long catapult itself was up on the surface, its angled steel framework looking spidery by comparison with the heavy construction of Earthside structures. Yet it still seemed bold and new, compared with the tired ancient hills and worn pockmarked plain of the Sea of Clouds.

The control center was in a small surface dome. It looked rather like the control tower of a minor airport Earthside, mainly because it served the same function. But instead of guiding aircraft into and out of an airport, this center handled only outgoing traffic: the drone supply packages that were launched to the manned space stations in orbit around the Earth.

As Kelly stepped off the power ladder and onto the plastic-tiled floor of the dome, he saw Colt standing in the middle of the clustered desks and electronics consoles that lined the long curving window across the way. The dome was dimly lit, and in the shadows a dozen men were sitting tensed over their desktop controls, watching the flickering lights and computer readouts, listening to the commands and data updates through the earpin microphones they all wore.

Through the window, Kelly could see a bulky wing-less cylinder squatting at one end of the long catapult track.

Both Colt and Kelly remained silent and unmoving, at opposite sides of the dome, as the launch crew carried out the final stages of their operation in the cool, clipped tones of their profession:

"T minus thirty seconds and counting."

"Beta Station acknowledges."

"Sled power on."

"All track relays green."

"Fifteen seconds . . ."

Across the sweep of desktop control panels, tiny lights were changing from amber to green, like a Christmas display. At the extreme right end of the row of consoles, the ARM and FIRE lights of the launch controller still glared red. The controller himself sat with his back to Kelly, his eyes riveted to his panel lights.

"Internal power on."

"Terminal guidance and control green."

"Thrusters green."

"Ten seconds . . ."

The launch controller manually lifted two switches with his right hand, and the last two red lights went amber.

"Automatic sequencer on."

"Energize full track."

"Beta acknowledges time and recovery angle."

"All systems green."

"Three . . . two . . . one . . . launch!"

They all looked up from their desks. The squat cylinder jerked into motion, became a blur almost instantly, and dwindled into invisibility as it hurtled down the long track.

"Radar?" the launch controller asked, with only the slightest edge to his voice.

From across the row of desks came a woman's voice, "Through the keyhole."

The launch controller yanked the earpin out and stood up. "Okay, well done. But nobody moves until

Beta Station picks her up and acknowledges the trajectory."

They leaned back in their chairs. A few pulled out cigarettes, and lit up.

The spell broken, Kelly walked grimly toward Colt. "Frank, can I talk to . . ."

Colt spun around at the sound of his name. He looked surprised, then puzzled, then surprised again as Kelly got close enough to be recognized in the dim lighting. "Pat? What're you doing up here?"

"Looking for you," Kelly answered.

"What's perking?"

"I've got to talk to you. Someplace where it's quiet."

Colt gave him a long look. "I'm here checking on the defensibility of the launch center. Be easy for the Reds to knock this place off—all they'd need's a couple bazookas."

Kelly realized that he was right. "But they'd have to trek over the surface to get here. The tunnel can be defended pretty easily."

"Hey, man," Colt grinned, "you're making noises like a soldier!"

"And anybody moving on the surface is damned vulnerable," Kelly finished, ignoring the thrust.

"They're vulnerable if you know they're coming, and if you realize their intentions," Colt said.

"We could set up perimeter alarms—lasers. Be simple to do, and nobody'd know about it."

Colt raised his eyebrows. "Yeah, that'd work, wouldn't it?"

Kelly repeated, "I've got to talk to you. Privately."

With a glance around at the chatting, relaxed crew, Colt said, "Okay, let's go back down the tunnel. I want to see how secure the heat and power lines are, anyway."

As they got to the power ladder, they heard one of the launch crew technicians sing out, "Beta's acquired our bird—on trajectory, time and angle on the double-oh."

Down in the long chilly tunnel, in the glare of the overhead luminescents, Colt's skin looked bluish. Otherworldly. "What's perking?" he asked Kelly again.

Pat suddenly wished he were somewhere else. Change the subject. Forget about the whole thing. But he heard himself saying, "It's Chet. He's been making some damned broad hints about refusing to fight, if and when the time comes."

Colt's expression turned sour. "Yeah, I know. So what else is new?"

"Frank, I think he means it. He really will refuse to obey orders—maybe he'll turn us over to the Reds!"

Colt raised his hands as if to grab Kelly's coverall front. "Listen," he snapped. "Chet may be a do-gooder and an easygoing fool—but he's not a traitor. Understand that? He won't sell us out. He might need a little push when the time comes—that's why I'm here."

They walked for several moments in silence, listening to their thermal boots clicking against the rough stone flooring of the tunnel.

Finally Kelly said, "Frank, you and Kinsman have been friends for a long time. But I've been looking over his shoulder for the past couple of months. I know what he's been saying and what he's been thinking. He's ready to do *anything* rather than fight. He's been palling around with Leonov and letting Russian nationals into our end of the hospital. He's closer to *them* than he is to our own people Earthside."

Colt said nothing.

"If he . . . if he fails to obey orders," Kelly went on, "he won't think of it as treason. He'll think he's doing the right thing. But he'll be crippling America's chances of winning the war."

"You're bringing your wife and kids up here, aren't you?" Colt asked suddenly.

Kelly stopped walking. "What's that got to do with it?"

Shrugging, Colt said, "I'd think that you'd be on Chet's side of this. You anxious to have a shooting war up here, with your family on the way?"

"They're going to be safer here than Earthside," Kelly said. "And I'd rather have them in the middle of a battle here than hand them over to the Russians. We're Americans; we're ready to fight for our freedom if we have to."

"Ready to die for it?"

Kelly nodded.

Colt laughed. "Ready to fight and die . . . Ready to fight and die."

"What's funny?" Kelly could feel his face going red.

"My brother, man, you sound just like my brother," Colt said. His laughter echoed weirdly in the tunnel, bounced off the metal heat pipes and electrical power lines, rang off the cold stone that surrounded them.

"He tried to beat the shit outta me when I joined the Air Force. Said I was a traitor to my people. I told him I didn't want to die for my people, I just wanted to live good. Told him it was time we got high enough into the chain of command to make it *our* Army and *our* Navy and *our* Air Force."

"I don't see . . ."

"Back then, the fighting was all inside the States. We were pals with the Reds. Turned out, they were just sitting back and waiting for us blacks to help tear down the U.S. of A. My brother tried. He fought for what he believed in: black power. He wound up in a shittin' hut in Dahomey, in Africa, hiding out from the FBI and CIA and Lord knows who else. Know how he died? Some motherfuckin' African Communists sprayed the crappy little airport down there with machine guns and grenades. He happened to be there. They killed him."

Kelly felt confused. Colt wasn't making sense.

"Listen," the black man said, "One thing I learned early and learned good. Don't fight city hall. Get inside city hall and take it over—but do it slow and easy, without any fuss. Too many guys call themselves revolutionaries, all they want is some quick publicity and a lotta chicks. The real revolutionaries carefully protect the system—'cause they want it for themselves."

"You're not—"

Colt grabbed him by the shoulder and shook him, schoolyard rough. "Listen, Irish Catholic God-fearing American. Black power don't mean shit if there's no America left, if it all goes up in a mushroom cloud. So I've gotta protect America, you dig? And at the same time, I wouldn't at all mind becoming commander of

Moonbase. So give Chet enough rope to hang himself. Give him plenty of rope."

"You sonofabitch," Kelly said, in a shocked whisper. "You say you're his friend—"

"I *am* his friend! But if he turns traitor, then he's not my friend or anybody's else's. And *you're* tellin' me he's gonna turn traitor."

Kelly said nothing.

"Well?" Colt demanded, his voice booming. "Isn't that what you're saying?"

It was hard to make his voice work. "Ye . . . yes," Kelly managed. "I guess that's what I'm saying."

"Yeah. You guess. And you're willing to have your wife and family in the middle of a shoot-out, to protect and defend America. Goddamned noble of you, whitey. Goddamned noble."

"Now, listen, Colt . . ."

"I had a wife and family—I saw them die. Wonder how you'd feel."

Kelly wanted to run. He wanted to get as far away from this man as he could. Anywhere . . .

But Colt was still holding onto his shoulder with a grip of fury. "Listen to me, Kelly. I want to know everything Chet's doing, everything he's thinking, even what he dreams about at night. I want to know what he's going to do before he knows it himself. Because if you're right, then I'm going to have to kill him—"

"Kill!"

"That's right, baby. Kill. Chet might look easygoing, but underneath it all he's stubborn as shit. And damned popular around here. He's turned Moonbase into a freakhouse for all the eggheads who think they can live with the Russians. When the button gets pushed, Chet's going to be *very* hard to stop. *Very* hard. Talking won't do it."

"But . . . killing him . . ." Kelly was suddenly afraid.

"I know. It sucks. So's everything else. Maybe we can get away without it coming to that. But we've got to be ready to face it."

Kelly pushed at his thinning hair. "I don't know . . ."

"But I do. And one other thing," Colt said, iron-hard. "Everything I've told you is based on the assumption that you're right, and Chet's going to hand us over to the Reds. If I find out that you're wrong—this whole planet won't be big enough to hide you. I will personally take you apart, little friend. Count on it."

Academician V. I. Mogilev was livid with rage. He flailed his arms angrily in the tight confines of the space station's compartment as he bellowed into the face of the station commander. "But this is insanity! It is preposterous! Bureaucratic interference with scientific research that has won the highest approval from the Supreme Soviet . . ."

The station commander listened with oriental patience. The son of an Uzbek herdsman does not rise to the rank of captain in the Soviet Space Corps without learning patience. He had been screamed at by true experts; this little professor was a rank amateur.

After some time, the academician wound down. "You can understand what idiocy this is, can't you?" His voice was almost pleading now. "We are in the middle of such delicate studies. All the instruments are at last aligned and working well. The pulsar's peak of radiation intensity will be reached in another fourteen hours, if Chalinik's calculations are correct, and . . . and . . ."

"My dear professor," the captain said as politely as he could, but still coldly enough to leave no doubt as to who was in command, "I appreciate the extreme importance of your work. But you must realize that orders from the Kremlin leave no room for argument. I cannot refuse to obey my orders. Do you want to have me shot?"

"No, no, of course not." There seemed to be some little doubt in the academician's tone, despite his words.

The captain shrugged elaborately. "Then what can I do? I have my orders. You and your assistants must be prepared to leave within another"—he glanced at his wrist watch—"another three hours."

"But—our work—the instruments . . ."

"We will take care of the instruments," the captain said. "No one will disturb them, I assure you."

The scientist continued muttering as the captain rose and squeezed out from behind his little desk, and escorted the older man to the airtight hatch that opened onto the space station's main corridor.

"You will allow the instruments to keep recording the pulsar's activities?"

"Of course. Certainly."

The scientist went slowly down the corridor, shaking his head and mumbling to himself. No sooner had the captain seated himself at his desk again than a younger officer stepped through the open hatchway. He was tall and blond, a true Russian.

He'll advance faster than I will, thought the captain as he glowered at the young man.

"Sir," the young officer said.

"Sit down, lieutenant. Your craft is ready to take the scientists home?"

"Yessir, although they seem quite unhappy about it."

The captain let a small smile creep across his face. "They are civilians. They do not understand military matters."

The lieutenant nodded.

"Of course, you understand such things, don't you?" The captain turned in his chair and reached for a tiny thermos resting on the shelf behind his desk.

"I believe I understand military matters," the lieutenant said to his back, then added, "sir."

"Hmm . . ." Taking two glasses from a desk drawer, the captain asked, "Drink?"

"No, thank you, sir. I will be piloting the shuttle rocket."

"So? Tea upsets you?"

"Oh!" The lieutenant was taken aback, a sight that pleased the captain. "Well, yes, in that case. Thank you."

As he poured the steaming brew, the captain asked, "So you understand military matters, eh?"

"I think so. Sir."

"Then tell me," he slammed the thermos on the desk hard enough to make tea jump out of both glasses, "how do those Earthbound desk-pilots expect me to defend a Soviet military installation that is defenseless? Heh?"

"I . . . sir . . ."

"Look at this place!" The captain waved his free hand. "It's made of straw. A single grenade exploded in co-orbit with us would shred us like goat's cheese. How are we to defend ourselves against attack?"

"I didn't realize that an attack was imminent," the lieutenant answered, keeping his hands carefully in his lap and not reaching for the tea.

"A commander must always assume that an attack is imminent! Learn that! Get it into your skull and into your blood! Never relax your guard!"

"Yessir."

The captain glared at him for a moment, then pushed one of the glasses toward him. The lieutenant quickly snatched at it.

"Why do you think they've ordered all the civilians off our little island in the sky? Heh? We are in an alert status. At any moment, the word may come that war has broken out. Do you have a family? Wife? Children?"

The lieutenant blinked once. "My mother . . . in Moscow."

"Mmm. My children will be safe enough from the bombs," the captain said. "But the fallout . . . the fallout, that's what will kill them. A lingering death."

"It may not happen," the lieutenant said, very quietly.

The captain eyed him. "Do you know what your cargo was? What you brought for me to sit with, in place of the scientists?"

"Nosir. It was sealed, and my orders made no mention of the cargo's contents."

"But something that big must have aroused your curiosity, heh? A single package, sealed and guarded. Heh?"

"Well . . ." the lieutenant smiled, almost. "There were rumors at Turyatum—"

"Rumors? Such as?"

"Well, that the package was part of a new weapon, a

system that will defend the space station against American attack."

"Hah! I wish it were."

"Then it's not?"

"No, lieutenant, it's not. It's a weapon, true enough. But it won't help to defend us. If anything, it will make us an even more important target to the Americans."

"What is it, then?"

The captain smiled his best inscrutable smile. "Come now, lieutenant. You must realize that I cannot tell you. The information is classified."

The lieutenant drank his tea in stony silence and departed. Some time later, the captain got up from his desk and strode the length of his tiny station to the loading dock. He watched the shuttle, filled with the complaining scientists now, as its rockets puffed briefly and it arced away to be quickly lost against the glare of the looming Earth.

Then another spark of light caught his eye. The package that the shuttle had left hanging in orbit a few hundred meters from the station's main airlock.

The bomb. Tomorrow the shuttle would be back with the guidance package. And the day after that, with the rocket thrusters.

I must check with Lunagrad to be certain that they are giving the highest priority to sending us extra fuel for the orbiting bombs, the captain told himself.

Then he got an inspiration. Turning from the viewport where he had been standing, he told the nearest technician, "Dismantle all that scientific junk and plant it on the outside skin of the station. It might help to deflect shrapnel, in case we're attacked."

Without a word of argument, the technician moved to obey.

It was a glum meeting.

The Farside astronomical observatory had once been a thriving center of exciting research. The vast array of steerable twenty-meter radio dishes seemed to fill all the Sea of Moscow—at least, all that was visible from Farside's main dome. The thousand-centimeter optical telescope and its clusters of electronic amplifiers and satellite telescopes. The UV and infrared, the x-ray and gamma ray detectors. The constant shuttle of intense, eager young men and women, balanced by the older, more patient, but no less eager permanent staff. The computer links. The excitement of searching the universe for knowledge, for life, for intelligence.

Now Farside was like a ghost town.

Kinsman slouched back in a webchair, letting his mind drift from the droning voices of the men and women around the table. He stared through the conference room's window at the spidery telescope framework outside. The largest optical telescope ever built, sitting in the open of the lunar plain, alone and useless.

The sky out there looked empty without Earth to brighten it. The astronomers loved that; it made Farside a much better site for their research. But it made Kinsman uneasy, frightened at the deepest level of his being. Earth was never in the sky, here on the far side of the Moon.

"The only remaining item to be discussed," Dr. Mishima was saying, his soft voice slow and measured, trying hard not to reveal the bitterness he felt, "is the protective dome for the thousand-centimeter telescope."

"I have examined the cost figures," said one of the Russian administrators. "The dome is too expensive for our current budget allocation."

Dr. Mishima drew in his breath. Then, "If this observatory is to be shut down, the equipment must either be transferred to Selene, or protected from meteoric erosion, so that it can be used again—when the gods of the budgets are more favorably disposed toward us."

What the hell's the matter with Ellen? Kinsman asked himself, staring out at the empty sky. Five days now, and she hasn't answered my calls. Since she got Pierce's job. Is that all she wanted from me?

One of the Americans was saying, "It's not that we *want* to abandon Farside. They just haven't given us the money to keep it open."

"I understand that you regret this turn of events more than can be expressed," Dr. Mishima said with elaborate politeness. "Still, it is necessary to consider the future. I cannot believe that astronomical research will cease entirely and forever—"

"Keep it open," Kinsman heard himself say.

They all jerked with surprise and turned toward him: Mishima, the Americans and Russians (sitting on opposite sides of the table, Kinsman noticed wryly), three men and four women representing the other nations with staff or equipment investments in Farside, and Piotr Leonov.

It was Leonov, sitting directly across the table from Kinsman, who asked, "What did you say?" The expression on his face was hard to read: almost a smile, eyes curious, as if he agreed with Kinsman, but wasn't certain he had heard him correctly.

"I said we should keep Farside open. It would be a tragedy to close this place down."

"I agree," Leonov said, "but the funds have been cut off. It's the one thing our two governments have been able to agree on."

Fuck them, Kinsman said to himself. Aloud, "Dr. Mishima, just how much do you need to keep on going here? You've got the big equipment, and you've got the computers and life-support equipment and electrical power systems. What else do you need?"

The Japanese astronomer seemed stunned. "Er . . . Our major costs over the past two years have been maintenance, housekeeping, basic supplies, things of that nature. And, of course, the largest cost has been that of bringing new people up from Earth."

"Pete, why can't we keep Farside going? We don't need Earthside replacements every ninety days. There's enough of a staff among the permanent Luniks to keep the research going here."

Leonov finally did smile. "I have orders to close the center."

"If your orders read like mine," Kinsman countered, "they merely inform us that no further Earthside funds will be allotted for Farside, and that we're to take the necessary actions. We still have our own resources."

Half the people around the table started talking at once, and the silent ones either grinned hugely or glowered at Kinsman. The grinners were astronomers; the glowerers were administrators from Selene, mostly ninety-dayers.

Leonov stood up and spread his hands for silence. "Wait! Wait. This is something that Colonel Kinsman and I should discuss together before we go any further."

"Right."

Kinsman got up and started around the table, saying, "Why don't we all break for lunch? Pete and I can talk right here and see if we can come up with a meeting of the minds."

The others—some puzzled, some upset—left the room in a buzzing, chatting group. When the door clicked shut behind them, Leonov turned to Kinsman and smiled sardonically. "Very well, you've been trying to get me alone for the past three days. What is it that you want?"

Kinsman walked toward the window. "I wondered why you didn't return my calls."

"I am being carefully watched. So are you."

Nodding, "Think this room's bugged?"

"I doubt it." Leonov came to the window and glanced out at the idle telescope. "Even if it is," he said, pulling a tiny flat dead-black plastic square from his pocket, "this will keep the bugs from hearing us."

Kinsman felt his eyebrows go up a notch. "Scrambler?"

"No, a new type of transmitter that broadcasts at the frequencies of most listening devices. I have programmed it with American hot-rock music; my security people will think you're carrying a jammer."

Kinsman laughed. "Wonder what *my* security people will think."

"That is your problem, old friend."

More seriously, Kinsman said, "I think I've got a solution to our other problem."

"Not your independence idea again!"

"Yes, but . . ."

Leonov closed his eyes. "I have received my orders. I will not be sent home, after all. I will be stationed at the Turyatum launch complex for the duration of the emergency. All space-qualified officers have been placed on a maximum alert basis. No leaves."

"Red alert?"

Leonov nodded. "Only for space-qualified officers. All other military units are on stand-by alert."

"When do you leave?"

"My replacement arrives in five days."

"God damn!"

Leonov turned and stared out the window. "Well, my idealistic comrade, what do you do about that?"

"That's not the question," Kinsman said. "The real question, Pete, is: What are *you* prepared to do?"

He turned back and gazed at Kinsman, his face somber, his eyes grave and weary. "Anything," he said in a near whisper. "Anything that will save my children from being killed."

"They're really going to do it—launch the missiles?"

"Of course they are!" the Russian exploded. "They can't get this close without someone pushing the final button. Oh, they will talk, and argue, and threaten each other for a few more days—a week or two, perhaps. They will stretch everyone's nerves to the breaking point before they convince themselves that they must attack. But one of them will press the button—for the glory of the Motherland, or to save the world for democracy. Then the rest happens automatically."

"Then it's up to us to stop them."

Leonov laughed. "How? By declaring independence? I said I would do anything—but it must be something that will *work!* I will not sit safely up here and watch my nation . . . my people . . . my *children* . . ."

"Okay, okay." Kinsman put both hands on his shoulders. "Take it easy. Cool down."

"No, I will not cool down!" Leonov shouted. "I am not an automaton. I am not a creature of ice water, as you are. I have blood in my veins! Russian blood! The world is about to explode and you expect me to stand here calmly and discuss politics with you. How can you—"

"Stop it!" Kinsman snapped. "They won't need bugs to hear us."

Leonov's face was glistening with sweat. His chest heaved.

"I just want to know one thing," Kinsman said. "Are you prepared to disobey orders and stay here?"

"Stay at Lunagrad instead of . . ." Leonov's voice trailed off for a moment. Then, clenching his fists with the effort of decision, "Yes. I will be doing the children no good by pushing buttons at Turyatum."

"All right." Kinsman licked his lips, and they tasted salty. Maybe I'm not all ice water after all. "This is what we need to do . . . The ABM networks are both unfinished, but *together* they can effectively cover the whole Earth and shoot down any missile attack by either side."

"Together?" Leonov echoed.

"Right. We declare Selene's independence and at the same time we take over the space stations. If we can grab the command and control centers for the ABM satellites, we can stop the war. And enforce our own independence."

"But they'll send troops . . ."

Kinsman could feel sweat trickling down his ribs. "They'll try. They'll have to send them in shuttle rockets. If the ABM satellites can shoot down missiles, they can shoot down troop-carriers, too."

"You . . . could do that?"

"I'd warn them first. But they probably wouldn't listen."

"Your people would shoot down Americans?"

"I don't know. But your people would, and *we'd* take care of any Russian boosters."

Leonov seemed to sag against the window.

"It's the only way," Kinsman urged. "Neither side can stop a war, not the way they've been going. One of them has to back down, and neither of them is going to do that. Only an outside force can stop them. We've got to be that force."

"A handful of people . . . How many are we? a thousand? less?"

"But we're in a special position. We can pull their fangs. We can stop them from fighting."

"They'll call us traitors. They'll kill us."

Kinsman nodded. "They'll try. Your government will probably take your kids."

"Yes."

"We could hold some of their officers from your space stations as counter-hostages."

"That might work." Leonov seemed dazed; his face was blank, his voice distant and toneless.

"Would they . . . kill the children?"

With a slow shake of his head, Leonov replied, "Who knows?"

"They'd be dead anyway, if the war . . ."

There were tears in the Russian's eyes. "So my choice is to have them bombed by the Americans or shot by the security police?"

"I . . ."

"No, no, it won't work. It could never work. It is madness even to think about it." Leonov paced away from the window.

Kinsman stood there and said nothing. He watched the Russian's back, the tension in the corded muscles of his neck. "It could work, Peter," he said. "We could make it work."

Leonov wheeled around to face him. "What would you have me do? Betray Russia and take away her only defense against American attack? Leave my homeland, my children, my whole life, to remain in exile here on this rock? Put my trust in a handful of people? Lunatics? Americans? How do I know I can trust your people? Or my own? How can I trust *you*?"

"You're afraid—"

"Of course I'm afraid!"

Kinsman felt the cold of that empty sky seeping into his guts. "—because I killed one of your cosmonauts."

Leonov rocked backward half a step. "Then it's true." His voice was hollow.

"It's true."

"I didn't believe the intelligence reports. Sometimes they contain exaggerations—outright lies, propaganda."

"I killed her," Kinsman said.

The Russian stepped close to Kinsman. Tears still glistened in his eyes. He shook his head. "I never meant to force you to confess to me."

Kinsman felt lightheaded, almost giddy. It was like coming out of anesthesia. "It was something I had to tell you; it had to be removed from between us."

Leonov said nothing.

"I can't kill anyone again," Kinsman said. "Not even if it's only sitting by and letting others push the buttons. I have to try to stop them. *Have to*, Peter."

"And you cannot do it without Lunagrad's help."

"Without *your* help."

"Forgive me, old friend, I could never have trusted you if you hadn't told me. It's ridiculous, but I could not have trusted you."

They stood side by side, looking out the window at the bleak, empty-skied landscape.

"Too many of us have died," Kinsman told him. "It's time to stop the killing."

Staring at the barren rocks, the ancient weary mountains, the stark framework of human artifacts, Leonov asked quietly, "Do you think there are enough people like us in Selene to carry it off? Can we make a success of it, or will we merely start the war here on the Moon? I have no desire for a glorious failure. Only the victors write the history books."

"Dammit all, Pete, if we don't try, there won't *be* any history books."

"The world's savior," Leonov said. But there was no sarcasm in it. He gestured with a nod out the window, toward the unused telescope. "You want to make the blind see. You've already brought a dead man back to life. And now you want to save the world from hellfire. They'll crucify us, you know."

Kinsman shrugged.

Then, with a smile that was more sadness than anything else, Leonov slowly raised his hand and extended it toward Kinsman. Taking it in his, Kinsman gripped the Russian's hand firmly.

"Wasn't it one of your revolutionaries who said, 'We must all hang together, or we will surely all hang separately?' "

Kinsman laughed. "Franklin."

"We must act swiftly," Leonov said. "And we must start *now*."

Now, Kinsman repeated to himself as he sank into the foamcouch of the ballistic rocket. Takeoff from Farside was felt, rather than heard. A pressure squeezing you into your couch. A distant rumbling that was more of a vibration in your bones than audible sound.

The engine thrust cut off and Kinsman felt the pressure ease to zero. Free-fall. Floating. His hands drifted off the couch's armrests. He still leaned back in his couch, unable to see the dozen other passengers, all cocooned in their own couches, their own thoughts.

He swung the couch to the sit-up position and touched the communications keys on the right armrest. The screen on the seatback in front of him flickered to life, and within a few moments he had Pat Kelly's worried, lip-nibbling face on the screen.

"What do you hear from your wife and family?" Kinsman asked.

Kelly looked puzzled that his boss would call from the Farside ferry rocket with a personal question. "They were at Kennedy yesterday. I haven't checked with Alpha yet, but they ought to be transshipping from the rocketplane to the shuttle this afternoon. That's the schedule."

"Listen, Pat. Get Alpha on the horn and find out exactly when that shuttle took off—and who's on it. I want the info on my desk when I land back at Selene."

"Okay. Sir."

"There's more," Kinsman said. He pulled the pin mike from the armrest and lowered his voice as he spoke into it. "I want you to set up a red-alert condition—"

Kelly's mouth dropped open.

"No, it's not really a red alert, but I want you to get the whole base buttoned up as if there were one. The best men we have at all the critical centers—communications, power, water factory, launch complex. Only permanent Luniks, no ninety-dayers. The program's all set up in the command computer; all you have to do is run off the orders."

Kelly scratched at his thinning hair. "Well, are we on alert or aren't we? What do I tell—"

"Just do what I told you and do it now! I want the base buttoned up tight before midnight."

With a shrug, Kelly said, "People are going to ask a lot of questions."

"Keep it as quiet as you can. No fuss, no alarms, no scaring the civilians. Just get the right people to the right places. Now!"

Kelly looked distinctly unhappy when Kinsman breezed into his office, more than an hour later.

"What's the word?" Kinsman asked, going straight to his desk.

Kelly had a thick sheaf of plastic reports in his hand. "We're scrambling hell out of everybody's work cycles, but the base is getting buttoned up. Lots of questions being asked, lots of grumbling."

Sitting in the desk chair, Kinsman said, "I told you to do things quietly."

"You can't shove half the military population around quietly!" Kelly snapped.

Kinsman looked up at him. "Okay, Pat. Okay. Sit down." He pointed to the couch. "Give me a rundown."

By the time Kelly was finished, Kinsman was satisfied that everything was going as smoothly as could be expected.

"What about the shuttle?" he asked.

"Left Alpha on schedule."

"The passenger list?"

"In the computer."

Leaning back in his chair, "Okay, good. Put in a call to the shuttle; tell 'em to increase boost and get here on a maximum-energy trajectory. Clear the launch center for them. Talk to your wife while you've got the channel open."

Kelly shook his head, as if to clear it. "Maximum-energy trajectory? Chet, what the hell are you doing?"

Kinsman grinned at him. "Your wife and kids are on board. Aren't you anxious to see them?"

"Yeah, but—"

"How many kids is it?"

"Uh . . . six."

"You don't sound too sure."

It was Kelly's turn to grin. "Well, I haven't seen her for a couple months. She might know something I don't."

"Goddamn sex maniac."

"Me?"

"Get moving. I want to know exactly when that shuttle can touch down. And I'll be inspecting the base at midnight. God help all of you if I'm not satisfied with the security status."

Mumbling incoherently, Kelly got up and left.

Kinsman immediately turned to the computer readout screen and started going through the personnel files of all the military men in Moonbase—especially the ninety-dayers. He knew most of them, had selected them from previous tours of duty. Wonder how many I've rejected over the years? The unthinking martinets. The clumsy ones who would kill themselves up here. The stupid ones who'd kill others with their mistakes. The idiots who couldn't live in close contact with people of other races, other nationalities. The soft ones who'd never have the guts to . . . to . . .

"To commit treason," he said aloud. "Face it. Treason. Like Washington and Jefferson. Like Benedict Arnold. It depends on who wins; that's the difference between treason and patriotism."

Out of the more than one hundred military personnel among the ninety-dayers, Kinsman identified forty that he knew would be reliable. Forty men who would be willing to follow him, who could see a free Selene not as a threat to America, but as the only way out of a negative-sum-game.

The highest-ranking man on the list, next to Pat Kelly, was a captain. "Christopher Perry," Kinsman muttered, looking over the captain's personnel file. The picture on it showed a young, square-faced blond man. Pleasant expression; almost innocent. Kinsman remembered a long conversation with him during his previous tour of duty; how he was fed up with flying helicopters on riot patrol over Greater Washington. "Yeah. He's one of us."

The door buzzer sounded. Looking up from the read-out screen, Kinsman called, "Come in."

The door slid back and Frank Colt stepped into the office.

"I was just thinking about you, Frank."

The black major kept his face expressionless. "What's going on around here?"

"Sit down, buddy. Relax."

Colt ignored the couch and pulled a straightbacked chair from the wall. "Kelly says you've got a mock-alert going. You suddenly getting security conscious?"

"Yep. That's it. I'm security conscious."

Colt didn't look convinced at all. "Why're you keeping the ninety-dayers out of it?"

"Because Murdock wants us to have enough people available to help out with the manned stations," Kinsman answered smoothly. "Can't send the permanent Luniks, can I?"

"You could in a pinch. Only one section of the stations are at Earth gee."

"Yeah, but the ninety-dayers would be better for orbital duty. Not us soft, decrepit medical cases."

Colt frowned.

"What's wrong, Frank? I thought you'd be delighted that I'm taking Murdock's hysterics so seriously."

"How come I wasn't notified? I'm the deputy commander and I—"

"The command program hasn't been updated since you arrived. You found out anyway, didn't you?"

"Because I bumped into Pat Kelly in the fuckin' corridor and he looked scared as shit!"

"So you didn't find out through official channels," Kinsman said. "But you *did* get the word."

"What are you pulling, Chet?"

"When I pull something," Kinsman responded, "you'll be the first to know. I'll even go through official channels."

Colt jumped to his feet. Still unaccustomed to lunar gravity, he knocked the chair over backward. "Goddammit, Chet, you're gonna get your ass killed! I know you're up to something crazy, and I know it's not Murdock's orders. Now, take some advice from a friend, man, and—"

"Frank!" Kinsman cut in. "I don't want advice. I know what I have to do."

"Don't do it, Chet. I'm asking you. Don't do it, whatever it is. You're gonna force me to kill you."

"There won't be any killing, Frank."

"I don't know what the hell's going through your crazy head," Colt's voice was trembling, almost breaking, "but don't put me on the spot. I don't want to have to choose between your life and mine."

"You won't have to choose," Kinsman said calmly. But he could feel the tightness gripping his chest.

"If you try to hand this base over to the Russians—"

"Don't be silly!"

"Or do anything else against the United States . . . Chet, I'll have to stop you! I'll have to!"

"You'll have to try, if and when the time comes."

"Chet! Dammit!"

Rising slowly from his chair, Kinsman said, "Frank, if and when the time comes, we'll all have to do what we think is best. If you've got to kill me . . . Well, everybody dies."

"Jesus H. Christ on the motherfuckin' cross!" Colt threw his hands up and stamped out of the office.

Kinsman stood there for a long time, leaning on the desk, waiting for the tension to ease away from his chest.

Saturday 11 December 1999: 0112 hrs UT

It was evening in Washington, dark and raining.

General Murdock shivered as he humped his over-weight body against the limousine's jumpseat. It wasn't the rain or cold, although God knew they made the bedraggled tinsel and Christmas decoration of the downtown stores look cheap and dreary enough. No one—absolutely no one—was walking on the streets. An Army combat car stood at every street corner, glistening in the wan streetlights and the steady downpour of rain, turrets buttoned up and guns aimed at the sidewalks.

Even General Hofstader looked gloomy. His uniform was crisp, and his ribbons gleamed in the darkness of the limousine. But his face was gray, creased, shrinking into premature old age.

It was the other man's voice that made Murdock shiver. That harsh, labored whisper, like a demon clawing its way up from Hell.

"Enemies within as well as without," he rasped, pointing a heavy hand toward the empty streets. "With the Reds about to attack us, every fool and Commie sympathizer in the land is preparing to stab us in the back."

"I didn't realize . . . " Murdock began, then immediately wished he hadn't. General Hofstader froze him with a glare.

"Didn't realize," the other man said, his rage-filled face getting even redder. "How many Americans do realize the seriousness of the threat? Few. Very few. Precious few."

137

He lapsed into silence for a moment. Neither general dared to speak. The limousine sped through the rain, its turbine whining shrilly. There was no traffic to hinder them. The only other sound was the *thwack, thwack* of the windshield wiper on the back window. The front of the car was acoustically sealed off from the rear.

"We precious few," the man wheezed. It was as close as he ever came to a laugh. "We will live through the holocaust, and then begin the new world—begin afresh, the right way, the way that made this nation great."

General Hofstader cleared his throat. "I should be at Cheyenne Mountain if an attack is imminent . . . "

"It is important to have the General Staff together for this meeting. In person. Top security." He turned his burning eyes on Murdock. "And you. I want to hear the latest intelligence from your mavericks on the Moon."

Murdock swallowed hard. "They seem to be taking the crisis much more seriously now. Apparently they've gone into a maximum-security status . . . "

" 'Apparently'?"

"From . . . from . . . the latest report, this afternoon."

"And the Russians?"

"I don't know." Murdock felt helpless. "I don't have access to that information."

"I suppose you also do not know that the Russians are placing nuclear weapons in orbit."

"Ohmigod."

"Indeed. Now, tell me, what is your personal assessment of the commander of Moonbase?"

Murdock blurted, "Kinsman?"

"If that is his name. I understand he is a dubious factor."

"Well, he's . . . "

"Yes?"

His eyes were boring into Murdock. Hofstader was staring at him, too. Miserably, Murdock answered, "He's been a good administrator, but I'm not certain he's the best man for the job in an emergency situation."

"Then get rid of him."

Murdock turned toward Hofstader.

"Remove him," the four-star general said. "Do you have a reliable second-in-command up there?"

"Oh, yessir. Very reliable."

"Put him in command. Send whatever-his-name-is back down here."

"He can't. Medical disability."

The other man leaned forward to place a heavy hand on Murdock's knee. "Get him out of there. If you have to arrest him or put him in a life-support capsule for the rest of his life—get him out of there!"

"Yessir. Right away," Murdock squeaked.

It was close to 0200 hours when Kinsman finished his inspection rounds of Moonbase.

Everything's buttoned up tight. Shuttle's down and won't move until I say so. He was satisfied that the base was as secure as it could be. Reliable men on duty. No screams for help from Leonov.

Kinsman was pacing down a corridor in the residential section of the base. Most of the people were sleeping, as if this night were the same as any other.

He turned at an intersection and headed for Ellen's quarters. She can't be working all the time, he thought.

He put all doubts behind him and hurried down the corridor, passing from the eerie bluish light of one set of fluorescents into the shadows between lights and then back into light again. It was warm down at this level, but Kinsman still felt a clammy cold sweat that made his coverall stick to his chest and arms and back.

He knocked at Ellen's door. No answer. He knocked again, then put his ear to the thin plastic of the door. A scuffing sound inside. Muttering.

The door opened a crack.

"Oh, hello," Ellen said. Her voice was thick, her hair tousled, eyes puffy.

"Can I come in for a minute?" he asked.

She opened the door wide enough for Kinsman to step through. She was wearing an ankle-length shift. It had been pink once, but it had faded considerably. No frills on it. High Chinese collar.

"Is something wrong?" she muttered. "I stayed at the comm center until one-thirty . . ."

He stood on the grass-covered floor and surveyed the room. The door to the bedroom was closed.

"Something's wrong," he said.

"What?

"You haven't returned my calls. You've been avoiding me."

"Not now, Chet. I can't . . ."

"Now," he said. "I want to know why."

She rubbed at her eyes.

"Why?" Kinsman took her wrist in his hand. "You pump my whole goddamned life story out of me, and then you turn your back on me. Why?"

"Because you scare me," Ellen said.

"Scare you?"

Her voice shaky, eyes avoiding his, she said, "I didn't realize . . . Not that night, not until this crazy red alert came through . . . You mean it! You're really going to try it."

"Of course I am. I told you."

She pulled her hand away from him. "I don't want any part of it. All you're going to accomplish is getting yourself killed. You're committing suicide, Chet, over some woman who died seventeen years ago."

"That's ridiculous."

"It *is* ridiculous. And frightening." Ellen backed a step away from him. "I don't want to be involved in it. You're going to kill yourself."

"No I'm not."

"Yes you are. You're going to keep pushing at it until they kill you. It's all the same thing."

"Everybody dies," he said.

She pushed at her tousled hair. "Sure. Be a hero. Save the world. I can't stop you. I won't even try . . . because you'll pull me under with you if I get any closer to you. I can't take that, Chet! I'm not a hero. I don't want to die. I don't want *you* to die."

"So you're going to run away and hide," he said.

"What else can I do?" She looked desperate.

But he barely heard her answer. "There'll be killing," he was thinking aloud. "Frank Colt won't let me take Moonbase away from America without a fight. Leonov will have to shoot his way to independence. Then we'll have to take the manned satellites—more killing. It's inescapable. We've got to kill to prevent killing. It's a cosmic joke."

"There's nothing funny about it."

"I know."

"I can't go with you on this, Chet. You'll have to do it alone."

"I know." He had known it all along.

Pat Kelly looked scared. There's no other word for it, Kinsman decided. He's scared.

He had spent the morning going over all the contingency plans for repelling attack on Moonbase and keeping the base secure. He and Kelly had checked, via the picture phones, every vital area of the base. They had then called in, one by one, every key person—military and civilian: the communications chief, the head of engineering, the director of the hospital, the Officer of the Day—every man and woman in charge of a department, or an important group of people, or a vital set of equipment.

To each of them, Kinsman had given the same speech. "We are in a maximum-security status. War is imminent. I intend to declare our independence from Earthside and try to prevent the war from starting. We'll act together with the people of Lunagrad. Selene will become an independent nation. Both the United States and Russia will try to stop us, and there might be fighting. We'll try to avoid it, but we've got to be ready to face that possibility."

The night fears were gone from his mind, or at least buried deep enough so that he could ignore them for the present. Kinsman felt strangely calm, at peace with himself for the first time since he had been at the controls of a high-flying jet plane.

The people he spoke to were shocked, surprised. Some smiled with sudden relief. Some were angry and showed it. Of those who agreed with his purpose, Kinsman asked only that they explain the situation to the people under them. To those who became tight-lipped and clenched-fisted, he offered a shuttle flight back to Earth. And called in their second-in-command.

As the long day wore on, the entire absurd idea began to seem almost natural, inevitable. *We're thumbing
our noses at the two most powerful nations in the world.
Why? Oh, because I killed a Russian girl once. And
incidentally it'll save the world. And what's new with
you?* Kinsman began to feel lightheaded.

Ellen was one of the last to come into his office.
"You'll want the comm center shut up tight," she said,
her voice distant, businesslike. "All Earthside messages
routed straight to you?"

"Right," said Kinsman, taking refuge in the details of
work. "And no traffic beamed Earthside without my
specific okay."

"No traffic at all?" Ellen asked. "Won't that make
them suspicious?"

He shrugged. "We can't take a chance on somebody
sneaking a message out."

"I can take care of that," Ellen said.

He stared at her. "You're sure?"

"Yes."

"You want to? Getting that involved . . ."

"We can keep all the routine messages flowing," she
said, ignoring his question. "And all the computer data
exchanges. I can stop the personal messages and make
certain they don't contain anything damaging. I could
even run them through the cryptography computer, just
to be certain no one's sending coded messages."

For a moment, a part of Kinsman's mind wondered if
he could truly trust her. But he said merely, "Okay.
Good."

She got up and left without another word.

It was well into the afternoon by the time Kinsman
asked the worried-faced Pat Kelly, "Who's left?"

Kelly scanned a list on the desktop computer readout
screen. "That's just about everybody." His voice was
shaky.

"What about Ernie Waterman?" Kinsman asked.

Kelly looked up at him. "Ernie's not a department
head."

"I know, but I wanted to get his reaction, too. He's a
key man. Didn't I ask you to call him earlier?"

Kelly started to shake his head.

"And Frank Colt. Where's he? Get the computer to track him down."

"Okay."

Kinsman watched Kelly working the desktop keyboard. The kid's scared to death!

"Pat."

Kelly jerked away from the desk. "Yeah? What?"

"Calm down," Kinsman said softly. "It's going to be all right. There won't be any shooting."

Biting his lip, "Yeah. Maybe."

"I'm going to try to get Leonov on the phone. Meantime, you call Chris Perry in here."

"Perry? What for?"

Kinsman was already leaning over the side of the couch and punching out Leonov's number on the phone. "Chris is going to lead one of our missions to the satellite stations. His group will take Beta. I'm going to Alpha, and we've got to find a reliable guy to . . ."

Kelly's face looked stricken. He went white, his mouth hung open, his hands froze on the desktop.

"Pat! You okay?"

With an effort, Kelly managed to croak out, "I didn't know you were going to attack the stations. You never told me—"

"We're not going to attack them. We're going to take them over. Quick and neat and with no fuss. And Leonov's going to do the same on his side."

"You're going to leave the States defenseless."

"No," Kinsman answered. "We're going to take over all the defenses ourselves. Then we'll make sure that nobody can attack anybody else."

Kelly got up slowly from behind the desk. He was visibly trembling. "Chet, I . . . You've got to let me out of this. I never thought . . ."

"Hold on, Pat. Nobody's going to get hurt."

"You can't . . ." Kelly's eyes were darting, looking for a way out. "You never told me you were going to take over the ABM network. I'm not . . . I won't . . ."

Kinsman stared at him. "Okay, Pat," he said at last. "I don't want you to do anything you don't want to. You or anybody else." But his mind was saying, *He's not on our side!* I was so certain of him. But he can't make the crossover. How many others am I wrong about?

Kelly hurried out of the office. Kinsman watched the door slide shut behind him, then returned to the phone.

The screen stayed blank, and a technician's voice said, "Sir, all communications with Lunagrad have been cut."

"The lines are cut?"

"Nosir. No physical damage. They've just closed down their comm center. No traffic in or out. Our monitors show no Earthside traffic, either."

They're fighting! he realized. It must be a real civil war over there. And there's not a damned thing we can do to help Pete. That's all he'd need—a bunch of armed Americans tramping into Lunagrad.

But he couldn't stay in the office any longer. Kinsman punched out the number for the comm center and told the answering tech, "Page Captain Perry and have him meet me at the access hatch to the main Lunagrad tunnel."

There were a dozen points where Lunagrad and Moonbase touched each other: the main plaza, the hospital, the recreation dome. The main tunnel was the oldest and most strategic point of contact. It was here that the two separate bases had originally been united. And in a show of everlasting friendship, much of the life support plumbing and electrical power cabling had been routed through this tunnel.

He never got there.

As he raced down the corridor that led toward the main tunnel, the P.A. loudspeakers set into the rough stone ceiling suddenly began to blare:

"Chet . . . Chet Kinsman!"

He skidded to a stop under one of the speakers. As he stared at it, set overhead between the fluorescents and some piping, he recognized Frank Colt's voice.

"Chet, listen to me. We've taken the water factory. Ernie Waterman's here, and so is Pat Kelly and a lot of other loyal officers. We're going to shut down the water supply for Moonbase in exactly one hour, unless you surrender yourself to us. If you try to take us here, we'll blow the whole fucking water factory sky-high."

The hour was nearly over.

Kinsman stood at the railing of the balcony that rimmed the communications center. *Everything looks so damned normal!*

Down below, on the main floor of the center, the technicians were bending over their consoles and view screens. All of Moonbase seemed serene and secure. All except the water factory. And there had been no contact with Lunagrad for more than six hours.

Chris Perry came up beside Chet. He was taller and broader than Kinsman, with a wide-boned, open Viking's face; eyes the color of a summer sky. "We've triple-checked every person in the base," he said, in a young tenor voice. "Only thirty-two people are missing, mostly Air Force ninety-dayers. They must be the ones at the water factory."

"Thirty-two?" Kinsman echoed. "So the hard-core dissidents are that few." *More than enough to stop us.*

Ellen was sitting at a desk not far from where he stood. She too had been working steadily. But now she got up and walked slowly toward Kinsman, with a plastic message card in her hand.

"Priority message from General Murdock," she said, looking straight into Kinsman's eyes. "We just finished decoding it. You've been relieved of command. Frank Colt is the new commander of Moonbase. You're ordered to report to Washington immediately."

Kinsman reached out and took the plastic card from her fingers. It had been reused so many times that the electrostatically formed letters looked blurred and smudged. *Or is my eyesight going bad on me?* The back of Kinsman's neck felt knotted; his chest ached sullenly.

Turning to Perry, he said, "The Great White Father has relieved me of command. What do you think the Indians will say?"

The young captain shrugged his husky shoulders. "We're not taking orders from Washington any more. We take our orders from you."

Kinsman stared at the blond youth. "You're sure that you realize what you're saying? You can avoid a lot of grief. If we fail—"

"We won't fail," Perry said, with a quick smile.

We'd better not! "Okay, Chris . . . here's what I want you to do . . ."

It was five minutes before Colt's deadline when Kinsman arrived at the water factory entrance.

He stepped off the power ladder and saw that the entrance—an open space that had once been a natural cave—was now guarded by two unarmed men. Guns were carefully locked away in Selene. Only a few were available at any time, and Kinsman had control of almost all of them.

He recognized one of the men: a middle-aged accountant who worked in the procurement group. He was an asthmatic, and this excitement wasn't helping his heaving chest. The other man was younger, a newcomer, probably one of the ninety-day shavetails. Kinsman knew he had seen him before, but he couldn't place him. He wore ordinary gray fatigues, without insignia or color code.

Wordlessly they walked him through the rough-hewn chamber. The overhead fluorescents glared, the rock floor felt cold to Kinsman's slippered feet. Forcing himself to smile, Kinsman murmured to them, "Relax. Nobody's going to get hurt."

They didn't answer. At the end of the chamber, the redhead from Jill's party was standing tensely in front of the doors that opened onto the factory's office area. She looked angry.

"I didn't expect to see you here," Kinsman said.

She wasn't wearing a party dress now; just a pair of green fatigues that marked her as a member of the life-support group.

"Follow me," she said.

She pushed the door open and led him down the curving corridor, silently. Kinsman couldn't help noticing the way her butt moved inside the fatigues. They passed the computer area, and he stared hard through the long window as they walked by. The computer's lights were flashing as usual, even though no one was sitting at any of the desk stations. *They haven't shut anything down. Yet.*

"I never did get your name straight at the party," he said to the redhead.

"Doesn't matter."

He pulled up alongside her. "Come on, now. Politics is one thing, but you don't have to be inhuman about it."

In coldly clipped tones she said, "What happened at the party was strictly business."

"Business?" Even as he said it, Kinsman realized, Kee-rist! Internal Security Agency!

Soon they were out of the corridor and into the factory area itself. They led him through a maze of piping, up onto catwalks that threaded through the electric arcs and the main pumps. He could feel the machinery throbbing, making the metal catwalk vibrate. Off in the distance, the muted thunder of the rock crushers went on without slack.

Pat Kelly was standing on a platform on the next level above the catwalk. Under the harsh lights, Kinsman could see that Kelly was fidgeting nervously, his rabbit's face a picture of worry. And he wore a gun in a holster buckled to his hip.

The redhead stopped at the base of the ladder that led up to the platform. "Major Kelly will take over," she said.

"Tell me one thing," Kinsman said.

She looked wary. "What?"

"Still think I'm cute?"

She flushed angrily, and she spun away so fast that her shoulder-length hair swung over her face momentarily. Kinsman watched her stamp back down the cat-walk for a few seconds, then reluctantly turned to the ladder and started climbing.

Kelly was genuinely frightened. He wouldn't look straight at Kinsman.

"Come on," he said, gesturing down another spidery catwalk. "We don't have much time."

"I didn't expect you to be in with them," Kinsman said, falling in step behind the younger officer. The cat-walk was too narrow to walk side by side.

"I didn't expect you to be handing Moonbase over to the Russians," Kelly answered, keeping his eyes straight ahead. "Or to hand them our satellites."

"You're wrong about that, Pat. We're creating a new nation here."

Kelly shook his head.

"You know, if you blow up the water factory, you'll be killing everyone up here."

"They can send us water from Earthside."

"How soon? Two, three days? A week? A month? And how much? Enough for a thousand people, every day? Don't be stupid. And don't think they'll do *any-thing*—especially if the shooting starts down there."

Kelly didn't reply.

"It's your wife and kids, Pat. You'll be killing them, too."

"You're the guy who made me bring them here! Was that your idea—hold them as hostages?"

"I'm trying to save their lives."

For the first time, Kelly turned to face Kinsman. "By handing them over to the Russians? So *they* can shoot them?"

Kelly banged a fist on the catwalk railing, making it reverberate hollowly. "If we go to war we're all as good as dead anyway. I'm not going to let you help the Rus-sians beat America."

"Then why don't you help me to prevent the war from happening?" Kinsman's voice rose enough to echo off the huge metal machinery all around them.

"You can't take the easy way out of this," Kelly said, starting to walk along the catwalk again. "You can't avoid the war by giving the enemy everything he wants."

"Leonov and his people aren't the enemy."

"They're Russians! That's the enemy! I took an oath to preserve and defend the United States of America!" Kelly shouted, his voice cracking. "So did you. It might not have meant anything to you, but it's the most important thing in my life."

"It won't work, Pat."

"I know what my duty is!"

"And your family?"

"I know what my duty is!" Kelly was nearly screaming.

Very quietly, ignoring the growing tension in his chest, Kinsman said, "Joseph Goebbels."

Kelly blinked at him. "Who?"

"Goebbels. Propaganda minister for the Nazis, under Hitler. During the last days of World War II, when the Russians were pounding Berlin to rubble, he gave cyanide to his wife and kids. Six or seven of them, I think. Then he took some himself."

With a disgusted snort, Kelly kept striding along the catwalk. Almost running.

"I could never understand how a man could do that," Kinsman kept on. "Not since I first read about it, in high school. Now I know."

He couldn't see Kelly's face. But the red flush on his neck told him enough.

"Hold it right there!"

It was Frank Colt's voice, coming from somewhere below them. Kinsman peered over the catwalk railing, and there he was, down on the floor, three levels below. The black major was wearing his regulation fatigues, Air Force blue, with gold oak leaves pinned to his collar and a huge automatic strapped around his middle. "Search him," Colt ordered.

Kinsman took a palm-sized transistor radio from one coverall pocket. "This is all I'm carrying." *Plus the homing beacon inside my left slipper.*

Kelly searched him anyway and missed the flea-sized signaling device as he patted Kinsman's arms, torso and legs.

They clambered down a long ladder to Colt. Kinsman went slowly; he found that he was panting, short-breathed. Kelly followed him down.

Kinsman stepped out on the stone floor and said to Colt, "Congratulations, Frank. Murdock's made you commander of Moonbase."

Colt's eyebrows shot up. "Yeah? That's good. Makes everything legal and official."

"Except for the fact that there's no longer a Moonbase. This is the nation of Selene. Washington's orders don't affect us any more. Nor do Moscow's." *I hope!*

Colt glanced at his wrist watch. "In another minute and a half there won't be any water factory, buddy. Unless you call this shit off."

"Frank, we've been friends for a long time."

"This isn't friendship any more, Chet. It's treason."

Looking around the hulking metal shapes that surrounded them, Kinsman asked, "Where's Waterman?"

"Busy." Colt gestured vaguely down toward the main level of the factory.

"Planting explosives."

"Right."

"Frank, if you do this you're not only going to kill everyone in Selene. You'll be killing everyone on Earth, too."

"Stuff it. Nobody's gonna die if you tell your people to forget this independence shit. I'll even see to it that the whole thing's hushed up. Nobody arrested, no hassles. You can go back Earthside—"

"And get bombed."

Colt's jaw muscles clenched. He looked at his wrist again. "The explosives are set to go off in less than a minute. You'd better make your move."

Despite the roaring in his ears, despite the pain flaring in his chest, Kinsman forced himself to say calmly, "When your explosives go off you're going to be killing the whole human race."

"You goddamned fool!" Colt's voice was molten steel. "Leonov's pigeon. They've set you up, man! Can't you *see* that? They've set you up! Peace and love and friendship—and you turn the whole ABM system over to them. Fuck that!"

"You're wrong, Frank. We can trust Leonov. He's with us."

Turning to Kelly, Colt snapped, "Gimme that radio he brought." He took it and thrust the palm-sized plastic box at Kinsman. "Call it off, Chet. Tell 'em to stop. You've got fifteen seconds to go."

Kinsman stood unmoving, hands by his sides.

"For Christ's sake!" Kelly screamed. "Do it! Don't make us—"

The lights went off. The rumble of machinery died. Before anyone could say anything, the tiny emergency lamps came up, scattering pools of grayish light sparsely amid the dark, looming machinery.

Kinsman spoke first. *Calmly. Keep it cool.* "Your explosives are electrically fused?"

"Sonofabitch!" Even in the dim lighting, Kinsman could see Colt's hand rubbing the holster at his hip.

"There'll be troops coming through here soon," Kinsman told them. "They'll have sniperscopes and gas grenades. Remember, Frank? The stuff you insisted we stock, two years ago, so we could fight the Russians without shooting up any valuable equipment?"

"You haven't won, Chet." Colt pulled the gun from its holster. "Not yet!"

He gestured with the gun, ordering Kinsman and Kelly down the walkway that led between big steel domes of machinery. It was tricky going in the semi-darkness, but within a few minutes they met Ernie Waterman.

"They shut off the fucking power," Waterman cried. "How the hell am I supposed to . . ." Then he recognized Kinsman and shut up.

Colt waved the gun. "Jury-rig something! You can use batteries, can't you?"

"Yeah, yeah. That's what I was on my way for—batteries."

"Well, get 'em!" Colt's voice was urgent.

Kinsman asked, "Ernie, you could actually blow this up, after you worked so hard to build it?"

A dull, muffled boom made the floor shake. "There's your answer," the engineer replied. "One of the other teams has found some batteries. It's only machinery,

Colonel. It can be rebuilt. Machines do what they're designed to do. Not like people. People can turn on you."

"And people can behave like machines," Kinsman snapped back, "following programming that's obsolete."

"Patriotism isn't obsolete."

"It is when it leads to the destruction of the nation you're being loyal to."

"Cut the crap," Colt said. "Go find some goddamn batteries."

Waterman hurried off down the walkway, his braces clicking on the metal flooring. Kinsman wondered, *What did they blow? How much damage did they do?* He felt as if part of his chest were being rubbed raw, from the inside.

Another explosion. Closer. They all winced. Kelly put his hands to his ears.

"They're all finding batteries." Colt smiled grimly.

They walked to a row of electric arcs, a line of stainless steel jackets that looked like bullets, except that they were as big as a man, standing on insulated supports. Conveyor belts carried pulverized rock slurry into one end of each jacket; a maze of piping at the base carried away water and minerals. Standing there neatly lined up, the arcs reminded Kinsman of missiles, waiting for the final push of the red button.

The conveyor belts were still now; the arcs silent and powerless. Somewhere in the darkness Kinsman could hear the drip, drip of slurry leaking through a seam in the belting. Then his eyes caught an ugly cluster of red packages wedged under one of the arcs—plastic explosive, electrical detonator, coils of wire.

Colt holstered his gun and leaned against one of the stainless steel jackets. Kinsman stood before him.

"You're killing everybody here," he said simply.

"No," Colt replied instantly. "*You* are."

"And everybody on Earth." *Where's Perry and the cavalry?*

Wearily, Colt said, "Chet, you can afford to be a high-flier. You take your own chances, it's only your own white ass if you get caught. But what happens to every black man Earthside if I turn traitor? What'll their lives be worth if Washington thinks I'm helping you?"

What's he trying to tell me? "What are their lives worth now?" Kinsman asked slowly. "What happens to them when the missiles reenter? They're living mostly in the cities, right? Not out in the countryside where they've built shelters and food stockpiles."

"But *you're* the one who's gonna let the Reds launch their missiles!"

"No, Frank—"

"Yes! Dammit, man, open your eyes! If you let the Russians grab the ABM satellites, they can bomb us to hell and stop any counterattack we launch."

"Nobody's going to use those ABM satellites except us," Kinsman said, his voice rising. "The people of Selene. And we'll use them against any and all missiles—Russian or American. Or Chinese or French or Afghan!"

"Bullshit!" Colt yelled. "You've been conned, man! Once the Russians get their hands on our satellites, you know they ain't gonna cooperate with you. They've been sweet-talking you, and you fell for it."

"We can trust Leonov."

"Like hell! Can't trust Reds. Not any of 'em."

Kinsman felt as if he'd run a thousand meters—no, a thousand kilometers. "Frank, you're scared of trusting anyone. You're scared of taking the risk. And I'm telling you that unless we trust Leonov and his people—unless we all start trusting one another—the world's going to go up in flames."

Colt merely shook his head.

"You're chicken, Frank. Scared of trying something new. So you fall back on the regulations. When in doubt, follow the rules. Right?"

"Right!"

"Play it Murdock's way. Obey all orders blindly. Do what they tell you. Tote that barge, lift dat bale—"

Colt punched him. A short, savage right that came up from the hip and clipped Kinsman squarely along his jaw. Kinsman actually felt himself lifting off his feet, flailing ridiculously in the low lunar gravity, and collapsing in a heap—ass, spine, shoulder, legs, head—on the stone flooring.

For a moment he lay there, tasting blood in his mouth. "That's the way, Frank. Kill and be killed."

A tangled skein of expressions worked across Colt's face. He said nothing.

"Frank," Kinsman said, still on his back, propping himself up on one elbow, "the black people of America, of Africa, of *everywhere,* are going to die. Before the month is out. Is that what you want?"

"And you're gonna save 'em by turning 'em over to the Reds?"

"I'm going to save them by making them free."

"Ahhh . . . " Colt's face went sour. "You sound like a fucking dumb revolutionary. I've been that route. It sucks."

"Why isn't Ernie back?" Kelly wondered out loud. He peered nervously down the walkway.

Maybe Perry's men found him, Kinsman thought. Another explosion boomed faintly. Far off. Maybe a grenade? More likely another chunk of the factory being destroyed.

Kinsman got slowly to his feet. "Frank, Pat, have either of you thought about what it is that you're defending? The United States of America. Is it really the nation you want? Does it work the way you want it to?"

"Don't start that," Kelly muttered.

"Think about it," Kinsman said. "Look at what's happening down there. Fuel shortages. Food shortages. Riots. More people in jail than there are on the streets. Army patrols in every city. Curfews. Surveillance. What the hell kind of nation is that?"

"So you want to let them blow it up?"

"No! I want it changed. But they're not heading toward change. They're heading toward war."

"The United States will never start a war," Kelly said.

"What difference does it make who starts it?" Kinsman snapped. "Who's going to *prevent* it? We're the only ones who can."

"The United States—"

"Pat, stop spouting schoolbook lessons! There are

people down there who *want* the war! They think they'll live through it okay, while the rabble get fried."

"That's Communist propaganda!"

Kinsman shook his head. "The two of you—open your eyes. That wonderful land of the free and home of the brave—it's gone." With a chill in his heart, Kinsman realized it was something that he had known all along, but ignored, buried, hid away from his conscious mind. "That beautiful nation died in 1963, while we were still kids. Maybe someday it'll be free and beautiful again, but not the way it's going now. Not if it's subjected to nuclear attack."

For a long moment the three men stood facing one another, an unresolved triangle of silence.

Suddenly a rumbling noise startled them. Turning, they saw Waterman edging along the walkway, painfully towing a handcart laden with bulky, heavy-looking shapes. He was moving very slowly.

Where is Perry? Kinsman screamed to himself.

"Go help him, for Chrissakes!" Colt snapped at Kelly.

"Got batteries, connectors, firing actuators—everything we need," Waterman said tiredly. "Had to come the long way around, though. Soldier-boys all over the place, swarming on the catwalks, everywhere. They're ripping out the explosives wherever they find them."

It's only a matter of time, Kinsman told himself. Maybe the factory isn't too badly damaged. Maybe we can still make it happen.

Wordlessly, he watched Waterman and Colt work at fever pitch to connect the batteries to the explosives. But if they blow the arcs here, we're finished, Kinsman thought. We'll never be able to replace them without Earthside help.

"A matter of time," he said aloud.

Waterman looked up from his work.

"C'mon," Colt urged the engineer. "We gotta get it off before the troops show up." He looked over toward Pat Kelly. "Go down the walkway as far as the end of this row of arcs. Let me know when they're in sight."

As Kelly started down the dimly lit walkway, Kinsman took two quick steps, brushed past the kneeling Colt and grabbed Waterman by the back of his collar. He yanked the engineer away from the explosives and sent him staggering backward.

Colt sprang to his feet and pulled the pistol from its holster as Waterman landed on the seat of his pants with a loud *thwack*.

For an instant no one moved. Kelly stood frozen a few paces up the walkway. Waterman sat unhappily on the floor. Colt pointed his gun at hip level toward Kinsman.

"You're not going to do it," Kinsman said. "Even if I'm dead wrong, this is the only chance we have to get out without a war."

Colt's voice was gunmetal cold. "You're not just gonna be dead wrong, Chet. You're gonna be dead."

"Goddammit to hell," Waterman moaned. "You bent my fucking brace. Hey, leave those wires alone! If you touch the red one to the battery terminal—"

Kinsman stooped down and grabbed a fistful of wires.

"Chet!" Colt raised the gun, arm fully extended. The muzzle was ten centimeters from Kinsman's face, a yawning black tunnel to eternity.

"It's the only way you'll stop me, Frank." Kinsman heard his own voice as if it were coming from a long distance off: strangely flat and calm, as if he were reading lines that had been rehearsed eons ago.

"Chet, I'll kill you!"

"Then do it. If you have your way, everybody's going to die anyway."

Kelly found his voice. "Shoot him! What are you waiting for?"

"Chet," Colt said again, "take your hands off the wires and step away. If you don't, I'll have to shoot."

"No way, Frank."

Colt pulled the gun back slowly, and with his left hand slid the action back, cocking it with a loud metallic *clack, clack*.

"I mean it, Chet."

"I know. It all boils down to the two of us, doesn't it? You and me, Frank. Life or death."

"If you're wrong," Colt said, his face suddenly shining with sweat, "if you're wrong . . . "

"Leonov is with us. He's doing the same thing in Lunagrad that we're doing here."

"That's what he's told you."

"That's the truth."

"No . . . "

"Yes! The only way to prevent the end of the world is by trusting him. And if you can't trust him, Frank, then trust *me*. This is the only way, Frank. *The only way*."

The gun wavered just the slightest fraction of a centimeter.

"Don't listen to him!" Kelly screamed. "Shoot him! Shoot!"

Colt let his arm drop. He turned to Kelly. "You shoot him, hero. You get the job done."

Kelly blinked a half-dozen times in a second. "Me?"

"Chickenshit," Colt said. "It's all right for the black boy to do your dirty work, but you haven't got the guts to do it yourself."

Waterman, still sprawled on the floor, said, "You've gone crazy. All three of you—you're nuts!"

"Nobody's going to shoot anyone," Kinsman said. He yanked at the wires and pulled them away from the explosives. Then he stood up, as Colt holstered his gun.

In the distance, Kinsman could hear the clatter of men running. Faint voices. Lights flashing around the silent machinery, casting eerie flickering shadows along its bulk.

Waterman broke into sobs. "You're gonna let them destroy the United States. You're gonna let them kill my girls, you stupid sonofabitch—"

"No," Kinsman said firmly. "We're going to stop them from destroying themselves." *If there's enough of this factory left to keep us alive.*

"You hope," Colt said.

"It's the only hope we have," Kinsman answered.

"You'd better be right," Waterman said, his voice trembling. "You'd just better be right. If they kill my girls, I'll kill you. I swear it on my wife's grave. With my bare hands, I'll kill you, Kinsman."

His office was jammed with people.

It surprised Kinsman. He felt bone-weary, soaked with fear, sweat and exhaustion, as he trudged the final length of corridor to his office door. He was totally alone, wrapped in apprehension. *What's happening at Lunagrad? Why hasn't Pete called?*

Then he slid the office door open and saw more than a dozen people packed into the room. All the view screens were blaring. Ellen sat at Kinsman's desk, the phone's auxiliary headset clamped to her ear so she could hear over the clatter of the crowd. Nearly every light on the phone keyboard was lit. Hugh Harriman was working the other phone, at the sofa, yelling and waving his arms.

He went straight to the desk. Ellen looked up at him. Simultaneously they asked, "Are you all right? How bad's the damage to the factory?"

Ellen brushed a hand across her forehead. "You don't look so good."

"I could use a drink . . . What's the word on the damage? I didn't stay to see it all."

"Hugh's getting reports from the maintenance teams."

Chris Perry was suddenly standing beside him. "We've done it, sir! Everything's secure. The whole base is ours. The only real resistance was at the water factory, and they're all rounded up."

"Fine. What are the damage reports?"

People gathered around Kinsman, grinning, flushed with victory. But Harriman was still gabbling a steady stream of rapid-fire talk into the phone screen at the end of the sofa.

Kinsman pushed his way toward him. "Hugh, how bad is it?"

Harriman flailed a pudgy hand at him. "I'm trying to find out, dammit! Give me a minute or two!"

Perry asked, "What about the, uh, prisoners from the water factory?"

"Return them to their quarters. Put an armed guard at the end of each corridor. Just see that they don't get into more mischief." Kinsman's head was buzzing. "Any word from Leonov?"

Ellen answered, "We received a call from Lunagrad

about an hour ago. Not from Colonel Leonov, but from one of the scientists there. It was a personal call for Dr. Landau."

Landau? "No other communications from them?"

"No."

Puzzled, Kinsman made his way to the desk. On the wall view screen, he could see that all the sections of Selene currently being shown looked completely normal, except that the main plaza was crowded with people in a holiday mood. They were milling about, looking happy, excited. One screen showed a section of the water factory: an explosion had ripped open a half-dozen pipes, and precious, sacred water was gushing out, flooding the area knee-deep, while a team of repair techs sloshed around trying to stem the flow. It felt to Kinsman as if one of his own arteries had burst: that was life's blood being wasted.

He plopped down in a chair next to the desk and found an open phone line. Punching the button, he looked up and saw that Ellen was handing him a headset.

"Lunagrad," he said to the computer. "Colonel Leonov."

But a communications tech appeared on the screen, shaking her head. "Sorry, sir, but links with Lunagrad have been very spotty. We're getting no response at present."

Jesus Christ! "Use the surface laser comm system. Swing it from the lock on the space stations to a lock on Lunagrad's receiving mirror."

"Sir, I'll need authorization and—"

"This is Kinsman. I'm going to put Captain Perry on the phone, and by the time he gets here that laser had better be pointing at the Lunagrad receiver. I want a link and I want it *now!*"

"Yessir." The girl was wide-eyed.

Kinsman waved Perry back to the desk and explained what he wanted done. He went back to the sofa, where Harriman was still in agitated, animated conversation.

What are all these people doing here? he asked himself. Scanning the room he saw the chief of the engineering section, two of the top scientists, a couple of young Air Force noncoms who worked at the catapult facility, several others from various administrative sections, a few he couldn't place. And Ellen. She got up from the desk and came to him.

"How is it going?"

He shook his head. "Don't know yet. No word from Leonov."

"Are you all right?"

"Yeah. Fine. How about you?"

"I want to help. What can I do?"

Shrugging, "Sit and sweat it out with the rest of us." And then he understood why the others were here, why the people were gathering in the main plaza. Waiting. Waiting to see if it was going to work. Waiting to learn if they would live or die. *On my responsibility.*

Harriman snorted and slapped his hands on his thighs. "All right, all right, print out the details," he yelled into the phone screen, "and get a hard copy up here for these madmen to see!"

Kinsman was standing in front of him. "Well?"

Harriman rolled his eyes and made a fluttering motion with one hand. "Not too good, not too bad. I got all the damage-control teams to report directly into the computer, and then let the stupid machine mull it over for a few minutes."

"And?"

"Preliminary analysis: water production down about forty percent. Minerals and ores down a little less, maybe twenty-five, thirty percent. They blew a lot of plumbing, but the big hardware—the rock crushers—they just didn't have enough explosives to really damage those monsters."

"Forty percent."

"For how long?"

"Yeah, what's the computer estimate for repair time?"

Harriman said, "Two weeks. But that's too damned preliminary to count. Say a month, at least."

Kinsman did a quick mental calculation. "We can live with that. Water'll be scarce for a month or so."

Harriman lurched to his feet. "So we'll drink our booze straight, eh?"

And suddenly they were all laughing, almost cheering, with relief.

Perry's strong tenor voice cut through the noise. "I've got Lunagrad! They're bringing Leonov to the phone!"

The office went absolutely silent. *It all hangs on Pete.*

Kinsman went to the desk. Perry got up from the chair and Kinsman took it, feeling somehow weak and dwarfed beside the younger man.

The phone screen was a blur of rainbow static. Then it abruptly cleared and Piotr Leonov's face took form. He looked serious, his iron-gray hair disheveled. "My apologies, old friend."

Kinsman's heart stopped beating.

"I should have thought of the laser link earlier. The hardliners tried to seize the main communications and power centers."

"Tried to?" Kinsman felt some of the blood moving in him again.

"Yes. There was some shooting. I'm afraid we had to kill a few of them. But it's over now. We are in control."

A collective gasp of relief from everyone in the office.

"Fine, Pete, fine," Kinsman said soberly. "We've got this end of Selene under control, too."

For the first time, Leonov smiled. "Congratulations, then. We must toast to the birth of Selene, the newest nation of humankind!"

"Not yet," Kinsman said. "Not until we take command of the space stations. Without them, what we've done is meaningless."

Leonov nodded vigorously. "I already have a set of shuttles being boarded by reliable men. And the stations themselves are manned by a great variety of peoples—Ukrainians, Uzbeks, even a few Poles and Czechs."

"Really?" Kinsman could feel the tension among the people around him fading. "How'd that happen?"

His smile broadening, Leonov answered, "A few years ago I served a tour of duty as personnel director for orbital operations. I managed to place the emphasis on training, education, technical skill—rather than Party affiliation and zeal. Enthusiasm and Leninist ideals—although basically correct, you understand!—are no substitute for a knowledge of orbital mechanics, when you are in a space station."

"Agreed." And Kinsman felt himself relaxing a little.

"One thing." Leonov's face grew serious again. "Those two girls I brought to your birthday party. They *were* security agents! One of them shot me."

"Holy hell. Where? Is it serious?"

The Russian scowled. "In the back . . . lower back. I think she was aiming at humiliating me. At any rate, the doctors tell me I will live and enjoy life—but I won't be sitting comfortably for a while."

They all roared. But even while Kinsman was laughing, his mind was warning him, *The space stations. We've got to grab them quickly. Or fail.*

Tuesday 14 December 1999: 1200 hrs UT

Lieutenant Colonel Stahl stood before the main screens of Space Station Alpha's cramped communications center. "Holiday traffic's starting to build up, I see."

Major Cahill smiled weakly at his boss's joke.

The comm center was a shoebox of metal and plastic, with six monitor desks nested so tightly that if one of the technicians tried to stretch an arm it would knock the headset off the person next to her. When any of them spoke to the spacecraft that were approaching or leaving the station, it was in a low, urgent whisper, in the economical jargon of the Earthside ground controller.

Major Cahill sat at a compact desk of his own, built

into the metal bulkhead off to one side of the compartment. The entire forward bulkhead was a checkerboard of radar and video screens, a giant insect's eye showing all the traffic around Station Alpha.

Stahl always felt claustrophobic in here; his armpits went clammy on him. The room was too small, too densely packed with humming electrical gear and muttering human beings. It always smelled sweaty, tense. He pointed to one of the screens that showed a nearly empty field of view. Only one speck was discernible from the background of stars.

"Is that the shuttle from Moonbase?"

Cahill nodded and touched a stud on his desktop. Alphanumerical symbols sprouted on the screen alongside the lunar shuttle, telling its position, estimated time of arrival, cargo and crew.

Major Cahill was lanky and lantern-jawed. During his tour of duty aboard Alpha he had allowed a sandy mustache to grow; it was now thick enough to curl at the ends. He intended to shave it off before returning home for the holidays. His job included keeping track of all the unmanned ABM satellites orbiting far below, close to Earth, that were in Alpha's hemisphere-wide field of view. Plus all the manned craft approaching or leaving the station.

Lieutenant Colonel Stahl—chunky, solid, squared-off face seamed by age and weather, and sporting a nose broken in a long-forgotten Academy football game—was commander of the station.

"We've got another bird approaching," Cahill told his commander, pointing to a different view screen. "The troopship from Kennedy. Its ETA is going to conflict with the lunar shuttle."

"The troopship has priority," Stahl said crisply.

Cahill agreed with a nod. "We haven't had a supply shipment from Moonbase for two days. Their catapult's on the fritz."

"I know that."

"Yes, well, if you'll take a look at that cargo the shuttle's carrying . . ."

Stahl tried to make sense of the coded symbols.

"The 'LXY FDSTF' means 'luxury foodstuffs,'

Harry. Chickens, fresh vegetables, maybe even some fruit. It might be a good idea to get them packed away safely *before* those green troopers come stomping aboard."

Stahl pursed his lips. "Hmm. Green troopers, you say."

"None of 'em been on orbital duty before. There's going to be a lot of upchucking, a lot of wasted food. And if they see the good stuff being offloaded, they're not going to be satisfied with the usual synthetics."

"Who's in command of the detachment?"

"Some captain straight from Murdock's staff. He'll have a pipeline right back to the boss."

Stahl tugged at an earlobe, then grinned. "All right. Vector the troopship into a parking orbit while we off-load the goodies and pack them safely away. Then we can let Murdock's snoops come aboard."

Cahill grinned broadly. "Right you are, Harry."

Strapped into the contour seat, Kinsman felt the slight bump when the shuttle hard-docked with Alpha's landing collar. He forced himself to stay relaxed, stay in the seat, as tinier bumps and vibrations told him that the station crewmen were attaching the access tunnel to the shuttle's main hatch.

Kinsman was in the front seat of the shuttle's main passenger section. The spacecraft carried no cargo, despite the information radioed ahead to Alpha. There were twenty-six men aboard, the maximum the shuttle could carry. The cargo hold was empty. The men were armed.

It had been a strange thirty-six hours in free-fall. Kinsman had always loved the feeling of weightlessness, the sense of freedom that it brought. But this time he felt confined, pinned down, trapped. He kept in constant contact with Selene, by tight laser-beam link, impossible for anyone from the space stations or Earthside to intercept.

Everything was under control. Apparently. Earthside suspected nothing. Apparently.

You could be stepping into the midst of a reception committee, he thought. They might have seen through

your story about the catapult being inoperative. Even if
they hadn't, he had only twenty-six men to seize control
of Space Station Alpha, which had several hundred people aboard it. But only a handful of troops. No more
than forty. If we can surprise them, move fast
enough . . .

And is everything really under control at Selene?
Kinsman wondered about his decision to trust Frank
Colt. And Ellen.

It had happened on Sunday, after a night of cautious
celebration during which the Americans and Russians
had mingled freely—all except the dead and the prisoners. That morning, as Kinsman went over the lists of
available personnel and tried to puzzle out in his mind
how many men he'd need to seize the space stations *and*
maintain a strong hand in Selene, he realized that there
weren't enough men to go around. He called Colt and
Ellen and Hugh Harriman to his office.

Harriman looked tired but happy. He had spent the
hours of drinking and quiet celebration the previous
night telling everyone that at last he could become the
citizen of a nation once more.

Ellen was calm and cool. Too cool, Kinsman thought.
As if she had to maintain a certain distance from him.
Projection, he thought. You're assuming that she feels
about you the same way you feel about her.

Colt looked wary and . . . something else. Kinsman
couldn't put his finger on it. Uncertain. Undecided.

They sat. Colt on a slingchair, looking as relaxed as a
stalking cat can look. Harriman slouched on the couch,
muttering about homebrew vodka and pain thresholds.
Ellen sat beside him, quietly.

Kinsman was behind his desk. El Presidente, he said
to himself. The revolutionary who now has to worry
about revolutionaries. "How's everything in the comm
center?" he asked Ellen.

"Fine," she replied. "No hint of suspicion from
Earthside. All traffic perfectly normal."

Kinsman licked his lips. "Good. Now, the next step is
to take the space stations. If Ellen's right, they don't
have an inkling of what happened here yesterday."

"Yet," Colt murmured.

"And they won't," Kinsman countered, "as long as we've got a loyal crew at the comm center." He looked at Ellen as he said it. She gazed back at him. "With the exception of keeping the comm center and launch facilities guarded," he went on, "there's no reason why everything can't go on completely normally here in Selene."

"The barriers between here and Lunagrad are down," Harriman said.

"They were only paper barriers. We're all part of the same nation, the same people. We have been, for years. They'll be no walls between us."

Colt said nothing.

"I'm going to need every military man available to take the space stations, plus a few to keep the comm center and launch facilities secure. The catapult is shut down."

"And the Russians?" asked Colt.

"Leonov is going through the same exercise. He's already got his shuttles heading for their stations. No other flights in or out of Lunagrad."

Harriman said, "It'll only be a matter of time before they realize that nothing's leaving *either* Moonbase or Lunagrad. They'll get suspicious then."

"That's why we've got to move fast." Kinsman got up and stepped around the desk. "Hugh, I was thinking of asking you to act as chief honcho around here while I'm gone—"

"Lord no!"

Kinsman raised a hand to calm him. "I know, I know. You're not the right man for the job. Philosophers aren't leaders of men."

"Shit! You've got the nicest way of de-balling people."

Turning to Colt, "But military officers are, by training and attitude, leaders of men."

The black man looked startled. "What're you saying?"

"I'm asking, Frank, asking if I can trust you to run our half of Selene until I get back from the space stations."

Colt laughed bitterly. "You're crazy, man."

"I need you, Frank. I need the job done, and done well. You can do it."

"I'm not on your side! Haven't you caught up with that fact yet?"

Kinsman sat on the edge of the desk. "Frank, you could have stopped me right there in the water factory. But I asked you to trust me and you did. I think you can see that Leonov's keeping his word . . ."

"They can still pull the rug out from under you any time, buddy. Any time at all."

"Maybe. Maybe Leonov's bluffing, although I don't think he'd get himself shot in the ass just to—"

"Shot where?"

Harriman bubbled, "You should've seen him last night! Had his ass in a goddam sling! For real!"

Colt shook his head, bewildered.

"Frank," Kinsman was serious, "I'm asking you now if you will run Selene for a few days—our half of it, at least. Get the repairs started on the water factory. Make sure everything runs smoothly. What you'll be doing will have nothing to do with which side you're on. You'll be taking care of several hundred men, women and children; making sure that this place runs smoothly. Whether I win or lose is something else entirely."

Colt started shaking his head.

"All I ask is that you promise not to try to contact the space stations, or Earthside. Just take care of the job that needs doing here. Can I trust you?"

"Let Pat Kelly do it," Colt said.

Kinsman could feel his jaw muscles clench. "I can't trust Pat. Besides, he's in no emotional condition to do anything. If we get through this alive and the war's stopped, we'll ship him and his family home."

Colt repeated, "I'm not on your side."

"I don't care which side you're on," Kinsman said. "Can you run our half of Selene for a few days—as a temporary neutral?"

"That'd be *helping* you, man!"

"I'll do it," Ellen said.

Kinsman blinked at her. Harriman muttered something undecipherable.

Ellen actually smiled at them. "Don't look so

shocked. I can be a leader of men, as you so beautifully put it, Chet. I'll run the base for a few days."

It took several seconds for Kinsman to say, "You'd want to . . . to help?"

With a nod, she answered, "Someone's got to. And I really am on your side—whether I like it or not. I can run the base as well as anyone."

Kinsman said, "I never thought . . ."

But Ellen had already turned toward Colt. "I'd expect you not to try making trouble while Chet's back is turned."

Kinsman returned his attention to the black major. "How about it, Frank? Will you promise not to try to grab the comm center or the launch pad?"

Colt frowned and blinked and struggled visibly with himself. Finally, "Aw, shit. Okay, I won't make any waves. But I want to be on the first damned shuttle that goes back Earthside! I want no part of your crazy revolution."

Harriman looked dubious, but for once he said nothing. Kinsman felt uneasy, and must have looked it.

"What's the matter, Chet?" Ellen asked. "Afraid to let a woman run the show? Even for only a few days?"

He shrugged and grinned and surrendered gracefully. After all, he told himself, what choice do I have?

A green light was flashing, breaking Kinsman's troubled reverie.

"Okay for egress," the shuttle pilot's voice came over the intercom.

Kinsman unstrapped his safety harness and got out of the contoured seat—floated up, weightless. It had been a long thirty-six-hour journey to Alpha. Now it was too short, too soon finished. They had gone over their "battle plan" fifty times. Now he wished for fifty more.

"All right, men." Boys. "Just follow the assignments we've mapped out and they'll never know what hit them. Move fast. Don't shoot unless you have to. Good luck."

Their young, serious, scared faces looked back at him. A few nodded. A couple of others checked their weapons. They all carried pistols, nothing bigger. Dartguns, designed to stop a man with a combination of impact shock and sedative. Not strong enough to puncture the fragile skin of a spacecraft or space station. Or to knock down a charging opponent.

Kinsman floated past them all to the airlock hatch. He felt and heard the thumps of the station crewmen on the other side, undogging the hatch. Hefting his pistol in his hand, Kinsman pressed the button on the bulkhead alongside the hatch that unlocked it from the ship's interior.

The hatch swung open, revealing a hefty tech sergeant and two airmen in work fatigues. "Wha . . . ? We were expectin' . . ." Then the sergeant saw Kinsman's gun.

"Just stand back and don't give us any trouble," Kinsman said.

"What the hell is this?"

They backed the three men out of the cramped metal chamber of the airlock, into the larger area of the unloading bay. This was at the center of the space station, in the zero-gravity hub of the many-wheeled structure.

The lunar troops fanned out along three main tubes, the "spokes" that led from the station's hub through each wheel, to the outermost ring. Their objectives were the communications center, the power generators and the officers' quarters. Five men were left in charge of the loading bay. Three teams of seven men each rushed toward their three objectives.

Most of the station was taken up by civilian living, working and recreation areas. Kinsman ignored them. *Take the high ground and the rest comes free.* There were the weapons centers, where high-powered lasers and small missiles were stored for defending the station against outside attack. *But they need the power generators. Control the electrical power and we control the station.*

Kinsman led the group heading for officer country. They clambered down the long, nearly endless spiral ladder that wound around the tube's inner wall, dropping in free-fall at first, then grabbing at the ladder's handrail and half walking, half leaping as gravity returned. *Officer's quarters are in Level Four, which* spins at a lunar grav, Kinsman knew, thankful that he wouldn't have to face a full Earth gravity—at least, not right away.

They pushed past two startled civilians who were making their way up the tube. Neither of them said anything as the armed men hustled past them. Let 'em go. By the time they figure out what we're up to, we'll be in command of the station. They clattered on, footsteps echoing metallically now through the narrow, dimly lit tube.

At last they burst out on Level Four and rushed down the central corridor toward the officers' area. His heart pounding against his ribs, Kinsman searched the nameplates on the doors they passed. There it is! L/C H. J. STAHL. He pushed the door open. Empty. Bed, desk, photos of wife and children, tape cassettes, but the man himself wasn't there.

Two other station officers were being pulled out of their compartments by Kinsman's grim-faced aides. One of them recognized him. "Kinsman! What're you doing here? What the hell's going on?" Flanked by the armed youngsters, they both looked surprised and more than a little annoyed.

"We're taking over the station, Ralph. Where's Harry Stahl?"

"Taking over? What do you mean?"

"Just what I said," Kinsman answered, walking down the corridor toward them. "Where's Stahl? There's no time for playing games."

Ralph was looking edgy now. His buddy was staring at the guns that the young officers were holding. "The colonel doesn't always take me into his confidence about his moves," Ralph said angrily. "Maybe he's in the head. How the hell should I know?"

Kinsman grimaced. "All right," he said. "Move—down to the mess hall." To his half-dozen men he added, "Clean out every compartment along this corridor. Herd them all down to the mess hall."

Ralph and his friend walked ahead of Kinsman. They didn't raise their hands over their heads, and Kinsman tucked his gun into its holster. But they all knew what was happening.

"This is crazy, Chet. You can't get away with it."

"Just keep walking, Ralph."

The corridor sloped upward in both directions; it looked as if you were always walking uphill, no matter which way you turned. But actually it felt perfectly flat, and there was no sensation of climbing at all.

The mess hall was nothing more than a widened section of corridor, with bulging blisters on both sides to make alcoves where people could sit and look outside. It had enough tables to accommodate fifty people at a time. Both ends of the mess hall were open to the corridor, which ran through Level Four like the inner tube of an old-fashioned bicycle tire. At the far end of the mess hall, the corridor passed through the galley and a series of storage bays. Kinsman seated the two officers at one of the tables, then walked to the galley and waved a wide-eyed cook and his helpers to seats near Ralph and his smoldering friend.

The Earth slid past the viewport beside their table as the young lunar troops began bringing other station officers and men into the mess hall. They looked shocked, angry, bewildered. A few of them had obviously been awakened abruptly from sleep. Three of the officers were women. Lieutenant Colonel Stahl was not among the prisoners.

"Colonel Kinsman," the overhead speaker blared. A young man's voice. "Colonel Kinsman, please call the communications center."

Kinsman went to the wall phone in the galley, keeping his eyes on the rapidly filling tables. Men and women were coming in from both sides now, urged by gun-wielding youngsters. "Kinsman here," he said, after touching the phone's ON button. "Put me through to the comm center."

The station's computer buzzed briefly, then, "Comm center."

"This is Kinsman," he said into the speaker grill.

"Yessir. Lieutenant Reilly here. We have Colonel Stahl. He was in the comm center when we got here."

Involuntarily, Kinsman let out a sigh of relief. "Very good. Bring him up to the officer's mess. You've secured the center?"

"Oh, yessir. No trouble at all."

"Good. Call me when the power generator team reports in."

"Will do."

The mess hall was filling with grumbling, scared-looking men and women when Lieutenant Colonel Stahl was led in by one of Kinsman's kids.

"Kinsman! Just what the hell do you think you're doing here?"

"Declaring independence."

"What?" Stahl stood defiantly in the center of the mess hall, legs slightly spread, fists clenched. He looked as if he wanted to spring at Kinsman.

"We're taking over all three of your stations," Kinsman said slowly, walking up to within a half-meter of him, "as part of creating the independent nation of Selene. It's a funny name, I guess, but the best one we've got. The Russians are doing the same with their space stations."

Stahl's face was white. "You . . . you and the . . . the Russians?" He seemed dazed.

"Moonbase and Lunagrad together, that's right."

"You can't—"

"We have."

The two men stood facing each other, neither one moving, neither one speaking. The loudspeaker broke their stalemate: "Colonel Kinsman, please call the power generator section."

The kids at the power generators were jubilant. No casualties on either side, everything under control. Kinsman congratulated them and told them to stand by for further orders.

He scanned his own men, then nodded to the oldest-looking one. "You men escort these officers back to their quarters, then seal the emergency hatches on both ends of officers' country and station a guard at each hatch." That'll keep them in their own compartments, where they can't make waves. "I'm going down to the comm center."

The communications center was down in the next wheel, Level Three, spinning fast enough to produce a half Earth gee. For the first time in nearly five years,

Kinsman felt a pull stronger than the Moon's gentle gravity. It was like wading through chest-deep surf.

He sank gratefully into the chair that Major Cahill had recently occupied and looked over the view screens that were now showing mostly the various interior sections of the big space station. His chest felt heavy; he was puffing like an overweight jogger.

The mop-up operations took several hours. There were a couple of hundred civilians aboard the station, almost all of them in the outermost wheel, Level One, at a full Earth gravity. Kinsman left them alone for the time being. He concentrated his meager forces on the military areas, hoping he had enough men to do the job. And it began to look as if the gamble had worked. There were only a few other officers who weren't in their quarters or at the comm center, loading dock, or power generators. There were many more noncoms and techs, of course, but Kinsman's gun-brandishing Luniks rounded them all up quickly and efficiently.

Kinsman watched it all from the communications center, slouching heavily in his seat, perspiring with the effort of lifting his chest to breathe. Reports came in from Stations Beta and Gamma: all secure. Those stations were much smaller, with only a squad or two of men in each. Some of the crewmen on Gamma had recovered from their initial surprise and tried to rush Kinsman's Luniks with their bare hands. They were all gunned down after a brief scuffle.

"I can't believe it's going so well," said one of the youngsters after Captain Perry reported success at Beta. "Weren't the stations on yellow alert, same as Selene?"

Kinsman nodded. Even that was an effort. Slowly, he said, "Yes, but yellow alert here means stand-by to shoot down unfriendly boosters—not repel boarders. Good old S.O.P.—screws you every time."

The kid laughed.

Civilians were starting to phone the comm center. They knew something strange was happening, but not just what. Some of them tried to climb up from their wheel to the inner levels, but they were stopped by Kinsman's guards, stationed at the connecting tubes.

"They're getting kind of panicky," said one of the

men at a communications console. "They don't know what's happening, and it's getting to them."

Kinsman said, "Pipe me through the P.A. system."

The kid studied the rows of buttons on the console before him, puckered his face into a frown, then carefully touched two of them in sequence. Turning back to Kinsman, he said, "You're on, sir—I think."

Watching the view screens that showed the main corridor of Level One, Kinsman said calmly, "Attention, please. May I have your attention, please."

In the view screens he saw conversations stop, people walking down the corridor coming to an abrupt halt, heads turning upward toward the overhead loudspeakers.

"My name is Chet Kinsman." Suddenly he didn't know what to say. "Umm . . . Today, a group of us from Selene—Moonbase, you call it—have taken over command of this space station, as well as Stations Beta and Gamma. Our Russian neighbors from Lunagrad have taken similar actions with their space stations. We have formed a new nation, called Selene, independent of the United States and Russia. Independent of all the nations of Earth."

He watched their faces. Shock, disbelief, incredulity, apathy, anger.

"We've taken the space stations as a matter of self-protection. We intend to transport anyone who wishes to return Earthside, just as soon as possible. In the meantime, please carry on your work as usual. Nobody's going to hurt you or bother you. But for the time being, we'll have to ask you to remain in your own sector of the station. Please stay on Levels One and Two, and don't try to get any higher than that, until we announce that it's all right. Thank you."

He studied their faces in the view screens. They looked stunned, for the most part. The whites—mostly Americans and some Europeans—seemed either frightened or angry. The few orientals and blacks aboard looked surprised, but perhaps not as fearful. A few people smiled. But very few. Within minutes, there were knots of babbling, arm-waving conversations to be seen in each view screen.

Kinsman set up temporary headquarters in the rec area, up in Level Six, where the effective gravity was even less than lunar. The walls, floor and ceiling of the big gymnasium were all padded. Appropriate, he thought. Amidst rowing machines, oversized barbells, and a magnetic pool table, Kinsman and a few of his men put together some benches and a Ping-Pong table next to the only wall phone in the area.

Men scurried in and out constantly, bringing reports and problems to Kinsman. The phone buzzed incessantly. Inevitably, papers piled up on the table. They just grow, like mushrooms, when your back is turned.

The captain of the waiting troopship was told to abort his docking with the station and retrofire for return Earthside. He sputtered indignantly about dropsick troops until told that there were several cases of an unidentified viral infection aboard the station. Then he blasted away, gladly. Kinsman had the comm center call Earthside with a request for an immediate medical evacuation mission, to take more than a hundred uninfected people off the station.

That brought up a beeswarm of calls from Earthside, including one from General Murdock. Kinsman's officers handled them all from the comm center, sticking to their story, claiming that they were on skeleton crew status because of the infection.

By 1800 hours Kinsman could relax enough to have a brief dinner brought up from the gallery. He was just finishing a not-quite-thawed piece of soyloaf when the phone buzzed on the wall, right beside his ear. "Kinsman here," he said into the speaker.

"Sir," the voice sounded worried, "one of the civilian scientists down in Level One is putting up a terrific squawk. Claims he has a critical experiment on weather modification going on and he's got to get to the observatory section before 1900 hours or several years' worth of work will be wasted."

"The observatory's in the zero-gee area, next to the loading and docking facilities," Kinsman thought aloud. "What nationality is this man?"

"American, sir. But he claims he's working for the United Nations—UNESCO, or something like that."

"The Weather Watch." He thought it over for a moment. "Send him up here, I want to talk with him."

"Yessir."

"Don't let him wander around alone; have him escorted."

"Yessir."

Kinsman finished his small meal, wondering, How's Leonov doing? Too early to expect any word from him, I guess. Shouldn't expect everything to go as smoothly for him as it has for us.

A few minutes later, a Lunik officer and a civilian entered the rec area and crossed the padded floor to Kinsman's makeshift command post.

The civilian didn't look like a scientist. He was well over six feet tall, with broad shoulders, an athletic body. He glided smoothly across the padded floor; low gee didn't bother him a bit. His face was hard, hawk-nosed, set in a looking-for-trouble frown. The stump of an unlit cigar was clamped in his teeth. He was completely bald, except for the thinnest white fuzz across his skull. He reminded Kinsman more of a Turkish wrestler than anything else—and an angry one, at that.

Kinsman stood up behind the Ping-Pong table.

"Ted Marrett," the civilian said, keeping both his beefy hands at his sides.

"Chet Kinsman."

"Now listen. I don't have time to be polite or to repeat what I say, so listen good. I've got a rainfall augmentation project going—been working on it for six fuckin' years. Moving rainfall patterns along the Upper Niger valley, trying to hold back the Sahara from creeping southward and wiping out even more farmlands and pastures. If I'm not directing the catalysis experiment that starts at 1900, six years' work will fall through—and a few million people will starve."

Kinsman let himself sink back onto the bench. "You're directing the experiment from here?"

"Where the hell else?" Marrett boomed, still standing. "You can see the whole goddamned hemisphere from here. Key to the whole motherin' experiment is the wind and current patterns off the Canary Islands. What do you think—"

"Whoa, slow down." Kinsman put his hands up. Grinning, he said, "Do you understand what's happened here today?"

Marrett gave him an even sourer look. "Some of you Lunatics took over the station. Your glorious leader wants to proclaim the independence of the Moon. Big shit. I've got *work* to do, buddy."

"Um . . . I'm the glorious leader."

Now it was Marrett's turn to grin. "Hmm, well, my mouth always was bigger'n my brains. But, c'mon, time's wasting. I've got to be in touch with my people Earthside. It's important."

It occurred to Kinsman that it would help allay any suspicions Murdock might have if the experiment went through on schedule. "You won't mention anything about what we're doing here?"

"Shit, I'm no politician. As long as I can get my work done."

"Well, I'll let you go ahead and do it, but I'm going to ask the lieutenant here to stay with you and make certain that you talk *only* about your work."

"Fine by me," Marrett said easily. "Only, this job might take ten, twelve hours."

"We'll send a relief then."

Shrugging, Marrett turned to the young officer, whom he loomed over. "C'mon, sonny," he said.

It wasn't until after they had left that Kinsman asked himself, How in hell would any of us know if he's sticking to his job or sending some sort of nonsense gobbledegook that'll stir up suspicions Earthside? It was one thing to trust Frank Colt, despite his profession of loyalty to the other side. Frank's with us, whether he realizes it or not.

But this Marrett character was a complete stranger, Kinsman realized. The one I'm really trusting is that kid lieutenant, and I can't even remember his name.

The phone buzzed again. From the speaker on the wall, a scared, shaky voice said tinnily, "Sir, several of the station crew have broken out of confinement down here on Level Four. They shot two of our men, sir. One of them's dead. The other—he's hurt bad, sir."

Tuesday 14 December 1999: 1810 hrs UT

Kinsman sagged back on the bench, felt his shoulders slump against the padded wall of the gym. The young officers around him froze in their tasks: one was holding a sheaf of papers; another, sitting across the table from Kinsman, had been reaching for the coffee mug; the third simply stood staring at the phone on the wall, slack-jawed.

Strangely, Kinsman felt no surprise, no shock. You knew all along that it wouldn't go without fighting. They'd never give up so easily. There had to be blood.

His voice as bleak as his soul, he said into the phone grill, "Seal all the hatches leading into Level Four. Nobody in or out."

"But sir," the kid on the other end of the phone line objected, "a couple of our men are still in there."

"Seal off Level Four," he repeated, with more iron in his voice. "Airtight. Get a couple men out on EVA and dog down all the outside hatches, too. I don't want a molecule getting out of that level. Understood?"

The barest of pauses. "Understood, sir."

He punched the phone off. Turning to the officer with the papers in his hand, "How many men does Stahl have down there?"

The youngster pawed through the sheets. "Duty roster, personnel assignments . . . Here we are!" He pulled a flimsy sheet from the stack. "According to this checkoff list, there are thirty-five men down there—no, make it thirty-three. Two are in sick bay."

"How many of 'em are women?" the kid with the coffee cup in his hand asked.

"Looks like ten, about."

"They won't fight."

"The hell they won't! Give them guns and they'll shoot you just as dead as any man." *They fight,* Kinsman knew. *They die, too.*

The youngster who was standing seemed to pull himself together. "The small arms supply is down on Level Four, isn't it? They'll have submachine guns."

They were starting to look scared. The seriousness of the situation was beginning to sink in.

"If Stahl has Level Four, then we're cut off from the comm center and—"

"And they're cut off from us and the loading bay."

Kinsman nodded. "Which means half our men can't get through to our escape route back to Selene."

"Jesus."

Half turning on the bench, Kinsman touched the phone button. "Comm center," he called.

Swiftly he outlined the situation to the men at the communications center.

"Yessir, we can see them on the view screens here. They've got guns, all right, and they're starting to break out some of the emergency pressure suits."

"All right," Kinsman said. "Turn off their air."

"What?"

"Tell our guys at the power generators to throttle down the air pumps on Level Four. In fifteen minutes they'll all be unconscious down there."

"Not if they're in pressure suits."

Kinsman answered, "There's only a handful of suits down there. Not enough for all thirty-three of them."

"But they've got three of our guys in there, too. One of them seems to be hurt pretty bad. We've got to try and get him to sick bay."

Kinsman hesitated. "Put me on the P.A. system for Level Four only. Patch their answers into this phone."

"Yessir."

The hatch at the far side of the gym swung open and a young officer burst through. His zipsuit was stained with sweat, and he lurched crazily toward Kinsman, trying to run in the low gravity. "Sir . . . I got up here . . . fast's I could."

Kinsman recognized the voice; the fear also showed in his eyes. "All right, all right. Take it easy. Calm down. Just what happened on Level Four?"

"I . . . Hard to say. Everything happened so fast. We were standing guard outside the hatch between the mess hall and officers' country. They just broke through the hatch. Popped the explosive bolts. Knocked us flat on our asses. Never had a chance . . . Shot Polanski while he was laying there—right through the chest."

"How'd you get away?"

One of the young officers handed the kid a cup of coffee. Another one was searching through a medical kit that he had opened on the table.

"The blast from the hatch knocked me behind a table." He took the cup; the coffee sloshed from his trembling hand. "They didn't see me the first couple seconds. I got up and emptied my dartgun at 'em. Jumbled 'em up enough. They sort of fell over each other and ducked down. I crawled to the galley and then went up the ladder to Level Five."

"Okay, fine. You did the right thing," Kinsman said soothingly.

The kid gulped at the coffee. "I saw Polanski die. They just shot him . . . never gave him a chance." His face was flushed. The officer with the medical kit took out a hypospray.

"It's all right. Everything's under control," Kinsman lied. To the officer nearest him, he ordered, "Find another phone, fast! Get our men standing by the hatches to disarm all the explosive bolts."

"Yessir." The youngster was on his way before Kinsman had finished speaking.

The kid finished draining the coffee cup just as the other officer pressed the hypospray against his sleeve. "Trank," he said. "Settle your nerves."

"Shot him," the kid was muttering. "Colonel Stahl himself . . . Just pointed the gun at Polanski and shot him while he was still on the floor."

Warrior of the week. Stahl'll get a medal for heroism, shooting kids.

The phone buzzed. "Sir, the air pumps to Level Four

also supply parts of Level Three, including the comm center, where we are."

Shit! "Better get into pressure suits, damned fast!"

The voice sounded distinctly unhappy. "Yessir."

"And what about the P.A. hookup to Level Four?"

"All set, sir. Whenever you want it."

"Are the pumps shut down?"

A brief hubbub of background chatter. "Yessir, they've just shut them now."

"All right," said Kinsman. "Plug me into the P.A."

"You're on, *now*."

Kinsman hesitated a moment. Then, "Colonel Stahl. This is Kinsman. You'd better stop now, before anybody else gets hurt."

For a moment nothing but a sizzling hum came out of the phone grill. Then Stahl's voice crackled clearly: "Kinsman, the game's over! You've got five minutes to give yourself up, or we'll recapture the station, level by level. I've got the men and the weapons to do it!"

He sounds happy! Kinsman realized. *Elated. The sonofabitch is* enjoying *this! He's high on it!*

"Stahl, listen to me. You can't get out of Level Four. All the hatches are sealed."

"That's your story."

"We've disarmed all the explosive bolts."

"We've got primacord and thermite from the engineering section. We'll get through the hatches. Come on, Kinsman, you're beaten. Give up."

It always comes down to this. You knew it would. There's no such thing as a bloodless coup. Now you make your choice: let him win or be ready to kill him. No idle threats. You can't talk your way out of this one. You've got to be ready to kill him. All of them. That's all they understand.

"Come on, Kinsman!" Stahl snapped impatiently. "We've got three of your own men down here. One of them's bleeding to death. You'd better give up quick so we can get him to sick bay in time to save his life."

Rage suddenly boiled past Kinsman's self-control. "You damned hypocritical bastard! You shot the kid, and now you're using him as a hostage!"

"Damned right! I only wish it was you—*traitor!*"

And just as suddenly, with that word, Kinsman's rage turned glacier cold. It wasn't gone. The fear and anger were still there, greater than ever. But instead of bubbling hotly in his guts, now they were gelled into an iron-hard purpose. Beyond all trembling. Beyond all self-doubt. Stahl was no longer a threat, a man to be feared. He was an obstacle that would be hurdled, a barred gate that would be broken through. Kinsman almost smiled. Idly he glanced at the faces of the men around him: apprehensive, questioning, frightened.

I am sitting here in a padded room with a gaggle of kids, rebelling against the United States of America. In the name of humanity. In the name of peace, I'm going to kill thirty-some people. For openers. And God only knows how many more. In the name of peace.

"If this is treason," he said slowly into the phone, "then make the most of it. Your air input was shut off ten minutes ago." A lie; it was more like three, four minutes ago, at most. "You've got about five minutes before your men start passing out."

"You . . . what?"

"So you want to be a hero, Stahl? Fine. You've already killed one man, and you're letting another bleed to death. How many pressure suits down there? Twelve? So figure out who among you is going to live and who's going to die. That's a perfect task for a hero, Stahl: pick out the people you're going to murder."

Kinsman punched the phone's off button. Immediately, he called the comm center again. "What's going on down on Level Four? How many suits do they have?"

"We're checking all the screens, sir. And we're getting into suits, too. It's not easy—takes time."

"What's Stahl doing?" Kinsman demanded, his voice rising.

"Colonel Stahl's waving his arms and yelling for everybody to be quiet. They're all milling around, arguing. They've got about ten suits out, but nobody's anywhere near sealed up in 'em."

"All right. Get our men on the other sides of those hatches leading into Level Four to put on pressure suits. I'm going to suit up also and come down there."

"Uh, sir, if we keep the air off long enough it'll kill them, or cause brain damage. And our own men—"

"Just do what I told you," Kinsman snapped. Then he added, "There's nothing else we can do, son. Not a goddamned thing."

By the time Kinsman had suited up and clumped down to the tube hatch that opened on Level Four, comm center reported that most of Stahl's people had collapsed. Only five had successfully sealed themselves into pressure suits, the colonel among them.

Kinsman had his men pop all the hatches at once, and they moved into Level Four—ten spacesuited men holding dartguns in their gloved hands. Kinsman clambered down the ladder that led to the galley hatch. A younger man, unidentifiable in his bulky pressure suit, pushed through ahead of him. The area was deadly calm. No one in sight. The only sounds in Kinsman's ears were his own breathing and the whisper of the suit's air pump.

Pushing through the galley, into the mess hall, they found bodies. Sprawled, blue-faced, but still alive. Barely. "Get the medic's oxygen masks on these people," Kinsman ordered.

Six bodies. Two women. He clumped past them and into the corridor that ran through officers' country. "Got two guys here!" his earphones crackled. "They're surrendering."

"Two men in pressure suits?" Kinsman asked.

"Yessir. No fight. They give up."

That left three more. He met two of his own men coming down the corridor toward him and almost fired at them. But he quickly saw that their pressure suits were orange and red—colors that could easily be spotted on the desolate lunar surface—rather than the white of the orbital station's crew.

Together they poked into each compartment along the corridor. Empty. Meanwhile reports were pouring in, over the suit radio, of men and women found asphyxiated in other sections of Level Four. Most were still alive. Eight were dead, including the wounded man from Kinsman's group.

Kinsman kicked open a compartment door and his

nerves flashed red inside him. A pressure-suited figure sat on the bunk, a submachine gun in its lap.

The dartgun in Kinsman's hand was cocked and pointed at its chest before his brain screamed: *Is it a man or a woman? Is he/she threatening you?* "Put the gun down on the floor," Kinsman shouted. Although the oxygen in the air was depleted, there was still enough air pressure to transmit sound.

The figure on the bunk took up the gun by its muzzle and laid it gently on the floor.

"Stand up."

"Don't shoot." It was a man's voice: high-pitched, frightened. "I'm just an adjutant, with the Judge Advocate Group. I'm not here to fight!"

A lawyer. Kinsman almost laughed with relief. A mother-humping lawyer. How the hell did he get into a suit, while the others suffocated?

There was one more suited man to find. And Colonel Stahl.

Stahl's quarters are down this way, he told himself as he and the other two Luniks behind him plodded down the corridor. Be just like him to start a shoot-out. The thought of their dartguns against a submachine gun didn't please Kinsman, especially in the narrow confines of the corridor and tiny compartments.

Shots! A muffled string of shots, coming from up ahead. Kinsman broke into a galumphing sprint, leaving the two pressure-suited youngsters behind him. Sure enough, there was Stahl's door. Shut. Probably locked. And the shooting? He kicked at the door, and it slid open. Stahl was sitting at his tiny desk, his back to Kinsman. The submachine gun was on the floor beside him.

With the inevitability of a Greek drama, Kinsman knew what he would find. He didn't even bother calling to the colonel. He saw the whole event in his mind's eye: Stahl sitting there at the desk, defeated. Maybe starting to write a note to his wife or family or commanding officer. Realizing that he had lost the station to traitors. Unable to write with the suit's clumsy gloves over his hands. Knowing that it was just a matter of time before he would be taken prisoner. Thinking about all that tradition, centuries of military history piling up inside his head, all the gallantry and honor and bravery that had failed.

He believed all that crap, Kinsman thought as he crossed the three-paces-wide compartment.

Stahl facing defeat, disgraced in his own eyes. Staring down at the gun. Holding his breath and lifting up the visor and resting the gun's muzzle on the lip of his helmet and setting it on semiautomatic and squeezing . . . His last thought: *Don't let me die in vain. Remember Space Station Alpha.* Kinsman knew it, as if Stahl had implanted it telepathically in his brain.

He put his hand on Stahl's shoulder and turned the colonel toward him. The chair swiveled easily. There wasn't a speck of blood anywhere, except inside the helmet. For the first time in his life, Kinsman retched in his pressure suit.

PAFB/SCM TO SACHQ/SJL
COMMUNICATIONS WITH STATIONS ALPHA, BETA, GAMMA INOPERATIVE. PLS ADVISE.

SACHQ/SJL TO PAFB/SCM
BACKUP SYSTEMS USE AUTHORIZED. EMPLOY LASER LINK IF NECESSARY.

PAFB/SCM TO SACHQ/SJL
NO RESPONSE ON ANY FREQUENCY, INCLUDING LASER LINK.

SACHQ/SJL TO PAFB/SCM
HOW LONG HAVE ORBITAL STATIONS BEEN OUT OF CONTACT?

PAFB/SCM TO SACHQ/SJL
LAST ROUTINE AUTOMATIC CHECK-IN AT 1545 HRS UT. NO RESPONSE TO PERSONAL CALLS, ROUTINE TRAFFIC, ETC SINCE 1745 HRS UT.

SACHQ/SJL TO PAFB/SCM
HAVE YOU CHECKED SOLAR ACTIVITY? JAMMING? OTHER POSSIBLE INTERFERENCE?

PAFB/SCM TO SACHQ/SJL
FULL TEAMS OF COMM SPECIALISTS CHECKING FOR
PAST THREE HRS. NO INTERFERENCE. THEY'RE JUST
NOT ANSWERING. LAST MESSAGE WAS CALL FOR ME-
DIVAC. CLAIMED INFECTION SPREADING THROUGH AL-
PHA. POSSIBLE COMM CENTER PERSONNEL INFECTED
AND UNABLE TO PERFORM DUTIES?

SACHQ/SJL TO PAFB/SCM
UNLIKELY TO CAUSE BLACKOUT AT BETA AND GAMMA.
WILL QUERY TOPSIDE. STAND-BY FOR POSSIBLE RED
ALERT.

PAFB/SCM TO SACHQ/SJL
WHAT ABOUT MEDIVAC MISSION? IT'S ALREADY
LIFTED FOR ALPHA.

SACHQ/SJL TO PAFB/SCM
CONTINUE MEDIVAC MISSION. IS COMM LINK WITH
THEM OK?

PAFB/SCM TO SACHQ/SJL
READ THEM LOUD AND CLEAR. WILL CONTINUE MIS-
SION AND STAND-BY FOR RED ALERT. MSG ENDS.

SACHQ/SJL TO JCS/SJL, ADC/SCM
COMMUNICATIONS WITH ORBITAL STATIONS ALPHA,
BETA, GAMMA CUT OFF. HAVE INITIATED STAND-BY
FOR RED ALERT. AWAIT FURTHER ORDERS.

JCS/SJL TO ALL COMMANDS
RED ALERT. REPEAT, RED ALERT. ARM ALL MISSILES
PREPARATORY TO STRIKE ORDER. FULL SECURITY ALL
BASES AND SUBMARINES. ALL LEAVES CANCELED.
ACTIVATE SUBROUTINE 93–00622
QUERY. QUERY. QUERY. NETWORK REQUIRES AUTHOR-
IZATION FOR AUTOMATED MESSAGES.
AUTHORIZATION SUBCODE JCS/AAA FOR SUBROUTINE
93–00622
THNX
ACK

SUBROUTINE BEGINS.
CHIEF OF STAFF TO ALL BASE AND FBMS COMMAND-
ERS: MEN, WE ARE ON THE BRINK OF THE NATION'S
SUPREME TEST. THE WORLD DEPENDS ON US TO FACE
DOWN THE AGGRESSORS WHO THREATEN CIVILIZA-
TION. I KNOW THAT EACH OF YOU WILL DO HIS DUTY,
AND FUTURE GENERATIONS OF AMERICANS WILL BE
PROUD OF YOUR HEROISM AND DEDICATION. GOOD
LUCK. GOD BLESS AMERICA. MSG ENDS.

By 2000 hours, Alpha was securely in the hands of
the men from Selene. All of Stahl's men were back in
their quarters, disarmed and cowed. Several were in
sick bay, oxygen masks and IV tubes feeding into them
while medical teams grimly tried to keep their oxygen-
starved injuries down to a minimum. The dead were
being prepared for shipment back to Earthside.

Kinsman split his tiny command into three groups
and set up a sleeping routine. He put a lieutenant in
charge as Officer of the Day, then made his way down
to Level Three and the comm center. The extra weight
there was still painful. He braced himself in the doorway as he received reports. Extra men were on their
way from Selene. The troopship had reentered Earth's
atmosphere and landed back at Patrick. The medivac
mission would rendezvous with the station in less than
one hour.

"There's all sorts of queries and messages from
Earthside," the youngster running the comm center told
him. "Should we keep radio silence all this time?"

He nodded slowly, and it made his head feel like a
cement mooring block. "Got to. We can't let them know
what's happening until we've got enough of our own
people here to run the whole ABM network."

The young technician shrugged. The heavier-than-
lunar gravity didn't bother him in any discernible way.

Kinsman quickly returned to his makeshift headquarters in the rec area, grateful for the diminishing weight
as he made his way up the metal ladder that wound
through the tubular spoke connecting the station's various levels.

They'll go on red alert, he knew. But they'll find out that the Russians are cut off from their stations, too. They'll wait to puzzle that out. *They'll wait.* But the burning in his chest contradicted the logical certainty his mind was trying to establish.

There were four civilians waiting to see him, sitting along the bench at his table as he padded across the gym floor. He spent the better part of an hour with them, assuring them patiently that they could stay at the station or leave for Earthside as soon as transport could be arranged.

One of them was a wispy little Japanese astronomer, fragile and aged. "We are scientists, not politicians," he said in a quiet, calm voice. "We do not wish to abandon our work here. Several of us are in the midst of experiments or observations that must not be interrupted. We have no desire, however, to be caught in a cross fire between armed troops."

"Nothing could be further from my own desires," Kinsman answered, unconsciously picking up some of the formal cadence of the Japanese manner of speech. "I sincerely believe that you can all be assured that no one will interfere with your work. It would please me if you would continue your investigations as if nothing had happened."

"Well, I'm not a scientist," said one of the other men, hotly. He was younger than the others, dressed in flashy Earthside fashion, built on the chunky side and starting to flesh out too much. Youthful muscle turning into the flab of premature middle age.

"I'm just a taxpaying citizen from Denver," he went on, "and I want to know what the hell's happening around here. My wife and I came up here for the vacation of a lifetime, and it cost plenty, let me tell you—"

Kinsman silenced him with a pointed finger. "You'll be going back home within the hour. Better get your bags packed."

"What? After all I spent to get here? You can't—"

Kinsman said, "There's no time for arguing. Get packing! I'm sorry to cut your vacation short and cost you all that money, but you'll be much better off at home than around here." He turned to the other three.

"That goes for all of you. Anyone who wishes to return Earthside may do so."

The tourist lurched to his feet. Angrily he shouted, "You're letting foreigners stay but a taxpaying American has to clear out!"

"The scientists can stay if they want to," Kinsman answered. "Civilians and tourists will be better off going home. This station is no longer American territory; it's part of the independent nation of Selene."

The tourist blinked, uncomprehending. The Japanese astronomer sighed knowingly.

"I don't get it," the tourist said.

"You will, once you're Earthside," Kinsman told him. "Now, hurry, you don't have much time to spare."

One of the younger scientists claimed Kinsman's attention: "We're being held incommunicado. Your men won't let us call Earthside."

"Only for a short time more."

"And what have you done with Dr. Marrett? He disappeared with one of your officers after putting up a row, and he hasn't been seen since."

"He's in the observation section, carrying out his experiment."

"Do you mean he's allowed to have radio contact with Earth?"

Nodding, Kinsman replied, "Only with his own special outposts, and only for the experiment he's working on. We have an officer up there with him to make sure that he doesn't . . . do anything political."

"This is insane," the young man argued. His accent was decidedly British. "You're going to have half the troops in the United States pouring in here as soon as they realize what's happened. We'll all be clay pigeons in a shooting gallery."

"Maybe," said Kinsman evenly.

"Of more serious consequence," the Japanese astronomer said softly, "is the possibility that America might unleash its nuclear striking force, for fear that this situation has been caused by the Soviets."

When they realized what the older man had said, the others turned toward Kinsman. But he had no answer for them.

Captain Ryan closed his codebook with an audible snap. The other officers in the wardroom were staring at him. Not a smile on the eight of them. The captain's personal codebook was used only for the very highest priority messages, the kind that were marked FOR YOUR EYES ONLY. All lesser priorities were decoded by the submarine's computer.

"It's the red alert, all right," he said. The tension in their faces actually eased a bit. The known fear was always easier to face than the unknown. "And a personal message from the Chief of the Joint Staffs. He expects us all to do our duty and make our kids proud of us."

Garcia's kids are living in the open housing development south of San Diego, Captain Ryan knew. They won't be around ten minutes after the button's pushed. He scanned the faces of his fellow officers. Same for Mattingly and Rizzo. Same for my own—and my grandson! "Well," he said, leaning his elbows heavily on the green felt tabletop, "it looks as if the shit has really hit the fan. And we've got a job to do."

They showed no enthusiasm at all.

"Listen to me," he said evenly. "When those missiles go, there's gonna be a helluva lot of Americans killed. Our job is to seek and destroy enemy subs. There are two of 'em in our area, according to this morning's sonar sweep, and they wouldn't be on this course if they weren't missile-launching bastards."

They glanced at each other, nodding. Still no show of fire. It was a captain's responsibility to instill a high morale among his crew, especially among his officers. The officers must set an example for the men, and the captain must set an example for the officers.

"Now, one of those subs has got at least one missile that's got San Diego for a target," he went on. That moved them. They stirred. They sat up straighter.

"We've got to stop that missile from getting launched."

"Sir," Garcia said, "I don't see how we can . . . I mean, a red alert doesn't mean war's been declared."

"There won't be a declaration of war, Mike," argued Mattingly, with his damned nasal Princeton accent. "The button is pushed and the missiles are launched. No paperwork. No diplomatic niceties."

"Then how do we stop them from launching it?"

Captain Ryan said, "We're going for those subs *now*. Not after they've launched their missiles. Not after we get the codeword from Fleet HQ. *Now!*"

"But—"

"You want to wait until they've blown San Diego off the map?"

"No, but we can't move without orders."

"A red alert gives the captain of a warship discretion to act on his own initiative in case of communications failure."

"But we don't have a communications failure," Rizzo said, his voice a bit hollow.

"We do now," Captain Ryan answered.

No one argued against him.

The rec room looked more like a command post now. Men going in and out constantly. Several more tables and chairs had been moved in. A computer terminal clacked at one table; a communications console complete with four small view-screens lapped over the sides of another.

Kinsman was wolfing down a hasty sandwich. It was well past 2100 hours now. The medivac spacecraft had taken most of the civilians off the station. Word of what had happened must be screaming to Washington by now.

"Sir, we have Colonel Leonov on screen four," said one of the technicians, a girl who had volunteered to stay with the Luniks.

Washing down a mouthful of unidentifiable soybean product with a gulp of synthetic coffee, Kinsman made his way to the comm console.

Leonov looked grimly triumphant on the tiny screen. "All three of our orbital stations are completely in our hands," he reported. "There was amazingly little shooting. Surprise and a good deal of agreement with our aims carried almost everyone. I was *very* eloquent." He arched his eyebrows, daring Kinsman to dispute him.

"Good work, Peter," was all Kinsman could counter with. "We had a few bad moments here, but everything's cool now. Beta and Gamma are secure, and I have Captain Perry checking out the ABM control system on Station Beta."

"I thought the main control center was on Alpha."

"It is," Kinsman said, "but we've still got several civilians and a few dissident prisoners aboard. We'll need to transfer them Earthside, but there wasn't enough room for them all on the evacuation ship."

"So you want to be sure that the unmanned satellites can be directed from Beta," Leonov concluded.

"Right. They're shipping us their prisoners, and we'll hold them here until we can get another ship up from Earthside."

"If I were you, comrade, I would hold onto the rest of the prisoners. They might be valuable as hostages. That is what we are doing here."

Kinsman nodded.

"Now, what about announcing our actions to the former owners of these satellites, eh?"

"The evacuees are probably yelling their guts out into the radio aboard that medivac ship right now," Kinsman said. "Washington ought to be sorting out the story very shortly."

"Yes, but do you realize that both sides are on full alert down there? They could send off their missiles before we are ready to stop them. We must make some sort of announcement jointly so they won't bombard each other."

"I know, Pete, but I'm afraid if we make the announcement before we can really control the ABM satellites, they'll either shoot at us or send troopships. I'd rather wait until the reinforcements get here from Selene and we have enough people to man the ABM control centers properly."

Leonov slowly blinked his eyes. "I understand. But it is much faster to launch a missile or troopship from Earthside than to get extra technicians down here from Selene. Even with our ships accelerating at maximum energy . . ."

He stopped. Someone off-screen had caught his attention. Leonov snapped something in Russian, and an excited voice babbled breathlessly at him. Leonov's face went white. "Chet, it's too late! One of our . . . a Russian submarine has been torpedoed and sunk off the coast of California. The war has started!"

Tuesday 14 December 1999: 2148 hrs UT

"They've fired the missiles?" Kinsman's voice was a shocked, high-pitched little boy's squeal of fear. His guts were frozen, a block of lunar ice. But his mind was racing:

Got to tell them right away that we've taken over. Right away! Got to scan the missile farms—Idaho, Montana, Texas, Siberia, China. Jesus Christ! The oceans. The subs . . . We'll need every sensor on every satellite. Got to be in touch with Perry and the others, make sure we can fire the lasers, get the radars tracking, all the sensors—get 'em ready to shoot at anything that moves. Fast!

"No," Leonov was answering. "Nothing has been launched yet. But the stand-by orders have gone out. It's only a matter of hours, perhaps minutes."

Can't do it from here, Kinsman realized as he watched the Russian's dismal face on the tiny viewscreen. Got to get down to the comm center.

A clattering noise made him jerk his attention away from the screen. One of the young officers had let a plastic food tray slip from his hands. He was visibly shaking as he knelt to pick up the mess. The others were fixed on Kinsman: standing, sitting—one of them leaning his fists on the top of the computer terminal, his face a tense death mask, white, taut, unblinking—all of them staring at Kinsman, waiting for him to act.

"Pete, get on all the broadcast frequencies you can manage and tell your people what we've done. I'm going down to our comm center and do the same thing. We can stop 'em if we yell loud enough." I think! "But we've got to tell 'em now!"

"Yes, yes, of course, but do you think . . . ?"

"Tell 'em we're prepared to shoot down any missile, launched from anywhere on Earth. Make 'em believe it!"

"But can we really do it?"

"You tell me."

Leonov rubbed a hand over his forehead. "I don't know. We have teams of technicians working, but how can we be sure that all those satellites will respond correctly?"

Forcing a grin, Kinsman answered, "The machines don't care what your politics are, Pete. If the lights come on green, then everything's working."

"Sheer materialism."

"Yep. And you thought I was a romantic. Get moving. There's no time to spare."

"*Da* . . . Good luck, *tovarich*."

"Goodspeed, friend." He pushed up from the chair and started across the padded gym floor for the hatch that led to the downward-spiraling ladder. "Get the comm center on the horn," he commanded the youngsters around him. "Make sure they understand what's happening. Tell them I'm on my way down there, and the techs had better be able to use every fucking laser on every fucking satellite we've got!"

"Yessir!" yelped one of the officers as Kinsman yanked the hatch open.

Level Three was like wading through ocean surf. One-half normal Earth gravity, and Kinsman was quickly out of breath. By the time the comm center crew made a chair available for him, his legs ached and his heart was thumping heavily. Even the air felt soupy, humid and thick, hard to breathe.

The comm center reminded Kinsman of a string sextet flying through a Mozart allegro: wildly ordered activity, measured frenetic action. The comm techs were buzzing commands into their pin mikes; the giant-insect-eye of view screens—bank on bank of them—showed strangely incongruous scenes:

The bright, soul-thrilling beauty of the broad Pacific: a globe-spanning expanse of blue water decorated with intricate patterns of dazzling white clouds, swirls of giant storms, files of cumulus puffs marching dutifully in response to sunlight and earthspin. How many submarines are under that beauty? How many missiles?

The tense, sweat-streaked face of a technician, urgently yammering into the earphone of the comm tech who sat nodding in front of that particular screen.

Captain Perry, standing in front of the elaborate fire control panel aboard Space Station Beta, talking to someone in what looked like an easy, professional, competent tone. Kinsman couldn't hear him, of course, unless the audio from that particular screen was piped into the earphones that rested in his lap. The board's idiot lights are almost all green, he noted. The ABM satellites are in operative condition.

View screens showed lovely rural Earthside scenery, where the ICBM silos were hidden. Half a dozen major cities. A Russian comm tech, frowning as he talked with his American counterpart. No. Not Russians or Americans any more. Luniks. Selenites.

Kinsman took all this in with a single glance as he slumped heavily into the seat near the comm center's hatch.

"Reports look good," said the officer sitting next to him. "And we've got a dozen or so volunteers from the station's crew helping us. They decided to stay with us."

Kinsman nodded, and even that was an effort. For the first time it registered in his mind that three of the six techs working the view screens were women.

"I've got to be patched in on the top priority network right away," he said wearily. "White House, Pentagon, SAC headquarters, C in C's of the Atlantic and Pacific strike forces—the works."

"The gold-braid circuit. Yessir, can do," the youngster nodded easily, grinning. He started flicking fingers across the master keyboard at his desk.

Make a good piano player. Kinsman realized that he wouldn't be able to play well in this gravity. Or at all, in a full Earth gee. He pushed everything to the back of his mind. Closing his eyes, he leaned his head back, annoyed momentarily that the chair they had given him had no headrest.

So far no missiles had been launched. So far the reports from all the space stations and the unmanned ABM satellites looked good. Now he had to make Washington aware of the new situation. Convince them that we can and will shoot down anything they launch.

He rubbed at the back of his neck, which ached sullenly. It's not fair, dammit all! Jefferson had months to write his Declaration. I've got minutes.

The view screens that filled the main bulkhead of the center's crowded compartment were beginning to show Earthside military men. Communications techs at first, but quickly each was supplanted by an officer; colonels and generals and even a pair of admirals scowled or glared or licked their lips nervously, waiting for the message from Space Station Alpha. They weren't accustomed to waiting.

"What about the White House?" Kinsman asked.

The youngster looked up from his own desktop keyboard, one hand on his earplug. "They're working their way up through a gaggle of flunkies. They say General Hofstader will speak with you. Is that okay?"

Kinsman nodded. "He'll do."

"They have to find him and patch him into the circuit. It's still sleepy-time down there."

"Tough. I doubt that any of them are asleep."

Suddenly the central screen showed the handsome, silver-haired image of General Hofstader. The paneling of the office wall behind him looked more Pentagon than White House. A furled flag was behind him, and he seemed to be glancing at other people who were in the office, but off-camera.

"General . . ."

"What is this, Colonel?" Hofstader's voice was crisp, deep, the very model of a commander's decisive tone.

"Why have the space stations been off their air and out of contact? What's going on?"

"We've taken control of the stations. And the ABM network."

" 'Control'? 'We'? What are you talking about?"

All the faces on the smaller screens around the general looked appropriately alarmed, surprised, concerned. Kinsman almost laughed. It was like watching a living Rorschach test.

"The people of the Moon," Kinsman said slowly and carefully, "have decided to form the independent nation of Selene. We have taken over all the space stations, both American and Russian."

For a moment he thought the words hadn't gotten through. They all just sat there, with no reaction. Then came the eruption. The smaller screens showed men going red with fury, white with shock, blue with rage. General Hofstader's eyes went absolutely round, his mouth fell open, he seemed to slump inside his well-pressed uniform.

"That's impossible! You can't—"

"We have. And we intend to enforce an absolute ban on all rocket launches. Anything, launched by any nation, from any spot on Earth, will be destroyed immediately."

"This is treason!"

A civilian pushed into view, crowding the general and forcing him to lean back in his high-backed plush leather chair. Kinsman recognized the hawk-featured face: the Secretary of Defense. "Do you realize that the Russians are counting down for a full-scale nuclear strike?" he bellowed into the camera. "Are you insane, man? You're destroying your nation, your homeland!"

"No missiles have been launched," Kinsman replied evenly. "And if they are, we'll shoot them down long before they reach their targets."

General Hofstader edged around the Defense Secretary's elbow to roar, "I'll give you five minutes to surrender and turn yourself in! Otherwise you'll see the full striking power of—"

"Bullshit, General!"

Hofstader sagged. The Defense Secretary grabbed at his arm, as if to keep him from falling off his chair.

"Now, listen, all of you," Kinsman said to the many faces in the screens. "This is no joke and no idle threat. We will stop any rocket launching. No matter where in the world it's launched from. We will not allow the destruction of Americans, or Russians, or anyone else. There will be no war. Is that clear? No war!"

Kinsman could feel his heart banging wildly, making his ears roar. He took a deep, painful breath and went on, "There is no way that we can hurt you. Our armaments were specifically designed to defend against missile launches. The nation of Selene is no threat to any nation on Earth. But we will not allow missiles to be launched! And if you try to send troops to these space stations to take them away from us, we'll be forced to destroy your troop-carrying rockets. Check with your technical staffs, gentlemen. We can do it. And we will. Now, good night. It's been a long and difficult day up here."

He turned and nodded once to the officer beside him. All the view screens went blank.

"Stay in touch with them," he commanded. "Answer their questions. Tell them that we make only one demand: that they refrain from launching any rockets. Tell them we'll shoot anything that moves."

"Yessir."

Slowly, Kinsman pulled himself to his feet. Like a ninety-year-old, he thought as he made his way back toward the rec area, and the blessed ease of low gravity.

It was well past midnight by the time he got to bed. His men set him up in one of the tourist VIP "suites" on Level Five. The station crew—those who had elected to remain aboard and join the Luniks—jokingly referred to it as the honeymoon suite. The low gravity, even less than lunar gee, was considered to be better than an Earthside waterbed.

Kinsman smiled back at them as they showed off the tiny two-compartment suite. He remembered the old Zero-Gee Club of bygone days, so many years ago that it seemed like another century. Damned near is another century, he realized as he stretched out gratefully in the bunk. The millennium is almost here.

He knew he should call Selene. He knew he should check on Ellen and Colt, and talk with Harriman. He knew he should tell them that he was all right, and everything had worked out better than they had any right to expect. But he was too tired. Too tired to talk, to think, even to sleep. I'll never sleep, he told himself, turning over onto his stomach. Too keyed up . . .

He awoke with a pang of fear in his middle. The phone was buzzing. The only lights in the compartment were the yellow 0351 of the digital clock and the pulsing red eye of the phone. He reached up, instantly wide awake, and punched the ON button. "Yeah?"

A woman tech said, "Station Gamma reports a rocket launch, from the Chinese mainland."

He sat up in bed, forgetting both his nakedness and the fact that the room's darkness hid it. "When?"

The girl glanced at something off-camera. "T plus one hundred fourteen seconds."

"Lemme see."

The phone's tiny view screen flickered, then showed a telescope view. The brown, cloud-streaked mountain country of western China. A single luminous thread of a rocket exhaust.

A male voice came on. "Trajectory extrapolation gives an impact in mid-ocean. Doesn't look heavy enough for an ICBM. Exhaust profile matches a scientific high-altitude sounding rocket more than anything else."

"Shoot it down," Kinsman said.

"We're already tracking it and have programmed a kill as soon as it clears the coastline," the man's voice answered, almost casually. "Got three different satellites lined up on it. If the first one misses—"

"Good work," Kinsman said. Very practical people, the Chinese, he thought. The only ones with sense enough to use a cheap scientific rocket to see if we mean business.

The rocket was too small to be seen visually, even in the best telescopic magnification. Instead, the various satellite sensors were being overlapped to give an optical view of the Earth background, and a combined radar-infrared image of the rocket—which looked on the view screen like a reddish blob, slightly longer than it was wide. Suddenly it blossomed into a white glare. *Got it!* The fireball was much too small for a nuclear explosion, but bright enough to see visually. It quickly dissipated. "Well done," Kinsman grunted. "Now let me get some sleep. Call me only if something critical happens."

The comm tech reappeared on the screen. "Sir," she asked pleasantly, "who's to decide what is critical?"

"The Officer of the Day, honey. He's the man on the spot."

But Kinsman couldn't sleep any more. He tossed in the bunk for what seemed like a week, got up and padded around the darkened compartment, bumping into the dresser that was built into the bulkhead beside the bunk.

Finally, when the glowing digits of the clock said 0700, he put in a call to Ellen. The phone screen stayed a blank gray as Selene's computer tracked her down. She wasn't in her quarters or at the communications center. Finally her face appeared on the small screen. Kinsman recognized the background instantly; she was in his office.

"You're up early," he said.

"You too. Is everything all right?"

"I was going to ask you that."

Completely serious, she said, "Everything's running smoothly here. No trouble from Colt or any of the other dissidents."

"Good."

She frowned slightly as she said, "We got the word that everything went well, at first. But then there were reports about fighting. Nobody seemed to know what was happening for a while. Finally the word came through that you had taken control of all three stations, and that Leonov had taken the Russians'. There was quite a celebration, the Russians and us."

"Sorry I missed it."

"When will you be back?"

"I'm hoping I can leave today. Be back, um, Thursday sometime. Work out the exact ETA later."

"All right."

Christ, we might as well be talking about the weather! How can she just—

"We saw the Chinese rocket intercept," Ellen said. "It happened in the middle of the party. Everybody was in the main plaza. And then when the Orca missiles were fired . . . "

"Orca?"

She brushed a wisp of hair back from her eyes. Kinsman began to realize that she probably hadn't slept all night. "Yes. We watched the whole thing on the big screen in the plaza. Everyone cheered when they were shot down."

"Yeah," he said weakly.

She peered into the camera. "Are you all right?"

"I just need a little rest."

"The worst is over now," she said. "Isn't it?"

"Yes. The worst is over," he answered, trying to believe that it was true.

As soon as Ellen signed off, Kinsman punched the code for the comm center. He asked for the Officer of the Day.

"Why wasn't I informed about the submarine missiles?" he demanded.

The youngster wore a lieutenant's bars and a wispy light brown mustache. "Sir, you gave orders that you were not to be disturbed unless something critical occurred. The submarine launched six missiles in salvo, from the mid-Pacific. We assume it was an American sub, since the projected trajectory of the missiles was toward Asia. Our own fire control crew aboard Gamma tracked the missiles and shot them down within eight minutes of launch. It all went very smoothly. No sweat. Sir."

Kinsman sagged back on the bunk and grinned. "I see."

"We have videotapes, sir, if you wish to review the action." The lieutenant was very sure of himself, as only a young officer can be when he's got the rules working on his side. And when he's guessed right.

"No. I'll take a look at it later. Any messages from Washington or elsewhere?"

"Oh, yessir. A whole tankful of them!"

It was two hours later that Kinsman realized he was hungry. He went down to Level Four, where the mess hall was. He got a tray of hot food from the galley and sat at a long table that was crowded with his young officers and crewmen, and a few civilians. The more elaborate automated restaurant down on Level One had been shut down by its departing crew, so the civilians were forced to eat up in officers' country.

Most of the civilians seemed relaxed enough, even friendly. But one pair—Americans, by their dress and accent—got up from the table when Kinsman sat down, and moved to a smaller table on the other side of the mess hall. A few of the Europeans seemed ill at ease, uncertain. The orientals were polite and professionally inscrutable.

Nobody knows where this is going to end, Kinsman realized, watching them work at their food and their conversations, but they all want to avoid the pariah.

Ted Marrett walked in. Fatigue lines were etched under his eyes. He moved his big frame stiffly, as if he'd been cramped in one position for much too long.

Kinsman followed the broad-shouldered meteorologist with his eyes as Marrett punched out two cups of steaming black coffee from the dispenser in the galley and carried them tiredly into the mess hall. One of the scientists at Kinsman's table, a slim, sharp-featured Moroccan, called to him, "Ted, here. Come join us."

Marrett shuffled over to them and sat next to the Moroccan, two seats down from Kinsman.

"How did the trial go?"

"Pretty good." Marrett took a huge gulp of scalding coffee, winced, then took another. "Missed two of the correlation factors we're looking for, but it looks like all the major factors check out. We'll know more in a month, and still more when the winter season's over."

"If you can stem the encroachment of the Sahara . . ." the Moroccan mused.

Marrett grimaced. "Could do better'n that if we had

authority to operate in the Mediterranean. That's where the motherlovin' crux of the problem is. But they won't give us permission. 'Fraid we'll screw up their humpin' sky."

The Moroccan shrugged. "We mustn't hope for more than can be accomplished. As I said earlier, if even a ten percent increase—"

"Ten percent! Hell, we could stop the goddamned Sahara cold, if they'd just let us work things right!" He drained the plastic cup, slammed it on the table, and grabbed the second cup. That's when he noticed Kinsman. Raising the cup in greeting, Marrett asked, "How's your revolution going?"

Kinsman arched his eyebrows in a "here's hoping" expression. "So far, so good. Had some trouble last night, but everything seems cool now."

"Yeah, I heard. Got some interesting queries from my confreres Earthside. Even a few priority calls from Washington and Paris."

"Paris?"

Marrett reached into his shirt pocket. "Damn! No more cigars. Yeah, Paris. European Federation's interested in what you're doing. And UNESCO, of course."

"Hmm." Kinsman thought a moment. "Leonov and I ought to make a world-wide broadcast."

"Might help to settle people's stomachs."

Kinsman nodded thoughtfully, then turned his attention to his cooling breakfast. Marrett kept talking nonstop to the Moroccan and a couple of other, younger men who joined them.

Before long, Kinsman realized that they were talking about flying: small planes, jets, soarplanes, even rocket gliders. He joined the conversation simply by saying, "I never got a chance to try a rocket glider; they came in after I became a permanent Lunik."

One of the younger men immediately broke into an animated, "Christ, there's nothing like them! You stovepipe up to fifty thou and drop the boosters . . . "

And they were brothers. Fliers, all of them. Without nationality, or race, or any creed except the excitement of flying.

"You can keep the rocket stuff," Marrett said, with a

wave of a meaty hand. "I'll take soarplanes; that's where the real fun is. I want to make love to those fat humpy cumuli. I want to get into those thermals. I want to *feel* that goddamned cloud. Feel it."

Kinsman decided that he liked the man. Trusted him. On the strength of his enjoyment of flying? Yes, Kinsman realized. On nothing more than that. It's enough. Reluctantly, though, he got up and started out of the mess hall. There's more to do than shoot the shit— dammit all. As he headed down the corridor for the tube that led up to his headquarters, he heard Marrett's voice behind him.

"Got a minute, Colonel?"

He turned. "Better call me Chet. I think my commission in the Aerospace Force might not be worth much this morning."

Marrett laughed: a strong, healthy, joyful sound. He was too big for this narrow corridor; he needed a much wider setting to accommodate him. "Okay. Chet, look, I've got a question. Maybe it's dumb, but I figured out long ago that there's no such thing as a stupid question, only stupid answers."

Kinsman grinned back at him. "What's the question?"

"Just what in the seven tiers of heaven are you trying to accomplish with this revolution of yours?"

"You want the answer in twenty-five words or less?"

"Less."

They stood there facing each other, the big meteorologist with his heavy hands planted on his hips, Kinsman looking up at him, the rest of the corridor empty and sterile-looking, a row of plastic doors set into aluminum-framed plastic curtainwalls.

"Well, Dr. Marrett . . . "

"Ted."

"All right, Ted. What we're trying to accomplish is peace. No war. No missile strikes. No fighting between Russians and Americans on Earth, at least no nuclear fighting. So there'll be no need to fight on the Moon."

"That's what I thought." Marrett gestured toward the tube hatch. "Goin' upstairs?"

"Yes. To Level Three."

"Good. I'm heading back to the observation bay." He started walking toward the hatch. Kinsman followed. As they padded up the metal steps, circling the thin metal wall that held the cold vacuum of space at bay, Marrett said, "Got another question for you."

In the dim lighting of the tube, Kinsman couldn't see Marrett's face too well. But his voice was low, serious, as it echoed along the metal tube. "What is it?" Kinsman asked.

"Your new nation gonna apply for membership in the UN?"

"I suppose so. Why?"

"Listen, I've been working for the UN for twenty-some years now, watching the best weather-modification work in the world get pissed down the drain because one nation or another blocks it."

"You don't look that old," Kinsman said.

Marrett cast a baleful eye on him. "How do you think I got bald? X-ray treatments?"

"Okay," Kinsman said as they continued climbing the spiraling metal steps. "So your work has been stymied by individual nations."

"And blocs. EuroFed, Paraguay—you name it. They all think of themselves as the one and only outfit on the planet. Nobody else counts. And UNESCO, the whole diddling UN, is helpless as long as one nation refuses to go along with our ideas."

"So?"

Marrett stopped. Two steps above Kinsman, he loomed in the shadowy lighting like a menace from an old Gothic tale. "So here you are," he said quietly, rationally, "pulling off your revolution. You stop the States and Russia from using missiles on each other, but they've still got other ways to fight. Germ warfare or nerve gas or some old manned bombers to drop nukes."

"Maybe," Kinsman admitted. "In time."

"Listen! In the meantime, you want to be recognized as an independent nation . . . What the hell you gonna call yourselves, anyway?"

"Selene."

"Ugh. Okay, Selene, if that's what you want. You think the U.S. and Russia are gonna recognize an independent Selene?"

"No, I suppose not."

"Damned right they won't! And what makes you think any of the other nations are gonna run the risk of alienating the big boys, just to make you feel good?" Marrett leaned down over Kinsman and jabbed a forefinger against his chest. "They won't. Not unless there's something in it for them."

"We can act as an international policeman," Kinsman said, "as long as we control the ABM satellites."

"That's a negative plus."

"Huh?"

"I mean it's the kind of advantage that isn't obvious," Marrett said. "So you prevent a missile war, and all the fallout and crap. That doesn't put any rice on the table in Burma."

"I don't follow." Kinsman got the feeling that Marrett was being deliberately *non sequitur*.

With a sigh, Marrett hunkered down and sat on the stair. His long legs straddled four steps. Kinsman leaned against the tube bulkhead. The metal felt chill against his back.

"Look," Marrett said, with great patience. "Suppose you could go to the smaller nations of the world— especially some of the Southern Hemisphere nations— although the EuroFeds would be interested too, come to think of it—well, anyway, suppose you went to 'em and promised them not only a cop in orbit, but weather control?"

"Weather control?"

"Right. Not modification. *Control*. We can control the goddamn weather all across this planet. Optimize crop yields, improve health, make fortunes for resorts, divert storms, improve fish populations, maybe even save the dolphins before they go the way of the whales—the whole big ball of it. But we need two things—these space stations to operate from, and the political muscle to override the objections of individual nations and their blocs, especially the big powers."

"They're against weather control?"

Marrett frowned. "It's a long and bloody story. Big-power politics. Basically, the big nations are against letting the UN have any real power. The only way weather control can possibly work is on a world-wide basis. You can't slice off a chunk of the atmosphere and separate it from the rest of the world. No single nation can achieve weather control by itself. And the big powers won't let the UN have a shot at it, either."

"Orbital cop and weather control." Kinsman's mind was churning.

"It'd give the UN some godawful power, buddy," Marrett said. "If a nation doesn't behave, we'll just turn off their water."

"You could do that?"

"More or less."

"But that would mean a terrific upheaval in the UN itself. They're not set up for anything like this. You'd have to revamp the whole structure."

"Damned right." Marrett was grinning hugely now.

In those gloomy shadows, with the twisting metal steps trailing off into darkness above and below them, Kinsman felt suspended between—what? Success and failure? Life and death? Heaven and hell?

"Are there people in the UN who'd be willing to consider this?"

"I know one," Marrett said.

"Who?"

"Emanuel De Paolo."

"The Secretary General?"

"The very same."

Wednesday 15 December 1999: 1700 hrs UT

It was precisely noon in Washington, although from the windows of the Oval Office nothing could be seen but the swirling wind-driven snow of the season's first blizzard.

"Big wet flakes," the President said, idly gazing out the windows as he leaned back in his desk chair. His eyes were puffy from lack of sleep, his hair tousled. "The kind that's heavy to shovel. I remember, back in Roxbury, when I was a kid, one year . . ."

The Defense Secretary looked pale, drawn. "Mr. President, there's no time for childhood reminiscences."

The President swiveled around to look at him and the other two men in the room: General Hofstader and the burly, rage-masked advisor.

"Oh, no?" the President asked lightly. "What else can we do? This, eh, colonel—what's his name?"

"Kinsman," Hofstader spat.

"That's right, Kinsman. He's got us stopped, doesn't he? We can't lift a missile off the ground. We can't attack, and we can't be attacked. So there's nothing to do except what we used to do in blizzards back home: sit back and enjoy it."

"What makes you so certain that we can't be attacked?" came the burly man's tortured whisper.

The President blinked in puzzlement and the reflex response of fear. "Why? Do you think . . . ?"

It was eight o'clock in the evening in Moscow, but the same questions were being raised.

"Are we so certain," the Nameless One was asking in

208

his stiletto-thin voice, "that this is not a clever American trick? What guarantee do we have that these lunar rebels will stop an American attack on us?"

The Premier shifted his bulk uneasily in his chair. The long table was almost empty. Only Marshal Prokoff, the Minister of State Security, and the Nameless One were present.

"Didn't they shoot down half a dozen American missiles?" the Premier demanded.

"What are a half-dozen missiles?" the Nameless One asked. "A ruse, a decoy, aimed at lulling us into relaxing our guard. Tomorrow, or next week or next month, they could strike while our defenses are in a state of sleepy lassitude."

"That's right," General Hofstader was saying. "This could all be a goddamned trick to catch us with our pants down."

"And keep us from instant readiness to launch a counterstrike," the Defense Secretary added.

"Or a preemptive strike," Hofstader said.

The burly man whispered harshly, "More than that. While our attention is focused on this drama in space, we still face very real crises here on Earth. The Antarctic coal fields, the battles between our fishing fleets last summer . . ."

". . . and they sank one of our submarines," Marshal Prokoff insisted, waggling one stubby finger in the air. "Do not let this trickery with the satellites blind us to the realities of Earth!"

Wearily the Premier asked, "Then what do you recommend? Clearly we cannot launch a missile strike — for which ill fortune, I think, we should all be grateful."

"Perhaps," the Nameless One said. Then with a thin smile he added, "But I feel it will be necessary to send troops to recapture the orbital stations."

"Can that be done?"

"We will find a way."

"Remember, they have the orbital bombs with them at the space stations," Marshal Prokoff said. "We cannot allow them to hold those weapons over our heads."

The Premier glowered at him. "The bombs that *you* insisted we place in orbit."

The Security Minister cleared his throat. "We should," he said, "arrest the family of this Colonel Leonov, and anyone else who is on the space stations or the lunar base. As a precaution."

"What good would that do?" the Premier grumbled.

"They might become useful hostages."

"Idiot! Think of the hostages *they* have at their mercy!"

"Hostages?"

Rapping the table with his knuckles on each word, the Premier counted, "Moscow, Leningrad, Smolensk, Volgagrad, Kiev . . ."

"Then we're agreed," the Defense Secretary said, "that recapturing the space stations is our first order of business."

"Yes," whispered the burly man.

General Hofstader nodded.

"I'm not so sure," the President said. "How can we get troops up there if they're going to shoot down all our rockets?"

"We'll have to work out a plan," said General Hofstader.

"There are a *lot* of things we'll have to work out," the Defense Secretary agreed.

"Yes," came the angry whisper. "A lot of things."

It was nearing midnight when General Murdock read the TWX for the last time. He was still in his office, at his desk. The lights of Patrick Air Force Base were still dimmed; the red alert had not yet been lifted.

His wife had called three times, and each time he had told her that he'd be home in an hour. He hadn't told her about the TWX. He stared at the flimsy sheet of paper. "Right out in the open. Not even a private communication. Everybody on the base must know about it. They knew about it even before *I* did!"

He was past crying. He had blubbered for an hour when the TWX first arrived. His secretary had tried coffee, bourbon, womanly comforting that went from a

motherly caress to an offer to bed down for the night.
The base chaplain had come in and talked to him
briefly: "It's an investigation—that's all that a court-
martial means. They can't find you guilty of treason or
dereliction of duty." Shaking, Murdock had ordered
him out of his office.

A psychologist, a golf-playing friend of the general,
had dropped by long after the dinner hour: "But why
do you think they're going to blame you, Bob? You had
nothing to do with it."

"I'm the one they can reach. I'm the commanding
officer of the men who rebelled. It's my responsibility.
Have you studied history? Do you remember what happened to General Short, after Pearl Harbor? What do
you think they're going to do to *me?*" He had screamed
these last words.

Prayer didn't help. Neither did tranquilizers. Murdock knew what they were going to do to him. Knew it
quite clearly. "You're killing me, Kinsman," he murmured as he sat at his desk. He was leaning his chubby
forearms heavily on the desk. His uniform was dark
with sweat, despite the gusting air-conditioning that
blew papers across his office. But not the TWX. It was
magnetically pinned to the deskpad. Nothing could
blow it away.

Court-martial. Inquiry. Trial.

Brigadier General Robert G. Murdock rose from his
desk and walked unsteadily to the bathroom off one
side of the office. Idly, he thought how much easier it
would be if he had a gun. But he hadn't fired one in
years, and had never used one in anger.

"I've tried never to hurt anyone," he said to himself,
and his voice sounded little short of whining. "Not even
Kinsman. All these years he's laughed at me, made a
fool out of me. And now he's killed me."

He turned on the hot-water tap, then reached for the
medicine chest above the sink for a razor blade.

Thursday 16 December 1999: 2250 hrs UT

"Retrofire in five minutes; please prepare for landing."

The pilot's voice coming through the tinny speaker in the seatback ahead of him woke Kinsman. For an instant he didn't know where he was; disoriented, he felt a flash of panic surge through him. Then it settled into place: the lunar shuttle. The young officers around him, the safety harness crossing his chest and thighs, the windowless metal tube of the spacecraft's passenger section. "I must have dozed off," he muttered.

The kid beside him grinned. "About four hours ago, sir."

Kinsman grunted and rubbed his eyes. It had been a long flight, at minimum-energy boost, but a busy one. He had spent more than twenty hours straight in urgent communications with Selene, the space stations—where he had left Chris Perry in charge—and with Ted Marrett, going into more and more detail about the politics of global weather control.

There had been a flood of messages from Earthside: urgent, angry, inquisitive, apprehensive. Kinsman had Perry or Harriman answer most of them. He refused to speak to anyone lower than the President of the United States or the Premier of the Soviet Union. With a grin, he admitted, That guarantees I won't have to handle any calls. The heads of state would never call him—it would be too big an admission for them to make; it just wasn't done in the protocol-above-all world of international diplomacy.

He spoke briefly with Ellen at Selene, using the compact view-screen before him. All was quiet. Apparently

212

both sides were still on red alert, but there had been no further warlike incidents, no further rocket launches, no further threats or blusterings from Washington or Moscow.

They're playing wait-and-see, Kinsman knew. They're digesting the new situation, running it through their computers and committees and think tanks, trying to figure out what to do next.

"Retrofire in thirty seconds."

We've got to get Marrett back down to New York, Kinsman realized. He's got to talk to De Paolo. We're going to need weather control, even if it's just a threat or a promise, to give us some leverage with the big powers.

The braking rockets fired, and Kinsman felt a firm but gentle hand press him down into his foam cushion seat. There was no noise from the rocket engines, really; only a shuddering vibration that he could feel in his bones.

He was still trying to decide whether the pilot had fired three bursts or four, when he realized they were down. The familiar feel of lunar weight enveloped him as the pilot sang out, "Last stop: the free and independent nation of Selene. Population: one thousand and umpty-two. Everybody off the bus!"

Kinsman grinned. *Home sweet home.* Then he realized that he was indeed home. Ellen was here, and Harriman and Frank Colt and all the other people and things that made this part of the universe his home.

He had been sitting up at the front end of the passenger compartment, and most of the other men and women aboard lined up at the hatch ahead of him. One of the youngsters turned as Kinsman stepped into the aisle between the seats: "If you'd like to go out first, sir . . ."

He shook his head. "No, that's all right. Go on ahead."

The hatch was unsealed within a few minutes and Kinsman shuffled with the others through the flexible access tube that connected with the airlock of Selene's main dome. It felt like a long walk. Behind him was the excitement, the terror, the passion of action—the swift, fearful climax of so many years of self-doubt, so many weeks of indecision. Now it was done, and men had died because of it. *I killed them.* But strangely he felt no guilt. Only weariness, and the beginnings of dread.

Kinsman realized that his revolution—if it really was one—had only begun. *The fighting may be over but the real struggle has only started. Now we have to make it stick. Make a nation of little more than a thousand people stay independent of the eight billions of Earth. We've got a long lever and a place to stand—but is it enough?*

The inner airlock hatch was closed when Kinsman stepped into the small metal compartment. "Something wrong?" he asked the man ahead of him.

The officer shrugged. "Dunno. It was open and people were going through, then somebody outside yelled 'Stand by,' and they shut the damned hatch in my face."

Before Kinsman could go to the wall phone, the hatch swung open again. The young officer shrugged and stepped through and Kinsman followed him out onto the floor of the main dome.

It was filled with people. Off to his right, a motley collection of musicians struck up a nearly unrecognizable version of "Hail to the Chief," playing a battered slide trombone, a dozen or more recorders and kazoos, a few homemade instruments, at least one violin, a few drums made from oil cans, and a dulcimer. Everyone was shouting and cheering. Kinsman didn't even have the strength to stagger. He stood frozen to the spot. The trombonist was *smiling* as he played!

The crowd was still yelling as the band stopped, making the dome reverberate with their cheers. Hugh Harriman was somehow beside Kinsman, pounding him on the back. Leonov was there too, grinning and kissing everyone in sight, man or woman. "Congratulations, Chet!" Harriman was yelling into his ear. "We ran an election this afternoon and you lost! You're the Chief Administrator of this crazy nation."

"And I am Deputy Chief," Leonov beamed. "In charge of immigration. I get to interview all the girls who want to come and live here!"

It was a dizzy, crazy whirl. Ellen came out of the

crowd and took his arm as the whole population descended on him, laughing, cheering, shaking hands, telling him and each other that they were ready to defend their new nation and to follow his lead.

Kinsman lost all track of time. Somehow, after what seemed like hours of ear-numbing noise and crowds and music and folk dancing that snaked all across the dome and down the corridors below ground, a small group of them ended up in Ellen's quarters: Harriman, Leonov, Jill and Alexei Landau, Ellen herself.

"Immigration?" Kinsman was asking. His head was spinning, and there was a tall drink in his hand. Ellen was perched on the arm of the couch, beside him.

Leonov nodded vigorously. He had a bottle in one hand and a tiny shot glass in the other. He was standing, his feet were planted solidly on the grassy floor, but his body weaved slowly from side to side. Kinsman couldn't decide if it was his own eyesight or the Russian's stabilization system that was going kaput.

Leonov boomed jovially, "Do you realize how many requests for immigration visas we have received in the past twenty-four hours? Thousands! From almost every nation in the world."

"We've already been officially recognized by several nations," Ellen said. "Starting with Israel."

Before Kinsman could reply, Harriman rubbed his fingernails on the chest of his zipsuit. "I'm not without influence among certain civilized nations of Earth, I'll have you know. Besides," he added, "this is the only nation in the world that they haven't been thrown out of."

"Too much," Kinsman muttered. "It's all too much."

"You're entirely right," Jill Myers said, fixing Kinsman with a professional medical gaze. "You look like you've been through several wringers. I want you in my office at oh-nine-hundred hours tomorrow morning."

"You mean *this* morning," Alexei said softly. "It's already past three."

"To bed, all of you," Jill commanded. "Can't have our Chief Administrator collapsing his first day on the job."

Harriman pursed his lips. "There are several lewd remarks I could make, but considering your exalted position, Mr. Chief Administrator, I will maintain a kindly and courteous silence."

"You're just sucking up for a good political job," Kinsman said.

"Right you are! How about making me Minister of Education?"

"No, I want you to be our Foreign Minister."

Harriman was aghast. "Me? A diplomat? One of those mincing faggots?"

"You'd start a new trend in foreign affairs. You've already influenced one nation, by your own admission."

"I won't wear striped pants!"

"Hugh, you don't have to wear any pants, if you don't want to. What I need is—"

"Tomorrow!" Jill said firmly. She got up from her chair, and Alexei rose with her, towering above her tiny form. Ellen got up too, and they all drifted toward the door. But Kinsman stayed as the others left.

Harriman's voice was still echoing down the corridor as Kinsman said to Ellen, "They didn't kill me."

"They tried," she said.

He reached out to push the door shut, but she didn't let go of it.

"You did a fine job, taking care of everything while I was gone."

"Thanks."

He didn't want to make polite conversation. He didn't want to talk about anything, or even to think. Not about politics, or war or death.

"Ellen—let's make love."

"Is that what you want?" she asked, her voice flat and unemotional.

"Yes."

"And then tomorrow you'll go back to your office and be the Chief Administrator."

He nodded.

She let go of the door and shook her head. "I've got so much will power when you're not around." With a rueful smile she put her arms around him. "We're not good for each other, you know."

"No, I don't know. Tell me about it." He pushed the door shut and they headed for the bedroom.

Jill Myers took up the first couple of hours of the new day, running Kinsman through an extensive physical, clucking and frowning and shaking her head as the readouts came from the medical sensors and their integrating computer.

"You think this heart murmur of yours is just a dodge to fool the brass Earthside," she scolded. "Well, take a look at this EKG." She handed him a ribbon of plastic tape across her bare little desk.

Kinsman examined the jagged line. "Bad?"

"It's got the shakes. Have you been feeling any chest pains? Sharp twinges along your left arm or elsewhere?"

He shrugged. "A little discomfort when I was down in the high-gee section of the space station, that's all."

"That's all." She glowered at him, spoke a prescription for pills into the computer input mike, and then waved him out of her cubicle of an office. He got as far as the door, a single step.

"You're not immortal," Jill said sharply. "We're all depending on you, Chet. But you'll be no good to any of us dead. Slow down."

"Sure." He grinned at her. "The worst is over. It's going to be downhill from here on in."

It wasn't until he was halfway down the corridor toward the water factory that he realized how many different connotations "downhill" could have.

Ernie Waterman was embarrassed to see him. The dour-faced engineer actually blushed when Kinsman came on the scene. They were at the rock crushers, where an explosion had wrecked two of the six conveyer belts that carried pulverized rock from the giant machines toward the electric arcs.

"I . . . I figured as long as I'm here . . ." Waterman stammered, over the clamor of technicians yelling to each other and the spark and hiss of welding lasers. The four working crushers pounded out a *basso* accompaniment to the higher-pitched noises. "Well . . . I figured

I might as well help out. It's better than sitting around doing nothing, isn't it?"

"That's fine, Ernie," Kinsman said, trying to keep his voice even while yelling over the din of the construction crew. "I appreciate your help."

"How soon do I have to leave?"

"Leave?"

An air compressor screamed to life, and Waterman raised his shrill voice even louder and leaned toward Kinsman's ear. Their hard hats actually touched. "When are you going to be shipping me back Earthside?"

"Nobody's going Earthside," Kinsman yelled back, "and nothing from Earthside is coming up here—not until we get some of the politics straightened out. And whether you leave Selene or not is your decision, Ernie. I can't send you back to a wheelchair. If you can stomach what we're doing here—or even better, come over to our way of thinking—you're welcome to stay as long as you like."

Waterman's mouth moved, but Kinsman couldn't hear what he said.

"I mean it, Ernie," he shouted. "As long as you don't work against us, you're welcome to live here."

"You'd . . . trust me?"

"Why not? Aren't you an honest man?"

Waterman merely shook his head in wonderment.

Much of the afternoon was spent going over personnel lists and combining the American files with Leonov's. The two of them worked in the Russian personnel office, alone except for the Lunagrad computer terminal that sat on a table in the middle of the large room. The Moonbase computer had not yet been fully linked with the Russian machine.

Leonov had to translate the Cyrillic symbols. Kinsman had the American files phoned into the Russian data bank. He frowned as Pat Kelly's file appeared on the tiny phone screen. Kelly was still confined to quarters, and under a psychiatrist's care. He had requested immediate transfer for himself and family back to Earthside.

I failed with him, Kinsman told himself. He worked

so close to me, saw everything I saw, everything I did. And yet he couldn't make the jump, couldn't change his thinking enough to grasp what had to be done. He'd rather see America destroyed than changed.

When he returned to his own quarters, just before dinner time, he found Frank Colt sitting in his living room. Alone.

"I was wondering when you'd show up," Kinsman said as he let the front door slide shut.

"Yeah. I steered away from the partying last night. Figured you earned a celebration without me screwing it up for you."

"I looked for you in the crowd. I wanted to thank you for staying out of mischief while I was away." Kinsman crossed the room and sat on the slingchair next to Colt, who was perched tensely on the couch.

"Took some guts for you to trust me," Colt said, eyeing Kinsman carefully.

"Took some guts for you to accept the responsibility, feeling the way you do."

"Yeah, maybe so."

"Do you still feel that way? That what we're doing is wrong?"

Colt didn't answer right away. When he did, it was with a silent nod of his head.

"Even though you can see that the Lunagrad people are with us, and that we're both acting to save the United States—and Russia?"

Hunching forward, fists on knees, Colt answered, "Okay, okay, you're a bunch of do-gooders and you've got the best interests of mankind at heart. I still can't buy it. I'm sorry, Chet, that's just the way it is. I want out. I want to go back to Earthside."

"But Frank, can't you see—"

"I can see the whole fucking thing! And I know which side I'm on. And it ain't your side. I'm sorry, man. Maybe I'm wrong and you're right. But that's where it's at."

Kinsman searched his friend's face. It was a thinly masked mixture of pain and stubbornness. "There's nothing we can do?"

"Not a damned thing. Just send me back Earthside, as soon as you can."

"There might be trouble for you down there. They might not believe that you were against us."

"I'll take my chances."

With a shake of his head, Kinsman said, "Frank, I just hate like hell—"

"Do it!" Colt snapped. "Stop thinking you can win everybody over with logic and a sweet smile. I am what I am, and you can't change that."

"And you *won't* change it."

For an instant, Colt looked as if he'd lash out at Kinsman. But the fire in his eyes dimmed and he answered only, "That's right. I won't change."

Something from the back of Kinsman's mind surfaced, and he heard himself say, "Okay, Frank. You can be on the next shuttle to Alpha. I'll set up a special flight to Earthside from there. There are a few civilians—scientists and such—who want to get back. You can go with them." *And Marrett.*

"Fine."

Kinsman sank back in the slingchair, thinking, You're using him, letting him be the excuse for getting Marrett to the UN people. "Is there anything else, Frank?"

Colt gritted his teeth before answering. "Yeah, one more thing." He sounded disgusted, ashamed.

"What is it?"

"Murdock . . ."

"Oh, shit. What's old wetpants done now?"

Colt's eyes wouldn't meet Kinsman's. "Ellen asked me to tell you. She didn't know how to break it. He's dead. Committed suicide two days ago."

"Suicide?"

"Sliced his wrists."

Murdock? That pudgy kettledrum of a man? The guy we used to tease until he'd throw a tantrum? Clowns don't slice their wrists. It can't be for real! "But why?"

Colt's voice was barely audible. "They were looking for a scapegoat. Told him they were going to investigate, court-martial him."

"Oh, for God's sake." The bastards. Kicking the

weakest one around. I should have known. "Did he leave a note or anything?" Kinsman asked.

"A taped message. It was addressed to you. The communications people just got to it this afternoon—they've been swamped and this had no priority at all."

"Addressed to me?" Kinsman felt his insides going hollow.

"I burned it," Colt said. "You don't want to hear what was on it."

"What did it say?"

"It was shitty—"

"What did it say?"

Colt took a breath. "He said, 'Thanks for everything, Kinsman. This is the reward I get for covering up your murder of that Russian girl. I should have crucified you when I had the chance.' "

Thursday 23 December 1999: 1400 hrs UT

It was 9 A.M. in New York. Ted Marrett paced impatiently past the floor-to-ceiling windows of the plushly carpeted office, high in the UN's Secretariat Building. A sleety rain pelted the windows; across the turgid, oily East River, Brooklyn and Queens were only a gray smear.

"You're going to wear out your boots," said Tuli Noyon. He was sitting placidly in a leather easy chair, his round, flat Mongol face a picture of stoic calm. He looked as if he would be perfectly at home atop a shaggy pony, with a short bow strung over his shoulder and a warrior's padded armor and helmet on. Instead he wore a bright yellow business zipsuit, and the only unusual item he carried was a pocket-sized isotope-powered electronic computer.

"Better than wearing out the seat of my pants," Marrett growled. He was in old-fashioned pants and thigh-length dashiki—and he puffed hard on the stump of a cigar clamped between his teeth.

Tuli silently thanked the gods for the ventilation system that sucked up the fetid cigar smoke. "He said he would be here shortly after nine."

"That's what it is now." Marrett tapped his wrist watch. "Shortly after nine. Where is he?"

"He does have other business."

"Nothing as important as this! Holy hell, Tuli, we've been trying to see him for a solid four days!"

"The Secretary General doesn't often make time to see a couple of lowly UNESCO engineers. His schedule is arranged—"

Marrett wheeled toward the Mongol. "Don't give me that humble oriental crap! I know you better. You're just as worked up about this as I am."

Noyon allowed himself to smile. "Perhaps I did use my consanguinity with the Mongolian ambassador to further our cause."

"You betcha."

"But it won't do us any good if you're a nervous wreck when . . ."

The door opened. Marrett turned, taking the cigar from his lips. Noyon stood up.

Emanuel De Paolo was a slight, frail-looking man. His skin was dark, his hair gray as volcanic ash. His eyes were utterly black, but alive, youthful and alert in an aging man's face. His suit had a very conservative cut, with cuffed trousers and a full-length jacket over his soft turtleneck sweater. But the suit was Andes blue, and the sweater was Incan gold. "Gentlemen," he said, in a soft, musical voice. "Please do not be formal. Sit, sit."

Marrett eased his big frame slowly into the chair that Noyon had been using, without taking his eyes off the Secretary General. The Mongol engineer wordlessly moved aside and took another chair. De Paolo relaxed in a webchair of Scandinavian wood and rope.

"May I ask you please to be brief," the Secretary General said pleasantly. "There is a meeting of the Security Council this afternoon, and I have several appointments on my calendar to clear before the session begins."

Marrett glanced at his friend. Noyon said, "I'm not sure of how much the Mongolian Ambassador told you."

"Very little," said the Secretary General. "I must confess that he seemed to be enjoying making this as mysterious as possible."

"It's not mysterious," Marrett snapped. "It's no more mysterious than the rain falling out there."

An hour later an aide knocked discreetly on the door of the room to remind the Secretary General of his ten-fifteen appointment. De Paolo told him to cancel it. The phone rang once, and De Paolo spoke harshly into it in Portuguese. They were not interrupted again, except for when the Secretary General suggested that they have some food and drinks brought in.

The Security Council meeting began without him. By mid-afternoon, De Paolo was saying, "Can all this really be done?"

Marrett was chewing the soggy end of his last cigar. It had gone dead hours earlier. "If you mean technically, the answer is yes. Sure, it'll be some time before we can tailor-make the weather on a small scale, but we know enough right now to ruin a nation's crops, any time we want to. And we've been able to steer major storm systems for years."

"Within limits," Noyon added.

The Secretary General had taken off his jacket. He dabbed at his forehead nervously. "This is fantastic. Do you realize what power you are speaking of? Do you have any conception of what you are offering?"

"It *is* awesome," Noyon quietly agreed.

De Paolo pulled himself out of his chair and walked to the window. It was no longer raining, but the sky was still gray. "I wish I hadn't agreed to listen to you," he said, staring out at the decaying city. "I wish I had never heard this. The temptation . . ."

Marrett tapped his watch. "In exactly five minutes you'll see some blue sky, and the sun will break through."

The Secretary General glared over his shoulder at the big man. "You're certain of it?"

Nodding, Marrett answered, "Just as certain as I am that the UN—or *somebody*—has got to grab this power. We can't keep it secret much longer. There are plenty of meteorologists, weather people, who're aware of the potential. Once they work up the guts to admit to themselves that the weather can be controlled all over the globe—it'll be the next big international crisis."

"And this Kinsman," De Paolo asked, "he is an honorable man? He can be trusted?"

"I think so. He wants to have his new nation admitted to the UN. He wants to enforce world peace."

The Secretary General shook his head. "It's frightening. Too tempting."

"You mean the potential power?" Noyon asked.

"That," the old man nodded, "and the responsibility. We have all wrung our hands about the United Nations' political impotence. But this changes everything. Everything."

"It's using our technical power to obtain political power," Marrett said.

"I'm not certain that it is the right thing to do. I'm not at all sure that we're ready for this. It's the use of force—a different kind of force, perhaps—but still . . ."

"Force is the only way to move an object," Marrett said.

"Newtonian physics," said the Secretary General. He smiled wanly. "You see? I am not entirely ignorant of science."

He turned back to the window. A lance of sunlight broke through the gray clouds. A slice of blue could be seen. "Your prediction was too conservative," he said to Marrett. "Five minutes have not elapsed yet."

Marrett shrugged. "I'm always on the conservative side."

"Are you?" The Secretary General squared his shoulders, like a man who has finally decided to accept a burden, no matter how heavy. "Very well. I suppose I should meet with this Kinsman. Do you think he would be willing to come here to New York?"

The Florida sunshine was strong and brilliant, coming out of a sky so blue that it needed occasional puffs of white cumulus clouds for contrast.

Frank Colt squinted, even behind his polarized glasses. The glare coming up from the cement runways and taxi aprons off to his right was considerable. In summer it would be almost intolerable. But I can handle it, Colt told himself. That, and anything else they care to send my way.

The two Air Policemen walking in stride a few paces behind him—both well over six feet tall, football physiques, big automatic pistols holstered on their hips—followed Colt wherever he went. Technically, he was under house arrest and confined to this base until the masterminds in Washington decided whether he could be blamed for any responsibility in the lunar rebellion.

Colt grinned sardonically. Not every dude has his own bodyguards following him around. Status symbol.

Overhead a silvery speck started to materialize into an executive jetcopter, and Colt could hear the *whush-whush whush* of its huge rotor blades even over the shrill scream of the turbine engines.

Colt and his two guards came to a parade rest, quite unconsciously, at the edge of the yellow painted circle marking the special helicopter landing area. A service truck was racing across the concrete off in the distance, coming up to plug in electricity for the copter's communications, lights and air conditioning.

The jetcopter settled down on the concrete landing apron in a scream of gale-blown grit and pebbles. As it squatted on its springy landing gear and the rotors slowed, Colt looked up and saw that it bore no insignia except a standard USAF star and the identification number H003.

The "three" in the number struck Colt at once. Number one's for the President and two's for the Vice President, he knew. He was impressed with the man inside, the man who had come to see him.

The copter's main hatch swung upward, and a lieutenant in spotless uniform stood in the hatchway as metal stairs trundled out and touched down on the concrete. He looked at Colt and nodded, sallow-faced, pinch-eyed, very professional looking. Colt went to the stairs and up into the copter. His two guards stood at the bottom of the stairs, out in the sun. In the week that they had been escorting Colt everywhere, they had yet to have a word of conversation with him.

Get a good tan, fellas, Colt silently wished them.

Inside, the copter was frigid. The lieutenant was tall enough to have to duck his head as they stepped through a smaller hatch, set into a gray-painted partition. Colt stepped into a sort of conference room—a compartment, really: spacious for a helicopter, perhaps, but cramped by the three people already seated there.

Colt snapped to attention and saluted. The weary-looking two-star general seated across the conference table flicked a salute back to him. He was flanked by a puffy-faced colonel and a civilian—a man in a dark suit who was hunched over, his burly shoulders bulging strangely inside the suit jacket, his face seemingly stamped with the red heat of constant pain.

There was one lightweight plastic chair unoccupied. The general gestured to it; Colt sat down. The lieutenant stayed at the hatchway, behind Colt's back. He had noticed that the lieutenant wore an Air Police armband, but carried no gun. Standing behind him, though, it would be possible for him to kill Colt in a half-dozen ways with his hands, if he were told to.

"I am Major General Cianelli," said the general. "This is my aide, Colonel Sullivan."

Colt nodded. But two-star generals don't get chopper number three, he thought. This bird must belong to the civilian stud. He turned expectantly to the red-faced man, who was sitting on his left.

"My name is not important," he whispered, harsh and labored.

For a moment there was silence in the conference compartment. Colt could hear the distant muffled drone of the service truck's generators, nothing else.

General Cianelli looked pained. "We are here to review your case, that is, the statements you made to the investigating board earlier this week."

"Yessir," Colt said, going into his professional act. "I'd be happy to clear up any questions you have."

"You said that you led a group of counterinsurgents," Colonel Sullivan said, surprising Colt with his high tenor voice, "and attempted to destroy the water production facility."

"Yessir. We were only partly successful, though. We were overwhelmed by sheer numbers before we could do more than superficial damage."

"Only superficial damage?" came the tortured whisper from his left.

"I heard, while I was under arrest afterward, that our action cut down Moonbase's water production capability by about one-third—"

"Ah?"

"—but that the damage could be repaired in a few weeks."

"A few weeks," Sullivan echoed. "That means that the rebels will be short on drinking water?"

"Not likely, sir," Colt responded. "The water facility can produce enough drinking and irrigation water for both Moonbase and Lunagrad. They may be short on rocket propellant, though, since the hydrogen and oxygen are electrolyzed from the water that the facility produces."

General Cianelli frowned. "What sort of man is this Colonel Kinsman?"

Careful, man! They know all about both of you. "He was a close friend of mine, sir. I've always regarded him as well-meaning, very likable, but politically soft."

They went on and on, for hours. Colt carefully maneuvered around the fact that he could have shot Kinsman, or could have attempted a counter-coup while the rebels were seizing the space stations. Nobody else from Selene's down here yet, he gambled.

Gradually it became clear to Colt that they were no longer questioning his loyalty or his actions during the rebellion. They were probing for information about the rebels themselves, Kinsman especially, and the defenses that the space stations and lunar settlement possessed.

"Sir," he said to the general, "am I going to face a court-martial?"

General Cianelli glanced at the angry-faced civilian. "That's a matter to be decided—"

The burly man silenced him with the barest movement of his hand. To Colt, he said, "There will be no court-martial. Quite the opposite. We are seeking a knowledgeable officer to assume General Murdock's command. A man who knows the space stations well enough to show us how to recapture them."

Colt closed his eyes momentarily, and saw a general's stars. "Recapture the space stations," he echoed, looking straight into the civilian's pain-shot eyes. "I can show you how."

Cianelli looked surprised. Sullivan smiled. But it was the angry man who answered him: "How? The rebels have command of all the ABM satellites. They will destroy any rocket vehicle boosting from Earth."

Colt faced him. "You've got to get them to agree to allow one flight to come up to Alpha. That's all you need: just one flight."

The man stared at Colt, his face red and scowling. Neither of the two Air Force officers dared to speak. Finally he said, "Show me."

Colt asked, "Do you have a view screen?"

The civilian touched a stud set into the tabletop before him. One whole wall of the compartment glowed palely.

"And a computer terminal?"

He looked up at the lieutenant, who was still on his feet behind Colt. "Get it."

It took some fiddling around with the terminal—a compact rolling unit, about the size of a typing table—before Colt could get the displays he wanted, from the files at Patrick Air Force Base.

He showed them view-screen pictures of Space Station Alpha, together with the record of the number of military personnel in the normal crew there.

"Even if we assume that Kinsman's put extra people in Alpha to protect the station," Colt said, "he couldn't have more than a hundred military men aboard."

"An aerospace rocketplane carries only fifty passengers," General Cianelli objected.

"Yeah, but they could be armed troops. And there's enough cargo space in the bottom deck for fifty more."

The general sat up straighter. "We'd have to modify the rocketplane, give the cargo deck life-support capability—but that can be done."

"Certainly," Colonel Sullivan said.

Colt went on to show how the station could be overrun quickly and efficiently by a hundred or so well-armed and well-trained men.

"They'd have to be well led, too," Colt added.

"And you will be their leader?" the burly man asked.

"No," Colt said. "Not me. I'm not an infantryman."

Ignoring that, Cianelli asked, "So we recapture Alpha. What good does that do?"

Smiling, Colt realized he had them hooked. "Okay." He touched the computer keyboard again. The view screen showed an animated drawing of Earth, with hundreds of satellites revolving around it. With a touch of his finger, Colt wiped out all the satellites except the three American space stations: Alpha, Beta and Gamma. "Now, look at the area each of the stations 'sees' as they hang up there in synchronous orbit."

The view screen showed pale-colored cones emanating from the three stations down to the Earth. Alpha's cone of influence, a pastel blue on the screen, covered almost the entire Western Hemisphere: nearly all the United States was shaded light blue.

"Alpha's the key to the whole situation," Colt said. "Beta's coverage overlaps a little, of course, but there's plenty of room here in the States to launch a whole squadron of rocketplanes—once we've got control of Alpha and the Russian station over the mid-Atlantic. Then we can stock Alpha with enough troops to grab the other stations, both American and Russian." He clicked off the view-screen display. "If we can move fast enough, and we do everything *exactly* right, we can take over the whole ABM network—everything!"

"We'll have the Reds staring into our gun barrels!" Sullivan exulted.

"And we can march in on Moonbase any time we want to," Cianelli said. "They'll be defenseless. They'll fall like a ripe plum."

"Lunagrad, too," Colt added.

The other man said nothing. They all turned to him. He breathed a deep, labored exhalation. Then, "Consider yourself an acting colonel, Mr. Colt. The general here will process your orders immediately. You will implement the plan you have just outlined. If it succeeds you will be raised in rank to brigadier general."

Cianelli's mouth tightened to a bloodless line. Sullivan's eyes were evasive.

Colt said, "One more thing."

The man's angry face seemed to swell and get even redder.

"I want," Colt said, "to meet the President of the United States. It's purely a personal thing. I want to meet the top man, just for a minute. I want to shake his hand."

The anger subsided, slightly. He almost smiled. "Of course. It will be arranged."

"When can we strike?" General Cianelli asked suddenly. "It seems this entire strategy depends on the rebels' allowing us to send a rocketplane to Alpha."

The angry man mused, "Intelligence reports that many nations have forwarded requests for emigration to the lunar rebels. There have even been some Americans asking for exit permission."

"Americans?" Sullivan looked shocked.

"They will be reeducated," the burly man said. "We have always had fools and traitors in our midst—this is a good way to get them to identify themselves for us."

"Christmas Eve," Colt said.

"What?"

"Or Christmas Day. Get Kinsman to accept the first flight of immigrants on Christmas Day."

"Impossible!" Cianelli shook his head. "We can't pick shock troops and train them for this mission and modify a rocketplane by tomorrow or the next day."

Colt frowned. "Kinsman's a sentimentalist, a romantic. He'd buy the Christmas thing."

"What about New Year's?" Sullivan asked.

The three of them were looking at Colt, waiting for his reaction. "New Year's *Eve*," he said. "That way they can spend their first day of the new century—the new millennium—aboard the space station in their new nation."

"Didn't I read somewhere that the new millennium doesn't really start until next year—2001? Is that right?" Sullivan wondered.

"Doesn't matter," Colt countered. "Kinsman will buy the New Year's Eve bit. And everybody counts the change from 1999 to 2000 as the millennium—nobody gives a crap about the purists." Colt used the slight profanity very deliberately. Nobody reacted to it at all. You got 'em, baby, he told himself.

"New Year's Eve it will be, then," the burly man grated.

Before the sun set that day, Colt's guards disappeared. He was ushered into plush quarters and a big office, where he found a pair of silver colonel's eagles on his new desk, together with the paperwork of his promotion. "They work fast," he muttered to himself.

He fingered the eagle insignia. "Only two pieces of silver. Judas got thirty."

Looking out the window of his new office, he could see the pale outline of the rising Moon in the still-bright sky. "I ain't gonna hang myself, though." Yet his voice sounded bitter, even to himself.

Saturday 25 December 1999: 1612 hrs UT

"It's been a busy day," Kinsman said.

"Haven't they all?" replied Ellen.

They were sitting in the living room of his quarters, watching the start of the buggy race on the wall screen across from the sofa.

"I guess they have, at that," Kinsman admitted. He hadn't seen Ellen since the night of his return from Alpha, except for two brief business talks in his office. At the second of them, he had appointed her deputy director of personnel for Selene, under a former Russian psychologist.

Selene's first Christmas of independence had been celebrated by a huge dinner in the central plaza, with everyone bringing their own food, plus something extra for the communal buffet. More than a thousand people sat on the grass and ate picnic style, celebrating the holiday together regardless of nationality, religion or politics.

After three and a half hours of feasting, the buggy race had begun. Kinsman and Leonov officiated at the countdown, up in the main dome. Then Kinsman had asked Ellen to have a drink with him.

Now they watched the ungainly lunar buggies lumbering across the uneven ground at speeds of up to ten kilometers per hour, heading for the crater Opelt. It would take them two days to complete the nine-hundred-kilometer round trip.

The racing buggies were standard lunar surface rovers—but barely recognizable. They all had bubble-shaped canopies up front where the crew sat; bulging cockpits that looked like insect's eyes and gave the term "buggy" a double meaning. There the similarities ended and individual expression took command. Some of the buggies were wheeled, others tracked. One walked stiffly on sharp-angled praying mantis legs that ended in spongy-looking hooves. Several had weird multicolored wings sprouting from them: solar panels designed to intercept different wavelengths of sunlight and convert them into the electricity that ran the motors. Some had boxy collections of fuel cells running their lengths, and one buggy had a steam generator and a solar mirror atop it, just behind the cockpit. Their colors were all garish, and not for esthetic reasons alone. Each crew wanted to be easily spotted by searchers if their buggy broke down on the desolate lunar plain.

Kinsman sat on the sofa with a drink in his hand and Ellen beside him, watching the slow-motion race. Without a cloud of dust, without a hint of noise, the buggies scrabbled toward the nearby horizon, climbing slowly over the rises in the bare lunar plain and wallowing in the shallow spots, like turtles seeking the sea.

His mind flashed a memory of roaring balls-out in an F-18 thirty meters above the Mojave floor, throttle to the firewall, afterburner screaming, cactus and rocks and sand blurring into one continuous barely seen swatch of gray-brown as he focused his eyes on the mesa leaping up in front of him. Then barely a nudge of the yoke and she stood on her tail and hurtled skyward while the safety suit hissed and squeezed at him, and he flipped her into a tight barrel roll just for the sheer hell of it.

Nevermore. He shook his head.

"Chet?" Ellen broke his reverie.

"Huh? What is it?"

"I just realized . . . You didn't get me anything for Christmas, did you?"

"Oh, for . . . No, I didn't." He felt alarmed and foolish. "I forgot all about it. I'm sorry."

But she was grinning at him. "No, no, don't worry about it. Because I didn't think to get you anything, either."

He grunted. "Two of the great all-time romantics, that's what we are."

"It's a silly custom, anyway."

The phone buzzed before he could reply. Kinsman punched it on.

Hugh Harriman's face took form on the screen at the end of the sofa. He was wearing his pixie expression. "Am I interrupting anything?" he leered.

"Yes. We're planting a mistletoe tree. What do you want, Hugh?"

"While you two have been playing all day at your infantile games," Harriman answered, "I have been having many hours of earnest and fruitful discussion with my fellow diplomats Earthside."

Kinsman sat up a little straighter. "On Christmas Day?"

"You sound like Bob Cratchit. Yes, on Christmas Day. It hasn't been easy to put all the pieces together, since nobody wants to go on record with any of this. It's all under the table, highly unofficial and all that."

"For Chrissakes, Hugh, you're sounding more like a Foggy Bottom bureaucrat every day! What the hell are you talking about?"

"Well!" Harriman put on his injured air, but let it evaporate immediately. "Okay, here's the story. One: Marrett called early this morning and told me that you could expect a personal invitation from the Secretary General of the United Nations to address the General Assembly in a special session. As a private person, mind you, not as a head of state. But he will invite you officially only if he knows beforehand that you'll accept. Can't afford to lose face and all that shit."

Kinsman felt his breath coming faster. "When?"

"Before the week is out."

Ellen moved closer to Kinsman. "Will the American government allow someone from Selene to land there?"

"My dear child, what do you think I've been trying to arrange all day long? Do you think I'd miss the feasting and girl-goosing of this festive occasion for sheer lack of team spirit?"

"Cut the crap, Hugh. What did you accomplish?"

"Plenty, if I say so myself." He hesitated only a moment. "I explained to Marrett that our position with the Yankee *Federales* is rather delicate. He understood, and said the UN had already requested a safe-conduct for you and all those in your party."

"So?"

"So while I was wondering whether I should try to get a call through to the American State Department—knowing that nobody who could exert any authority would be available on Christmas Day—I received a call from an old chum of yours: *Colonel* Franklin Delano Roosevelt Colt."

"Colonel?"

"Seems Frank's rising fast in the Earthside chain of command. He was wearing a bird colonel's eagles."

"He's at Patrick?"

"Right. Apparently they've let him take over Murdock's desk."

Sonofabitch!

"And," Harriman went on, "this request from the UN for handling a party of visitors from Selene has already reached his level. Approved by, no less, the President of the United States hisself."

"You mean it's all set?"

Harriman nodded and scratched at his goatee. "Not only have they moved faster than anyone in Washington has since the riots of eighty-five, but they seem to be going out of their way to be nice to us."

"What do you mean?"

"They're asking permission to send up a shipment of people from all over the world who've asked to emigrate from their native lands to Selene. Leonov's kids might be among them."

Kinsman leaned against the sofa's foam padding. "I don't get it. Why are they so accommodating, all of a sudden?"

"I asked myself the same question," Harriman replied. "There are several possible answers."

"Such as?"

"Well, for one thing, Colt's probably having some influence. He must be telling them that we really mean the United States no harm—and that an independent

Selene friendly to the U.S. would be better than a Selene that's hostile."

Kinsman nodded.

"Then, too, the think-tank people must have figured out by now that we could easily become allies of the Soviet Union, which would be disastrous for the U.S. Another reason for them to treat us carefully."

"Go on."

Harriman shrugged. "There's also world opinion—the big, bad U.S. picking on a helpless little new nation. That doesn't count for much, I think, but it might explain the request to send us a token bunch of immigrants."

Trojan Horse? flickered through Kinsman's mind. "I want to know exactly who these immigrants are—complete data on each of them."

"Right."

"You've had a busy day."

Harriman grinned toothily. "Yes. It's been very rewarding. I even spoke briefly to the Russian ambassador to the United Nations. Marrett told me where to find him; he'd canceled a holiday trip home. It looks as if the Russians won't be averse to recognizing our independence—as long as they can inspect our space stations and ABM satellites and satisfy themselves that we are really independent."

"Check with Leonov about that. And find out about making sure his kids are in that shuttle-load of immigrants."

"Right."

"It all sounds terrific, Hugh."

"Yes, it looks as if they're bending over backward to be sweet to us. Maybe it's the Christmas spirit."

"Could be. Hope it's something deeper and more permanent."

"Amen."

"Anything else?" Kinsman asked.

"Two things. About that invitation to address the General Assembly—the hitch is that they want you to do it 'at your earliest convenience.' But no later than this coming Thursday."

"Thursday?" Ellen echoed. "That's too soon."

"We can't let any grass grow on this," Harriman said, totally serious. "Everything's going our way; we've got to take advantage of the tide before something happens to change their minds."

"All right," Kinsman said. "Thursday. What was the other thing?"

"The other? Oh!" Harriman's eyes twinkled. "I spent an hour's time—my lunch hour, the way I figure it—tracking down the jackal who calls himself the Temporary Maximum Leader of my native land. Finally got him on the screen."

"To tell him that you're coming Earthside under a UN safe-conduct?"

"No." Harriman smiled with beatific delight. "I just wanted to see his pockmarked face once more, and watch the expression on it as I gave him my Christmas greeting."

"You called to wish him a Merry Christmas?" Ellen asked.

"Not quite. I told him to go fuck himself."

Sunday 26 December 1999: 1015 hrs UT

"There is no way," Jill Myers was saying, "that you are going Earthside, Thursday or any other day. It's medically out of the question!"

They were in Kinsman's office: Jill, Leonov, Harriman, Ellen and Kinsman himself.

"Come on, Jill," Kinsman said, "this is no time for lectures."

She was on her feet, frowning intensely at Kinsman. "Chet, I'm not lecturing. I'm telling you the simple facts. You can't live on Earth."

Ellen sounded surprised. "Not ever?"

"Maybe with six months' special training and exercise," Jill said, "but even then the heart—"

"Jill, let's not start believing our own propaganda," Kinsman interrupted. "You know damned well we cooked up that heart murmur to get around the duty regs about rotation."

Jill stood squarely in front of him, a tiny snub-nosed Raggedy-Ann doll with a will of chrome steel. "Your heart problem is real," she said slowly, making every word diamond hard and clear. "It was a trivial matter five years ago, and with the proper balance of rest and exercise it could have been corrected. But for those five years you have been living in one-sixth the gravity of Earth. Your heart has become accustomed to doing one-sixth the work it would face Earthside. The muscle tone, the workload capacity, is gone. You simply can't survive under Earthside gravity! You'll kill yourself!"

For a long moment the office was absolutely still. None of them moved or spoke.

Kinsman found himself staring at the view screen on the wall opposite the couch: Earth was hanging there, close and lovely, the jewel of the cosmos. Near enough to touch, to reach in a day or two . . .

"Jill," he said at last, "I'm not asking you to tell us what we can't do. You've got to help us accomplish what needs to be done. I've *got* to go Earthside. Do you understand that?"

Leonov cleared his throat. "Let me go instead. I am in good physical condition—Russian pride in manly strength, as opposed to decadent Western self-indulgence."

"I appreciate the offer, Pete," Kinsman answered. And the attempt to make us smile. "But the simple fact is that the deal was set up for me. The Americans would get very twitchy if you showed up in my place. Even the Russians would start to wonder what's going on."

"Does it have to be a personal visit?" Ellen asked. "Can't we handle it by phone?"

Harriman shook his head. "No, dear lovely lady. The crux of this whole meeting is the chance for Chet and

Marrett to get face to face with the key national leaders down there. In private, with no bugs or eavesdroppers. The speech and the public meetings are nothing more than window dressing. The important thing—the *vital* thing—is for Chet and Marrett to offer the smaller nations their double-barreled deal of ABM protection and weather control."

"How about *your* health, Hugh?" Kinsman asked him. "Will you be able to make the trip?"

Harriman put a fist to his forehead and flexed his bicep. No motion was discernible inside the jumpsuit sleeve. "I've been exercising at least six hours a week in the centrifuge ever since I came here. I always expected to go right back home again, remember?"

"I checked his latest physical exams," Jill said. "He's in good shape."

"You bet your sweet ass!" Harriman concurred.

"All right," Kinsman said. "So it's my frail heart that's the problem. But I'll be Earthside for only a few days . . ."

Jill gave him a tight-lipped scowl. "How did you feel when you were aboard the space station the week before last?"

"Huh? Fine! No problems." *As long as I stayed in the low gee sections. But that wasn't my heart! I just felt tired, heavy, had some trouble breathing . . .*

"Your chest didn't feel heavy?" Jill probed. "You didn't feel any aches or sharp pains anywhere?"

"Nothing much."

"How much time did you spend on Level One, where there's full Earth gravity?"

"Um, well, I didn't get down there at all. But I was on Level Three a lot—it's about half an Earth gee, a lot more than we have here."

"And how did you feel?"

"Kind of tired—achy. But my heart was okay."

Jill shook her head. "When you got back here, your EKG looked like a Richter point-eight seismograph reading. Do you have any idea of how much your heart function has deteriorated from Earth normal? And your entire muscle tone? You wouldn't be able to stand up under normal Earth gravity for more than a few minutes! You'd—"

"Shut up!" he snapped.

Jill glared at him. But became silent.

"Now, listen to me," he said more softly. "We live in an age of medical miracles and high technology. There's no reason why I can't wear a powered suit down there. The exoskeleton will hold me up, and the servo motors will move my arms and legs, if my own muscles are too flabby to do the job."

"But your heart—"

"Do something about it! You've got pressure cuffs and booster pumps and God knows what the hell else. Pump me full of adrenalin or whatever it takes."

Harriman shook his head furiously. "No drugs, dammit! We can't have you high or dopey during these meetings, for Chrissakes."

Already Kinsman was feeling weary. He ran a hand across his eyes. "Yeah, you're right." Turning back to Jill, "Okay, you're going to have to prop me up with whatever mechanical aids you can produce. I guess I'll need a doctor with me, then."

"But I can't go back," Jill said, almost apologetically.

"I know that," Kinsman answered, reaching out to touch her arm. "I don't expect you to . . ." *To risk your life, the way I'm risking mine?*

"Alex will go with you," Jill said. "There's no medical reason for his being confined here."

"He's driving one of the buggies in the race," Kinsman said.

"Then call him back," Jill countered.

"But—"

Leonov raised a solemn hand. "She is right. The race is not as important as your medical safety."

"It'll be good politics to have a Russian in our little group," Harriman pointed out.

"All right," Kinsman said. "Then it'll be Alex, you," nodding to Harriman, "and me. A Russian, a Brazilian Irish Jew, and an American. We'll outnumber 'em."

Somehow he ended up walking toward the living quarters with Ellen. She was quite silent as they went down the long, rough, curving corridor. It was late afternoon; nearly the whole day had been spent planning the Earthside trip.

"Would you like to have dinner at my place?" he asked.

She wouldn't look at him. "No, I don't think so."

A family walked toward them, parents and two children, one barely big enough to walk by himself. After they passed, Kinsman asked Ellen, "What's wrong?"

She stopped and turned toward him. "You know what's wrong. You're going to keep going at this thing until it kills you, aren't you?"

"Oh, for God's sake, Ellen. I've *got* to."

"I know you do," she admitted. "That's the trouble."

"I'll be all right," he said.

"They're going to kill you."

"Don't be melodramatic."

She started walking again. He caught up with her and grabbed her arm. "Ellen, listen to me. You wouldn't be so damned upset if—"

"Don't say it!" she snapped, pulling her arm away from him. "Don't let all this drama and self-sacrifice put you into a romantic mood, Chet. You're going to keep at this business until you're dead. So go ahead and kill yourself. They'll build a statue to your memory."

She strode off down the corridor, leaving him standing there alone.

Frank Colt wore dress blues as he sat back in the plush reclining chair of the jetcopter's passenger section. The seats were arranged two by two, facing each other. Sitting beside Colt was a major, ten years his senior, now serving as his aide. Facing the two officers was a pair of civilians: one from the State Department and the other from the Internal Security Agency.

"We've cleared visas for all of the foreign visitors who want to emigrate to Moonbase," the State Department man was saying. He was a professional Foreign Service officer, crisp and knowledgeable. "They'll start arriving in New York on Thursday morning. The lunar delegation can meet most of them that evening."

The ISA man, small, paunchy, balding, nodded happily. "That should allay any suspicions the Luniks might have. Then we'll stash the foreigners at Kennedy Spaceport, tell them there are technical difficulties, and keep them incommunicado."

"While the troops take off in their place and seize the space stations," the major finished. "All very neat."

"Timing's critical," Colt said. "No room for screw-ups."

"Everything is worked out to the second," the major replied smugly.

"Then work it out to the millisecond," Colt snapped. "I'm meeting the President tonight, and I want to be able to assure him that those stations will be in our hands when the New Year begins."

The major nodded, his lips pressed together and his cheeks going a blotchy red.

The State Department man traced a well-groomed finger down the crease of his slacks as far as the knee. "There's one additional item."

"What is it?" Colt asked.

"Our situation analysts have run this whole plan through the computers one extra time, to see if there are any loopholes to be plugged."

"And?"

"They've come up with a cute suggestion. They think you, Colonel, should be in New York with this Kinsman character as the rocketplane takes off."

Colt controlled his surprise with a reflex clamping down on his emotions. He kept his voice noncommittal. "Why?"

"If Kinsman has any slight shred of doubt about a Trojan Horse situation, your presence in New York should ease his fears."

"Or put him on his guard."

"No." The State Department man smiled. "We've analyzed Kinsman's personality profile quite thoroughly. He tends to trust people rather easily. And you were— or perhaps still are—friendly with him. He'd see your presence at the UN as a gesture of amity, and that should put him off his guard."

He does trust people too easily, Colt admitted to himself.

The ISA man giggled. "Beautiful. You two can watch the takeoff on TV together."

"The final few hours of countdown will be more-or-less automatic," the major chipped in. "There's no real need for you to be physically present at the Kennedy launch center, or even at Patrick."

Colt said, "I don't like it. I'd rather be where the action is, at the launch complex."

"But the computers," said the State Department man, "show the plan's chances for success increasing from eighty-five to ninety-three percent, if you're with Kinsman in New York."

You want me to kiss him on the cheek, too? But Colt hid his anger, hid his fear, and looked into the three white faces, each in turn.

"All right," he said at last. "I'll do it."

Wednesday 29 December 1999: 0525 hrs UT

Kinsman snapped awake.

For a moment he couldn't remember where he was. Then it came to him: a VIP compartment in the low-gravity section of Space Station Alpha.

He got up slowly. There was a plastic tube in his thigh, carefully wrapped in protective bandaging. He glanced at the digital clock set into the bulkhead. In another hour and a half, that tube would be connected to a pacemaker and electric motor. Inside his leg, the tube wormed through his femoral artery and up his torso into the aorta, where the plastic balloon pump rested. It was quiescent now. Once the pacemaker and power unit were connected, the balloon would act as an auxiliary, helping with the blood-pumping work that his natural heart would be too weak to do on Earth.

Jill had frowned through the entire surgical procedure. "The pump can't take more than fifty percent of the workload off your heart," she had said. "You're still going to be in trouble when you reach Earth."

Kinsman padded into the sanitary stall and dry-bathed, letting the sonic vibrations cleanse and massage his skin. Silly, he told himself, knowing that he could have luxuriated in a water shower. But the habit prevails. And I shouldn't get the bandage wet, I guess. He didn't want to admit that a water shower would smack too much of a last-chance-of-my-life ritual.

He shaved carefully, then started to dress. Briefly, he thought of putting in a call to Ellen, back in Selene. But he shook his head against it. Better to leave it this way. If I get back—*when* I get back, maybe we can put something together. But not now.

He pulled on a T-shirt, shorts and slipper socks. Nothing else. The bandage showed beneath the brief shorts; it bulged against the inside of his thigh. Feels like an extra pair of balls.

He took a deep, calming breath, then opened the door and headed out to meet with Jill and her medical team.

Two hours later he was sitting in a special foam cushion chair aboard a rocketplane as it reentered Earth's atmosphere.

Kinsman was encased in a mechanical exoskeleton: a framework of metal tubing that ran along his legs, torso, arms and neck. The silvery metal tubes were jointed in all the places where the human body was jointed, although the broad metal plates running along Kinsman's back could never be as supple as a human spine. Tiny electrical servo motors moved the suit in response to Kinsman's own muscular actions.

As the rocketplane bit deeper into Earth's atmosphere, and the gee forces inside the ship built, Kinsman tested his new external skeleton. He raised his right arm off the seat's armrest. A barely audible hum of electric motors and the arm lifted smoothly, easily. Yet when Kinsman tried to flex his fingers, which had no auxiliary help, it felt as if he was trying to squeeze a sponge-rubber ball, rather than empty air.

The exoskeleton would allow a normal man working in Earth's gravity to lift half-ton loads with one hand. Kinsman hoped the suit would allow him to stand and walk properly.

The back of the suit included a rigid framework—much like a hiker's pack frame—to which would be attached the electrical power supply for the suit and the heart pump, the pacemaker controls and motor, and a small green tank containing an hour's worth of oxygen. Resting on the seat beside him was a clip-on oxygen mask. Jill had insisted on its being part of the equipment he carried, in case of emergency.

It was difficult to turn his head, because the neck supports of the exoskeleton were so stiff. So, like a man with a sore neck, Kinsman carefully edged his whole body slightly sideways, restrained by the safety harness cutting across his shoulders and lap.

He looked at Landau and Harriman, sitting in the double seats across the aisle from him. They were unfettered except for their safety harnesses, deep in animated conversation.

The rest of the rocketplane was empty, except for the flight crew in the cockpit up front, and a trio of stewardesses who had all shown professional nurse's certifications before Jill agreed to let them serve on the brief flight.

Kinsman leaned back in his seat, to the accompaniment of a miniature chorus of electric hums, and closed his eyes. He knew perfectly well what was happening up in the cockpit now—or, at least, what used to happen when he flew such craft, decades ago. Now they were controlled from the ground; everything was automatic. The flight crew was only there in case of emergency.

But in his mind he again felt the bucking of the control column in his hands as the ship buffeted through maximum aerodynamic forces. He saw the firetrail of reentry, when the ship blazed through the atmosphere like a falling meteor, torturing the air around it to incandescence. He remembered one flight when he and Frank Colt had . . .

"Touchdown in three minutes," the little speaker grill announced. Even the voice sounded mechanical, automatic. No emotion at all.

Despite himself, Kinsman grinned. Only an old fart reminisces about the good old days.

There were no viewports on the rocketplane, but the tiny view screen set into the chairback in front of him showed a pilot's-eye view of the craft's approach to JFK Spaceport. Sunlight glittered off steel-gray water, uncountable structures took form on the screen: houses, factories, warehouses, parking garages, towers, churches, stores, bridges, roads—all out in the open, under the strangely pale and diluted Sun.

Peering intently at the little screen, Kinsman still couldn't see any people, nor any cars on the roads. Just an occasional gray bus or olive-colored truck that looked more like an Army than a civilian vehicle. The long dark arrow of the runway rushed up at them. A jarring bounce, then another, and then the muffled roar of the braking jets told Kinsman that they were down. On the ground. On Earth.

He didn't move until the craft rolled to a stop at the terminal. The stewardesses helped him undo the buckles of the safety harness. Then they stood back, odd expressions on their faces, as he tried to stand up.

Must look pretty weird, he thought as the suit unfolded itself—unfolded him—and he got to his feet.

"How does it feel?" Landau asked, his deep voice and grave eyes somehow irritating to Kinsman.

"Fine. Same as on Level One, back at Alpha. I'll challenge you guys to a game of basketball before we go back home."

Harriman snorted, "Bragging already! Come on, if you're so good, move your ass off this tin can and let the people admire us."

There were no people.

At least, no crowds. Kinsman and his two followers walked from the ship into an access tunnel that led to the terminal building. A small knot of officials and medical people were there, including an American State

Department representative, and several UN functionaries. One of them, Kinsman noted immediately, was a strikingly attractive blonde. Swedish, I'll bet.

No news people. No television cameras. No curious onlookers. All the other gates in this wing of the terminal building were shut tight. The whole area had been cleared of people. As far down the corridor as Kinsman could see, there was no one except a row of uniformed security guards spaced every twenty meters or so, wearing hard hats, with gas masks on their belts next to their riot guns and grenade pouches. Even the newsstands and gift shops were shut tight.

Then the tall, cigar-chewing figure of Ted Marrett pushed its way through the little knot of officials. "Welcome to Fun City!" he boomed, and all the others seemed to pale and melt back.

Kinsman extended a metal-braced arm and Marrett grasped his hand warmly. "I'm here as the unofficial greeter and personal representative of the Secretary General. We've got a squad of cars outside waiting to take you to UN headquarters. The three of you will be guests of the Secretary General."

But it wasn't that easy. The officials immediately formed themselves into a reception line, and the three lunar visitors had to be introduced to each one of them. Kinsman wondered idly how they arranged their pecking order, since they seemed to come from a dozen different nations and two dozen different types of governmental agencies, ranging from the United States' National Institutes of Health to the Ministry for Development of Natural Resources of Tanzania.

Kinsman shook hands with them all, including the blonde—who was from Kansas City, and represented the American Urban Council. A good front for an intelligence operator, Kinsman guessed. Glancing at her clinging sweater, he decided, Hell, she's got a good front for anything.

Finally they were ready to go down the corridor toward the main terminal building. One of the American medical people said, "We can get a wheelchair for you, Mr. Kinsman."

"No, I can walk."

Landau came up beside him. "It would be better to conserve your strength."

"I feel fine."

"You are on an adrenalin high at the moment," Landau insisted quietly. "The wheelchair is advisable."

So they wheeled Kinsman, fuming inside, through the empty terminal building. Security's tight enough, he realized when he saw that the entire terminal building of one of the world's busiest airports—and one of its few spaceports—had been completely shut down. All the ticket counters were empty; all the TV monitors showing departing and arriving flights were blank; the coffee shops and restaurants and bars were shuttered and dark. Grim-faced, heavily armed security guards were posted every few meters.

The only sign of life, outside of the funeral cortege flowing through the deserted building with Kinsman, was a lone photographer who skipped back and forth with the agility of Oz's scarecrow, clicking away with a tiny camera.

Kinsman and Landau were ushered into a sleek limousine, together with Marrett and the American State Department representative, a square-jawed young man with a deep tan and the kind of wrinkles around his eyes that come from being outdoors, not behind a desk.

If he isn't ISA I'll eat the upholstery, Kinsman told himself as he settled into the limousine's back seat. The braces of his exoskeleton poked into him uncomfortably. Landau sat beside him, while Marrett and the State Department man took the jumpseats facing him.

"You okay?" Marrett asked. He had to hunch over a bit to keep his bald head from bumping against the plush-lined roof.

"As well as can be expected," Kinsman replied. He caught a glimpse of Harriman entering a car up ahead of theirs, with the blonde from Kansas City at his side.

"How's that one-man jail cell feel?" Marrett asked as the chauffeur started up the car and pulled away from the terminal building.

"Not bad. It's a lot better than trying to get along here without it, I guess."

The State Department man, whose name Kinsman

had already forgotten, asked, "How does it feel to be back home again?"

Kinsman threw him a sharp look. "My home's half a million kilometers from here."

"Oh. Yes, certainly . . . I mean . . ."

But Kinsman was staring out the windows at the acres of totally empty parking lots surrounding JFK. "They've really shut down the whole damned airport? For us? What are you afraid of?"

"Nowadays anything can be the cause of a riot," the State Department man answered. "And you're not terribly popular with the plebeians, you must realize."

"Also, it's easier to control the news about you," Marrett added quickly, "if the government's the only source of info. Right, Nickerson?"

Nickerson seemed to get darker under his tan. "The news media tend to be irresponsible, sensational."

Marrett laughed, a full-throated chuckle that filled the limousine's plush interior. "Sure. No sense letting them get excited just because a man who's led a successful revolt against the government has come down from the Moon to visit as a guest of the United Nations."

Nickerson did not smile back. "Mr. Marrett," he said coldly, "you are an American citizen, even though you seem more loyal to the UN than to your own nation. I advise you to be careful with your statements."

"Stuff it, sonny!" Marrett pulled a fresh cigar from his shirt pocket. Despite the winter weather outside, the big meteorologist wore only a light leather jacket over his shirt and slacks.

Landau raised a protesting hand. "It would be better if you didn't smoke."

"Huh? Oh." Marrett looked at Kinsman, then slipped the cigar back into his pocket.

The entire expressway leading into Manhattan was clear of all other vehicles, on both sides, except for an occasional police cruiser or Army armored car. Even the overpasses were empty of traffic and people.

As the parade of limousines and their escort neared Manhattan, an eerie sensation began crawling up Kinsman's spine. He had been here before. It all looked familiar, yet somehow different. *Empty. They've pulled all the people away.* No one on the streets, no cars or buses. Yet there was something more. Something was missing even from the bare canyons of cement and brick. *Defoliated!* he realized. Not a tree in sight. They've taken down all the trees. For fuel?

They swung up onto the Queensboro Bridge, and Kinsman saw the skyline of tall gray towers that he remembered, half lost in a cold brown haze of smog. Uptown of the bridge, a few private cars shared the East River Drive with phalanxes of steam-driven buses. But downtown of the bridge, where the drive led to the UN complex of buildings, the roadway was completely empty except for police and Army vehicles.

The river below looked oily and turgid, flowing sluggishly—and then it hit Kinsman. *Water!* Miles and miles of water, waves lapping gently, water that falls from the sky and makes noisy little streams like that time in Colorado flowing down the mountain slopes to form rivers that sweep out into the oceans—*rivers, oceans, a whole planet brimful of water.*

He stared into the gray river. *All that water, and what they've done to it. Nest foulers.*

He pulled his eyes away from the filthy river. "I just don't understand why you felt it necessary to clear out the whole path," he said.

Nickerson glanced at Marrett, sitting beside him on the other jumpseat. "Mr. Kinsman," he said then, "it may come as a shock to you, but the majority of the American people regard you as a traitor. We thought it would be better for your own safety to provide a maximum of security for you."

"And minimum opportunity for me to tell Selene's story directly to the people."

Nickerson's nostrils flared, but that was the only betrayal of his feelings. He said evenly, "We do not want to run the risk of starting a riot and possibly having you or the others in your party injured or killed."

Marrett looked disgusted, but said nothing.

Kinsman turned back to stare at the river. *So much water! For free!* This world is so rich—and they've fucked it up so thoroughly.

As they pulled off the East River Drive and down the short stretch of rampway that led directly into the UN garage, suddenly there were people. Thousands of them. Tens of thousands. Thronging the pedestrian mall and spilling over to block the bottom of Forty-eighth Street. A cordon of mounted policemen—*they still use horses!*—kept the crowd from surging onto the rampway and blocking the limousines' access to the garage.

Kinsman remembered the UN Plaza as a perfectly manicured park, green with trees and shrubs. The glimpse he got of it as the limousines slowed down showed it to be bare and treeless. And packed with people who clutched tiny American flags in their fists and waved placards:

DON'T DEAL WITH TRAITORS!
THE MOON BELONGS TO U.S.
BRUTUS, BENEDICT ARNOLD AND KINSMAN
ANOTHER UN SELLOUT OF AMERICA

And others that were worse. Most of them were professionally printed, and many copies of them had been made available by somebody. *The government?* The hand-lettered ones were obscene.

Through the bulletproof windows of the limousine Kinsman could hear the seething roar of the crowd, booing and shouting at them. A woman's high-pitched screech: "Kinsman, you Quaker bastard, I hope they kill you like a dog!"

Nickerson smiled oddly. "See what I mean?"

"Good job of stage managing," Marrett muttered.

The cars slid past the mouth of Forty-eighth Street and under the overhang of the pedestrian mall, to a wild cacophony of screams and curses.

With great effort, Kinsman turned around to look out the rear window. Suddenly the crowd broke through the police line and surged onto the rampway. More police appeared almost magically and tried to hold them back from the entrance to the garage. The mounted police reappeared, with gas masks on their faces—and on the horses!

"Stop the car," Kinsman ordered.

His voice was strong enough to penetrate the partition separating the back of the limousine from the driver's seat. "Stop it!" he shouted again.

The driver lurched to a stop.

"What are you—" Nickerson reached for Kinsman's metal-sheathed arm.

But he had already opened the car door and was climbing out, servo motors whining as he ducked through the door frame and stood erect.

There was a riot starting up at the entrance to the garage. The police were pushing at the crowd, and the crowd was pushing back. Police clubs and electric prods were already in hand. The roar of anger was echoing down the concrete tunnel.

The air was foul. It stank of smells that Kinsman had completely forgotten: gasoline and rubber and burning garbage and urine. His eyes burned. But instead of going for his oxygen mask, he trudged up the ramp toward the maddened, flag-waving, struggling crowd.

Dimly he was aware that Landau was running up behind him. And Marrett. And Nickerson, who probably had a gun on him.

The ramp's slope was unnoticeable to them all. But to Kinsman it was like climbing Annapurna. Step by plodding step: click, whine, hum, thump; click, whine, hum, thump. *Frankenstein's monster invades New York.*

And suddenly the battling and shouting up ahead of him died away. Not all at once, but within the space of a half-minute it went from riot to silence, a shock wave passing through the crowd, numbing it to inertness. One gruff voice hollered, "Hey, what the hell is that?" Then utter silence from more than ten thousand people.

Except for the noises of Kinsman's exoskeleton. Slowly, laboriously, he worked his way up the ramp. Breathing was an exercise in concentration; his chest felt raw inside, too heavy to lift.

One of the policemen edged toward him, face shield down, gas grenade clutched in one hand, bullhorn in the other.

"The . . . bullhorn," Kinsman puffed. *Christ Almighty. Twenty paces and you're half dead.*

The policeman hesitated, then held out the bullhorn. Kinsman took it, with a click and whir of servos. He put the bullhorn to his mouth. "I . . ." His voice cracked, his throat burned.

Landau reached out to support him. Marrett and Nickerson came up on the other side.

"I am Chester Kinsman," he said, and heard his magnified voice boom hollowly off the tunnel walls.

The crowd seemed to flow backward a pace or two, buzzing. *Like a rattler trying to make up its mind about striking.*

"I'm the man who's being accused of treason," Kinsman took a deep, rasping breath. "I can only tell you . . . that we declared . . . independence for the Moon . . . in the same spirit that our forefathers . . . declared independence . . . for the United States."

Can't get air into my lungs!

"The people of Selene . . . would like to live in peace . . . with all humankind . . . There's no more reason for you to fear an independent Selene . . . than there has been for England to fear an independent United States . . ."

The crowd was murmuring, wavering. Kinsman let his arm drop. Someone took the bullhorn from his grasp. *There's more to tell them . . . but I can't . . . Too bloody tired.*

Thursday 30 December 1999: 1332 hrs UT

Floating. He was floating in free-fall, connected to reality only by the life-giving umbilical snaking back to the spacecraft.

Kinsman gloried in the freedom of it. Turning slowly

in space he gravely saluted each of the stars in turn: Rigel, Betelgeuse, Sirius, Procyon, the Twins, the Crab, the Scorpion with Antares glowering redly in its middle. Antares, the rival of Mars. Enemy of Mars. Enemy of war.

And then she drifted into his view. Dead. Arms still out-stretched in terror, life-giving oxygen lines ripped away by his hands. She was turning slowly, ever so slowly, showing her back to him at first but slowly, slowly revolving so that now he could see the bulge of her helmet where the right earphone was built in, and now the hinge of her dark-tinted visor, and the first red initial of CCCP across the top of her helmet.

No! I want to wake up!

But she drifted closer to him, still turning toward him, her arms extended now in a cold embrace of death. He wanted to tear his eyes away, but instead looked deeply into that visor through the darkness and saw her face.

Ellen's face. Dead.

"No-o-o!" he screamed.

Kinsman was trying to sit up, eyes wide open, room still echoing with his nightmare shout. Dr. Landau and two nurses burst into the room.

He saw that he was lying on a waterbed, felt it sloshing wildly beneath him. A light plastic web harness was fastened over him, making it impossible for him to turn over. In his ears he heard the peculiar double-beat of his natural and artificial hearts, thumping hard in syncopation.

"Chet, Chet! Don't try to get up!" *First time Alex's ever called me Chet,* he realized with a detached part of his mind.

"I'm all right," he said. "Just a dream . . . a bad dream."

One of the nurses—a tall, leggy African—had a syringe in hand. Landau waved her away.

As they unfastened the web harness, Kinsman lay back and let the buoyancy of the water carry him. The room was big, huge by lunar standards, and plushly furnished. The ceiling was richly paneled in wood, the floor thickly carpeted; deep comfortable chairs and

couches were scattered in a smooth, luxurious arrangement.

The other nurse touched a button, and the drapes slid
back, letting sunlight filter through the ceiling-high windows. There was a spacious desk by the windows, with
various electronic gadgets on it, and a special contour
chair.

For the freak, Kinsman realized, when he saw his exoskeleton neatly stacked beside the chair, like some
smothering insect that was waiting to envelop him.

Most of the electronic gadgetry was medical checkout
equipment, which Landau used to test Kinsman's vital
systems. The Russian shook his head solemnly through-
out the entire brief procedure.

As the nurses helped Kinsman into his clothes and
then into his braces, he asked Landau, "Well, Alex,
how'm I doing?"

Landau was sitting on a regular chair, next to the
desk. He bit his lower lip as he scanned the readout on
the desktop view-screen.

"Terribly, if you must know the truth," he answered.
"The heart pump cannot sustain you through any physical exertion at all."

The black nurse was lifting his right leg and clamping
the foot brace on, while the other girl—she looked
Greek, maybe Armenian—was doing the same for his
left.

"So I won't exert myself," he said lightly. "Who needs
to, with such expert help around." He would have patted
their heads, but his arms felt too heavy; he feared he
couldn't coordinate them properly.

"This is no joking matter," Landau replied grimly.

Kinsman found he couldn't even shrug comfortably.
"All right. So I'll sit still and do nothing more strenuous
than talk."

"Your heart reacts to emotional stress, also, you
know."

The nurses bent him forward to hook up the back
brace.

"Ummph. But, Alex, I feel a helluva lot better now
than I did yesterday. What happened? Did I pass out or
what?"

"You collapsed," Landau said. Bitterly, he went on, "And for a reason that I should have foreseen, but was too stupid to. The air you were breathing, it was heavily contaminated, polluted with carbon monoxide and other filth. Your lungs strained, which put an additional work-load on your heart. You were faced with a serious cardiac insufficiency, and you collapsed. The exoskeleton would not permit you to fall, so you hung inside it, quite unconscious."

"I had a heart attack?"

Landau shook his head. "No, not what a layman would call a heart attack—merely an insufficiency of oxygen-carrying blood getting to your brain."

"Like a blackout in a high-gee maneuver."

Landau frowned in concentration for a moment. "I suppose so."

"But I feel fine now."

"You have been sedated and resting in the most comfortable environment that the United Nations could provide. The air in this room is mixed from bottled gases; you are not breathing city air at all, not even filtered city air."

Kinsman laughed as the girls lifted his arms and clamped the braces on them. "I remember something we used to say when we were kids: New Yorkers don't trust air they can't see."

Landau found it completely unfunny.

With the exoskeleton fully hooked up to him, Kinsman tried a few experimental steps across the wide carpeted room. *Just like the Tin Woodman. Hope somebody remembered to bring the oilcan.*

Landau let the nurses leave. A few minutes later, a pair of liveried waiters wheeled in breakfast. And right behind them came Hugh Harriman.

"Well!" he snapped with mock indignation. "Sleeping Beauty's finally up and on the job, eh?"

"I think I can make it through until nap time," Kinsman said.

"Good." Harriman ordered the waiters around as they patiently set up the breakfast table and took the food from the hot and cold sections beneath the white-clothed rolling table. They showed no evidence of listening to him or even admitting that he was talking to them.

Finally, when they had left, and the table was neatly arranged with a variety of dishes, Harriman pulled up a chair. "Bagels and lox—that's really a low blow," he complained. "They've loaded this table with foods we can't get in Selene."

Kinsman found that his contour chair had a series of toggle switches set into its right arm. The first one he tried adjusted the back. The second rolled the chair forward. *Like a joystick.* He deftly maneuvered the chair up to the table.

Landau pulled his chair to the table, looked everything over, and murmured, "Caviar."

"Don't worry," Kinsman said. "We'll be getting this kind of stuff in trade goods a year from now."

"And what'll we trade them back?" Harriman groused. "Oxygen?"

Kinsman unconsciously shook his head, and the whir of electric motors startled him. "We'll have trade items," he said slowly. "Electronics, pharmaceuticals, tourist accommodations, research facilities."

"I still think it's damned shitty of them to lay all these goodies in front of us," Harriman said.

Landau reached for the tea. "They are probably trying to be very polite to us."

"Or the fucking American and Russian security people are bribing the UN to make us homesick."

"All right," Kinsman said. "Let's get down to work. What did I miss yesterday?"

"Nothing much," Harriman replied. "We met a lot of UN staff people in the afternoon. Then in the evening they trotted a dozen of the immigrants past us. They wanted to meet you, but they had to settle for my charming self."

"The people who are coming to live in Selene?" Landau asked.

Harriman nodded as he munched on a mouthful of bagel, cream cheese, Nova Scotia salmon and onion. "Uh-hmmm." He swallowed mightily. "Fascinating group of people, all of them still rather stupefied that their governments are letting them leave. They fly out of Kennedy tomorrow; they're on their way down there now."

"On their way down to where?" Kinsman asked.

"Kennedy Space Center."

"In Florida? Not the JFK Spaceport here?"

Harriman blinked. "No, they told me the American government was taking them to Florida."

"Why wouldn't they take off from here?" Kinsman wondered.

"Damned if I know. Probably some bureaucratic red tape someplace along the line. Anyway, that's not the important thing. The Secretary General is scheduled to meet you at ten this morning—less than an hour from now. Are you up to it?"

Kinsman started to nod, thought better of it. *I'm getting to hate the sound of electric motors*, he realized. "I'm fine. Where will the meeting be?"

"Right here. Mohammed's coming to the mountain."

Kinsman raised his eyebrows. *At least I can still do that for myself.*

A few minutes before ten, Ted Marrett burst into the room unannounced, with Tuli Noyon. "Best meteorologist Mongolia's ever produced," he said, by way of introduction.

"For your information," Noyon said quietly as he shook hands with the seated Kinsman, "Mongolia produces very few meteorologists. And actually, my training was in fluid dynamics."

"Well, the best in Asia then," Marrett amended. "You seen the morning news? Your performance at the garage yesterday really's getting the big splash."

Without asking, he crossed the room in a few long-legged strides and touched a small inset wall panel. A holographic Monet reproduction instantly disappeared from the wall, to be replaced by the three-dimensional image of a woman being wheeled through a hospital corridor. "Goddamn soaps," Marrett grumbled as he touched the panel again.

Kinsman sat back in his special chair and suddenly saw a holographic picture of himself striding painfully toward the crowd at the UN garage. The camera was somewhere in the crowd, heads and placards were constantly getting in the way as this weird skeletal figure clambered up the garage ramp.

The newscaster's voice was saying things about "Unearthly appearance . . . terrific physical strain of ordinary gravity . . . message of peace and friendship . . ."

Good Christ! Kinsman said to himself as he watched. *I actually did raise my hands like an old-time Indian scout.*

Marrett abruptly shut off the picture. "The government's gone ape," he said, grinning broadly. "They had everything all buttoned up. No newsmen at the airport, nobody allowed to get near you guys."

"But there were cameramen in the crowd."

"Sure! Half of 'em were government goons, there to record the riot."

"There was *supposed* to be a riot?" Harriman asked.

"It is an old tactic," Landau said. "The government plants agitators in the crowd; natural leaders seize the opportunity to vent their passions; the riot begins, and the natural leaders have identified themselves. They can be taken by the police during the riot, or if that is inconvenient, at least their pictures are recorded. Then they can be picked up later."

"And at the same time," Marrett added, "they show the news-watching American public that the people are dead set against you. It's called 'forming a climate of opinion.'"

"An old trick," Noyon agreed quietly.

"Wonder who they learned it from?" Harriman murmured.

The Secretary General arrived precisely at ten. He came alone, without flunkies or fanfare. He merely knocked on the door once and opened it. As he entered the room, all five men present got to their feet. Kinsman ignored the whine of his servos.

"Please—sit down," said the Secretary General, "I insist."

As they did so, he added, "And since this is an informal meeting, let us please dispense with titles. My name is Emanuel De Paolo. I know your names—Mr. Kinsman, Mr. Harriman, Dr. Landau—so let us relax and speak freely. I can assure you that this room has been carefully inspected, as recently as an hour ago, to ensure that it is not wired by anyone."

Kinsman found himself immediately liking this slim, tan-faced man with the dark sad eyes. De Paolo took a chair for himself and brought it close to Kinsman's. Marrett pushed the breakfast table out of the way. The morning sunlight struggled through the murky haze of the city to make the room seem warm and bright.

"Now then, Mr. Kinsman," De Paolo said, "you have shown considerable courage and wit. You are an instant hero with the American public this morning. How long such popularity can last is questionable, however. Many Americans, perhaps most of them, honestly consider you to be a traitor."

"I'm sure that most Englishmen considered George Washington a traitor," Kinsman answered.

De Paolo shrugged. "Yes, of course . . . Eh, you have come here to seek recognition for your new nation, is that correct?"

"Yes. We want to create a political situation in which Selene can feel free from the threat of attack by the United States or the Soviet Union. In return for this, we can offer to all the nations of the world a safeguard against missile attack—against nuclear war."

De Paolo pursed his lips. "You offer us much more than that."

Glancing at Marrett, Kinsman said, "Oh, you mean weather control."

"I mean much more than that. Much, *much* more."

Kinsman leaned forward in his seat. The chair back moved with him. "I don't understand."

With a smile that somehow looked more sad than happy, De Paolo said, "Let me see if I can explain it simply." He paused. Then, "What causes war? You may say, 'Political differences,' or 'Conflict over territory' or even 'Need for natural resources.' None of these is completely true. Wars are caused by nations. National governments decide that they can obtain by force something that they desire but cannot obtain any other way. Once they have decided to use force, there is no way to stop them from fighting."

"Go on," Kinsman said.

"Our world—this Earth—is faced with a myriad of staggering problems. War is only one of them. There is vast hunger, in my native land, in most of the Southern Hemisphere, even in parts of the wealthier nations. There is a struggle for natural resources. There is over-population and energy shortages and pollution on a global scale. These are world-wide problems."

Harriman said, "Ahhh . . . "

"You begin to understand." De Paolo smiled at him. "The nations of the world cannot—or will not—solve these global problems. Because the most fundamental problem of all is the problem of nationalism."

His voice was suddenly iron-hard. "Each nation considers itself sovereign, a law unto itself, with no higher authority to hinder its actions. All nations, even the youngest in Africa and Asia, demand complete authority to do as they wish inside their own borders. What they accomplish is stupidity! Population crises, food shortages, racial injustices. And eventually, inevitably —there is war."

"We're a new nation, too," Kinsman said, "and we want our sovereignty, too."

"Yes, of course. But why have you come here? It is, I think, because you have realized that no nation is completely sovereign, de facto. There are always restraints on action, political realities that cannot be ignored, the need to cooperate when you cannot coerce. The irony of it all is that you—living on the Moon!—you realize that you must cooperate with the other nations of Earth if you wish to survive. Would that the nations of Earth were as clear-sighted."

Kinsman nodded, and the servo motors' buzz made his forehead twinge with the beginnings of a headache.

"Your own Alexander Hamilton knew the problem. He wrote, 'Do not expect nations to take the initiative in developing restraints upon themselves.' No. The nations of the world will not solve the problem of nationalism. They cannot," De Paolo said, very firmly. "For more than two centuries they have been trying to cure the sickness of nationalism, and every year it gets worse, more virulent, closer to the point of lethality."

The old man rose to his feet. "Every year . . ." he muttered, walking toward the windows. Kinsman felt confusion in his mind. De Paolo looked frail and yet strong; old and yet vital.

De Paolo turned and faced Kinsman, framed by the windows. "For twenty-two years I have watched them play their stupid games. The proud nations! Each so utterly convinced of its divine right to be as smug and stupid and brutal as it chooses. For twenty-two years I have watched people starve, villages bombed, whole nations looted, while diplomats politely stood here, in this very building, and made a mockery of ideas such as law and justice and peace. They are no better than the barbarian warlords they replaced centuries ago!"

He was staring beyond Kinsman and the others in the room, and looked disgusted at what he saw. "I know the games they play. I have given the best years of my manhood to make the United Nations a force for order and sanity in a world of madmen. But they refuse order and sanity. They have turned our political efforts into travesties. They loudly proclaim the need for international law, but then use the power of money and weapons to take what they want, like bandits and cowards."

He gazed straight at Kinsman. "For more than two decades I have tried to use the UN's nonpolitical arms—UNESCO, the World Health Organization, the International Food Distribution Committee—but even there the proud nations have thwarted us. Their refusal to allow weather modification work is only the most recent example of their nonsense."

"So you're proposing . . ."

The slim old man paced stiffly back to his chair. "I am proposing that we take the skill and courage that we possess, and work toward an effective world government. With the anti-missile satellites that you control, we can offer the smaller nations of the world safety from nuclear holocaust. With Dr. Marrett's manipulations of the weather, we can maximize food production and avert disastrous storms—and at the same time threaten any nation on Earth with unacceptable calamity, if it does not cooperate with us."

For a long moment, Kinsman didn't know what to say. "That . . . that's quite an undertaking."

"Of course. And we cannot hope to even begin working toward that goal unless you join us. Your satellites are the key to everything."

"But—"

"I know," De Paolo said. "You fear that I am a megalomaniac, intent on world domination."

"No—"

"But I am!" He smiled again, and this time the sadness was lessened. "I want to see the world dominated by *law*. By justice. By cooperation among peoples. Not by force and terror, as it is now."

De Paolo spread his hands expressively. "We know how to build an effective world government, a government in which each nation would participate, and no nation would be held like a pawn or slave. We can substitute the rule of sanity and law for the present rule of power and nuclear armaments."

"The nations of the world can't solve the problem of nationalism," Kinsman said. "They need an outside force . . ."

"And together we can be that outside force," De Paolo answered. "I know it sounds dangerous. I know how tempting it would be to strike for a world dictatorship, and *make* the recalcitrant nations do as we wish. It would have been easy for your George Washington to have himself proclaimed king, also."

"But he didn't."

"And neither will we."

Kinsman closed his eyes. "That's a lot to swallow in one sitting."

"I know. And I intend to give you even more to chew on. This afternoon you were scheduled to address the General Assembly. But the American delegation has asked that your address be put off until Monday—after the weekend and the holiday."

"I can't!" Kinsman flashed. "I can't stay here that long."

De Paolo nodded. "I understand. This is a move to

prevent you from getting your message across to the people of the world. Unfortunately, the Russians are in agreement with the Americans on this, and between them and their allies in the General Assembly, they have enough votes to force the postponement of our special session. Actually, most delegates are away at home for this week, and a postponement suits them very agreeably."

"But—"

"Fear not," De Paolo said, with an upraised hand. "You can address the General Assembly next week from the Moon or one of your satellite stations. Your public address was not the real reason I wanted you here. There are a few dozen key people that you must meet—and we will take advantage of your time here to bring them to you. They are officials from many different nations. Most of them are from very small and weak nations—but a few might surprise you."

"If they think you're okay," Marrett broke in, "then they'll get their governments to go along with us—to revamp the UN and move toward a real world government."

"Wait a minute," Kinsman said. "I'm not sure that *I* want to go that far!"

De Paolo smiled, and once again there were generations of human suffering in his face. "Your discussions with these men and women will help *you* to make up *your* mind, in that case. Obviously, none of us can move in any direction until we are all agreed."

"Fair enough," Kinsman said.

De Paolo got to his feet. "I must get back to my other duties. You may hear thumping along the walls and ceiling from time to time. Do not be alarmed; it is merely our security team sniffing for electronic bugs."

He walked to the door, alone. Stopping there, he looked back at Kinsman: "You believed you were acting to save your world—your Selene—from being destroyed by decisions made here on Earth. Then you found that perhaps you could save the people of Earth from destroying themselves. Now we offer you something much grander, and much more difficult to achieve: a chance to rid the people of Earth of the curse of nationalism. A chance to move human society on to its next evolutionary phase. A world government is the only chance we have to avoid global catastrophe."

Through the long day they came, and well into the evening. One by one, very rarely two together, and only once did three visit Kinsman at the same time. Diplomats, representatives of many nations. Some of them had enough technical background to converse freely about missile trajectories and the logistics of orbital operations. A few of them had been on the Moon for brief periods, although Kinsman remembered only one of them—a striking olive-skinned, black-haired Italian geologist. She was now part of the UNESCO team studying global natural resources, and apparently reported directly to the Italian cabinet.

"A father in high office," she murmured, with the trace of an accent laid over her British-styled English. She smiled as if she thought that her father's position was being aided by her work, rather than vice versa.

Marrett stayed with Kinsman and Harriman until the last visitor had departed. He spoke to the visitors of weather control, of optimizing their climate, of allowing them to plan their harvests years in advance and then see the predictions come true. Kinsman spoke about international peace, based on the protection of the orbital ABM network, about substantial disarmament and the chance for the smaller nations to depend on world law rather than expensive armies that sometimes turned on their own governments and ousted them.

The visitors to the plush, quiet room with the special air supply came from Africa, from Asia, from the scattered islands of the Pacific, from the overpopulated nations of Latin America. Kinsman was surprised to receive a three-man team from Japan—all smiles and polite bows and sincere wishes for good fortune—who knew a disturbing amount of data about the ABM satellite lasers and were quite well aware of Marrett's work in weather control.

Tuli Noyon brought his uncle, the Mongol ambassador to the United Nations. The Italian girl was not the only European: the Scandinavian nations, Hungary,

Czechoslovakia, Yugoslavia, Holland and Switzerland all sent representatives.

All very unofficial. All completely social. No agreements were made. No commitments. But they got the information they came for, and they left with a new light in their eyes.

By 10 P.M. Kinsman was exhausted. He had the back of his contour chair cranked way down while Landau ran through the medical checks. Marrett and Harriman were wolfing hot sandwiches and beer.

"That waterbed looks good," Kinsman said tiredly as Landau disconnected the last electrodes from the medical recorder.

"It should," the Russian said. "Your blood pressure is low." The mini-analyzer on the desk gave a *ting* with its little bell, and its analysis of Kinsman's blood sample was automatically displayed on the computer viewscreen.

"Ahhm," Landau muttered, studying the readout. "Blood sugar is down also, as I suspected. You need food and rest."

Kinsman closed his eyes. "I'm too tired to eat. God, we must have told the same story three dozen times."

"Sixteen times," Harriman corrected from the portable dining table. "There's another dozen coming tomorrow."

Landau scratched at his beard. "Very well. Let's get you bedded down, and we can feed you with the IV."

"No you don't." Kinsman's aversion to having holes poked in him overcame his fatigue. "I'll eat some real food." He cranked the seat back up and rolled to the dining table. "If there's anything left," he said, glancing at the fast-disappearing selection of sandwiches.

"Sixteen times," Harriman repeated thoughtfully, while hanging onto a steak sandwich with both hands. "After listening to you two *spiel* all day and night, I could give your song-and-dance routine in my sleep."

"I'd do it sixteen thousand times," Kinsman said, "if I thought it'd do any good."

"It did good," Marrett said firmly. He had a bottle of beer in one big hand; he disdained a glass. "Every one of the people who came in here today is connected right back to the power in their governments. No flunkies or dodos in the bunch of 'em. They might not all have had much rank, but hell, most big-shot diplomats are nothing but assholes anyway."

"Hey, watch that!" Harriman snapped, beetling his brows.

Marrett raised his beer bottle in salute. "Present company excepted."

Harriman kept his stern visage. "There's a lot of nasty comments I could make about engineers."

"I'm a meteorologist."

"Worse yet!"

Landau pulled up a chair and reached for one of the few remaining sandwiches.

"You think we got our message across to them?" Kinsman asked Marrett.

"Yep. They knew the story before they came in here. De Paolo's seen to that. They just had to meet you, size you up, and play that against their estimates of what they stand to gain and lose by going along with De Paolo's scheme."

Kinsman shook his head and got a fresh lance of pain from the servo motors that were just behind his ears. "I wonder about De Paolo's plans," he said. "He claims that he's not aiming for a world dictatorship . . ."

"You mean can you trust him," Marrett said. "He's honest. He means what he says."

"What about the people around him?" Kinsman asked. "And the people *after* him?"

Marrett started to shrug, but Harriman said, "What the hell did you expect, Chet?"

"What do you mean?"

With a shake of his head, Harriman explained, "Don't you see that De Paolo's plans are a logical extension of your own? Follows as the night the day. All he's doing is building a permanent structure where you've been improvising lean-tos and pup tents. De Paolo sees further than you do, my boy. What he wants is a solid edifice."

"You mean a jail?"

Harriman made a sour face. "Don't be such a muddlebrain. The only way you can prevent nuclear war is by producing a force that's stronger than nations. Selene by itself can't be that strong. But De Paolo's moving toward a *real* international government—with muscle. It's what we need. Hell, Woodrow Wilson recognized that! But up until now, no international organization has had the muscle to *make* the nations toe the line. Well, now we do. Or we will."

"Damned right," Marrett agreed. "We're gonna build a whole new thing out of all this. A real world government. The age of nationalism is over, finished. Has been, ever since Sputnik. We're just trying to build something effective in its place to hold the world together."

Marrett took a long, thoughtful pull on his beer. Putting the bottle down, he said, "Listen, a world government isn't gonna solve all the world's problems overnight. And there's always the danger of dictatorship on a global scale. But compared to what we've got, a world government looks damned good to me."

Harriman added, "Chet, it's a question of quid pro quo. If we want these nations to recognize Selene, if we want to be admitted to the UN, to get the United States and the Soviet Union off our backs—then we've got to play along with De Paolo. There's no choice. It's a question of political reality. Help De Paolo to get what he wants, and he'll help us to get what we want. Quid pro quo."

"While the whole fucking human race hangs in the balance," Marrett added.

Kinsman asked, "These people we talked to today—they're going back to their respective governments?"

"They're on airplanes right now," Marrett said. "De Paolo will carry the ball from here on. All we need from you is your agreement to keep up your end of the bargain."

"And that will get us recognized by a large enough bloc of nations to have us voted into UN membership."

"If none of the Security Council members vetoes our application," Harriman pointed out.

"That means Russia and the States."

"Right."

"Why would they be nice to us?" Kinsman asked.

"Because," replied Marrett, "De Paolo's gonna let them know that weather control's on the way. They can't afford to be left out in the cold—and storm—and drought—and flood."

Kinsman stared at him. "You can really do that?"

"Damned right." Marrett let his big fists rest on the table top. "Been doing it on a small scale since the fifties. It's been used in war—mostly to increase rainfall and lead to floods, or at least wipe out crops that can't use too much moisture. It's really *easier* to do it on a big scale—you've got more reinforcement factors working for you."

Harriman broke in, "Besides, the U.S. and Russia are already starting to be nice to us. They're letting those immigrants go—including Leonov's kids."

"Yes . . ." Kinsman wanted to nod, but instead found himself blinking, as Pete did. "But they asked for a postponement of my speech to the General Assembly."

"I am in agreement with them on that," Landau said. "You must avoid any additional strain and return to Selene as quickly as possible."

Ignoring him, "But why did *they* push for a postponement?"

Marrett shrugged. "Who the hell cares? They're just giving De Paolo more time to line up everybody. Time's on our side."

"Is it?" Kinsman wondered. "Is it really?"

Friday 31 December 1999: 1700 hrs UT

In the Pacific and through much of Asia it was already the New Year. Holiday crowds celebrated in the summertime streets of Melbourne and Sydney. In Tokyo, where Western-style observances were frowned upon, the streets were silent. A waning crescent Moon looked down across China, the vast Himalayan wastes of high rock and ice, and the steaming subcontinent of India. If the new millennium was being celebrated there, it was quietly, in private homes or government palaces. Or in shrines.

In Florida it was high noon. Fifty men, women and children who had traveled from all over the world to Kennedy Space Center were being led away from the sleek silvery rocketplane that they had expected to board.

They looked tired and more than a little bewildered as they marched in a ragged line under the high Florida sun, across the cement shimmering with heat haze, under the dark-glassed eyes of uniformed guards. They were better dressed than most refugee groups, but they still gave an impression of bedraggled despair to the technicians and security men watching them.

In a dozen different tongues they asked each other, "Why? What has caused the delay? When will we be allowed to take off?"

In a flat Midwestern twang, a crew-cut Army major, wearing mufti, told them, "We're experiencing some technical difficulties with the rocketplane that will take you to Space Station Alpha. We'll let you know more as soon as we learn about it."

The refugees were led into very comfortable quarters, complete with air conditioning, separate bedrooms, color television and an open cafeteria.

"Guests of the government of the United States of America," the major told them cheerfully.

The one hundred troops who were checking their automatic pistols and gas grenades and electric stunners were quartered only half a kilometer away, in a gray cement building that had no amenities except a row of coke machines that took half dollars.

The Sun raced across the other side of the world, and the line of midnight swept westward, carrying the new year and the new millennium with it.

In New York, by 5 P.M. it was already dark. A cold wind had swept the city all day, and now as Kinsman stood by the ceiling-high windows of his room in the UN Secretariat Building, he could see a single star hanging high in the darkening sky. Jupiter? Or maybe Saturn.

"You should sit," Alexei Landau's heavy voice came to him from across the room.

Kinsman turned slowly, a symphony of servo noises. "Alex, I've got to move around. I can't stay in that damned chair all the time." But it's hard to stand, he admitted to himself, back aches, head hurts. I'm falling apart like a geriatrics case.

"That was the last of the visitors," Harriman said glumly from the desk.

He's tired too. And feeling the strain of being cooped up in this room, Kinsman realized. "Ted," Kinsman called, "how about taking us on a guided tour of the building?"

"Huh?" The meteorologist looked startled.

"Absolutely impossible," Landau said. "I forbid it."

"Alex, we're all going crazy in here!"

Landau shook his head. "The air out there is full of viruses and bacteria, dust, dirt, pollutants. No, it's impossible."

Frowning, Kinsman said, "I'll wear my oxygen mask, for Chrissakes!"

"And he can stay in the chair," Harriman added.

Marrett agreed. "We can take him down to the basement level and cross over to the General Assembly chamber. It's an impressive place. Nobody'll be there."

Landau scowled but said, "Give me a few moments to pack my kit. If anything happens, I want to be prepared."

"Great!" Kinsman clapped his hands. Or tried to. The servos were out of sync just enough to make his palms hit slightly off-center, producing a dull thump instead of a sharp smack.

He got into the chair and said, "And while we're thinking about it, check the rocketplane. It's still set to take us up at ten?"

Harriman said, "I called JFK fifteen minutes ago. They'll be ready for us at ten."

"You'll miss the New Year's Eve celebration," Marrett said.

"In here? Watching the celebration on TV isn't my idea of fun—even if it's a three-dimensional set," Kinsman said. "I'd rather be on my way home."

"We'll get to Alpha an hour or so behind the immigrants," Harriman said. "There'll be plenty of celebrating."

They made a strange foursome: Marrett leading the way, tall, an aging athlete's flat-stomached, hard-eyed figure, chomping on an unlit cigar; Harriman walking alongside Kinsman's rolling chair, pudgy and round, a middle-aged cherub; Kinsman himself in his otherworldly skeleton of metal and machinery, his face hidden behind a green oxygen mask; and Landau, tall and taciturn, a dour bearded figure walking behind the chair and waiting for a tragedy.

There hadn't been a traffic jam in New York City for years: most of the commuters were carried in and out of Manhattan on government-operated buses and trains; private autos had disappeared almost entirely. But on this particular evening people poured into Manhattan. They jammed the buses, choked the trains. They drove petroleum-extravagant cars, pedaled bikes. They clogged the bridges and tunnels where the toll gates had been left open by a strangely munificent government.

*They were filling the city, which normally was empty
and quiet after sundown. Times Square was already
packed with people, and for the first time in a decade
the Manhattan traffic computer system broke down.
The wind died away, and clouds drifted over the Moon.
It would be cold this night, but few of the New Year's
Eve fun-seekers would notice.*

The General Assembly meeting chamber was empty.
Almost. A little knot of schoolchildren clustered by the
speaker's rostrum, goggle-eyed at the splendor of the
real wood and plush upholstery and paintings and
sculpture commissioned over the years by the United
Nations. The work of the world's best artists decorated
the chamber profusely.

To no avail, thought Kinsman as he sat at the far end
of the chamber, near the last rows of visitors' seats. He
tasted oxygen in his mouth—felt the slight chill of the
gas and flat tang of plastic—as he looked out across the
splendid and futile chamber. *So much of the world's
hope has been brought here—and laid to rest. Buried
under talk.* He noticed a broad, sweeping painting of an
underwater scene, very abstract, but very recognizable:
The big fish eat the little fish.

The schoolkids were trudging up the aisle, on their
way out. Their teacher somehow got into a conversation
with Marrett. She was a gray-haired, dumpy woman
with a bright smile and expressive hands.

Marrett walked back a few steps toward Kinsman.
"Chet, these kids are children of UN employees. Mostly
local people—parents work as clerks, janitors and such.
Some of the kids'd like to talk with you."

From inside the oxygen mask, Kinsman couldn't con-
duct a conversation. He raised a hand and pointed skyward.

"Upstairs," Marrett translated. "You'll talk to them
up in your room?"

Kinsman made a circle of thumb and forefinger and
winked broadly. *At least I can do that without servos.*

Landau said, "They can only visit for a few minutes."

"Okay," Marrett said. "You take him back up, and
I'll keep the kids busy with a quick tour through the

weather center. Be with you in fifteen, twenty minutes. Right?"

Kinsman nodded and Landau agreed.

The New Millennium had already come to Moscow, Teheran, Tel Aviv. Berlin, Vienna, and all the other cities of Europe were preparing for it. News headlines proclaimed WAR THREAT EASES *in forty different languages. Happy, expectant crowds were streaming through London. And in New York the clubs and restaurants that normally closed at sundown were filling. The streets were crushed with people. Pickpockets and prostitutes had more business than they could possibly handle.*

In Florida at five-thirty, Eastern Standard Time, the troops started boarding the rocketplane. The entire Kennedy Space Center had been cleared of all prying eyes. The news people were locked in the same plush prison as the refugees.

In Washington, the burly, red-eyed man shifted painfully in his chair as he watched the troop loading on closed-circuit television.

"They take off at six?" he asked for the hundredth time.

"Barring delays," answered an Air Force colonel. "They should have Alpha secured by shortly after midnight, according to the schedule. Kinsman and his group will arrive no sooner than one A.M."

The man nodded.

"May I ask, sir," the colonel said, "why we're allowing Kinsman to depart at all? Why not keep him here, under our thumb?"

"A dead martyr is a worse enemy than a live traitor."

"Oh, I see. Uh, Colonel Colt should be in New York by now, incidentally."

The man came as close as he could to smiling. "Yes, I know."

Colt was there when Kinsman returned to his room. Harriman was holding the door open as Kinsman wheeled in, with Landau behind him. Colt was standing by the windows, looking out at the night and the unaccustomed brilliance of the city's lights.

As he rolled his chair into the room, and took off his oxygen mask, Kinsman said, "This is a pleasant surprise. What brings you here? I thought you were in Florida."

Shrugging, Colt replied, "Couldn't let you get this close without running up to say hello and wish you a Happy New Year."

Harriman said, "Good old sentimental Frank."

"Yeah," Colt said. "Sentimental. That's me, all right."

"I'm glad to see you," Kinsman said. "Bird colonel, eh?"

Colt said nothing. Kinsman gestured him to a chair as he wheeled up close to the windows. "Can't see the Moon—too overcast."

Landau started setting up his instruments on the desktop.

"I thought you'd be busy with the final countdown at Kennedy," Kinsman said to Colt.

"It's going along fine. They don't need me breathing down their necks. If there's any problem they can reach me here."

Kinsman grinned at him. "That doesn't sound like the old perch-on-the-bastard's-ass Frank Colt that I used to know and love."

Colt turned away slightly. "I'm a big-ass bird colonel now. Got to show some dignity. Besides, I'd rather be up here with you."

"How come our first shipload of immigrants is being launched from Florida?" Harriman wanted to know. "Why not right here, from the civilian port?"

Colt didn't answer. He licked the edge of his lower teeth with his tongue and frowned.

God, he's uptight, Kinsman thought.

"Listen," Colt said at last, "I . . ."

The door buzzer startled all of them. Kinsman turned his chair around as Harriman hustled to the door and opened it.

Four very solemn-faced youngsters came in, three

boys and a girl. The oldest must have been ten, at most.
The girl and one of the boys was Latin-dark. Puerto
Rican, probably. One of the boys was black. The fourth
was a red-haired, freckled, street-wary Huckleberry
Finn.

And their teacher. "Oh, it's *so* kind of you to let us
visit you! I understand how busy you must be." She
prattled on to Harriman as she urged her youngsters
into the room, like a hen pushing its chicks.

The kids were silent, staring, but the teacher never
stopped talking. Kinsman immediately realized that she
was speaking to Harriman only to allay her own ner-
vousness, and using exactly the same tone and expressions that she must have used in her classroom, on the
kids.

"Oh, and you must be Mr. Kinsman—Chester Arthur Kinsman. Were you named after President Arthur?
And you live on the Moon! Isn't that interesting, children? Do you want to live on the Moon someday?"

The girl reached a hand out toward Kinsman's exoskeleton. "Why you wearin' that?"

Kinsman smiled at her. *The old lunar charm.* "I need
it to help me move around. See?" He raised one arm,
and all four of the kids hopped back a step at the sound
of the servo motors. "My muscles are used to the gravity on the Moon, which is a lot lighter than the gravity
here. I'm too weak to move by myself here. You're a lot
stronger than I am, I bet."

That emboldened one of them. "My dad says you're
a traitor. You're being bad to the United States," the
black boy said.

"I'm sorry he feels that way," Kinsman answered.
"The people on the Moon want to be free. We don't
want to hurt the United States or anyone else. We just
want to be free."

"When I grow up," the Puerto Rican boy asked, "can
I go to the Moon?"

"Sure. You can live there, if you want to."

"Would I have to wear one of those things?" He
pointed at the braces.

"No." Kinsman laughed. "That's only for weak old
men like me. And on the Moon, even I don't need it."

They asked a few more questions, and then their teacher started to shoo them toward the door.

"Can girls go to the Moon too?" the girl asked.

"Yes, sure."

"Come now, children. Mr. Kinsman is very tired. It's very difficult for a man from the Moon to stay here on Earth. Smell the air in here? Even the air is different!"

"I don't smell anything."

"That's what I mean," the teacher said.

By now they were outside in the hall and the door was swinging shut when one of the kids yelled, "Fuckin' traitor! We'll get ya!"

"George!" the teacher clucked. "Such language. And shouting in the hallway!"

Shout it from the rooftops, kid, Kinsman thought. Be a real patriot.

Harriman kicked the door shut. "George must be running for mayor."

Landau got up from his chair and went back to the desk. "Chet, I must run a medical check."

"More blood? Hugh, order up some dinner, will you? Frank, you'll stay and eat with us."

"I oughtta get going . . ."

"Come on," Kinsman urged. "We'll let you loose early. We've got to be at JFK for a ten o'clock takeoff. And you can watch the immigrants' takeoff on TV."

Hesitantly, Colt got up and went to the TV controls on the wall. With equal reluctance, Kinsman turned his chair toward the syringe-wielding Landau.

All traffic was being routed around Times Square. Policemen on duty—on horseback, in armored cars, in helicopters—all wore riot gear: hard hats, plastic visors, gas masks, the armament of a combat infantryman. Thousands of people were pouring into the Square, and more throngs were congregating elsewhere in Manhattan. In strategically located armories around the island, the Army had companies of men sitting aboard armed personnel carriers and balloon-wheeled light tanks. Washington Square, Columbus Circle, the whole length of the Amsterdam Avenue Mall—crowds were forming in all of them. Bottles and butts and pills were passed freely, in spite of the fact that the police patrolled the fringes of the throngs, and flittered by overhead with glaring searchlights arcing back and forth. But the people were happy, laughing, celebrating. Huge TV screens had been set up in the streets to show the launch from Kennedy Space Center.

Frank Colt was puffing on a joint as he sat on the sofa and watched the final moments of countdown. The rocketplane was sitting on its tail, bathed in the glare of a dozen huge spotlights. The service tower had been rolled back, and only a thin wisp of vapor from the liquid oxygen boiloff indicated that the craft was occupied and ready for launch.

The TV announcer was prattling, "In one of the most generous acts of international good will seen in this decade, the United States is allowing fifty persons from foreign nations to engage in this historic journey to the Moon—despite the fact that the lunar settlement is still legally American territory."

Landau frowned as he packed away his medical equipment. Harriman was on the phone, checking again on the preparedness of their own rocketplane at JFK.

Kinsman sat tiredly in his special chair. The medical exams not only depressed him, they made him physically weak.

The door buzzer sounded. Dinner arrived.

"Not again!"

General Maksutov listened for a solid four minutes, by the digital clock on his metal desk, his face growing more incredulous and grimmer at the same time. Finally he put the phone down. His last words were "Yessir. Immediately!"

"Dimitri," he said to his aide, who was sitting across the desk from him holding a champagne glass in one hand, "that was headquarters. We must prepare for three manned launches immediately."

Dimitri dropped the champagne glass.

"Intelligence claims that the Americans are on their way to recapturing their space stations. If we don't take our own back from the counterrevolutionaries, the Americans will get them. In a matter of hours."

"But *three* manned launches? *Now?*"

General Maksutov nodded bitterly. "Rouse the men—full crews and full backups. I'll call Andrei and give him the joyful news. The ground crews must be alerted, also. See to it."

The aide nodded dumbly and pushed himself up from his chair. Absently, he noticed that his glass had not broken. He picked it up off the thick carpeting and placed it on the desk.

"Get the infirmary to issue wake-up pills. And you'd better take some yourself."

"Yessir."

"Happy New Year, comrade," the general said bitterly. "And happy new millennium."

Dimitri shook his head. "This is too much like the old millennium."

"Yes, isn't it? Except that back in the twentieth century we didn't have the duty of killing our own countrymen, you and I."

The launch was shown on the mammoth TV screens set up in Times Square and other places where the crowds had gathered. The people watched, a sea of murmuring humanity, as the final few seconds of countdown ticked off, and the sleek rocketplane stood bathed in the spotlights against the balmy Florida night, waiting, waiting . . .

"Three . . . two . . . one . . . Ignition!"

For an instant, nothing happened. Then an orange spark blossomed beneath the rocketplane's tail and grew into a huge radiant yellow-orange glow that overwhelmed the powerful searchlights.

The crowds ooohed.

The rocketplane lifted off the ground, and the hot fiery glow spread and spread, reflected by the low-lying mists from the nearby sea. The whole sky turned the color of heated copper. The stars disappeared. A coppery-orange daylight spread across the flat Florida cape. Buildings and palm trees and trucks that had been lost in night darkness were now clear to see. And the

*sound, the rolling reverberating thunder of a million de-
mons bellowing, washed across the crowds with palpable force. People gasped with awe.*

*And the TV announcer never missed a beat. "The
liftoff is fine, fine . . . She's heading straight and true,
with the first load of interplanetary immigrants in the
history of the human race . . ."*

Dinner had been quiet, tense. Kinsman and the three
other men had eaten without much conversation,
watched the TV screen, which alternated between shots
of the rocketplane's countdown, views of the New
Year's Eve crowds in Manhattan, and long dreary seg-
ments of "entertainment."

"Well, Frank," Kinsman said as the big wall-screen
showed a telescopic view of the rocketplane, "you can
relax now. They got off without you."

"Yeah," said Colt.

He's down. What on earth's bothering him? Kinsman
knew something was wrong, but his body ached too
much for him to think. *I know how Atlas must've felt,
holding up the world.*

"Chet," Landau said, "we must begin to prepare for
the ride to the airport. You will have to wear the oxygen mask."

Kinsman wanted to nod, but didn't even try.

"De Paolo's got two cars coming," Harriman said.
"Plus the escort. No local or federal cops this time. We
sneak out quietly."

Suddenly, Kinsman turned to Colt. "Frank—come
with us!"

"To the airport?"

"No, to Selene! Come on. You know what we're
trying to do there, and you know how chickenshit life
can be down here. Join us."

Colt actually pushed his chair away from the dinner
table. "Me? You're serious? You want me . . . ?"

"Why not?"

"After what I've done?"

"That's in the past. We're building for the future.
You can help us. You'll be a helluva lot happier in Selene than playing soldier down here."

Colt got to his feet. "You're crazy! I can't—"

"Sure you can," Kinsman urged.

Throwing his napkin down on the table, Colt shouted, "You damned fool! There won't *be* any Selene by the time you get back there."

"I don't get—" But the tortured look on Colt's face stopped Kinsman. "What do you mean, Frank?"

"Shit, man! Did you really think they were gonna let you get away with it? Did you really think that?"

Kinsman could feel fire flashing along his nerves. "Frank, what are you saying?"

Colt's face was a landscape of pain. "Chet, you soft-headed bastard—that plane's not filled with your god-damned refugees. It's loaded with a hundred troops! In another couple hours we'll have Alpha. In twenty-four hours we'll have *all* the manned stations. Then we take Selene."

Kinsman closed his eyes. *Trojan Horse.*

"You sonofabitch!" Harriman raged. "That's how you got those fucking eagles!"

"Yeah." Colt's voice sounded weak, miserable.

Landau muttered one word: "Jill . . . "

Kinsman looked at the three of them. Harriman and Landau still sitting at the dinner table, food and wine unfinished. Colt standing, legs spread slightly as if he were waiting for them to physically attack him.

"Phone," Kinsman said, more to himself than the others. Wheeling toward the desk, "Phone link . . . JFK's got a link with Alpha."

Colt shook his head. "They won't put you through. Air Force took over the communications at JFK an hour before I came here."

Kinsman slid the chair to a halt at the desk. Turning it back to face Colt, he said, "Then you've got to tell them to reestablish contact."

"*I've* got to?"

"You're the only one who can, Frank."

Colt was wide-eyed now. "You're crazy, man. That's insane."

The scene on the view screen showed Times Square and the still-growing crowd there. Harriman went over to the wall controls and turned the volume down.

"Frank," Kinsman said, "you're on our side. You've always been on our side. You're the only one who hasn't recognized it."

Walking stiff-legged, shakily, toward him, Colt answered, "I'm on *my* side, Chet. That's the only side there is. Numero uno."

"Bullshit. You can't live with that, and we both know it. So they make you a general. It's still a dying world, Frank. It's *dying!* Unless we do something to change it."

"By selling out the United States?"

"By rising above it!" Kinsman shouted, and his chest flared with pain.

Colt was standing in front of his chair now, looming over him. "We know what you and De Paolo are doing—all those visitors you've had the past couple days. It won't work, Chet. We're not gonna let it work."

Kinsman took a long shuddering breath and forced the pain down. "I don't care about that. I don't care about anything except Selene's independence. Because without our independence, you'll be part of a nuclear strike that'll kill all the people in the United States. There's no way around it, Frank. Either we control those satellites, or there's going to be war. Which do you want?"

"I don't want either, dammit!"

His voice as hard as the braces he wore, Kinsman snapped, "It's got to be one or the other, Frank. And *you* decide which. It's your choice. Choose."

Colt glared at him.

"Choose!"

Colt turned to the desk and punched savagely at the phone keyboard. "JFK central switchboard," he said into the speaker grill.

The tiny phone screen glowed pearl gray, but no picture came on. A man's voice said, "JFK Spaceport," in a bored, flat voice.

"This is Colonel Colt. Put me through to Major Stodt, in communications."

The voice suddenly became more alert. "Sir? Would you please repeat the order so that our audio verification equipment can check your voice-print?"

Colt did it, and with a single flicker of the screen, a pinch-faced man with a high domed forehead appeared. His blue tunic bore the gold oak leaves of an Air Force major.

"Stodt here."

Colt gave Kinsman a sidelong glance. Then, "I want a tight laser link with Alpha. Full scramble and no tapes. At once. Pipe it into this phone line."

The major's narrow-boned face seemed to tighten even more. "Sir, that's not in our operational plan."

"Did I ask if it was?" Colt snapped. "Do it!"

"But . . . but, sir, there's no way for us to monitor a laser link unless we have time to——"

"Stodt, you've got ten minutes to get that fucking link set up. In the eleventh minute, you can start writing me a report explaining why an asshole of a communications tech has been promoted beyond his talents. Now, move, *Captain*. Or do you want to try for lieutenant?"

The major actually trembled. Visibly. "Right away, sir," he muttered. The screen went blank.

Colt turned back to Kinsman. "I don't know how long it'll take 'em to catch on to what you're doing and cut the link. Better talk fast—if you get the chance to talk at all."

The pain was a dull, sullen throb, like a cinder: charred black on the outside but red and glowering deep within. Kinsman said merely, "Thanks, Frank."

Colt shook his head, but said nothing. He walked back to the couch near the silent wall-screen and plopped down. The screen was showing the Guy Lombardo simulacrum smiling and waving its baton in perfect three-four time in front of an orchestra of robots. Real people were dancing on the floor of the Starlight Roof.

"We should be leaving for JFK ourselves," Landau said.

Harriman gruffed. "Those bastards won't let us go. They've got us by the balls here."

"No," Colt said. "I told them that it'd be okay for you to return to Alpha, and then Selene. We were gonna have Alpha under our control by the time your rocketplane got there. That was our plan."

Kinsman listened with only half his mind. The rest was racing through the possibilities. *Can't let them dock at Alpha. But they'll probably try to force a docking. Or maybe they've got enough pressure suits to jump across and grab the emergency hatches. God, if there's much fighting up there, they'll destroy the whole station. Ellen . . .*

The phone screen flashed into a sparkle of colors. A voice—not Major Stodt's—said, "Direct link with Alpha is coming on, sir."

The screen cleared, and a female communications technician, looking faintly surprised, said, "Go ahead, JFK."

"This is Kinsman," he said, squaring the chair in front of the phone. "Who's in charge there?"

The girl blinked once. "Mr. Perry."

"Where's Leonov?"

"He returned to Selene yesterday, sir. I can patch you through to him if—"

"No. Get Perry. Immediately."

"Right."

It took a few minutes. The other three men gathered tensely around Kinsman's chair. Finally Chris Perry's strong, youthful face appeared on the screen. *The typical square-jawed adventure hero. I hope he's up to it.* He was smiling broadly, and there were other people and a general hubbub in the background.

"We thought you'd be on your way here by now," he said happily. "Had a helluva party at midnight—our time, that is. But everybody's staying up to welcome the immigrants, and Ellen Berger wants—"

"No time!" Kinsman snapped. "The flight from Florida is filled with soldiers, not immigrants."

"What?"

"It's a trick. A Trojan Horse. We're still here at UN headquarters. That rocketplane must not be allowed to dock. Understand? Under no circumstances."

"Yessir." Perry was completely sober. The laughing and chattering in the background had turned into absolute silence.

"Establish radio contact with them. Order them to retrofire and return Earthside immediately."

"Right. But what if they don't comply? They could try to force a docking. If there's any kind of heavy weapon play in here—"

"I know." Kinsman realized he was clenching his hands on the metal braces of his thighs. "That's why it's best to get them to turn around. If they don't comply, use the ABM lasers on them. There are enough satellites within range to get them before they close in on you."

Perry didn't flinch. He nodded, tight-lipped.

"Warn them. Tell them exactly what we're going to do," Kinsman commanded. "But don't let them get close enough to the station to damage it. They might have missiles on board, and they'll use them if they can't board you."

"They do," Colt's voice said behind him.

Perry looked grim. "Yessir. I'd better get on the horn to them right away."

He turned away from the screen momentarily.

"Will he do it?" Landau whispered.

Kinsman turned and looked up at him. The braces made it a painful operation. "You mean will he kill Americans? We'll find out pretty soon." *You started this as a move to end war, and it's turning into a civil war.*

"He'd better do it," Colt said.

Perry came back to the screen. "I've got to get down to the comm center. They've got the rocketplane on the standard comm frequency, but I can't run all the parts of this show from here."

"Right. I'll keep this line open," Kinsman said, adding silently, *As long as they'll let me.*

Suddenly the screen erupted in flickering colors. The only sound from the speaker grill was an angry scratchy hiss.

"They tumbled to it," Colt said. "Cut the link."

Kinsman turned the chair around. "Hugh, find a phone someplace and tell our rocketplane to hold. No telling when we'll be there—if ever. Then see who you can find in the UN chain of command—"

"Christ! On New Year's Eve?"

"I know it! But we've got to get some muscle around

that rocketplane. It's our link home. And—" A sudden surge of pain made him gasp.

"Chet!"

Landau reached for him. Kinsman pushed the Russian away. "No . . . I'm all right . . . Hugh, for God's sake—we need De Paolo. Find him. Find some foreign diplomats. Marrett, newsmen, anybody. We've got to get word out about this. Don't . . ." The pain hit again, searing flame. "Don't let them keep this bottled up."

Harriman bit his lower lip. But he nodded and rushed toward the door.

Landau forced the chair down to a reclining position. The ceiling seemed to be spinning. Kinsman heard the phone making funny noises, then a voice calling tinnily, "Colonel Colt! Colonel Franklin Colt!"

Landau's face was hovering over him. It was blurred, but very serious. Intent. *So damned somber. Wonder if he's that way in bed with Jill. He must smile sometime.*

"This is Colt."

"One moment, Colonel. Priority call from Washington."

"Great. Just what I need."

By turning his head slightly, Kinsman could see the wall screen. The dance floor was jammed with happy people. Old people, mostly. The scene shifted. The Amsterdam Mall was crowded with dancing people, too. But these were young, black, Puerto Rican, other Latins. And their dancing wasn't stately or measured. Their music wasn't provided by a painstakingly detailed simulacrum of a long-dead orchestra. Kinsman could see steel drums and guitars and enough amplifiers to make him wonder sleepily, *Where'd they get all that electricity?*

He forced himself awake. "Stop sticking needles into me, dammit all!"

Landau laid a heavy hand on his shoulder. "Be still. Quiet."

"Colonel Colt." Kinsman couldn't see the desk, but the voice came through the phone speaker clearly. It was an angry burning whisper.

"Right here." Colt's voice was calm.

He's made his decision.

"Congratulations, Colonel. You have earned yourself a firing squad."

"Guess again, baby. I'm on UN territory and I'm seeking asylum in Selene."

"You are a traitor," the harsh whisper grated. "A turncoat. Worse even than Kinsman himself. You *knew* what we were doing. You *planned* it for us. And then you changed sides. There will be no mercy for you, black man. No place to hide. You are a dead man."

"Everybody dies," Colt said, in his toughest ghetto style.

"Correct. And you will die sooner than most. Our troops will not be thwarted. They will seize Station Alpha or destroy it."

"Better change the orders. They'll get their asses fried if they don't turn back."

"They will not turn back. And if your new-found friends kill American troops, not even the UN building will be safe for you."

"If I were you," Kinsman heard Colt say quite distinctly, "I'd be heading for a bomb shelter instead of making threatening phone calls." Then he heard the faint snap of the phone switch.

"Alex," Kinsman said. "Don't put me under. I've got to stay awake . . . got to . . ."

"Your EKG is frightening," Landau said. "You will stay down and you will rest."

"He will not," Colt said, firmly.

Kinsman fumbled for the controls on the arm of his chair and swung the chair around to a point where he could see Colt. *Don't try sitting up. Don't get that brave.* The pain was dulled now, but he knew that was from whatever Landau had injected into him. It was still there, screaming inside him. The drug had merely turned the volume down temporarily.

"Keep him awake and alert," Colt said, walking over to face Landau. "He's the one they'll listen to—the people up there and the people down here. If he's out of it, they're not going to listen to you or me."

"There's Harriman," Landau said, through barely opened lips.

"Keep him awake," Colt repeated.

"You'll kill him."

Colt said nothing. Kinsman grinned at him. "Everybody dies."

They both turned toward him.

"Frank, see if you can reestablish contact with Alpha. Perry's no fool. He's probably trying to make direct contact with this building's microwave receivers right now."

"Yeah . . . right." Colt went back to the phone.

Breathing very carefully so that he wouldn't disturb the beast that was drowsing inside him, Kinsman told Landau, "Do whatever you have to, Alex. But don't put me under. Frank's right. I've got to be awake through this. I'm the only one they'll listen to. Maybe when Hugh comes back . . ." *If he gets back. If he had to go outside the building, they might have grabbed him.*

"I could try electrical blockage for the pain," Landau muttered, and went back to his medical equipment.

Colt was grumbling and swearing into the phone. "Don't any of those fuckers on the switchboard speak English? Holy shit."

Kinsman smiled to himself. *Frank made his choice. He came through.*

The wall screen showed a huge clock built into the facade of one of the Times Square towers. It said 9:48. The crowd was like a single mass of people now, swaying, chanting, self-hypnotized.

"Yeah . . . whozzat? Perry! This is Colt."

Kinsman swung his head. Too fast. The pain lanced through him. *Christ, I can't even move!*

Colt dashed over to him. "Perry's on the phone. No visual, just voice."

He wheeled Kinsman to the desk.

"Chris, this is Kinsman." *Can he hear me? My voice sounds so damned weak.*

"Yessir. We've been trying to reach you."

"What . . . happened?"

"The ship refused to turn back. They even fired a missile at us."

Missile! "Where? How much damage?"

"No damage. We intercepted the missile with a laser

beam and then got the ship itself with another laser."

"Got the ship?"

A long delay. "Yessir. Radar confirmed the kill. She split apart—nothing but debris now."

A hundred men. Nothing but debris. In orbit . . . floating like she did . . .

"Sir?"

"Yes." His voice was a croak. A groan.

"There was nothing else we could do. They refused to back off."

"I understand. You did the right thing. It's my responsibility. I gave the orders."

"Yessir." The phone went dead.

"Now you *must* sleep," Landau said. "There is no—"

But Colt said, "Look at this." He turned up the volume on the wall TV screen.

A grave, shocked looking announcer's face filled the big screen. He was saying, ". . . destroyed by the rebels. The government has made no announcement of why the troops were aboard the rocketplane, or of what happened to the group of international émigrés who were scheduled to reach the space station at about 10 P.M., Eastern Time.

"I repeat, the White House announced a few minutes ago that a rocketplane carrying one hundred American Aerospace Police troops was destroyed by laser fire as it neared Space Station Alpha tonight. All one hundred Americans—plus the rocketplane's crew, also Americans—were killed. The rocketplane was deliberately destroyed by the rebels who are in temporary command of the space station. More information will be announced shortly, White House sources report."

The TV screen cut back to a view of the crowd at Times Square. They were frozen in place, stunned, immobile. The big TV screens all around the square had shown the same announcement, and now one of them— the public educational channel—was showing a simulation of the rocketplane approaching the space station. It disappeared in a flash of blinding light.

"They worked that up fast, the bastards."

The scene changed to a TV announcer down on the street, warmly bundled in an electrically heated suit, three well-armed private policemen standing beside him. "The crowd here seems stoned, bombed, utterly unable to believe this sudden and tragic news," he said into his lip mike.

Then there was shouting and a surge of bodies. The view cut back to the overhead shot, from atop one of the buildings around the Square. But the announcer's voice rattled on: "There's shouting. I don't know if you can make out what they're saying. It's rather profane, a lot of it, but the general gist of it is—the lunar dissidents have killed a hundred Americans. There's anger here, real rage."

Kinsman heard a woman's piercing shriek quite distinctly: "Those bastards are in the UN Building!"

"The crowd is milling around," the announcer was saying.

"They'll be here," Kinsman said.

Colt nodded. "They're already starting to push out of the Square. And the whitehats are letting 'em go."

The police were doing nothing as the crowd began streaming out of Times Square. The TV picture changed to show similar scenes elsewhere in Manhattan.

Kinsman tried to sit up. "Frank . . . we've got to get to the rocketplane. Now." The pain bloomed inside him. It was like railroad tracks of red-molten steel clamping down across his chest, his arm, and then everywhere. *No!* he screamed to himself. *Not now!* But he could see nothing. It all went black.

Distantly he heard Landau's shocked voice. "It's too much . . . too much . . ."

Friday 31 December 1999: 2358 hrs UT

Something was shaking him. A loud whining roar rattled his very bones. He couldn't move; his body felt glued down.

A voice. Marrett's? Shouting over the engine roar: "I told him we'd given 'em the driest goddamned spring season the continent's ever seen. And we can do it, too. De Paolo's on the phone with the President right now."

Kinsman forced his eyes open. It took an effort of will. His head was turned to a small window. It all came together slowly in his foggy brain. *Helicopter. They took us off the roof in a copter.*

"So they tracked me down. Hugh burst in on the party with a whole squad of UN security police. Half the people there thought it was a drug raid!"

Kinsman tried to focus on the scene outside. It was still night. There were city lights sliding past below them. In the distance was the river, the skyscrapers . . . *Oh, God!*

Fire. Flames licking upward, doubly reflected in the river and the glass wall of the Secretariat building. *They're burning it. They're burning the UN building.*

"Fire's getting worse," somebody said.

Marrett's voice answered, "Sure. Goddamn fire trucks can't get to it because of the mob."

" 'What fools these mortals be.' " Harriman's voice, sounding very tired, very down.

"Hey, it's midnight."

"Terrific."

"Happy fucking New Year."

The voices buzzed on. But Kinsman paid no attention. He watched the UN building being swallowed in flames.

The pain came and went and returned again. He could feel it snaking through his body. Tendrils of hot iron worming down through his arteries and veins, branching, exploring, searching. Down through the fine nets of the capillaries the pain spread. He felt it, he knew it was there, even though his brain kept insisting that the drugs were keeping the pain suppressed. *Yes, but I can still feel it, going further and further.*

Harriman's voice came out of total silence. "It's De Paolo. They're going to meet tomorrow. The President's coming up to New York to see the damage. De Paolo says to tell Chet that buildings can be rebuilt. And so can institutions. Stronger than they were before."

But we'll have to be so careful, Kinsman replied silently. *It'll be so easy to turn it into a dictatorship. We've got to preserve human freedoms—it won't work any other way.*

They were moving him. He felt himself being lifted, placed. Carefully. So carefully. Like a fragile treasure. *Like a fossil.*

Pressure and the muted thunder of rocket engines. The pain flared now everywhere, waking him.

Frank Colt was sitting beside his litter, brooding. Kinsman grabbed at his arm.

"There's so much to do, Frank." His voice sounded like a dying old man's.

"Hey, Chet, take it easy, man." Even Frank's voice sounded funny.

"Got to . . . listen, Frank. We've got to do everything we can. We've got to keep the doors open for the human race . . ."

"Yeah, sure, baby. Don't get yourself excited."

Others were surrounding him now. Shadows.

"Frank, we can get raw materials from the Moon. We can develop it . . . There's a whole solar system of natural resources . . . Nobody has to go hungry or be poor. We can do it! We can make it all work out."

"Yeah, okay."

"You understand, Frank. You know what I mean. I can leave it with you, can't I?"

He nodded as the others gently pulled Kinsman's hand away. "I know," Colt said. "Been thinking about it myself. I'll see that it gets done. Don't worry about it. Just rest yourself."

"Good," Kinsman said. "Good. You'll know how to get it done. Mine the Moon. A world of resources there. And the asteroids, too. Plenty of power . . . everything we need . . . for everybody . . ."

Someone—*Landau, most likely*—pressed a needle into his arm.

Floating. He was floating. Voices flickering around him. They were moving him again, but now it was like drifting out in the sea.

Don't go out too far, Chester. There's a tide.

Yes, Momma . . . There sure as hell is.

"It's all right now, Chet. You're safe. You're back home. I'm here."

Ellen's voice. Her scent.

He tried to open his eyes. He tried to speak. With all the power of his being, he tried to raise a hand to touch her.

Nothing.

He felt her hair brushing his face. "You're going to be all right, Chet. You're not going to die. Please. You can't die."

He moistened his lips. He got the feeling that his eyes were open, but he just couldn't see anything. Maybe a blur, a faint gray against the enveloping darkness. Cold. Cold and dark as space itself.

"Chet, it's me. Ellen. Please don't die. There's so much for us to live for. I could love you, Chet. I could have loved you . . ."

And I could have loved you. I could. I could. He wondered if she could hear him saying it.

But then the gray blur of the enveloping darkness

took shape, and he saw her waiting for him, floating weightlessly, her arms outstretched to embrace him at last. Kinsman's last thought sighed out of him like a sigh of relief. The debt is paid, the only way it could be paid. He joined her, completely and finally.

About the Author

BEN BOVA is Editor of *Analog Science Fiction-Science Fact* magazine, the most widely read and influential science fiction magazine in the world. He received the Science Fiction Achievement Award (Hugo) for best editor of the year in 1973, 1974, and 1975.

A prolific writer of science fiction and science fact himself, Bova has also been a working newspaperman, an aerospace executive, a writer of teaching films, and a television consultant. As Manager of Marketing for Avco Everett Research Laboratory, in Massachusetts, he has worked with leading scientists in advanced research fields such as high-power lasers, magnetohydrodynamics (MHD), plasma physics, and artificial hearts. Prior to joining Avco, he wrote motion picture scripts for the Physical Sciences Study Committee, working with the MIT Physics Department and Nobel Laureates from many universities. Earlier, he was a technical editor on Project VANGUARD with the Martin Co. in Baltimore. He also worked on several newspapers and magazines in the Philadelphia area.

Bova has lectured on topics ranging from the history of science fiction to the future of America's cities. His audiences have ranged from junior high students to the New

York Academy of Sciences. He was born in Philadelphia, where he attended Temple University and received a degree in journalism.

His short stories and science articles have appeared in all the major science fiction magazines, as well as the *Smithsonian Magazine*, the IEEE *Spectrum, School Library Journal*; and many other periodicals. His book *The Fourth State of Matter* was honored as one of the top one hundred science books of the year 1971 by the American Librarians' Association. *Starflight and Other Improbabilities* was selected as a Junior Literary Guild book in 1973. He was the 1974 recipient of the New England Science Fiction Society's E. E. Smith Memorial Award for Imaginative Fiction.